How to Book Your Holiday

UK

Choose any of the holidays in the brochures listed below (subject to the terms and conditions) and then call Thomas Cook Direct on

01733 335501

quoting reference BOOK1 to book. (You cannot book at your local Thomas Cook shop). After making the phone booking, send in the application form below to Thomas Cook Direct, PO Box 44, Peterborough, Cambs PE3 8BX. Upon receipt, £100 will be deducted from the cost of your holiday.

Holiday Choices for UK Customers:

First Choice (All Inclusive, Cyprus, Lakes and Mountains), Cosmos (Summersun, Florida and California, America and Canada, Golden Times), British Airways Holidays (Golf, Far East, Worldwide), Air Travel Group (Magic of Italy, Magic of Spain, Magic of Portugal), Kuoni (Switzerland, Safari, Worldwide), Crystal (Ski, Lakes and Mountains, Italy), Manos (India), Thomas Cook Holidays (Summer Sun, Winter Sun, Sailing, Club Med Choice, Villas with Pools, Cyprus, Greece, Turkey, Cyprus, Jersey and Guernsey, Golden Circle, France Camping and Mobile Homes, France Hotels and Apartments, Worldwide Faraway, Ski, Florida), Unijet (Caribbean, Las Vegas, America), Virgin Holidays (New England, Far East, Florida), Cruises (P&O, Royal Caribbean), Sovereign (Summer Sun, Winter Sun).

IRELAND

Choose any of the holidays in the brochures listed above, plus any Falcon or Sunworld holiday departing from an Irish airport (subject to the terms and conditions) and then call Thomas Cook Dublin on

01 677 1721

quoting reference BOOK1 to book. After making the phone booking, send in the application form below to Thomas Cook Dublin, 118 Grafton St., Dublin 2. Upon receipt, £100 (punts) will be deducted from the holiday. Customers from Northern Ireland may choose to book through either Thomas Cook Direct or Thomas Cook Dublin.

At the time of booking you will need:

1. Details of your chosen holiday from the brochure. 2. This holiday discount page 3. Deposit for your holiday and the necessary insurance premium (payable by debit or credit card or by cheque).

BOOK IT. THEN THOMAS COOK

£100 OFF YOUR NEXT HOLIDAY BOOK IT WITH THIS BOOK

KU-441-581

M3

Terms and Conditions

1. Holidays can be booked any time until 31 May 1997 and must be completed by 31 October 1997. 2. Discount applies to new bookings made on or after 1 January 1997. 3. Holidays must be for a minimum of 2 adults for one week (or more). 4. Thomas Cook Insurance must be purchased for each passenger at the time of booking. 5. Only one £100 discount page per booking; discount cannot be combined with any other offer. 6. Discount page cannot be used toward payment of your deposit or insurance premium. 7. Offer open to all residents of the UK and Ireland aged 18 or over. 8. Holidays will be booked by Thomas Cook, acting as agent on behalf of the tour operator, and the consumer agrees to be bound by the booking conditions of the tour operator or any other third parties. All holidays subject to availability. 9. Reed Books shall not be responsible for any matter relating to holidays. 10. Discount and insurance premium must be paid at time of booking. The balance of the full cost of the holiday will be payable 10 weeks prior to departure, or at the time of booking if sooner. 11. Discount pages are not refundable either wholly or partly in cash. Any holiday cancelled will be subject to tour operator's cancellation charges and any refund due in respect of a cancelled holiday booking can only be paid from the balance of the holiday cost and the value of the pages will not be taken into account for refund purposes. 12. Defaced, altered or damaged pages will not be accepted. Proof of posting will not be accepted as proof of receipt. 13. A charge of £2 will be made where the holiday cost is paid by credit card. 14. For purposes of monitoring customer service, calls to Thomas Cook Direct are recorded.

Promoter's Address: Reed Books Ltd., Michelin House, 81 Fulham Rd., London SW3 6RB. Registered in England No: 1974080

BOOK IT. THEN THOMAS COOK IT.

£100 OFF YOUR NEXT HOLIDAY WITH THIS BOOK

-------------------- **Application Form** --------------------

Please fill this in when you have made your booking over the phone and send it to Thomas Cook Direct at the address listed in 'How to Book Your Holiday'. £100 will be deducted from the cost of your holiday upon receipt of this form.

Name .... Address .... Postcode ....

Booking Reference (this will be given over the phone when you make your booking) .... Date of Booking ....

I am 18 years old or over and have read, and agree to abide by the Terms and Conditions on this discount page. Signature: ....

Tick here if you do not wish to receive further information from Reed Books or Thomas Cook ☐

'Stephen Fry's witty first novel . . . strikes a chord with those who have been buggered at public school and gone on to do English at Oxbridge. It ought to be repulsive to anybody with an ounce of democracy in their souls, but it turns out to be hugely enjoyable.' *Observer*

'A book which genuinely makes you laugh out loud is rarer than reviews and wrappers suggest. This one made me laugh three and a half times, which is one half more than *Lucky Jim*.' *Sunday Telegraph*

'A thousand curses on the man. What next? An ascent on the Eiger *sans* thermals?' Sue Townsend's Book of the Year

'*The Liar* is very funny, full of intelligence and ideas, Post-Punk E. F. Benson' *Spectator*

'It's very unfair. It took Joseph Heller seven years to write *Catch 22*. Stephen seems to have knocked this off on a couple of wet Wednesday afternoons in Norfolk.' Hugh Laurie

50p
R.S.P.C.A
STROUD
JULY 08

The Liar

'You have a fine brain. A really excellent brain, Mr Healey.'

'Thank you.'

'A fine brain, but a dreadful mind. I have a fine brain *and* a fine mind. Likewise Russell. Leavis, a good mind, practically no brain at all. Shall we continue like this, I wonder?'

Like what?'

'This fortnightly exhibition of stolen goods. It all seems rather pointless. I don't find the pose of careless youth charming and engaging any more than you find the pose of careworn age fascinating and eccentric, I should imagine. Perhaps I should let you play the year away. I have no doubt that you will do very well in your final tests. Honesty, diligence and industry are wholly superfluous qualities in one such as you, as you have clearly grasped.'

'Well, it's just that I've been so . . .'

Trefusis pulled the handkerchief from his face and looked at Adrian.

'But of course you have! Frantically busy. Fran-tic-ally.'

Trefusis helped himself to another cigarette from a packet that lay on top of a tower of books next to the sofa and tapped it against his thumb-nail.

'My first meeting with you only confirmed what I first suspected. You are a fraud, a charlatan and a shyster. My favourite kind of person, in fact.'

The Liar

STEPHEN FRY

Mandarin

A Mandarin Paperback
THE LIAR

First published in Great Britain 1991
by William Heinemann Ltd
This edition published 1992
by Mandarin Paperbacks
an imprint of Reed International Books Ltd
Michelin House, 81 Fulham Road, London SW3 6RB
and Auckland, Melbourne, Singapore and Toronto

Reprinted 1992 (seventeen times), 1993 (fifteen times),
1994 (nine times), 1995, 1996 (four times)

Copyright © Stephen Fry 1991

The author and publishers are grateful to the
following for permission to use copyright material:

Shakespeare and Tragedy © John Bayley
quoted by kind permission of Routledge Ltd

'Maria' (Richard Rogers/Oscar Hammerstein II)
© 1959. Williamson Music International, USA
Reproduced by permission of
EMI Music Publishing Ltd, London WC2 0EA

'Puppy Love' composed by Paul Anka
and reproduced by kind permission of
M.A.M. Music Publishing Ltd

'I Don't Know How to Love Him' by Tim Rice
reproduced by kind permission of
MCA Music Ltd

A CIP catalogue record for this title
is available from the British Library
ISBN 0 7493 2433 3

Printed and bound in Great Britain
by Cox & Wyman Ltd, Reading, Berkshire

This book is sold subject to the condition
that it shall not, by way of trade or otherwise,
be lent, resold, hired out, or otherwise circulated
without the publisher's prior consent in any form
of binding or cover other than that in which
it is published and without a similar condition
including this condition being imposed
on the subsequent purchaser.

To ....
   (insert full name here)

Not one word of the following is true

A Fame *T-shirt* stopped outside the house where Mozart was born. He looked up at the building and his eyes shone. He stood quite still, gazing upwards and glowing with adoration as a party of *Bleached Denims* and *Fluorescent Bermuda Shorts* pushed past him and went in. Then he shook his head, dug into his hip pocket and moved forwards. A thin high voice behind him caused him to stop mid-stride.

'Have you ever contemplated, Adrian, the phenomenon of springs?'

'Coils, you mean?'

'Not coils, Adrian, no. Coils not. Think springs of water. Think wells and spas and sources. Well-springs in the widest and loveliest sense. Jerusalem, for instance, is a spring of religiosity. One small town in the desert, but the source of the world's three most powerful faiths. It is the capital of Judaism, the scene of Christ's crucifixion and the place from which Mohammed ascended into heaven. Religion seems to bubble from its sands.'

The *Fame T-shirt* smiled to himself and walked into the building.

A *Tweed Jacket* and a *Blue Button-down Shirt of Oxford Cotton* stopped in front of the steps. Now it was their turn to stare reverently upwards as the tide of human traffic streamed past them along the Getreidegasse.

'*Take Salzburg. By no means the chief city of Austria, but a Jerusalem to any music lover. Haydn, Schubert and . . . oh dear me yes, here we are . . . and Mozart.*'

'*There's a theory that special lines criss-cross the earth and that where they coincide strange things happen,*' said the Oxford Cotton Button-down Shirt. '*Ley-lines, I think they call them.*'

'*You'll think I'm grinding my axe,*' said the Jacket, '*but I should say that it is the German language that is responsible.*'

'*Shall we go up?*'

'*By all means.*' The pair moved into the interior shadows of the house.

'*You see,*' continued the Tweed, '*all the qualities of ironic abstraction that the language could not articulate found expression in their music.*'

'*I had never thought of Haydn as ironic.*'

'*It is of course quite possible that my theory is hopelessly wrong. Pay the nice Fräulein, Adrian.*'

In a second-storey chamber where little Wolfgang had romped, whose walls he had covered with precocious arithmetic and whose rafters he had made tremble with infant minuets, the Fame T-shirt examined the display cases.

The ivory and tortoise-shell combs that once had smoothed the ruffled ringlets of the young genius appeared not to interest the T-shirt at all, nor the letters and laundry-lists, nor the child-size violins and violas. His attention was entirely taken up by the models of stage designs which were set into the wall in glass boxes all round the room.

One box in particular seemed to fascinate him. He stared at it with intensity and suspicion as if half expecting the little papier mâché figures inside to burst through the glass and punch him on the nose. He appeared to be oblivious of

2

the group of Bleached Denims and Acid-coloured Shorts that pressed around him, laughing and joking in a language he didn't understand.

The model that so particularly engrossed him was of a banqueting hall in which stood a dining table heaped high with food. Two little men had been placed by the table, one crouched in terror, the other standing with hand on hip, in an attitude of cavalier contempt. Both figures looked upstage at the model of a white statue which pointed down at them with the accusing finger of an Italian traffic policeman or wartime recruiting poster.

The Tweed Jacket and the Blue Button-down had just entered the room.

'You start at that end, Adrian, and we'll meet in the middle.'

The Jacket watched the Oxford Cotton move to the other end of the room and then approached the cabinet, whose glass was still being misted by the intense scrutiny of the Fame T-shirt.

'Don Giovanni,' said the Tweed coming up behind him, 'a cenar teco m'invitasti, e son venuto. *Don Giovanni, you invited me to dinner, and here I am.*'

The T-shirt still stared into the glass. 'Non si pasce di cibo mortale, Chi si pasce di cibo celeste,' he whispered. '*He who dines on heavenly food has no need of mortal sustenance.*'

'I believe you have something for me,' said the Tweed.

'Goldener Hirsch, name of Emburey. Small package.'

'Emburey? Middlesex and England? I had no idea you were interested in cricket.'

'I get it out from a newspaper. It looked a very English name.'

'And so it is. Goodbye.'

3

The Tweed moved on and joined the Blue Shirt, who had fallen into conversation with a Frenchwoman.

'*I was telling this lady,*' *said the Shirt,* '*that I thought the design for* The Magic Flute *over there was by David Hockney.*'

'*Certainly so,*' *said the Tweed.* '*Hockney seems to me to paint in two styles. Wild and natural or cold and clinical. I seem to remember remarking that there are two kinds of Hockney. Field Hockney and Ice Hockney.*'

'*Please?*'

'*It's a joke,*' *explained the Blue Shirt.*

'*Ah.*'

The Tweed was examining an exhibit.

'*This figure here must be the Queen of the Night, surely.*'

'*She is a character altogether of the most extraordinary, I believe,*' *said the Frenchwoman.* '*Her music – my God, how but that it is divine. I am myself singer and to play the Queen is the dearest dream of my bosom.*'

'*It's certainly one hell of a part,*' *said the Oxford Cotton.* '*Pretty difficult I'd have thought. What's that incredibly high note she has to reach? It's a top C, isn't it?*'

The Frenchwoman's answer to this question startled not just the Blue Button-down Shirt and his companion, but the whole room. For she stared at the Blue Shirt, her eyes round with fright, opened her mouth wide and let go a piercing soprano note of a purity and passion that she was never to repeat in the whole of her subsequent, and distinguished, operatic career.

'*Good lord,*' *said the Tweed,* '*is it really that high? As I remember it –* '

'*Donald!*' *said the Button-down Shirt.* '*Look!*'

The Tweed Jacket turned and saw the cause of the scream and the cause of other, less technically proficient, screams that were starting up everywhere.

4

In the middle of the room stood a man in a Fame T-shirt, twitching and leaping like a puppet.

It was not the crudity of such a dance in such a place that had set everyone off, it was the sight and sound of the blood that creamed and frothed from his throat. The man seemed, as he hopped and stamped about, to be trying to stem the flow by squeezing at his neck with both hands, but the very pressure of the blood as it pumped outwards made such a task impossible.

Time stands still at such moments.

Those who retold the scene afterwards to friends, to psychiatrists, to priests, to the press, all spoke of the noise. To some it was a rattling gargle, to others a bubbling croak: the old man in the tweed jacket and his young companion agreed that they could never hear again the sound of a cappuccino machine without being forced to think of that awful death wheeze.

All remembered the staggering quantity of the blood, the force of it pushing through the man's fingers. All remembered the chorus of bass voices upraised in panic as helping hands braved the red shower and leapt forward to ease the jerking figure to the floor. All recalled how nothing could staunch the ferocious jetting of the fountain that gushed from the man's neck and quenched the words 'I'm Going to Live For Ever' on his T-shirt with a dark stain. All remarked on how long it seemed to take him to die.

But only one of them remembered seeing an enormously fat man with a small head and lank hair leave the room, letting a knife leap from his hand like a live fish as he went.

Only one man saw that, and he kept it to himself. He grabbed his companion's hand and led him from the room.

'Come, Adrian. I think we should be otherwhere.'

One

I

Adrian checked the orchid at his buttonhole, inspected the spats at his feet, gave the lavender gloves a twitch, smoothed down his waistcoat, tucked the ebony Malacca-cane under his arm, swallowed twice and pushed wide the changing-room door.

'Ah, my dears,' he cried. 'Congratulations! Congratulations to you all! A triumph, an absolute triumph!'

'Well, what the fuck's he wearing now?' they snorted from the steamy end of the room.

'You're an arse and an idiot, Healey.'

Burkiss threw a flannel onto the shiny top hat. Adrian reached up and took it between forefinger and thumb.

'If there is the slightest possibility, Burkiss, that this flannel has absorbed any of the juices that leak from within you, that it has mopped up a single droplet of your revolting pubescent greases, that it has tickled and frotted even one of the hideously mired corners of your disgusting body then I shall have a spasm. I'm sorry but I shall.'

In spite of himself, Cartwright smiled. He moved

further along the bench and turned his back, but he smiled.

'Now, girls,' continued Healey, 'you're very high-spirited and that's as it should be but I won't have you getting out of hand. I just looked in to applaud a simply marvellous show and to tell you that you are certainly the loveliest chorus in town and that I intend to stand you all dinner at the Embassy one by one over the course of what I know will be a long and successful run.'

'I mean, what kind of coat is that?'

'It is called an astrakhan and I am sure you agree that it is absolutely the ratherest thing. You will observe it fits my sumptuous frame as snugly as if it were made for me . . . just as you do, you delicious Hopkinson.'

'Oh shut up.'

'Your whole body goes quite pink when you are flattered, like a small pig, it is utterly, utterly fetching.'

Adrian saw Cartwright turn away and face his locker, a locker to which Adrian had the key. The boy seemed now to be concentrating on pulling on his socks. Adrian took half a second to take a mental snapshot of the scrummy toes and heavenly ankle being sheathed by those lucky, lucky socks, a snap-shot he could develop and pore over later with all the others that he had pasted into the private album of his memory.

Cartwright wondered why Healey sometimes stared at him like that. He could sense it when he did, even when he couldn't see, he could feel those cool eyes surveying him with pity and contempt for a younger boy who didn't have so sharp a tongue, so acid a wit as almighty Healey. But there were others dumber than he was, why should Healey single him out for special treatment?

Setting a spatted foot on the bench that ran down the middle of the changing-room with elegant disdain, Adrian began to flip through a pile of Y-fronts and rugger shorts with his cane.

'I was particularly taken,' he said, 'with that number in the first act when you and the girls from Marlborough stood in a line and jumped up at that funny leather ball. It was too utterly utter for words. Lord how I laughed when you let the Marlborough chorus run off with it . . . dear me, this belongs to someone who doesn't appear to know how to wipe his bottom. Is there a name-tape? Madison, you really should pay more attention to your personal hygiene, you know. Two sheets of lavatory paper is all it takes. One to wipe and one to polish. Oh, how you skipped after that Marlborough pack, you blissful creatures! But they wouldn't give you the ball, would they? They kept banging it on the ground and kicking it over your lovely goalpost.'

'It was the referee,' said Gooderson. 'He had it in for us.'

'Well whatever, Gooderson darling, the fact is that after this wonderful matinée performance there is no doubt that you are all going to become simply the toast of the town. Certain unscrupulous men may call upon you here in your dressing- room. They will lavish you with flowers, with compliments, with phials of Hungary water and methuselahs of the

8

costliest champagne. You must be wary of such men, my hearts, they are not to be trusted.'

'What, what will they do to us?'

'They will take the tender flower of your innocence, Jarvis, and they will bruise it.'

'Will it hurt?'

'Not if it is prepared beforehand. If you come to my study this evening I will ready you for the process with a soothing unguent of my own invention. Wear something green, you should always wear green, Jarvis.'

'Ooh, can I come too?' said Rundell, who was by way of being the Tart of the House.

'And me!' squeaked Harman.

'All are welcome.'

The voice of Robert Bennett-Jones bellowed from the showers. 'Just shut up and get bloody dressed.'

'You're invited too, R.B.-J., didn't I make that clear?'

Bennett-Jones, hairy and squat, came out of the shower and stumped up to Adrian.

Cartwright dropped his rugger shirt into the laundry bin and left the changing-room, trailing his duffle-bag along the ground. As the doors flapped behind him he heard Bennett-Jones's harsh baritone.

'You are disgusting, Healey, you know that?'

He should stay to hear Healey's magnificent put-down, but what was the point? They said that when Healey arrived he had got the highest ever marks in a scholarship entrance. Once, in his first term, Cartwright had been bold enough to ask him why he was so clever, what exercises he did to keep his brain fit. Healey had laughed.

'It's memory, Cartwright, old dear. Memory, the mother of the Muses . . . at least that's what thing-ummy said.'

'Who?'

'You know, what's his name, Greek poet chap. Wrote the Theogony . . . what *was* he called? Begins with an "H".'

'Homer?'

'No, dear. Not Homer, the other one. No, it's gone. Anyway. Memory, that's the key.'

Cartwright went into the House library and took down the first volume of the Chambers Encyclopaedia. He had still only got as far as Bismarck.

In the changing-room, Bennett-Jones snarled into Adrian's face.

'Just plain fucking disgusting.'

The others, some of whom had been peacocking about the room, stroking their towels round their napes like boas, staggered to guilty halts.

'You're a fucking queer and you're turning the whole House into fucking queers.'

'Queer am I?' said Adrian. 'They called Oscar Wilde a queer, they called Michelangelo a queer, they called Tchaikovsky a – '

'And they were queers,' said Sargent, another prefect.

'Well, yes, there is that,' conceded Adrian, 'my argument rather falls down there I grant you, but what I say is this, my door is always open to you, R.B.-J., and to you as well, Sargent, naturally, and if either of you has any problems in coming to terms with your sexuality you mustn't hesitate to visit me and talk about it.'

'Oh for God's sake – '

'We can thrash it out together. Personally I think it's your habit of dressing up in shorts and prancing about on a field and this bizarre obsession with putting your arms round the other members of the scrum and forcing your head between the bottoms of the back row that is at the root of this insane fixation. The lady doth protest too much, methinks.'

'Let's fucking throw him out,' said Sargent, advancing.

'Now I warn you,' said Adrian, 'if either of you touches me . . .'

'Yes?' sneered Bennett-Jones. 'What'll you do?'

'I shall sustain a massive erection, that's what, and I shan't be answerable for the consequences. Some kind of ejaculation is almost bound to ensue and if either of you were to become pregnant I should never forgive myself.'

This was just enough to bring the others down onto his side and have the prefects laughed into retreat.

'Well, my lovelies, I shall have to leave you now. I am promised to the Princes Despina this evening. A little baccarat after supper is my guess. She means to win back the Kurzenauer Emeralds. Jarvis, you have a stiffy, this is most unpleasant, someone throw some cold water over him. Goonight, Lou. Goonight, May. Goonight. Ta ta. Good night, ladies, good night, sweet ladies, good night, good night.'

English boarding schools have much to recommend them. If boys are going to be adolescent, and science has failed to come up with a way of stopping them, then much better to herd them together and let them get on with it in private. Six hundred suits of skin oozing with pustules, six hundred scalps weeping oil, twelve hundred armpits shooting out hair, twelve hundred inner thighs exploding with fungus and six hundred minds filling themselves with suicidal drivel: the world is best protected from this.

For the good of society, therefore, Adrian Healey, like many Healeys before him, had been sent to a prep school at the age of seven, had proceeded to his public school at twelve and now, fifteen years old, he stood trembling with pubertal confusion on the brink of life. There was little to admire. The ravages of puberty had attacked his mind more than his skin, which was some kind of a blessing. From time to time a large, yellow-crowned spot would pop from his forehead, or a blackhead worm its way from the sweaty shelter of the side of his nose, but generally the complexion was good enough not to betray the hormonal crisis and mental havoc that boiled within and the eyes were wide and sensual enough for him to be thought attractive. Too smart at exam passing to be kept out of the Sixth Form, too disrespectful and dishonourable to be a prefect, he had read and absorbed more than he could understand, so he lived by pastiche and pretence.

His constipation, furred tongue and foul-smelling feet were no more than conventional school attributes, passed down from generation to generation, like slang and sadism. Adrian might have been unorthodox, but he was not so blind to the proper decencies as to cultivate smooth-flowing bowels or healthy feet. His good nature prevented him from discovering the pleasures of bullying and his cowardice allowed him to ignore it in others.

The great advantage of English public school life lies of course in the quality of tutelage it provides. Adrian had received a decent and broad English education in the area of his loins. Not all the credit for this could go to his schoolmasters, although a few of them had not been afraid to give practical guidance and instruction of a kind which would gladden the heart of those who believe that the modern teacher is slipshod in his approach to the Whole Boy. Mostly he had been given space to make his own way and learn his own lessons of the flesh. He had quickly happened upon the truth which many lonely contemporaries would never discover, the truth that everybody, simply everybody, was panting for it and could, with patience, be *shown* that they were panting for it. So Adrian grabbed what was to hand and had the time of his life genitally – focusing exclusively on his own gender of course, for this was 1973 and girls had not yet been invented.

His love life, however, was less happy. Earlier that afternoon he had worshipped at his altar in a private welter of misery that his public swagger never hinted at.

It had been upstairs, in the Long Dorm. The room was empty, the floorboards squeaking more faintly than usual beneath his tread. Cartwright's cubicle had its curtain drawn. The distant moan of whistles and cheers on the Upper Games Field and the nearer bang of a downstairs door slamming shut had unsettled him. They were over-familiar, with a bogus, echoing quality, a staginess that put him on his guard. The whole school knew he was here. They knew he liked to creep about the House alone. They were watching, he was convinced of it The background shouts of rugger and hockey weren't real, they were part of a taped soundtrack played to deceive him. He was walking into a trap. It had always been a trap. No one had ever believed in him. They signed him off games and let him think that he had the House to himself. But they knew, they had always known. Tom, Bullock, Heydon-Bayley, even Cartwright. Especially Cartwright. They watched and they waited. They all knew and they all bided their time until the moment they had chosen for his exposure and disgrace.

Let them watch, let them know. Here was Cartwright's bed and under the pillow, here, yes, here the pyjamas. Soft brushed cotton, like Cartwright's soft brushed hair and a smell, a smell that was Cartwright to the last molecule. There was even a single gold hair shining on the collar, and there, just down there, a new aroma, an aroma, an essence that rippled outwards from the centre of the whole Cartwrightness of Cartwright.

For Adrian other people did not exist except as extras, as bit-players in the film of his life. No one but he had noted the splendour and agony of existence, no one else was truly or fully alive. He alone gasped at dew trapped in cobwebs, at spring buds squeaking into life. Afternoon light bouncing like a yo-yo in a stream of spittle dropping from a cow's lips, the slum-wallpaper peel of bark on birches, the mash of wet leaves pulped into pavements, they grew and burst only in him. Only he knew what it was to love.

Haaaaaaah . . . if they really were watching then now was the time to pull back the curtain and jeer, now was the time to howl contempt.

But nothing. No yells, no sneers, no sound at all to burst the swollen calm of the afternoon.

Adrian trembled as he stood and did himself up. It was an illusion. Of course it was an illusion. No one watched, no one judged, no one pointed or whispered. Who were they, after all? Low-browed, scarlet-naped rugger-buggers with no more grace and vision than a jockstrap.

Sighing, he had moved to his own cubicle and laid out the astrakhan coat and top hat.

If you can't join them, he thought, beat them.

He had fallen in love with Hugo Alexander Timothy Cartwright the moment he laid eyes on him, when, as one of a string of five new arrivals, the boy had trickled into evening hall the first night of Adrian's second year.

Heydon-Bayley nudged him.

'What do you reckon, Healey? Lush, or what?'

For once Adrian had remained silent. Something was terribly wrong.

It had taken him two painful terms to identify the symptoms. He looked them up in all the major textbooks. There was no doubt about it. All the authorities concurred: Shakespeare, Tennyson, Ovid, Keats, Georgette Heyer, Milton, they were of one opinion. It was love. The Big One.

Cartwright of the sapphire eyes and golden hair, Cartwright of the Limbs and Lips: he was Petrarch's Laura, Milton's Lycidas, Catullus's Lesbia, Tennyson's Hallam, Shakespeare's fair boy and dark lady, the moon's Endymion. Cartwright was Garbo's salary, the National Gallery, he was cellophane: he was the tender trap, the blank unholy surprise of it all and the bright golden haze on the meadow: he was honey-honey, sugar-sugar, chirpy chirpy cheep-cheep and his baby-love: the voice of the turtle could be heard in the land, there were angels dining at the Ritz and a nightingale sang in Berkeley Square.

Adrian had managed to coax Cartwright into an amusing half-hour in the House lavs two terms previously, but he had never doubted he could get the trousers down: that wasn't it. He wanted something more from him than the few spasms of pleasure that the limited activities of rubbing and licking and heaving and pushing could offer.

He wasn't sure what the thing was that he yearned for, but one thing he did know. It was less acceptable to love, to ache for eternal companionship, than it was to bounce and slurp and gasp behind the fives courts. Love was Adrian's guilty secret, sex his public pride.

He closed the changing-room door and fanned himself with the lavender gloves. It had been a close thing. Too close. The greater the lengths he went to to be liked, the more enemies he gathered on the way. If he fell, Bennett-Jones and others would be there to kick him. One thing was for certain, the Queer Pose was running dry and a new one was going to have to be dreamt up or there would be Trouble.

A gang of fags was mobbing about by the notice-boards. They fell silent as he approached. He patted one of them on the head.

'Pretty children,' he sighed, digging into his waist-coat pocket and pulling out a handful of change. 'Tonight you shall eat.'

Scattering the coins at their feet, he moved on.

Mad, he said to himself as he approached his study door. I think I must be mad.

Tom was there, in a yoga position, biting his toe-nails and listening to *Aqualung*. Adrian sank into a chair and removed his hat.

'Tom,' he said, 'you are looking at a crushed violet, a spent egg, a squeezed tube.'

'I'm looking at a git,' said Tom. 'What's with the coat?'

'You're right,' said Adrian, 'I *am* stupid today. And every day. Stupid, stupid, stupid. Horrid, horrid, horrid. Morbid, morbid, morbid. Torrid, torpid, turbid. Everying in my life ends in id. Get it?'

'Get what?'

'Id. It's Freud. You know.'

'Oh. Right. Yeah. Id.'

'Idealistic idiot, idiosyncratic idler. Everything *begins* in id as well.'

'Everything begins with "I", you mean. Which is ego,' said Tom, placing an ankle behind his ear, 'not id.'

'Well of course it's very easy to be clever. If you could just help me out of this coat, I'm beginning to sweat.'

'Sorry,' said Tom. 'I'm stuck.'

'Are you serious?'

'No.'

Adrian fought his way out of his costume and into

17

his uniform while Tom reverted to a half-lotus and recounted his day.

'Went into town and bought a couple of LPs this afternoon.'

'Don't tell me,' said Adrian, 'let me guess . . . *Parsifal* and *Lark Ascending*?'

'*Atom Heart Mother* and *Salty Dog*.'

'Close.'

Tom lit a cigarette.

'You know what pisses me off about this place?'

'The cuisine? The distressingly plain uniforms?'

'I bumped into Rosengard in the High Street and he asked me why I wasn't watching the match. I mean what?'

'You should've asked him why *he* wasn't.'

'I said I was just on my way.'

'Rebel.'

'I like to keep my nose clean.'

'Well, "I'm just on my way" isn't a very stylish handkerchief, is it? You could have said that the match was too exciting and that your nervous system simply couldn't bear any more suspense.'

'Well I didn't. I came back here, had a wank and finished that book.'

'*The Naked Lunch*?'

'Yeah.'

'What did you reckon?'

'Crap.'

'You're just saying that because you didn't understand it,' said Adrian.

'I'm just saying that because I did understand it,' said Tom. 'Any road up, we'd better start making some toast. I invited Bullock and Sampson over.'

'Oh, *what?*'

'We owe them a study tea.'

'You know I hate intellectuals.'

'You mean you hate people who are cleverer than you are.'

'Yes. I suppose that's why I like you so much, Tom.'

Tom gave him a pained, constipated stare.

'I'll boil the kettle,' he said.

Cartwright looked up from the Chambers Encyclopaedia and mouthed, 'Otto Von Bismarck born in . . . in 1815, the year of Waterloo and the Congress of Vienna. Founder of modern Germany . . .'

In his line of sight were hundreds of books, the only one of which he could remember reading was *To Kill a Mockingbird* in the company of the rest of his fifth form at prep school. Such a great many books and yet this was still only the House library. The School library had thousands and thousands more and university libraries . . . Time was so short and his memory so feeble. What was it Healey had said? Memory is the mother of the Muses.

Cartwright levered Malthus to Nantucket from off the shelf and looked up Muses. There were nine of them and they were the daughters of Zeus and Mnemosyne. If Healey was right then Mnemosyne must mean memory.

Of course! The English word 'mnemonic', something that reminds you of something. Mnemonic must be derived from Mnemosyne. Or the other way around. Cartwright made a note in his rough-book.

According to the encyclopaedia, most of what was

19

known of the Muses came down from the writings of Hesiod, particularly this Theogony. That must have been the poet Healey was referring to, Hesiod. But how did Healey *know* all that? He never seemed to be reading, at least no more than anyone else. Cartwright would never catch up with him. It just wasn't bloody fair.

He wrote down the names of the Muses and returned with a sigh to Bismarck. One day he would get right to the end, to zythum. Not that he needed to. He had peeped ahead and seen that it was a kind of ancient Egyptian beer, much recommended by Diodorus Siculus – whoever he was.

Everyone had been rather surprised the day Adrian announced that he was going to share a study with Tom.

'Thompson?' Heydon-Bayley had shrieked. 'But he's a complete dildo, surely?'

'I like him,' said Adrian, 'he's unusual.'

'Graceless, you mean. Wooden.'

Certainly there was nothing obviously appetising about Tom's appearance or manner, and he remained one of the few boys of his year with whom Adrian had never made the beast with two backs, or rather with whom he had never made the beast with one back and an interestingly shaped middle, but over the last year, more people had come to see that there was something arresting about Tom. He wasn't clever, but he worked hard and had set himself to read a great deal, in order, Adrian assumed, to acquire some of Adrian's dash and sparkle. Tom always went his own way with his own ideas. He managed to get away with the longest hair in the House and the most public nicotine habit in the school, somehow without ever drawing attention to himself. It was as if he grew his hair long and smoked cigarettes because he liked to, not because he liked being seen to. This was dangerously subversive.

Freda, the German undermatron, once discovered him sunbathing nude in the spinney.

'Thompson,' she had cried in outrage, 'you cannot be lying about naked!'

'Sorry, Matron, you're right,' Tom murmured, and he had reached out a hand and put on a pair of mirrored sunglasses. 'Don't know what I was thinking of.'

Adrian felt that it was he who had brought Tom into notice and popularity, that Tom was his own special creation. The silent spotty gink of the first year had been transformed into someone admired and imitated and Adrian wasn't sure how much he liked it.

He liked Tom all right. He was the only person he had ever spoken to about his love for Cartwright and Tom had the decency not to be interested or sympathetic enough to quench the pure holy flame of Adrian's passion with sympathy or advice. Sampson and Bullock he could do without, however. Especially Sampson, who was too much of a grammar-school- type swot ever to be quite the thing. Not an ideal tea-companion at all.

Tea was a very special institution, revolving as it did around the ceremony and worship of Toast. In a place where alcohol, tobacco and drugs were forbidden, it was essential that something should take their place as a powerful and public totem of virility and cool. Toast, for reasons lost in time, was the substance chosen. Its name was dropped on every possible occasion, usually pronounced, in awful public school accents, 'taste'.

'I was just having some toast, when Burton and Hopwood came round . . .'

'Harman's not a bad fag actually. He makes really majorly good toast . . .'

'Yeah, you should come round to my study, maybe, we'll get some toast going . . .'

'God, I can hardly move. I've just completely overdone it on the toast . . .'

Adrian had been looking forward to toasting up with Tom in private and talking about Cartwright.

'Oh, Christ,' he said, clearing a space on his desk for the teapot. 'Oh, Christly Christ.'

'Problem?'

'I shall know no peace other than being kissed by him,' moaned Adrian.

'That a fact?'

'It is a fact, and I'll tell you what else is a fact. It's a fact that he is wearing his blue Shetland turtle-neck today. Even as we speak his body is moving inside it. Warm and quick. It's more than flesh and blood can stand.'

'Have a cold shower, then,' said Tom.

Adrian banged down the teapot and grabbed Tom by the shoulder.

'Cold shower?' he shouted. 'Jessica Christ, man, I'm talking about love! You know what it does to me? It shrinks my stomach, doesn't it, Tom? It pickles my guts, yeah. But what does it do to my mind? It tosses the sandbags overboard so the balloon can soar. Suddenly I'm above the ordinary. I'm competent, supremely competent. I'm walking a tightrope over Niagara Falls. I'm one of the great ones. I'm Michelangelo, moulding the beard of Moses. I'm Van Gogh, painting pure sunlight. I'm Horowitz, playing the Emperor Concerto. I'm John Barrymore before the movies got him by the throat. I'm Jesse James and his two brothers – all three of them. I'm W. Shakespeare. And out there it's not the school any longer – it's the Nile, Tom, the Nile – and down it floats the barge of Cleopatra.'

'Not bad,' said Tom, 'not bad at all. Your own?'

'Ray Milland in *The Lost Weekend*. But he could have been talking about Cartwright.'

'But he was talking about alcohol,' said Tom, 'which should tell you a lot.'

'Meaning?'

'Meaning shut up and get buttering.'

'I shall put the *Liebestod* on the stereo, that's what I shall do, you horrid beastly man,' said Adrian, 'and still my beating heart with concord of sweet sounds. But quick, man! – I hear a hansom drawing up outside! And here, Watson, unless I am very much mistaken, is our client now upon the stair. Come in!'

Sampson appeared at the doorway, blinking through his spectacles, followed by Bullock who tossed a jar at Tom.

'Hi. I brought some lemon curd.'

'Lemon curd!' said Adrian. 'And what was I saying only this minute, Tom?' "If only we had some lemon curd for our guests." You're a mind-reader, Bollocks.'

'Some toast over there,' said Tom.

23

'Thanks, Thompson,' said Sampson, helping himself. 'Gooderson tells me you were not unadjacent to mobbing up R.B.-J. and Sargent in the changing-rooms, Healey.'

'Dame Rumour outstrides me yet again.'

Not unadjacent? Jesus . . .

Bullock slapped Tom on the back.

'Hey, Tommo!' he said. 'I see you've got *Atom Heart Mother* at last. What do you reckon? Far outsville or far insville?'

While Tom and Bullock talked about Pink Floyd, Sampson told Adrian why he thought Mahler was in actual fact wilder, in the sense of more controlled, than any rock group.

'That's an interesting point,' said Adrian, 'in the sense of not being interesting at all.'

When the tea and toast were finished, Bullock stood up and cleared his throat.

'I think I should announce my plan now, Sam.'

'Definitely,' said Sampson.

'What ho!' said Adrian, getting up to shut the door. 'Treasons, stratagems and spoils.'

'It's like this,' said Bullock. 'My brother, I don't know if you know, is at Radley, on account of my parents thinking it a bad idea to have us both at the same school.'

'On account of your being twins?' said Adrian.

'Right, on account of my mother OD-ing on fertility drugs. Any old way, he wrote to me last week telling me about an incredible bitch of a row blazing there on account of someone having been and gone and produced an unofficial magazine called *Raddled*, full of obscene libellous *Oz*-like filth. And what I thought, what Sammy and I thought, was – why not?'

'Why not what?' said Tom.

'Why not do the same thing here?'

'You mean an underground magazine?'

'Yup.'

Tom opened and shut his mouth. Sampson smirked.

'Jesus suffering fuck,' said Adrian. 'It's not half a thought.'

'Face it, it's a wow.'

'These guys,' said Tom, 'the ones who put out this magazine at Radley. What happened to them?'

Sampson polished his spectacles with the end of his tie.

'Ah, now this is why we must proceed with great circumspection. They were both, hum, "put out" themselves. "Booted out" I believe is the technical phrase.'

'That means it's got to be a secret,' said Bullock. 'We write it in the holidays. You send me the material, typed onto stencils. I get it duplicated on my dad's office Gestetner, bring it back at the beginning of next term, we find a way of distributing it secretly round all the Houses.'

'All a bit Colditz, isn't it?' said Tom.

'No, no!' said Adrian. 'Don't you listen to Thompson, he's an old cynicky-boots. I'm in, Bollocks. I'm in for definite. What sort of material do you want?'

'Oh you know,' said Bullock, 'seditious, anti-public school. That kind of thing. Something to shake them up a bit.'

'I'm planning a sort of *fabliau* comparing this place

25

with a fascist state,' said Sampson, 'sort of *Animal Farm* meets *Arturo Ui* . . .'

'Stop it, Sammy, I'm wet at the very thought,' said Adrian.

He looked across at Tom.

'What do you reckon?'

'Yeah, why not? Sounds a laugh.'

'And remember,' said Bullock, 'not a word to *anyone.*'

'Our lips are sealed,' said Adrian. *Lips. Sealed.* Dangerous words. Not five minutes could pass without him thinking of Cartwright.

Bullock took a tobacco tin out of his pocket and looked around the room.

'Now,' he said, 'if someone would close the curtains and light a joss-stick, I have here for your delight some twenty-four-carat black Nepalese cannabis resin which should be smoked immediately on account of it being seriously good shit.'

II

Adrian threw himself along the corridor towards Biffen's formroom. Dr Meddlar, one of the school chaplains, stopped him.

'Late, Healey.'

'Really, sir? So am I.'

Meddlar took him by the shoulders. 'You're riding for a fall, Healey, you know that? There are hedges and ditches ahead and you are on course for an almighty cropper.'

'Sir.'

'And I shall be cheering and laughing as you tumble,' said Meddlar, his spectacles flashing.

'That's just the warm-hearted Christian in you, sir.'

'Listen to me!' spat Meddlar. 'You think you're very clever, don't you? Well let me tell you that this school has no room for creatures like you.'

'Why are you saying this to me, sir?'

'Because if you don't learn to live with others, if you don't conform, your life is going to be one long miserable hell.'

'Will that give you satisfaction, sir? Will that please you?'

Meddlar stared at him and gave a hollow little laugh. 'What gives you the right to talk to me like that, boy? What on earth do you think gives you the right?'

Adrian was furious to find that there were tears springing to his eyes. 'God gives me the right, sir, because God loves me. And God won't let me be judged by a f-f-fascist – hypocrite – bastard like you!' He squirmed away from Meddlar's grasp and ran on down the corridor. 'Bastard,' he tried to shout, but the words choked in his throat. 'Fucking bloody bastard.'

Meddlar laughed after him. 'You're evil, Healey, quite evil.'

Adrian ran on and out into the quad. Everyone was in morning school. The colonnade was empty, the Old School Room, the library, the headmaster's house, the Founder's lawn, all deserted. This again was Adrian's home, an empty world. He imagined the whole school with noses pressed up against their form-room windows staring out at him as he ran through the West Quad. Prefects with walkie-talkies striding down the corridor.

'This is Blue Seven. Subject proceeding along past the Cavendish library towards the Music School. Over.'

'Blue Seven this is Meddlar. Interview went according to plan, subject now unstable and in tears. Red Three will continue surveillance in the Music School. Over and out.'

Either they've got a life and I'm imaginary, thought Adrian, or I've got a life and they're imaginary.

He'd read all the books, he knew he was really the same as anyone else. But who else had snakes wrestling in their stomachs like this? Who was running beside him with the same desperation? Who else would remember this moment and every moment like it to the last day of their lives? No one. They were all at their desks thinking of rugger and lunch. He was different and alone.

The ground floor of the Music School was filled with little practice-rooms. As Adrian stumbled along the passageway he could hear lessons in progress. A cello pushed a protesting Saint-Saëns swan along the water. A trumpet further along farted out 'Thine be the glory'. And there, third from the end, Adrian saw through the glass panel, was Cartwright, making quite a decent fist of a Beethoven minuet.

Fate was always doing this. There were six hundred boys in the school and although Adrian went out of his way to intercept Cartwright and to engineer apparently accidental meetings – he had learnt his time table off by heart – he was sure that he bumped into him by genuine chance more often than was natural.

Cartwright appeared to be alone in the practice-room. Adrian pushed open the door and went in.

'Hi,' he said, 'don't stop, it's good.'

'Oh, it's terrible really,' said Cartwright, 'I can't get the left hand working smoothly.'

'That's not what I've heard,' said Adrian and immediately wanted to bite off his tongue.

Here he was, alone in a room with Cartwright, whose hair was even now leaping with light from the sunshine that poured in through the window, Cartwright whom he loved with his whole life and being and all he could find to say was 'That's not what I've heard.' Jesus, what was the *matter* with him? He might just as well have put on an Eric Morecambe voice, shouted 'There's no answer to that' and slapped Cartwright's cheeks.

'Um, official lesson?' he said.

'Well, I've got my Grade Three exam in half an hour, so this is a practice. It lets me off double maths at least.'

'Lucky you.'

Lucky you? Oh, pure Oscar Wilde.

'Well, I'd better let you get on with it then, hadn't I?'

Great, Adrian, brilliant. Magisterial. 'I'd better let you get on with it then, hadn't I?' Change one syllable and the whole delicate epigram collapses.

'Right,' said Cartwright and turned back to his music.

'Cheerio, then. G'luck!'

'Bye.'

Adrian closed the door.

Oh God, Oh Godly God.

He wound a fraught trail back to the form-rooms. Thank God it was only Biffen.

'You're extraordinarily late, Healey.'

'Well, sir,' said Adrian, sitting at his desk, 'the way I look at it, better extraordinarily late than extraordinarily never.'

'Perhaps you'd like to tell me what kept you?'

'Not really, sir.'

Something of a gasp ran round the form-room. This was going it a big strong, even for Healey.

'I beg your pardon?'

'Well, not in front of the whole form, sir. It's rather personal.'

'Oh I see. I see,' said Biffen. 'Well, in that case, you had better tell me afterwards.'

'Sir.'

Nothing like getting a schoolmaster's curiosity glands juicing.

Adrian looked out of the window.

'Oh to be in Cartwright, now that March is here.'

Any minute now, some lucky examiner was going to be watching a lovely little frown furrow Cartwright's brow as he skipped through his minuet. Watching the woollen sleeve of his winter jacket ride up his arms.

'Whenas in wool my Cartwright goes, Then, then methinks how sweetly flows, That liquefaction of his clothes.'

He became aware of Biffen's voice knocking at the door of his dreams.

'Can you give us an example, Healey?'

'Er, example, sir?'

'Yes, of a subjunctive following a superlative.'

'A superlative, you say, sir?'

'Yes.'

'A subjunctive following a superlative?'

'Yes, yes.'

'Um . . . how about *"le garçon le plus beau que je connaisse"*?'

'Er . . . the finest boy that I know? Yes that meets the case.'

'Finest, sir? I meant the most beautiful.'

Damn, he was supposed to be phasing out the queer pose. Well, at least it got a laugh.

'Thank you, Healey, that will do. Be quiet, the rest of you, he really doesn't need any encouragement.'

Oh but I do, thought Adrian, I need all the encouragement going.

The lesson moved on, Biffen leaving him alone to daydream.

At the end of the forty minutes he reacted to the bell as fast as he could, streaking to the doorway from the back of the form-room and trying to lose himself in the crowd, but Biffen called him back.

'Aren't you forgetting something, Healey?'

'Sir?'

'You owe me an explanation for your unpunctuality, I think.'

Adrian approached the dais.

'Oh yes, sir. The thing is, sir, I was going to be late anyway – only a bit, but I bumped into Dr Meddlar.'

'He kept you for twenty minutes?'

'Yes, sir – or rather no, sir. He was very rude to me. He upset me, sir.'

'Rude to you? The Chaplain was rude to you?'

'I'm sure that's not how he would put it, sir.' Adrian had a shot at his pure but troubled expression. It was particularly effective when looking up at someone, as he was now. It was loosely based on Dominic Guard's Leo in the film of *The Go-Between*. A sort of baffled honesty.

'He . . . he made me cry, sir, and I was too embarrassed to come in blubbing, so I went and hid in the music-room until I felt better.'

This was all terribly unfair on poor old Biffen, whom Adrian rather adored for his snowy hair and perpetual air of benign astonishment. And 'blubbing' . . . Blubbing went out with 'decent' and 'ripping'. Mind you, not a bad new language to start up. 1920s schoolboy slang could be due for a revival.

'Oh dear. But I'm sure the Chaplain must have had good reason to be . . . that is, Dr Meddlar wouldn't speak sharply to you without cause.'

'Well I admit I was cheeky to him, sir. But you know what he's like.'

'He is, I am sure, a scrupulously fair man.'

'Yes, sir. I – I wouldn't want you to think that I've been lying to you, sir. I'm sure Dr Meddlar will tell you his side of the story if you ask him.'

'I won't do that. I know whether a boy is telling me the truth or not.'

'Thank you, sir.'

Did he hell. They never bloody did.

'I don't want to lecture you, Healey, and I don't want to keep you from your morning break, but you must face the fact that many members of staff are beginning to lose their patience. Perhaps you feel they don't understand you?'

'I think the problem is that they do understand me, sir.'

'Yes. You see that is exactly the kind of remark that is guaranteed to put certain masters' backs up, isn't it? Sophistication is not an admired quality. Not only at school. Nobody likes it anywhere. In England at any rate.'

'Sir.'

'You're the cleverest boy in my French set. You know that perfectly well. But you've never worked. That makes you the stupidest boy in the school.'

Parable of the talents next, what was the betting?

'What are your university thoughts?'

'Oh, well sir . . . you know. After "A" levels I think I'll've had it with education, really. And it will probably have had it with me.'

'I see. Tell me, what do you do on Friday afternoons, Healey? I take it you're not in the Cadet Force.'

'Threw me out, sir. It was an outrage.'

'Yes, I'm sure it was. So it's Pioneering, is it?'

'Yes, sir. There's a little old lady I visit.'

'Well,' said Biffen filling his briefcase with exercise books, 'there's a little old lady and a little old man in the Morley Road you might also find time to visit one day. My wife and I always give tea on Fridays, you'd be most welcome.'

'Thank you, sir.'

'You don't have to let us know in advance. We shall expect you when we see you. Off you go then.'

'Thank you, Mr Biffen, thank you very much.'

Adrian instinctively offered his hand which Biffen took with tremendous firmness, looking him straight in the eye.

'I'm not Mr Chips, you know. I'm perfectly well aware that you feel sorry for me. It's bad enough from the staff, but I won't take pity from you. I won't.'

'No sir,' said Adrian, 'I wasn't . . .'

'Good.'

III

Tom and Adrian and Pigs Trotter, an occasional hanger-on, were walking into town. From time to time tracksuited boys ran past them, with all the deadly purpose and humourless concentration of those who enjoyed Games. Juniors twittered along, running sticks against palings and whispering. Adrian thought it worth while trying out his new slang.

'I say, you fellows, here's a rum go! Old Biffo was jolly odd this morning. He gave me a lot of pi-jaw about slacking and then invited me to tea. No rotting! He did really.'

'I expect he fancies you,' said Tom.

'That's beastly talk, Thompson. Jolly well take it back or expect a good scragging.'

They walked on for a bit, Adrian practising new phrases and Pigs Trotter lumbering behind laughing so indiscriminately that Adrian soon tired of the game.

'Anyway,' he said. 'Tell me about your parents, Tom.'

'What do you want to know?'

'Well, you never talk about them.'

'Nothing to say about my folks,' Thompson said. 'Dad works for British Steel, Mum is next in line for Mayor. Two sisters, both mad, and a brother who's coming here next term.'

'What about you, Healey?' said Pigs Trotter. 'What do your parents do?'

'Parent,' said Adrian. 'The mother is no more.'

Trotter was upset.

'Oh God,' he said, 'I'm sorry. I didn't realise . . .'

'No, that's fine. Car crash. When I was twelve.'

'That's . . . that's awful.'

'If we go to Gladys Winkworth, I'll tell you the whole story.'

The church in the town was perched on a hill and in the cemetery – which people of shattering wit like Sampson never tired of calling 'the dead centre of town' – there was an old wooden bench on which was a plaque which said 'Gladys Winkworth'. Nothing else. The assumption was that it had been erected by a doting widower as a lasting memorial to his dead wife. Tom thought she was actually buried under it. Adrian believed it was simply the bench's proper name and he stuck to that belief.

From Gladys, the Upper, Middle and Lower Games Fields, the science block, the sports hall, the theatre, the Old School Room, libraries, chapel, Hall and Art School were all visible. You felt like a general observing a battle.

The day was cold and the breath steamed from their mouths and nostrils as they climbed through the graveyard.

'Alas, regardless of their fate the little victims play,'

said Adrian. 'The quick and the young play peep-bo behind the marking stones of the cold and the dead.'

Tom and Adrian sat down and waited for Pigs Trotter to catch up.

'It's not a nice story, the story of my mother,' said Adrian as Trotter finally crashed down beside them, 'but I'll tell it if you promise to keep it to yourselves. Only Pa Tickford knows. My father told him when I arrived here.'

Trotter nodded breathlessly. 'I won't tell a soul, Healey. Honest.'

Adrian looked at Tom who nodded gravely.

'Very well then,' said Adrian. 'One evening about three years ago . . . almost exactly three years ago in fact, I was sitting at home watching television. It was *A Man Called Ironside*, I remember. My father is a Professor of Biochemistry at Bristol University and he often works late. My mother had been in the kitchen since three in the afternoon drinking vodka from a teacup. At ten o'clock she smashed the cup onto the floor and cried out so I could hear her in the sitting room.'

Trotter shifted uncomfortably.

'Look,' he said. 'You don't have to tell us this, you know.'

'No, no, I want to. She had been, as I say, drinking all afternoon and she suddenly howled, "Ten o'clock! It's ten o'fucking clock! Why doesn't he come? Why in God's name doesn't he come?" Something along those lines.

'I went into the kitchen and looked at her face all swollen, her tear-stained and mascara-blotched cheeks and her trembling lip and I remember thinking, "She's like Shelley Winters but without the talent." Don't know why a thought like that should come to me, but it did. I turned back to the telly – couldn't bear to look at her like that – and said, "He's working, Mother. You know he's working."

'"Working?" She shrieked her stinking breath right into my face. "Working! Oh that's very good. Screwing that *cunt* of a lab assistant is what he's doing. The little bitch. I've seen her . . . with her stupid white coat and her stupid white teeth. Little *bitch whore*!"'

Tom and Trotter both stared at Adrian in disbelief as he screeched out the words, but his eyes were closed and he didn't seem to be aware of them.

'She really could scream, my mother. I thought her voice would fracture with the violence of it, but in fact it was my own which cracked. "You should go to bed, Mother," I said.

'"Bed! He's the one who's in fucking bed," she giggled, and she pulled at the bottle and the last of the vodka just dribbled down her mouth and mixed with the tears that ran down the folds of her fat face. She burped and tried to jam the bottle into the waste-hole of the waste-disposal thing, the thingummy.'

'Garburator,' said Pigs Trotter. 'I think they're called Garburators.'

'Garburator, that's it. She tried to jam the bottle down the Garburator.

'"I'm *going* to *catch* them at their little *game*," she chanted – she put on a kind of sing-song voice whenever she was pissed, it was one of the signs that she was really gone – "*That's* what *I'm* going to *do*. Where are the keys?"

'"Mother, you can't drive!" I said. "Just wait, he'll be back soon. You see."

'"Where are the keys? Where are the fucking car keys?"

'Well, I knew exactly where they were. In the hall, on the table, and I ran for them and stuffed them into my mouth. God knows why. That really got her going.

'"Come here you little bastard, give me those keys!"

'I said, "Mother, you can't drive like this, just leave it, will you?"

'And then . . . then she picked up a vase from off the table and flung it at me. Broke on the side of my head and sent me flying against the foot of the stairs where I tripped and fell. See that scar, just there?'

Adrian parted his hair and showed Trotter and Tom a small white scar.

'Five stitches. Anyway, there was blood all running down my face and she was shaking me and slapping my face, left and right, left and right.

'"Will you give me those fucking keys?" she kept screaming, shaking me on every syllable. I sprawled there, I was crying I don't mind telling you, really wailing. "Please, Mother, you can't go out, you can't. Please!"'

Adrian stopped and looked around.

'Dare we risk a cigarette, do you think?'

Tom lit three at once.

'Go on!' said Pigs Trotter. 'What happened then?'

'Well,' said Adrian inhaling deeply, 'what Mother hadn't seen was that the moment the vase hit me, the car keys had shot out of me like a clay-pigeon from a trap. She thought I still had them in my mouth so she

38

started to try and wrench it open, you know, like a vet trying to give a pill to a dog.

'"So the little bugger's swallowed them has he?" she said.

'I shouted back, "Yes, I've swallowed them! I've swallowed them and you can't get them back! So . . . so just forget it." But like a pratt of a heroine in a Hammer horror film I couldn't help looking round for them myself, so of course she followed my eyes, crawled across the hallway and swooped on them. Then she was off. I kept shouting at her to come back. I heard the scrunch on the gravel as she drove away and then – again like some git in a film – I fainted.'

'Christ,' said Pigs Trotter.

'She killed a family of four as well as herself,' said Adrian. 'My father, who had never had an unfaithful thought in his life, has still not really recovered. She was a bitch, my mother. A real bitch.'

'Yes,' said Tom. 'Thing is, Ade, you may have forgotten, but I met your mother last term. Tall woman with a wide smile.'

'Fuck,' said Adrian. 'So you did. Oh well, it was a good try anyway.' He stood and flicked his cigarette behind a gravestone.

Trotter stared at him.

'You mean,' he said. 'You mean that you made that up?'

'"Fraid so,' said Adrian.

'All of it?'

'Well my father's a professor, that bit's true.'

'You fucking shitbag,' said Trotter, tears filling his

eyes. 'You fucking shitbag!' He stumbled away, chok-
ing with tears. Adrian watched him go with surprise.

'What's the matter with Pigs? He must have known
it was a lie as soon as I began.'

'Oh nothing,' said Tom, turning his large brown
eyes on Adrian. 'His mother and two brothers were
killed in a car crash three years ago, that's all.'

'Oh no! No! You're kidding!'

'Yes I am, actually.'

An MCC Tie sat down next to a Powder Blue Safari suit at a window table in the Café Bazaar. White Shirts with Black Waistcoats hurried to and fro, the change jingling in their leather pouches.

'Herr Ober,' called the MCC Tie.

'Mein Herr?'

'Zwei Kaffee mit Schlag, bitte. Und Sachertorte. Zweimal.'

The waiter executed a trim Austrian bow and departed.

The Powder Blue Safari Suit mopped his brow.

'No exchange was made,' he said.

'Well now,' said the MCC Tie. 'Odysseus will certainly have got hold of the documents and will be preparing to take them out of Salzburg. He must be followed and relieved of them.'

'If the Trojans are prepared to kill Patrochlus in broad daylight . . .'

'They won't dare harm Odysseus.'

'He has a companion, you know. A young Englishman.'

The MCC Tie smiled.

'I'm fully aware of it. How shall we style him?'

'Telemachus?'

'Quite right. Telemachus. Remind me to tell you all about Telemachus.'

'You know him?'

'Intimately. I think we will find that it won't be necessary to inflict harm upon either Odysseus or Telemachus. Just so long as we can lay our hands on Mendax.'

'They are leaving tomorrow.'

'Are they now? What kind of chariot are they riding?'

'Odysseus has a red Wolseley.'

'Typical. Quite typical.'

The MCC Tie looked across at the Safari Suit with an expression of affectionate contempt.

'I don't suppose, Hermes, that you possess such a thing as a short-wave wireless?'

'A report to make?'

'Don't be foolish. BBC World Service. The West Indies are playing England at Old Trafford today.'

'Playing? Playing what?'

'Cricket, you arse of a man. Cricket.'

Two

I

'The periphrastic "do" was a superfluous tense-carrier,' said Adrian. 'Semantically empty yet widely used. The major theories of the origin of the periphrastic "do" are three: One) It was derived from the influence of the corresponding use of "faire" in French. Two) It developed out of the Old English causative "do". Three) It derived from semantic development of the full factitive verb "do". An examination of these three theories should tell us much about alternative approaches to diachronic syntax and generative grammar.'

He looked across to the sofa. Trefusis was lying on his back, an overflowing ashtray on his chest, lightweight earphones around his neck and a square of mauve silk over his face, through which he managed to smoke. If it weren't for the rise and fall of the ashtray and the clouds of smoke weaving through the silk, Adrian might have thought him dead. He hoped not, this was a good essay he was reading out and he had taken a lot of trouble over it.

Friends had warned against the Philology option.

'You'll get Craddock, who's useless,' they said.

43

'Trefusis only teaches research students and a few select undergraduates. Do the American paper like everyone else.'

But Trefusis had consented to see him.

'The Early Middle English periphrastic "do" could occur after modals and "have" + past participle. It was essentially a second position non-modal operator mutually exclusive with "be" + past participle and incompatible with a passive format. As late as eighteen-eighteen some grammarians wrote that it was a standard alternate to the simple form, but others denounced its use in any but empathic, interrogative and negative sentences. By the mid-eighteenth century it was obsolete.'

Adrian looked up from his sheaf of papers. A brown stain was forming in Trefusis's handkerchief, as the silk filtered the smoke.

'Um . . . that's it . . .'

Silence from the sofa. Far away all the bells of Cambridge began to chime the hour.

'Professor Trefusis?'

He couldn't have slept through an essay of that quality, surely? Adrian cleared his throat and tried again, more loudly.

'Professor Trefusis?'

From under the handkerchief came a sigh.

'So.'

Adrian wiped the palms of his hands on his knees.

'Was it all right?' he asked.

'Well constructed, well researched, well supported, well argued . . .'

'Oh. Thank you.'

'Original, concise, thoughtful, perceptive, incisive,

44

illuminating, cogent, lucid, compelling, charmingly read . . .'

'Er – good.'

'I should imagine,' said Trefusis, 'that it must have taken you almost an hour to copy out.'

'Sorry?'

'Come, come, Mr Healey. You've already insulted your own intelligence.'

'Oh.'

'Val Kirstlin, *Neue Philologische Abteilung*, July 1973, "The Origin and Nature of the Periphrastic Verb 'Do' in Middle and Early Modern English". Am I right?'

Adrian shifted uncomfortably. It was hard enough to know what Trefusis was thinking when his face was unveiled; with a handkerchief over him he was as unreadable as a doctor's prescription.

'Look, I'm terribly sorry,' he said. 'The thing is . . .'

'Please don't apologise. Had you bothered to do any work of your own I should have been obliged to sit through it just the same, and I can assure you that I had much rather listen to a good essay than a mediocre one.'

Adrian couldn't think of an adequate reply to this.

'You have a fine brain. A really excellent brain, Mr Healey.'

'Thank you.'

'A fine brain, but a dreadful mind. I have a fine brain *and* a fine mind. Likewise Russell. Leavis, a good mind, practically no brain at all. Shall we continue like this, I wonder?'

'Like what?'

'This fortnightly exhibition of stolen goods. It all

seems rather pointless. I don't find the pose of careless youth charming and engaging any more than you find the pose of careworn age fascinating and eccentric, I should imagine. Perhaps I should let you play the year away. I have no doubt that you will do very well in your final tests. Honesty, diligence and industry are wholly superfluous qualities in one such as you, as you have clearly grasped.'

'Well, it's just that I've been so . . .'

Trefusis pulled the handkerchief from his face and looked at Adrian.

'But of course you have! Frantically busy. Fran-tic-ally.'

Trefusis helped himself to another cigarette from a packet that lay on top of a tower of books next to the sofa and tapped it against his thumb-nail.

'My first meeting with you only confirmed what I first suspected. You are a fraud, a charlatan and a shyster. My favourite kind of person, in fact.'

'What makes you so sure?'

'I am a student of language, Mr Healey. You write with fluency and conviction, you talk with authority and control. A complex idea here, an abstract proposition there, you juggle with them, play with them, seduce them. There is no movement from doubt to comprehension, no breaking down, no questioning, no excitement. You try to persuade others, never yourself. You recognise patterns, but you rearrange them where you should analyse them. In short, you do not think. You have never thought. You have never said to me anything that you believe to be true, only things which sound true and perhaps even ought to be true: things that, for the moment, are in character with whatever persona you have adopted for the afternoon. You cheat, you short-cut, you lie. It's too wonderful.'

'With respect, Professor . . .'

'Pigswill! You don't respect me. You fear me, are irritated by me, envy me . . . you everything me, but you do not respect me. And why should you? I am hardly respectable.'

'What I mean is, am I so different from anyone else? Doesn't everyone think the way I think? Doesn't everyone just rearrange patterns? Ideas can't be created or destroyed, surely.'

'Yes!' Trefusis clapped his hands with delight. 'Yes, yes, yes! But who else *knows* that they are doing that and nothing else? *You* know, you have always known. That is why you are a liar. Others try their best, when they speak they mean it. You never mean it. You extend this duplicity to your morals. You use and misuse people and ideas because you do not believe they exist. Just patterns for you to play with. You're a hound of hell and you know it.'

'So,' said Adrian, 'what's to become of me then?'

'Ah, well. I could ask you not to bother me any more. Let you get on with your boring little life while I get on with mine. Or I could write a note to your tutor. He would send you down from the university. Either course would deprive me of the income, however nugatory, that I receive for supervising you. What to do? What to do? Pour yourself a glass of Madeira, there's Sercial or Bual on the side. Hum! It's all so difficult.'

Adrian stood and picked his way across the room. Trefusis's quarters could be described in one word.

Books.

Books and books and books. And then, just when an observer might be lured into thinking that that must be it, more books.

Barely a square inch of wood or wall or floor was visible. Walking was only allowed by pathways cut between the piles of books. Treading these pathways with books waist-high either side was like negotiating a maze. Trefusis called the room his 'librarinth'. Areas where seating was possible were like lagoons in a coral strand of books.

Adrian supposed that any man who could speak twenty-three languages and read forty was likely to collect a few improving volumes along the way. Trefusis himself was highly dismissive of them.

'Waste of trees,' he had once said. 'Stupid, ugly, clumsy, heavy things. The sooner technology comes up with a reliable alternative the better.'

Early in the term he had flung a book at Adrian's head in irritation at some crass comment. Adrian had caught it and been shocked to see that it was a first edition of *Les Fleurs du Mal*.

'Books are not holy relics,' Trefusis had said. 'Words may be my religion, but when it comes to worship, I am very low church. The temples and the graven images are of no interest to me. The superstitious mammetry of a bourgeois obsession for books is severely annoying. Think how many children are put off reading by prissy little people ticking them off whenever they turn a page carelessly. The world is so fond of saying that books should be "treated with respect". But when are we told that *words* should be treated with respect? From our earliest years we are taught to revere only the outward and visible. Ghastly literary types maundering on about books as "objects". Yes, that does happen to be a first edition. A present from Noël Annan, as a matter of fact. But I assure you that a foul yellow *livre de poche* would have been just as useful to me. Not that I fail to appreciate Noël's generosity. A book is a piece of technology. If people wish to amass them and pay high prices for this one or that, well and good. But they can't pretend that it is any higher or more intelligent a calling than collecting snuff-boxes or bubble-gum cards. I may read a book, I may use it as an ashtray, a paperweight, a doorstop or even as a missile to throw at silly young men who make fatuous remarks. So. Think again.' And Adrian had thought again.

Now he found his way back to the small clearing where Trefusis lay on his sofa blowing smoke-rings at the ceiling.

'Your very good health,' said Adrian sipping his Madeira.

Trefusis beamed at him.

'Don't be pert,' he said, 'it isn't at all becoming.'

'No, Professor.'

There followed a silence in which Adrian eagerly joined.

He had stood in many studies in his day, tracing arabesques on the carpet with his foot, while angry men had described his shortcomings and settled his future. Trefusis was not angry. Indeed he was rather cheerful. It was perfectly apparent that he couldn't care less whether Adrian lived or died.

'As your Senior Tutor, I am your moral guardian,'

he said at last. 'A moral guardian yearns for an immoral ward and the Lord has provided. I shall strike a bargain with you, that's what I shall do. I am going to leave you in uninterrupted peace for the rest of the year on one condition. I want you to set to work on producing something that will surprise me. You tell me that ideas cannot be created. Perhaps, but they can be discovered. I have a peculiar horror of the cliché – there! the phrase "I have a peculiar horror" is just such a revolting expression as most maddens me – and I think you owe it to yourself, to descend to an even more nauseating phrase, to devote your energies to forging something new in the dark smithy of your fine brain. I haven't produced anything original myself in years, most of my colleagues have lived from the nappy onwards without any thought at all making the short journey across their minds, leave alone a fresh one. But if you can furnish me with a piece of work that contains even the seed of novelty, the ghost of a shred of a scintilla of a germ of a suspicion of an iota of a shadow of a particle of something interesting and provoking, something that will amuse and astonish, then I think you will have repaid me for being forced to listen to you regurgitating the ideas of others and you will have done a proper service to yourself into the bargain. Do we have a deal?'

'I don't quite understand.'

'Perfectly simple! Any subject, any period. It can be a three-volume disquisition or a single phrase on a scrap of paper. I look forward to hearing from you before the end of term. That is all.'

Trefusis fitted the earphones over his ears and groped under the sofa for a cassette.

'Right,' said Adrian. 'Er . . .'

But Trefusis had put the handkerchief back over his face and settled back to the sound of Elvis Costello.

Adrian set down his empty glass and poked out his tongue at the reclining figure. Trefusis's hand came up and jabbed an American single-fingered salute.

Oh well, thought Adrian as he walked across Hawthorn Tree Court on his way to the porter's lodge. An original idea. That can't be too hard. The library must be full of them.

At the lodge he cleared his pigeon-hole. The largest object there was a jiffy-bag stuck with a hand-made label saying 'Toast by Post'. He opened it and a miniature serving of marmalade, two slices of soggy toast and a note fell out. He smiled: more flattering attentions from Hunt the Thimble, a relic from his days at Chartham Park a year ago. He had thought then that life at Cambridge was going to be so simple.

The note was written in an Old English Gothic which must have taken Hunt the Thimble hours to master.

'He took the bread and when he had given thanks, he toasted it and gave it to Mr Healey saying, Take, eat, this is my body which is given for you: eat this in remembrance of me. Likewise after supper he took the sachet of Marmalade and when he had given thanks, he gave it to them saying, scoff ye all of this; for this is my Marmalade of the New Testament, which is spread for you: do this as oft as ye shall taste it, in remembrance of me. *Amen.*'

Adrian smiled again. How old would Hunt the Thimble be now? Twelve or thirteen probably.

There was a letter from Uncle David.

'Hope you're enjoying life. How's the college doing in the Cuppers this year? Had a chance to inspect the Blues XI? Enclosed a little something. I know how mess bills can mount up . . .'

Mess bills? The man must be getting senile. Still, three hundred quid was surprising and useful.

'. . . I shall be in Cambridge next weekend, staying at the Garden House. I want you to visit me on Saturday night at eight. I have a proposition to put to you. Much love, Uncle David.'

The pigeon-hole was also stuffed with circulars and hand-bills.

'A tea-party will be held on Scholar's Lawn, St John's College, to protest at American support for the regime in El Salvador.'

'The Mummers present Artaud's *The Cenci* in a new translation by Bridget Arden. Incest! Violence! A play for our times in the Trinity Lecture Theatre.'

'Sir Ian Gilmour will talk to the Cambridge Tory Reform Group about his book *Inside Right*. Christ's College. Admission Free.'

'Dr Anderson will give a lecture to the Herrick Society entitled *The Punk Ethic As Radical Outside*. Non-members £1.50.'

After a judicious binning of these and other leaflets, Adrian was left with Uncle David's cheque, the toast, a bill from Heffer's bookshop and a Barclaycard statement, both of which he opened as he walked back to his rooms.

He was astounded to discover that he owed Heffers

£112 and Barclaycard £206. With the exception of one or two novels, all the books itemised on the Heffer's bill were on art history. A Thames and Hudson edition of Masaccio alone had cost £40.

Adrian frowned. The titles were very familiar, but he knew that he hadn't bought them.

He quickened his pace across the Sonnet Bridge and into the President's Court, only to charge straight into a shrivelled old don in a gown. With a cry of 'Whoops!' the man, whom he recognised as the mathematician Adrian Williams, fell sprawling on the ground, sending books and papers flying over the grass.

'Dr Williams!' Adrian helped him up. 'I am sorry . . .'

'Oh hello, Adrian,' said Williams, taking his hand and springing up to his feet. 'I'm afraid neither of us was looking where we were going. We Adrians are notoriously abstracted, are we not?'

They skipped about the lawn collecting Williams's papers.

'Do you know,' said Williams, 'I tried one of those packet soups yesterday. "Knorr" it was called, K–N–O–R–R, a very strange name indeed, but Lord, it was delicious. Chicken Noodle. Have you ever tried it?'

'Er, I don't think so,' said Adrian picking up the last of the books and handing it to Williams.

'Oh you should, you really should! Miraculous. You have a paper packet no larger than . . . well let me see . . . what is it no larger than?'

'A paperback?' said Adrian shuffling from foot to

foot. Once cornered by Williams, it was very hard to get away.

'Not really a paperback, it's squarer than that. I should say no larger than a single-play record. Of course in area that probably *is* the same size as a paperback, but a different shape, you see.'

'Great,' said Adrian. 'Well I must be . . .'

'And inside is the most unprepossessing heap of powder you can imagine. The dried constituents of the soup. Little lumps of chicken and small hard noodles. Very unusual.'

'I must try it,' said Adrian. 'Anyway . . .'

'You empty the packet into a pan, add two pints of water and heat it up.'

'Right, well, I think I'll go to the Rat Man now and buy some,' said Adrian, walking backwards.

'No, the Rat Man doesn't sell it!' Williams said. 'I had a word with him about it this morning and he said he might get it in next week. Give it a trial period, see if there's a demand. Sainsbury's in Sidney Street has a very large supply, however.'

Adrian had nearly reached the corner of the court.

'Sainsbury's?' he called, looking at his watch. 'Right. I should just be in time.'

'I had the happy notion of adding an egg,' Williams shouted back. 'It poaches in the soup. Not unlike an Italian *stracciatella*. Singularly toothsome. Oh, you'll discover that Sainsbury's display a vegetable soup on the same shelf, also made by Knorr. It's quite hard to tell the two packets apart, but be sure to get the Chicken Noodle . . .'

Adrian rounded the corner and streaked for his rooms. He could hear Williams's voice cheerily exhorting him not to let it boil, as this was certain to impair the flavour.

Perhaps that's what Trefusis meant about not lying. Williams wasn't raving about his bloody soup in order to be respected or admired, he genuinely meant to impart a sincerely felt enthusiasm. Adrian knew he could never be guilty of any such unfiltered openness but he was damned if he was going to be judged because of it.

Gary was listening to Abba's *Greatest Hits* and leafing through a book on Miró when Adrian came in.

'Hello, darlin',' he said. 'I've just boiled the kettle.'

Adrian went up to the stereo, took off the record and frisbee'd it out of the open window. Gary watched it skim across the Court.

'What's up with you, then?'

Adrian took the Heffers and Barclaycard bills from his pocket and spread them out on Gary's book.

'You are aware that theft, obtaining goods and monies by false pretences and forgery are all serious offences?' he said.

'I'll pay you back.'

Adrian went to his desk and opened a drawer. His Heffers card and Visa card were missing.

'I mean, you might at least have told me.'

'I wouldn't have thought of being so vulgar.'

'Well I don't want to be vulgar either, but you now owe me a grand total of . . .' Adrian leafed through his notebook, 'six hundred and eighteen pounds and sixty-three pence.'

'I said I'd pay you back, didn't I?'

'I'm busy wondering how.'

'You can afford to wait. You should be glad to do a member of the working classes a favour.'

'And you should have too much pride to allow me . . . oh for God's sake!'

The sound of Abba singing 'Dancing Queen' had started up in a room the other side of the court. Adrian slammed the window shut.

'That'll teach you to throw things out of the window,' said Gary.

'It'll teach me *not* to throw things out of the window.'

'Suppose I pay you back in portraits?'

Adrian looked round the room. The walls were covered with dozens of different portraits of himself. Oils, water-colours, gouaches, grisailles, pen and ink, chalk, silverpoint, charcoal, pastels, airbrushed acrylics, crayons and even Bic biro drawings, ranging in style from neo-plasticist to photorealist.

He had been given no choice in the matter of sharing rooms. Gary and he were drawn out of the tombola together, so together they were. The bondage trousers, henna'ed hair and virtual canteen of cutlery that hung from his ears told the world that Gary was a punk, the only one in St Matthew's and as such as fascinating and horrifying an addition to the college as the modern Stafford Court on the other side of the river. Gary was reading Modern and Medieval Languages, but intended to change to History of Art in his second year: meanwhile he expressed his devotion to Adrian – real or pretended, Adrian never knew which – by treating him as an idiot older brother from another world. He had never met a public school boy before coming to Cambridge and hadn't really believed that they existed. He had been more shocked by Adrian than Adrian had been by him.

'And you really used to have fagging and that?'

'Yes. It's on the way out now I believe, but when I was there you had to fag.'

'I can't bleeding believe it! Did you wear a boater?'

'When appropriate.'

'And striped trousers?'

'In the Sixth Form.'

'Fuck me!' Gary had wriggled with delight.

'I'm hardly the only one, you know. There are dozens here from my school alone, hundreds from Eton and Harrow and Winchester.'

'Yeah,' said Gary, 'but it's less than seven per cent of the population, isn't it? People like me never usually meet people like you except in a Crown Court, when you're wearing a wig.'

'This is nineteen-seventy-nine, Gary, people like you are forming the Thatcher cabinet.'

Adrian had told him about life at school, about the magazine, about Pigs Trotter's death. He had even told him about Cartwright.

Gary had immediately done a drawing of Adrian as he imagined him in a blazer and cricket whites, dawdling in front of a Gothic doorway, while capped and gowned beaks flitted in the background like crows. Adrian had bought it on the spot for ten pounds. Since then he had subsidised Gary's cannabis and vodka by buying at least three works of art a week. But he didn't now think he could take even one more view of himself, in any medium, from any angle, and he said so.

'Well then,' said Gary, 'you're going to have to wait for me to pay you back till the end of the year.'

'Yes, I suppose I am,' said Adrian. 'Oh coitus!'

'Oh come on, you can afford it.'

'No, it's not that. It's work.'

'Work? I thought this was supposed to be a university.'

'Yes, well, it's rapidly turning into a technical college,' said Adrian, falling into an armchair.

'Didn't Trefusis go for your essay then?'

'No, he loved it, that's the problem,' said Adrian. 'It was too good. He was very impressed. So now he wants me to do something major. Something startling and original.'

'Original? In philology?'

'No, any subject. I should be flattered really, I suppose.'

Honestly, what was the point? He could tell the truth to Gary, surely? He was lying as a matter of course. Was it pride? Fear? He closed his eyes. Trefusis was right. Right but ludicrously wrong.

Why wasn't he happy? Jenny loved him. Gary loved him. His mother sent him money. Uncle David sent him money. It was the May Term of his first year, the weather was fine and he had no examinations. Everything unpleasant was behind him. Cambridge was his. He had now made up his mind to stay here after Finals and become a don. All you had to do was memorise enough good essays and repeat them in three-hour bursts. Trefusis wasn't an examiner, thank God.

He hung Jeremy, his blazer, on Anthony, the peg.

'Let's have some toast,' he said. 'Hunt the Thimble has provided.'

II

'We come now gentlemen,' said President Clinton-Lacey, 'to the matter of JRFs and Bye-Fellowships. I wonder if – '

Garth Menzies, a Professor of Civil Law, coughed through a cloud of dense smoke which poured into his face from the pipe of Munroe, the Bursar.

'Excuse me, Mr President,' he said, 'I understood we had agreed to a no-smoking rule at Fellows' meetings?'

'Well, that is certainly true, yes. Admiral Munroe, I wonder if you would mind . . .?'

Munroe banged his pipe down on the table and gave Menzies a look charged with deepest venom. Menzies smiled and transferred a sweet from one side of his mouth to the other.

'Thank you,' said Clinton-Lacey. 'Now. JRFs and Bye-Fellowships. As this body is well aware, there has been – '

Munroe sniffed the air loudly.

'Excuse me, Mr President,' he said. 'Am I alone in detecting a nauseating smell of spearmint in this room?'

'Er . . .?'

'It really is most disagreeable. I wonder where it could be coming from?'

Menzies angrily took the mint from his mouth and dropped it into the ashtray in front of him. Munroe smiled beatifically.

'Thank you,' said Clinton-Lacey. 'Fellows, we have a problem in retaining our present levels of postgraduates. There is a large number of Junior Research Fellows and Bye-Fellows that benefits from our grants and disbursements as you know. You will be far from unaware of the nature of the economic weather system that blows towards us from Westminster.'

Admiral Munroe ostentatiously pushed the ashtray into the centre of the table, as if the smell of mint still offended him.

Alex Corder, a theologian down the end of the table, barked a rather harsh laugh.

'Barbarians,' he said. 'They're all barbarians.'

'The government,' said Clinton-Lacey, 'the justice of whose doctrines we are not assembled here to discourse upon, has certainly struck an attitude towards the universities which must give us cause for alarm.'

'The Prime Minister is a scientist,' said Corder.

Garth Menzies raised his eyebrows. 'I'm sure no one would accuse the Prime Minister of academic partiality.'

'Why ever not?' said Munroe.

'Well, whatever her possible bias,' said Clinton-Lacey, 'there is a feeling in government that the Arts side, oversubscribed by candidates for entrance as it already is, must be, er, honed, and extra encouragement given to the disciplines which can more productively . . . ah! Professor Trefusis!'

Trefusis stood in the doorway, a cigarette dangling from his lips, peering vaguely as if unsure whether this was the right room or the right meeting. The sight of Menzies' disapproving glare seemed to reassure him; he entered and slid down into the empty seat next to Admiral Munroe.

'Well, Donald, I am sorry that you seem to have been delayed again,' said Clinton-Lacey.

Trefusis was silent.

'Nothing serious I hope?'

Trefusis smiled affably around the room.

'Nothing serious I hope?' repeated the President.

Trefusis became aware that he was being addressed, opened his jacket, switched off the Walkman that was attached to his belt and slipped off his earphones.

'I'm sorry, Master, did you speak?'

'Well yes . . . we were discussing the fall-off in resources for the Arts.'

'The Arts?'

'That's right. Now . . .'

Menzies coughed and pushed the ashtray towards Trefusis.

'Thank you, Garth,' said Trefusis, flicking the ash from his cigarette and taking another puff. 'Most thoughtful.'

The President persevered.

'We will not have enough money to create any more Junior Research Fellows in the Arts for at least two years.'

'Oh, how sad,' said Trefusis.

'You are not concerned for your department?'

'*My* department? My department is English, Master.'

'Well precisely.'

'What has English to do with "the Arts", whatever they may be? I deal in an exact science, philology.

61

My colleagues deal with an exact science, the analysis of literature.'

'Oh poppycock,' said Menzies.

'No, if anything it's hard shit,' said Trefusis.

'Really, Donald!' said the President. 'I am sure there is no need . . .'

'Professor Trefusis,' said Menzies, 'this is a minuted meeting of adults, if you feel you can't preserve the decencies of debate then perhaps you should leave.'

'My dear old Garth,' said Trefusis, 'I can only say that you started it. The English language is an arsenal of weapons; if you are going to brandish them without checking to see whether or not they are loaded you must expect to have them explode in your face from time to time. "Poppycock" means "soft shit" – from the Dutch, I need scarcely remind you, *pappe kak*.'

Menzies purpled and fell silent.

'Well, be that all as it may, Donald,' said the President, 'the subject was resourcing. Whatever our views on the rights and wrongs of government policy, the fiscal reality is such that . . .'

'The reality,' said Trefusis, offering cigarettes around the table, 'as we all know, is that more and more young people are begging to be admitted to *this* college in *this* university to read English. Our English department receives a higher number of applicants for each available place than any other department in any other university in the country. If the rules of the market place, which I understand to be sacred to the gabies, guffoons and flubberhaddocks in office, are to apply, then surely we should be entitled to *more* fellowships, not fewer.'

'The feeling, Donald,' said the President, 'is that

English graduates cannot offer an expertise of benefit to the country. The fruits of research in botany or genetics or even my own subject, economics, are recognised as having a palpable value to the world . . .'

'Hear, hear,' said Menzies.

'Poppycock,' said Munroe, accepting a box of matches from Trefusis.

'But you and your colleagues,' said the President, ignoring both interruptions, 'are seen more and more as an intolerable burden on the tax-payer. There is nothing for you to discover of interest, nothing you can offer your undergraduates that fits them usefully into industry or profitable enterprise. You know that those are not *my* views. Around this table we have rehearsed many times the arguments and counter-arguments and I do not propose to do so again. I can only tell you that the monies will not be available this year.'

'Mr President,' said a don at the end of the table, 'I would like you to register my view that this is an absolute disgrace. This Philistinism will do nothing but impoverish our country. I hope you will minute my utter disgust.'

'Well,' said Trefusis, 'that should make Sir Keith Joseph and his friends shake in their boots, shouldn't it? No, no. The time has come for action. With the Fellows' approval I can train a hand-picked company of crack undergraduates and be in Whitehall before June.'

'This pose of embittered and embattled artist,' said Menzies, 'is unseemly and out of date. Society can no longer afford its jesters and is weary of being hit over the head with empty pigs' bladders. The world is bored of the piffling excesses of the Arts, of its arrogance and irrelevance to the real world. Your fat could do with trimming.'

'You're right of course,' said Trefusis, 'I see that now. We need lawyers. Wave upon wave of them.'

'Well of course it's very easy to mock . . .'

'It's certainly easy to mock some things,' agreed Trefusis. 'Oddly enough though I've never found it easy to mock anything of value. Only things that are tawdry and fatuous – perhaps it's just me.'

III

'So you see my little honeypot baby-squeeze,' said Adrian, 'I have to come up with some bloody piece of research or I may be out on my rather divinely shaped ear.'

'Well it's about time you did some work,' said Jenny, biting his nipple.

'That's a horrid thing to say. Now go a bit lower down and get those lips working, it's my turn to come and I have to be off to the University Library.'

Jenny sat up.

'That reminds me,' she said. 'Mary and I have written a letter to all the Senior Tutors in Cambridge.'

'Good God,' said Adrian, pulling her head down again, 'this is no time to babble of schoolgirl crushes.'

'No listen,' she said popping up. 'It's the pornography.'

'What?'

'You know I've been going to Tim Anderson's lectures on Derrida and Sexual Difference?'

'Look, if your mouth's busy you could at least use your hands. There's some baby oil under the bed.'

'Well, he showed us some pornography last week. Boxfuls of it. From the University Library. It's a copyright library, you see, so they get a copy of everything published. Everything.'

'What, you mean . . . everything?'

'Everything. Centuries of pornography up to the present day. The cellars are packed with tons of the most degrading and disgusting . . . I'm talking about amputees, children, appliances, things you could never even imagine.'

'You don't know what I could imagine.'

'I went to have a look at some of it. All I needed was Helen Greenman's signature. Told her it was to do with Tim Anderson's lectures. Well I mean, this stuff shouldn't be at Cambridge. It has no possible academic justification. It's degrading to women and should be burnt.'

'And degrading to animals and children and appliances, I shouldn't wonder.'

'Adrian, it's not funny. I think the UL dignifies this shit by storing it. So Mary and I are trying to get it banned.'

'What sort of things did you see exactly?'

'Well you have to view it in a private room . . .'

'Describe it to me . . . and use your left hand. That's it. A bit faster. Yes! Oh yes *indeed*. Now, what did you see?'

'Well there was one where this woman took a pork-pie . . .'

'That's the posish, Gary,' said Adrian when he had walked back from Newnham to St Matthew's. 'It's all there, a whole *index expurgatorius* waiting to be drooled over. And *this* is what the librarian needs to be shown.'

He handed him a small piece of paper on which was written:

'I authorise access to Jennifer de Woolf, an undergraduate of this college, to the following titles of Special Research Material . . .'

Underneath were listed titles of books and magazines and at the bottom was the signature, 'Helen Greenman, Senior Tutor, Newnham College'.

Gary's mouth fell open.

'*Elsa and the Bull, Young Nuns, Concentration Camp Action* . . . you're joking . . . *My Hot Little Daughter, Hung, Young and Handsome, Tampon Tina, Fist Fuck Faggots, Clingfilm Fantasies. Clingfilm*? Bleeding Christ.'

Adrian was rifling in the drawer of his desk.

'Too good to be missed I think you'll agree. Where are we . . . ah, yes.' He took a piece of writing-paper from his drawer. 'Now then, Gary, my old chum, my old mate, my old mucker. Do you want to knock off say . . . fifty quid from your debt? Of course you do. I want you to examine this letter, paying particular attention to the signature at the bottom.'

Gary took it.

'Dear Mr Healey, Dr Pittaway tells me that you are in need of instruction for the Philology option in

the English Tripos. I have not forgotten your expertise as an umpire when we met at Chartham Park last
summer and remember you as an alert young person
bright with capability and promise. I would therefore
be most happy to offer you what help I may. My
rooms are in Hawthorn Tree Court, A3. I shall expect
you at ten o'clock on Wednesday the 4th unless I hear
otherwise. Please be sure to bring your mind with
you. Donald Trefusis.'

'What about it?' said Gary.

'You can forge my signature, which is delicate and
elegant. This scrawl can't be beyond you?'

'You dirty fucker.'

'Well quite.'

V

Adrian walked through Clare College towards the
University Library. The impertinence of the building, as it launched upwards like a rocket, had always
annoyed him. Compared to the feminine domed grace
of Oxford's Bodleian or London's British Museum, it
was hardly a thing of beauty. It strained up like a
swollen phallus, trying to penetrate the clouds. The
same principle as a Gothic spire, Adrian supposed.
But the union of the library and the heavens would be
a very secular Word-made-Flesh indeed.

He went inside and made his way up to the
catalogue room. He flipped through the card indices,
scribbling down hopeful titles. Everywhere grey-
faced research graduates and desperate third year
students with books under their arms and private
worlds of scholarship in their eyes hurried back and

forth. He spotted Germaine Greer clutching a pile of very old books and Stephen Hawking, the Lucasian Professor of Mathematics, steering his motor-driven chair into the next room.

Do I really have a place here? Adrian wondered. All this work? This sweat? No short cuts, no cheating, no copying out, no grafting? Of course I do. A physicist doesn't work any harder than I do. He just copies out God's ideas. *And* he usually gets them wrong.

Gary watched Trefusis leave his rooms, briefcase in hand, trailing a cloud of smoke. He waited until five minutes after he had crossed the Sonnet Bridge before climbing the stairs to the first floor.

The latch of the outer oak door surrendered easily to Adrian's Barclaycard, as Adrian had said it would. Gary turned on the lights and surveyed the Manhattan of books before him.

It's got to be in here somewhere, he said to himself. I suppose I'll just have to wait for it to reveal itself.

Adrian went to the desk in the reading-room and waited to be noticed. It was very tempting to slap the counter and shout 'Shop!' He managed a polite cough instead.

'Sir?'

Librarians always seemed to treat Adrian with as much apathy and contempt as was possible without being openly rude. He would sometimes ask any one of the UL staff for a book written in, say, a rare dialect of Winnebago Indian, just for the hell of it, and they would hand it over with wrinkled noses and an air of superior scorn, as if they'd read it years ago and had long got over the stage where such obvious and juvenile nonsense could possibly be of the remotest interest to *them*. Had they somehow seen through him or was their contempt for undergraduates universal? The specimen who had come forward now seemed more than usually spotty and aloof. Adrian favoured him with an amiable smile.

'I'd like,' he said in ringing tones, '*A Fulsome Pair of Funbags* and *Fleshy Dimpled Botts* please, and *Davina's Fun with Donkeys* if it's not already out . . . oh and *Wheelchair Fellatio* I think . . .'

The librarian pushed his spectacles up his nose.

'What?'

'And *Brownies and Cubs on Camp*, *Fido Laps it Up*, *Drink My Piss, Bitch* and *A Crocodile of Choirboys*. I believe that's all. Oh, *The Diary of a Maryanne*, too. That's a Victorian one. Here's an authorisation slip for you.'

Adrian flourished a piece of paper.

The librarian swallowed as he read it.

Tut-tut, thought Adrian. Showing Concern And Confusion. Infraction of Rule One of the Librarian's Guild. He'll be drummed out if he's not careful.

'Whose signature is this please?'

'Oh, Donald Trefusis,' said Adrian. 'He's my Senior Tutor.'

'One moment.'

The librarian moved away and showed the paper to an older man in the background.

It was like trying to get a large cheque cashed, the same whispered conferences and sly glances. Adrian turned and took a leisurely look around the room.

Dozens of faces immediately buried themselves back in their work. Other dozens stared at him. He smiled benignly.

'Excuse me, Mr . . . Mr Healey, is it?'

The older librarian had approached the counter.

'Yes?'

'May I ask for what purpose you wish to look at these . . . er . . . publications?'

'Research. I'm doing a dissertation on "Manifestations of Erotic Deviancy In . . ."'

'Quite so. This *appears* to be Professor Trefusis's signature. However I think I should ring him up if you don't mind. Just to make sure.'

Adrian waved a casual hand.

'Oh, I'm sure he wouldn't want to be bothered about this, would he?'

'These authorisations are not usual for undergraduates, Mr Healey.'

'Adrian.'

'I would be much happier.'

Adrian swallowed.

'Well of course, if you think it's necessary. I can give you his number in college if you like. It's – '

The librarian scented triumph.

'No, no, sir. We can find it ourselves, I'm sure.'

Gary managed to track down the telephone under an ottoman. He answered it on the fifth ring.

'Yes?' he panted. 'Trefusis here, I was just taking a crap, what is it? . . . Who? . . . Speak up man . . . Healey? . . . "Manifestations of Erotic Desire . . ."? Yes, Is there some problem? . . . Of course it's my signature . . . I see. A little trust would not go amiss,

70

you know. You're running a library, not a weapons depository, this bureaucracy is . . . No doubt, but that's what the guards at Buchenwald said . . . Very well, very well. You catch me in a bad mood this morning, take no notice . . . All right. Goodbye then.'

'That appears to be fine, Mr Healey. You appreciate that we had to make sure?'

'Of course, of course.'

The librarian gulped.

'These will take some time to . . . er . . . locate, sir. If you'd like to come back in half an hour? We'll provide a private reading-room for you.'

'Thank you,' said Adrian. 'Most kind.'

He bounced springily along the corridor on his way down to the tea-room.

I can fool all of the people all of the time, he thought.

A man walked past him.

'Morning, Mr Healey.'

'Morning, Professor Trefusis,' said Adrian.

Trefusis! Adrian skidded to a halt. He was heading for the reading-room! Not even Trefusis could answer his telephone at St Matthew's and be in the UL at the same time.

He tried to shout after him but could manage only a hoarse whisper.

'Professor! . . . Professor!'

Trefusis had reached the door. He turned in surprise.

'Yes?'

Adrian ran up to him.

'Before you go in, sir, I wondered if I could have a word?'

'Very well. What is it?'

'Can I buy you a bun in the tea-room?'

'What?'

'Well, I wondered . . . are you going in for a book or to do some work?'

'To do some work as it happens.'

'Oh, I shouldn't if I were you.'

Trefusis smiled.

'You've tried it and find it a disagreeable pursuit? I'm afraid in my case it has to be done. Someone, after all, has to write articles for future undergraduates to copy out.'

He put his hand to the finger-plate of the door.

Adrian only just managed to stop himself from tugging at his sleeve.

'Full. Not a reading table to be had. That's why I wanted to speak to you. Wondered if you could show me a good place to work.'

'Well, I find the ninth-floor reading-room is generally free from distraction. You might try there. However I am bound to say that I would feel a little bothered working in the same room as you. I'll go and see if there are any private rooms free on this floor, I think.'

He pushed against the door. Adrian practically screamed.

'No that's all right, sir! You go to the ninth floor. I've just remembered, I've got to go anyway. Got a . . . meeting.'

Trefusis came away from the door, amused.

'Very well. I am greatly looking forward to your

masterwork, you know. People think our subject is airy-fairy, namby-pamby, arty, not to put too fine a point on it, farty. But as you are no doubt discovering, it is grind and toil from Beowulf to Bloomsbury. Grind, grind, grind. Toil, toil, toil. I like the Kickers. Good morning.'

Adrian looked down at his shoes. They were indeed smart.

'Thank you, Professor. And your brogues are a riot.'

With breathless relief he watched Trefusis disappear round the corner towards the lifts.

Adrian got back to St Matthew's to find that Gary had pushed all the furniture back to the walls and cleared the floor, which was covered with a vast sheet onto which he was drawing in charcoals.

'How'd it go?'

'Fabulous. Like a breeze. Did you put a handkerchief in your mouth?'

'Nah! If there's one thing Trefusis sounds like, it's a man with no handkerchief in his mouth. I just went up two octaves and sounded pissed off.'

Adrian scrutinised Gary's activities.

'So. Second question. What are you doing to my room?'

'Our room.'

'Our room, that I furnish and pay for?'

'This is a cartoon.'

'A cartoon.'

'In the original sense.'

'So the original sense of cartoon is "total fucking mess" is it?'

'The original sense of cartoon is a sheet of material onto which you draw the outlines of your fresco.'

Adrian picked his way through the debris and poured himself a glass of wine from a half-empty bottle on the mantelpiece. A half-empty bottle of the college's best white burgundy, he noted.

'Fresco?'

'Yeah. When I've designed it, I simply hang the sheet over the wall, prick the outline onto the wet plaster and get to work as quickly as possible before . . .'

'What wet plaster would that be?'

Gary pointed to a blank space of wall.

'I thought there. We just rip off the old plasterwork, bit of bonding on the laths, and Bob's your uncle.'

'Bob is not my uncle. I have never had an uncle called Bob. I never intend to have an uncle called Bob. If being Bob's nephew involves destroying a five-hundred-year-old . . .'

'Six hundred years actually. It's going to be a representation of Britain in the late seventies. Thatcher, Foot, CND marches, unemployment. Everything. I paint it, then we cover it with wood panelling. That's the expensive bit. The panelling will have to be hinged, see? In a hundred years' time this room will be priceless.'

'It's already priceless. Couldn't we leave it as it is? Henry James had tea here. Isherwood made love to a choral scholar in that very bedroom. A friend of Thomas Hardy's committed suicide here. Marlowe and Kydd danced a galliard on these exact floorboards.'

'And Adrian Healey commissioned Gary Collins's first fresco here. History is an on-going process.'

'And what's our bedder going to say?'

'It'll brighten her day. Better than picking up the manky Y-fronts of the economists opposite.'

'Fuck you, Gary. Why do you always make me sound so prissy and middle-class?'

'Bollocks.'

Adrian looked round the room and tried to fight down his bourgeois panic.

'So, hinged panelling, you say?'

'Shouldn't cost too much if that's what you're worrying about. I picked up this builder who's working on the site of Robinson College. He reckons he can get me some good stuff for under five hundred and he'll do all the rendering and plastering for free if I let him fuck me.'

'Not exactly in the great tradition is it? I mean, I don't think that Pope Julius and Michelangelo came to a similar kind of arrangement about the Sistine Chapel. Not unless I'm very much mistaken.'

'Don't bet on it. Anyway, someone's got to fuck me, haven't they?' Gary pointed out. 'Since you won't I've got to look elsewhere. Makes good sense.'

'Suddenly the whole logic becomes clear. But what about work? I'm supposed to be working this term, don't forget.'

Gary got to his feet and stretched.

'Bugger that, that's what I say. How was the porn?'

'Incredible. You've never in all your life seen anything like it.'

'Naughty pictures?'

'I'm not sure I'm ever going to be able to look a

75

labrador in the face again. But, ruined as my faith in humankind may be, I have to say that we of the twentieth century are a pretty normal bunch compared to the Victorians.'

'Victorian porn?'

'Certainly.'

'What did they *do*? I've often wondered. Did they have dicks and fannies and the rest of it?'

'Well of course they did, you silly child. And the zestier volumes indicate that they had a great deal more. There's a – '

Adrian broke off. He had suddenly given himself an idea. He looked at Gary's cartoon.

Why not? It was wild, it was dishonest, it was disgraceful, but it could be done. It would mean work. A hell of a lot of work, but work of the right kind. Why not?'

'Gary,' he said. 'I suddenly find myself at life's crossroads. I can feel it. One road points to madness and pleasure, the other to sanity and success. Which way do I turn?'

'You tell me, matey.'

'Let me put it this way. Do you want to pay off all your debt in one, plus the five hundred for wooden panelling? I've got a job for you.'

'Okay.'

'That's my boy.'

Trefusis approached the counter of the reading-room. The young librarian looked at him in surprise.

'Professor Trefusis!'

'Good morning! How wags the world with you today?'

'I'm very fit thank you, sir.'

'I wonder if you can help me?'

'That's what I'm here for, Professor.'

Trefusis leant forward and lowered his voice conspiratorially, not an easy task for him. Among his many gifts he had never been able to count speaking in hushed tones.

'Oblige the whim of a man old and mad before his time,' he said, quietly enough for only the first twelve rows of desks behind him to catch every word, 'and tell me if there is any reason why I shouldn't have come in here an hour ago?'

'Pardon?'

'Why should I not have come into this room an hour ago? Was something afoot?'

The librarian stared. A man who services academics is used to all forms of mental derangement and behavioural aberration. Trefusis had always struck him as blithely and refreshingly free from nervous disorder. But, as the saying had it, old professors never die, they merely lose their faculties.

'Well apart from the fact that an hour ago you couldn't have been here . . .' he said.

'I couldn't?'

'Well not while you were at St Matthew's talking to Mr Leyland on the telephone.'

'I was talking to Mr Leyland on the telephone?' said Trefusis. 'Of course I was! Dear me, my memory . . . Leyland rang me up, didn't he? On the telephone, as I recall. That's right, it was the telephone, I remember distinctly, because I spoke to him through it. He rang me up, on the telephone, to talk to me about . . . about . . . what was it now?'

'To check your authorisation for that undergraduate to read those . . . those Reserved Publications.'

'Mr Healey that would have been?'

'Yes. It was all right, wasn't it? I mean, you did confirm . . .'

'Oh yes. Quite all right, quite all right. I was merely . . . humour me once more and let me have a copy of the titles Mr Healey wanted to see, would you, dear boy?'

VI

'Bust me, Sir!' said Mr Polterneck. 'Bust me if I haven't just the little warmint for your most partic'lar requirements just now a-curling up in innocent slumber in the back room. You can bounce me from here to Cheapside if that ain't the truest truth that ever a man gave utterance of. Mrs Polterneck knows it to be so, my Uncle Polterneck knows it to be so and any man as is acquainted with me could never be convinced to the contrary of it, not if you boiled him and baked him and twisted him on the rack for another opinion.'

'I am assured of your good faith in this matter?' asked Peter.

'Lord, Mr Flowerbuck. I'm in the way of weeping that you might have doubt of it! My good faith in this matter is the one sure fact you may most particular be assured of! My good faith is a flag, Mr Flowerbuck. It is a tower, Sir, a Monument. My good faith is not made of air, Mr Flowerbuck, it is an object such as you might touch and look upwards on with wonder and may you whip me until I bleed if that ain't so.'

'Then I suppose we might do business?'

'Now then, Sir,' said Mr Polterneck, producing a most preposterous handkerchief of bright vermilion silk with which he mopped his brow. 'He's a most especial warmint, is Joe Cotton. Most particular especial. To a gentleman like yourself as I can tell is most discerning in the nature of young warmints, he is a nonparelly. I could sonnet you sonnets, Mr Flowerbuck, about the gold of his tresses and the fair smoothness of his young skin. I could ballad you ballads, Sir, on the theme of the fair round softness of his rump and the garden of paradise that awaits a man within. I've a stable of young colts, Sir, as I can say the like would not be found in any district of the City, nor without the City too, and Master Cotton, Sir, is my Prize. If that ain't recommendation enough you can hang me by the neck right now, Sir, from old Uncle Polterneck's lintel, and have done with me for a lying rascal.'

It was all Peter could do to restrain himself from taking Polterneck fully at his word. The fear of what foul gases might ooze from the creature's lungs as he did so and what contamination he would suffer in the handling of him kept his vengeful fury at bay quite as much as the reflection that he must proceed as levelly as he might with the business in hand.

'I suppose you can tell me nothing of his provenance?' he asked indifferently.

'As to his provenance, Sir, I'm in the way of thinking, and Mrs Polterneck is the same, and Uncle Polterneck is hardly of a different persuasion, that he was sent down from Heaven, Sir. Sent down from Heaven itself to put bread in the mouths of my kinfolk

79

and give pleasure and boon to gentlemen such as yourself, Sir. That is my opinion of his provenance and the man ain't been given birth to who could shake me out of it. You never seen such beauty in a lad, Sir. And how he's all compliance and skill in the Art he has been called to! A wonder to see him set to work, Sir. They say a young sister was sent down with him.'

'A girl? His twin, perhaps?'

'Well, now that you are in the line of remarking on the matter, I did hear mention as how the girl *was* his twin, Sir! A golden beauty of like complexion, for those that admires the same in the gentle sex. Where she might be, I have no knowledge, nor interest neither. Young cock-chicks is my game, Sir, the hen-birds is too devilish tickerly a proposition for a peaceable gentleman like myself. Bust me if they don't start a-breeding and a-parting with chicks of their own afore they've paid their way and how,' wheezed Mr Polterneck, 'is a man of business to procure the blessing of prosperity for his hearth when his stock is all a-laid up and a-breeding?'

'So you have no knowledge of this sister's whereabouts?'

'As to Whereabouts, whereabouts is different to provenance, Sir. Whereabouts is Mystery, and ask Mrs Polterneck and Uncle Polterneck if I don't deal in nothing but certainty. The whereabouts of Miss Judith is in doubt, the whereabouts of Master Joe is in the back room. If you are needful of a pretty little lady . . .'

'No, no. Your Joe will do.'

'Indeed, Sir, as I hope he *will* do.'

'As for price?'

'Ah now, Mr Flowerbuck,' said Polterneck, wagging a greasy finger. 'Seeing as we're agreed on the warmint's celestial provenance, I can't have my proper say in the affair of Fees. If he was my own I'd say a crown, and Mrs Polterneck and Uncle Polterneck would cry that I was a-cheating myself cruel and I would shake my head sorrowful and raise the fee another crown to please 'em! I should happily settle at that price, though Mrs P. and Uncle P. would complain I was cheating myself still. I was born generous and I can't help it and won't give apology to no man for it. But for all I can cheat myself, Mr Flowerbuck, I can't be cheating Heaven! It wouldn't be right, Sir. I could rob myself with a will an it pleased my gentlemen, for my customers is all to me, but I can't go robbing the Angels, Mr Flowerbuck, I can't. It ain't in me to do so. A full sovereign for the evening, back again by six next morning.'

Peter forbore once more to put a period to the rottenest life in the rottenest den in the rottenest borough in the rottenest city in all the rotten world. He pressed a coin into Polterneck's hand.

'Bring the boy to me!' he whispered.

Polterneck clapped his hands.

'Flinter!'

In the shadows at the back of the room a figure rose from out the straw. It was the figure of a boy, no older in appearance than fourteen years, although in a city where children of six have the eyes and gait of old men, indeed the same life of experience to look back upon, and where youths of twenty are so kept back in growth by filth and hunger that they retain the aspect of frail infants, it was impossible for Peter to determine the true age of this specimen. But that was never his concern, for his eyes were ever fixed upon the face. Or upon the part where the face ought by rights to have been. For it was not a face he fixed his gaze upon. A face, my Lords and Ladies and fine gentlemen, has eyes, does it not? A face must boast ears, a mouth, some arrangement of all the features that sniff and see and hear and taste before it can lay claim to that title. That they sniff the stench of villainy, see the deepest shame, hear the most degraded blasphemies and taste aught but the bitterest sorrows – that is never the face's affair! The face presents these organs each set in their place to look at what they will and listen where they please. What countenance deserves the name therefore – my lords who look upon gold plate, my ladies who breathe fine perfumes, my friends who taste plump mutton and hear the sweet harmony of a loving voice – what face can be called a face which has not a nose set upon it? What term might we invent to describe a face whose nose is all ate up? A face with a hole in its middle where a nose should have stood – be it a nose pinched and long, swollen and bulbous, or Roman and aloof, be it any kind of nose plain or pretty – a face, I say, with a black nullity where nostrils and bridge should be presenting themselves for admiration or disgust, that is no face but the face of Shame, no countenance but the countenance of Want. It is the visage of Sin and Lust, the aspect of Need and Despair but not – I beg the favour of your believing me – not, an hundred times never, the face of a human child.

'Flinter! Fetch down young Joe for the gentleman.

And Flinter! don't you never dream of touching no part of him neither, or bust me if you don't find your head a suddenly lacking of two ears also!'

Polterneck turned to Peter with an indulgent smile, for all the world as if to say 'Bless my buttons if I don't lavish more care on my young lads than they deserve!' He must then have caught sight of the expression of revulsion and horror on Peter's face, for he hastened to whisper an explanation.

'The pox, Mr Flowerbuck! The pox is a sore trial in my line of working. He was a good worker was Master Flinter and nor I don't have the heart to dismiss him now the pox has taken away his smeller.'

'I should imagine,' said Peter, 'that . . .'

'Slow down, for God's sake,' said Gary. 'My fucking wrist is about to drop off.'

Adrian stopped pacing the room.

'Sorry,' he said. 'I was getting carried away. What do you reckon so far?'

'Not sure about "bulbous".'

'You're right. I'll check it tomorrow.'

'It's two o'clock in the morning and I'm about to run out of ink. I'm going to crash.'

'Finish the chapter?'

'In the morning.'

In a service-station car-park off the Stuttgart – Karlsruhe
Autobahn, a Tweed Jacket and a dark Blue Marks &
Spencer's Leisure Shirt were licking their wounds.

'*I just can't believe it,*' the Leisure Shirt was saying. '*I
mean out of nowhere and for what?*'

'*Perhaps they fancy themselves as latter day highway
robbers,*' offered the Tweed.

'*Well that greasy one in a safari suit wasn't exactly my
idea of a Dick Turpin.*'

'*No,*' said the Tweed. He looked at the Leisure Shirt, who
had turned away and started kicking a tree stump.

'*Why did I have to go and suggest what is obviously the
most secluded bloody service-station on the whole sodding
Autobahn?*

'*I blame myself, Adrian, I should have parked nearer the
main building, I do hope you are all right?*'

'*Well they didn't take my passport or wallet, at least. In
fact as far as I can see they didn't take anything.*'

'*Not quite true.*'

The Tweed gestured forlornly towards the back seat of the
Wolseley.

'*My briefcase, I regret to say.*'

'*Oh. Anything in it?*'

'Some papers.'

'Phew. Lucky escape then, I suppose. Shall we call the police?'

Three

At the front of the tractor, fed from its power-take-off, was a picker. A conveyor belt ran along the side and disgorged the potatoes onto a rolling rack. Adrian and Lucy's job was to 'dress' them, to pull out the rotten, green or squashed potatoes as they trundled on their way to Tony, who stood at the end of the line, bagging the survivors. Every twenty or thirty minutes they would stop and unload a dozen full sacks into a pile in the middle of the field.

It was revolting work. The rotten and the good looked alike, so Lucy and Adrian had to pick up and examine each potato that jigged and bounced along in front of them. The bad ones burst under the slightest pressure, exploding in a squelch of stinking mucus. When it rained, mud sprayed up from the wheels and spattered their faces and clothes; when it was dry, clouds of dust choked them and matted their hair. The endless clanking, grinding, whining roar could have been the soundtrack for one of those Hieronymous Bosch visions of Hell, Adrian thought, where the moaning damned stand with their hands over their ears while demons frolic gleefully around them, probing their intimate parts with forks.

But in hell the inmates would at least try to strike up conversations with each other, hard as it might be to make themselves heard above the rumble of the treadmills and the roar of the furnaces. Lucy and Tony, brother and sister, never said a word to Adrian beyond a ''Ning' when he turned up, freezing, at dawn and a ''Nernight, then' at dusk when, stiff as a statue, he mounted his bicycle to pound wearily home to bath and bed.

Lucy just stared at the potatoes. Tony just stared at his bagging apparatus. Sometimes Adrian caught them staring at each other, in a manner which reminded him of the joke definition of a Cotswold virgin: an ugly girl under twelve who can run faster than her brother.

Lucy was no beauty, but if the looks she exchanged with Tony were anything to go by, Adrian guessed that she was no sprinter either.

The fact that he was expected to work at all in the Easter holidays had come as a blow. He was quite used to being told to find a job for the summer: waiting on tables at the Cider With Rosie restaurant, folding bolts of baize at the wool factory, treadling the cardboard-box machine at the ICI plant in Dursley, picking currants at Uley, feeding the birds at the Wildfowl Trust in Slimbridge.

'But Easter!' he had moaned into his cereal, the first morning of the holidays. 'No, Mother, no!'

'You're fifteen, darling! Most boys of your age like the idea of some kind of light work. Father thinks it's a good idea.'

'I know he does, but I've already *got* work to do. My school project.' Adrian was thinking of the article he had promised Bullock he would write for the school underground magazine.

'He doesn't want you wasting your time loafing around indoors.'

'That's pretty rich coming from him. He spends the whole bloody year cooped up in his sodding laboratory.'

'That's not fair, Ade. You know it isn't.'

'I've never had to get a job in the Easter hols before.'

His mother poured herself a fourth cup of tea.

'Won't you try it for me, darling? See how it goes?'

'Well it just means I'll have to write my essay over the Easter weekend, doesn't it? Or am I expected to pick bloody potatoes all through the most important sacred festival in the whole bloody Christian bloody calendar as well?'

'Of course not, darling. I'm sure you'll enjoy working for Mr Sutcliffe, he's a very nice man. And Father will be so pleased.'

She brushed his cheek with the back of her hand. But Adrian wasn't going to take it gracefully. He stood up and washed his bowl under the tap.

'Don't bother, darling. Betsy will do that.'

'It's a bloody swizz. I mean, it's cricket next term. I've got to get some practice in.'

'Well I'm sure you'll get nice and fit at the farm, dear.'

'That's not the same as practising is it?'

'Don't whine, Ade. It's a very ugly sound. And I must say I'm not sure I know where this sudden

enthusiasm for sports comes from, dear. Mr Mount-
ford said in your report that you failed to attend a
single rugby game or a single PE lesson last term.'

'Cricket's different,' said Adrian. 'I mean, you send
me off to school for most of the year and then as soon
as I come back you can't wait to get rid of me. I just
hope you won't both be surprised if I lock you in an
old people's home when you're old and smelly.'

'Darling! Don't be horrid.'

'And I'll only come and visit you to give you work
to do. Shirts to iron and socks to darn.'

'Ade, that's an awful thing to say!'

'And only then will you know what it's like to be
unloved by your own flesh and blood!' said Adrian,
drying his hands. 'And don't giggle woman, because
it isn't funny!'

'No darling, of course it isn't,' his mother said with
her hand over her mouth.

'Oh I give up,' he had said and put a tea-towel on
her head. 'I bloody give up.'

Human spirit, or lack of it, is such that, foul as the
work was, Adrian found himself so lulled by the
routine that sometimes the hours would pass like
minutes. He tried hard to concentrate on composing
in his head his contribution for the magazine. But he
was always being distracted by other thoughts. He
found himself playing a drama in which he cast
himself as God and the potatoes as humans. This one
he hurled into outer darkness, that one he sent to be
garnered home.

'Well done, thou good and faithful spud, you may
go to your reward.'

'Sinner! Corrupted one. I pluck thee out, I pluck thee out. Look, with a spot I damn thee.'

He wasn't sure if it was better to be a rotten potato or a healthy one, whether he would rather be safely bunched up in a warm bag with the goody-goodies or be thrown over the side and ploughed back into the soil. One thing was certain, either of those fates was preferable to being God.

The green potatoes were especially interesting. Donald Sutcliffe, the farmer, had explained them to him one lunchtime.

'Spuds have to grow underground, see. If they poke up through the soil and catch the rays of the sun you'll get photosynthesis and that gives you chlorophyll which'll turn them green. A green potato is a relative of Woody Nightshade. Not as poisonous, but he won't do you any good.'

This immediately made Adrian think that he was a green potato and Cartwright was the sun.

I have been kissed by the light and transformed, he thought. I am dangerous and God has rejected me.

He was always doing that these days. Everything he saw became a symbol of his own existence, from a rabbit caught in headlights to raindrops racing down a window-pane. Perhaps it was a sign that he was going to become a poet or a philosopher: the kind of person who, when he stood on the sea-shore, didn't see waves breaking on a beach, but saw the surge of human will or the rhythms of copulation, who didn't hear the sound of the tide but heard the eroding roar of time and the last moaning sigh of humanity fizzing into nothingness. But perhaps it was a sign, he also thought, that he was turning into a pretentious wanker.

On the last working day before Easter, Maundy Thursday, the four of them had been loading bags onto the trailer in thickening twilight when Adrian caught sight of a gathering of huge birds, as black as priests, pecking at rotten potatoes at the further end of the field.

'Look at the size of those crows!' he had cried.

'Boy,' said Mr Sutcliffe, tugging at a sack, 'when you see a load of crows together, them's rooks. And when you see a rook on its own, that's a fucking crow.'

'Oh,' said Adrian. 'Right. But supposing a rook gets lost or wanders off by itself. What would you call that?'

Mr Sutcliffe roared with laughter.

'Well I don't know about you, lad, but I'd call it a crook!'

II

'A SCHOOL FOR SCANDAL'
or
'The Education of an English Gentleman'
by
Woody Nightshade

The Daisy Chain Club is exclusive. Exclusive because you can only join if you sleep in a junior dormitory, one without cubicles. It isn't hard to become a member. Membership is

enforced. If one person refuses, the club cannot
meet.

The rules are simply learnt. After lights out
you stretch out your right hand until it finds
your neighbour's <u>membrum virile</u>. The same is
being done to you by the boy on your left. At a
given signal from the President of the club
(always the Prefect whose duty it is to have to
sleep in a junior dormitory), it's all hands to
the pumps and last one home's on the
bathroom-cleaning roster for a week.

It's a calm, civilised and amiable club, The
Daisy Chain. There are ones like it in every
house in the school and in every public school
in the land. An acquaintance from Ampleforth
tells me of the Hot Cupboard Society, another
from Rugby of the Milk-Shake Club, whose
name speaks for itself. A Wykhamist friend told
me of a pursuit at Winchester called the Biscuit
Game. The players stand around in a circle
tossing off onto a Wholemeal Digestive. The last
one to spit his stuff on the biscuit eats it. A new
kind of cream filling well in advance of
anything McVitie's have got round to thinking
of. Packed with potassium and vitamins, too.

From time to time news of these little
entertainments leaks out. A careless word from
Bletchley-Titherton to his older sister, a letter
home from a young Savonarola and the whistle
is blown. There follow tears, recriminations
and hasty expulsions.

This is strange. Let's face it boys, most of our
fathers went, if not to this school, at least to

others like it. Most of the staff too. Milk-Shake Clubs and their like are as old as the chapel steps.

But this is England, where the only crime is to be Found Out.

'My dear old fellow, we all know what goes on but it really doesn't do to shout about it. Upsets the apple-cart, muddies the water, what?'

I can't help thinking of the House of Commons. Six hundred or so men, most of them public school. They pronounce daily on the moral evils of the world, but just think my dears, just think of the things they have done and continue to do to their bodies and the bodies of others.

We are being groomed for power. In twenty years' time we will see fellow members of The Daisy Chain Club on television talking about oil prices, giving the Church's viewpoint on the IRA, presenting Blue Peter, closing down factories, handing down severe sentences from the bench.

Or will we?

The world is changing. We grow our hair long, we take drugs. How many people reading this have not smoked cannabis on school premises? We are not very interested in power, we are very interested in putting the world right.

Now that is really intolerable. No my-dear-old-fellowing for that kind of crime.

The Daisy Chain Club may provoke tears,

recriminations, hasty expulsions and even hastier cover-ups and laughings-off. But long hair, pot and real rebellion, they provoke anger, hatred and madness. When young people shag each other off in the dorms they are engaging in a charming old custom, a time-honoured ritual: the only reason that there are expulsions is that the tradition is hard to explain to tearful mothers and snide newspapers. But when boys say that they would rather be drummers than barristers, gardeners than businessmen, poets than soldiers, that they don't think much of examinations and authority and marriage, that when they are of age they intend to remake the world to fit them, not remake themselves to fit the world, then there is Trouble.

Someone once said that Capitalism is the exploitation of man by man and Communism is the exact reverse. I expect most of us agree with that. I don't know any schoolboy Communists, but I do know hundreds of schoolboy revolutionaries.

In the 60s the ideal was to overthrow by force. I don't know if you've seen the film 'If ...' I doubt it, every year the cinema club tries to show it and every year Headman forbids it. The film ends with a band of schoolboys turning into guerillas and assassinating parents and staff. People said that although it was set in a school it was supposed to be a metaphor for real life. Well I don't know about you, but for me school is real life. And probably will be for years. I have no interest in shooting any of the masters dead of course (well, no more than two or three, tops), but I have a lot of interest in challenging their authority. Not wresting it from them, necessarily, but <u>challenging</u> it. Asking where it comes from, how it is earned. If we are told that it is earnt on the basis of age and strength alone, then we know what kind of world we are living in and I hope we will know what to do about it. We are always being asked to show respect. Well, we can show respect with the best of them, what we find it hard to do is to <u>feel</u> respect.

Our generation, the 70s Generation, is calling for a social revolution, not a pol —

'Adrian!'

'Oh, bollocks!'

'We're ready to go now, darling.'

'Go? Go where?' shouted Adrian.

'To church, of course.'

'But you said I didn't have to!'

'What?'

Adrian came out of his room and looked down into the hall. His mother and father were standing by the door swathed in their dominical best.

'I'm in the middle of my school project. You said I didn't have to go to church.'

His father snorted.

'Don't be ridiculous! Of course you do.'

'But I was working . . .'

'You'll put on a tie and come down *now*!'

III

'You're a fucking maniac,' said Tom.

'*You're* a fucking maniac,' said Adrian.

'We're all fucking maniacs,' said Bullock.

They were in Bullock and Sampson's study leafing through copies of *Bollocks!*

The trunk they sat on felt to them like a powder keg. It contained seven hundred copies ready for distribution.

'Come on kids,' Bullock had said when Adrian had suggested the title at the end of the previous term, '*BUM* is much better. Bullock's Underground Magazine. Bollocks is my nickname for God's sake. Everyone will know I had something to do with it.'

'That's the whole idea, my little love-noodle,' Adrian had replied. 'No one is going to believe that Brainy Bollocks himself would be so stupid as to name a subversive underground magazine after himself.'

So *Bollocks!* it was. There was no artwork because only Sampson and Tom had much skill at drawing and their styles were too readily identifiable.

The magazine they now looked through was a simple fifteen pages of gestetnered typescript on green paper. No handwriting, no illustrations or distinguishing characteristics of any kind. It could have been done by any person or persons in any House in the school. Bullock had had no trouble typing and reproducing the stencils in total secrecy at home.

After many crossings-out and changes of direction, Adrian's piece had been sent off to Bullock's address in Highgate the Tuesday after Easter: reading it back now he found it rather tame and half-hearted next to the libretto of a rock opera on school life that Bullock had contributed and Tom's frankly hairy analysis of the heroin counter-culture in *The Naked Lunch*. Sampson's allegory of red and grey squirrels was simply incomprehensible.

'Now,' said Tom, 'we face the problemette of distribution.'

'More of a problemola than a problemette,' said Bullock.

'A problerama, even,' said Sampson.

'I'd go so far as to call it a problemellaroni,' said Bullock.

'It's a real cunt,' said Tom, 'no question.'

'I don't know though,' said Adrian, 'we've all been on cube calls, haven't we? We should know how to break into the Houses.'

'I've never been on one actually,' said Sampson.

'Well, I've been on plenty,' said Adrian. 'In fact, I believe I hold the House record.'

Discipline is a sensitive subject in public schools; the flogging of offenders, the toasting of small boys in front of fires, the forcing of uncomfortable objects up their bottoms, the hanging of them upside down by their ankles, all these cruel and unusual forms of punishment had died out at Adrian's school by the time he arrived. Headman sometimes flicked a cane, masters gave lines, detentions or remissions of privilege and prefects gave cube calls, but imaginative violence and cunning torture were things of the past. It had been three years since a boy had been emptied upside down in a lavatory or had his dick slammed in a desk. With this kind of leniency and liberalism in sentencing in our premier educational establishments, many thought that it was no wonder the country was going to the dogs.

When the cube call, whose violence was bureaucratic rather than physical, had been invented, no one could say. A single cube call was a small slip of paper given by a prefect to an offender. It contained the name of another prefect, always from another House. A double cube call contained two names of two different prefects, again from two different Houses. Adrian was the only boy in living memory who had been given a sextuple cube call.

The recipient of the call had to get up early, change into games clothes, run to the House of the first prefect on the list, enter the prefect's cubicle, wake him up and get him to sign next to his name. Then on to the next prefect on the list, who was usually in a House right at the other end of the town. When all the signatures had been collected, it was back to his own House and into uniform in time for breakfast at ten to eight. So that offenders couldn't cheat by going round in the most convenient geographical order, or by getting up before seven o'clock, the official start time, the prefects on the list had to put down the exact time at which they were woken up next to their signatures.

Adrian detested cube calls, though a psychologist might have tried to persuade him otherwise, considering how far out of his way to collect them he seemed to go. He thought it an illogical form of punishment, as irritating for the prefects who were shaken from their slumbers as for the offenders.

The system was open to massive abuse. Prefects

could settle scores with colleagues they disliked by sending them cube callers every day for a week. Tit-for-tat cube call wars between prefects could go on like this for whole terms. In Adrian's House, Sargent had once had a feud with a prefect in Dashwood House called Purdy. On every day of one horrendous week Adrian had collected single cube calls from Sargent for absurd minor offences: whistling in his study during prep; having his hands in his pockets while watching a match; failing to cap a retired schoolmaster who had been walking down the High Street and whom Adrian had never even had pointed out to him before as a cappable entity. On each of Sargent's cube calls that particular week Purdy's had been the name listed. On the fifth day Adrian had sidled apologetically into Purdy's cube to find it empty.

'The bird had flown, my old love,' he had tried to explain to Sargent when returning his unsigned chit. 'But I did abstract Purdy's sponge-bag from his bedside, just to prove that I was in his cube.'

That afternoon Sargent and Purdy had fought each other on the Upper. After that Adrian was left alone.

Of course prefects could do each other favours as well.

'Oh Hancock, there's a not-half scrummy scrum-half in your Colts Fifteen, what's his name?'

'What, Yelland you mean?'

'That's the one. Rather fabulous. You . . . er . . . couldn't find your way clear to sending him over one morning, could you? As a little cubie?'

'Oh all right. If you'll send me Finlay.'

'Done.'

Adrian as a new boy had been startled to find, on his first ever cube call, that the prefect whose signature he needed slept naked with only one sheet to cover him and was extremely hard to wake up.

'Excuse me, Hollis, Hollis!' he had squeaked desperately in his ear.

But Hollis had just groaned in his sleep, rolled an arm over him and pulled him into his bed.

The only really enjoyable part of the cube call for Adrian was the burglary. Officially all the Houses were locked until seven, which was supposed to make it pointless to set off early on a cube call and take the thing at a leisurely pace. But there were larder, kitchen and changing-room windows that could be prised open and latches that could yield to a flexible sheet of mica. Once inside all you had to do was creep up to the dorm, tiptoe into the target prefect's cube, adjust his alarm clock and wake him. That way you could start the call at half past five or six and save yourself all the flap and hurry of trying to complete it in forty minutes.

'Yup,' Adrian told Bullock. 'Don't you worry your pretty little head about it. I reckon I know a way into every House.'

Two days later the whole school awoke to *Bollocks!*

From three in the morning until half past six, Tom, Adrian, Bullock and Sampson, working from maps and instructions drawn up by Adrian, had invaded the Houses and left copies in studies, common rooms, libraries and in piles at the foot of staircases. They had seen no one and been seen by no one. They had come down to breakfast in their House as apparently amazed and excited by the appearance of the magazine as everyone else.

In school, before morning chapel, they joined the knots of people under the noticeboards in the colonnade, twittering about its contents and trying to guess who the authors were.

He had been wrong to worry that the sophistication of the others' contributions would outshine his. His brand of salacious populism was far more interesting to the school than the recondite pedantry of Bullock and Sampson, and much less aggressive than Tom's style of Open Field Beat. The most feverish speculation of the day centred around the identity of Woody Nightshade. Everywhere Adrian went he heard snatches of his article being quoted.

'Hey there, Marchant. Fancy a quick round of the Biscuit Game?'

'They can chop off your hair, my children, but they can't chop off your spirit. We are winning and they know it.'

'A school isn't an ante-room for real life, it is real life.'

'Passive resistance!'

'Let's set our own syllabus. Fail their exams, pass our own.'

The school had never known anything like this. At the eleven o'clock break on the morning of its appearance there was no other topic of conversation in the Butteries.

'Go on, admit it, Healey,' Heydon-Bayley said to Adrian, his mouth full of cream-slice, 'it was you wasn't it? That's what everyone's saying.'

'That's odd, someone told me it was you,' said Adrian.

He found it achingly frustrating not to be able to crow about his part in it. Bullock, Sampson and Tom revelled in the anonymity, but Adrian longed for applause and recognition. Even jeering and hissing would have been something. He wondered if Cartwright had read his article. What would he think of it? What would he think of the *author* of it?

He watched very closely to see how people reacted when accused of being a contributor. He was always trying to improve his mastery of the delicate art of lying and the spectacle of people telling the truth under pressure repaid close study.

He noticed that people said things like:

'Yeah, it was me actually.'

'Piss off, Aitcheson! Everyone knows it was you.'

'Oh God! How did you find out? Do you think Headman knows?'

Adrian memorised all the replies and reproduced them as faithfully as he could.

And then the authorities had struck back.

Adrian's Housemaster, Tickford, rose to his feet after lunch that same day, as did the other eleven Housemasters in the other eleven Houses.

'All copies of this magazine will be collected from studies by the prefects before Games this afternoon and destroyed. Anyone found in possession of a copy after three o'clock will be severely punished.'

Adrian had never seen Tickford look so furious. He wondered if he could possibly have guessed that *Bollocks!* had originated in his House.

He and Tom had handed their two copies in cheerfully.

'There you go, Hauptmann Bennett-Jones,' said Adrian, 'we have also an edition of *The Trial*, by the notorious Jew, Kafka. Berlin would appreciate it, I am thinking, if this too was added to the bonfire. Also the works of that decadent lesbian Bolshevik, Jane Austen.'

'You'd better watch it, Healey. You're on the list. If you had anything to do with this piece of shit then you are in trouble.'

'Thank you, Sargent. You needn't take up any more of our valuable time. I'm sure you have many calls of a similar nature to make in the neighbourhood.'

But for all the sensational impact of the magazine, Adrian felt somehow a sense of anti-climax. His article would never make a shred of difference to anything. He hadn't exactly expected open warfare in the form-rooms, but it was depressing to realise that if he and Bullock and the others were exposed tomorrow they would be expelled, talked about for a while and then completely forgotten. Boys were cowardly and conventional. That's why the system worked, he supposed.

He sensed too that if he came across the article in later life, as a twenty-year-old, he would shudder with embarrassment at the pretension of it. But why should his future self sneer at what he was now? It was terrible to know that time would lead him to betray everything he now believed in.

What I am now is *right*, he told himself. I will never

103

see things as clearly again, I will never understand everything as fully as I do at this minute.

The world would never change if people got sucked into it.

He tried to explain his feelings to Tom, but Tom was not in communicative mood.

'Seems to me there's only one way to change the world,' said Tom.

'And what's that?' asked Adrian.

'Change yourself.'

'Oh, that's bollocks!'

'And *Bollocks!* tells the truth.'

He went to the library and read up his symptoms in more detail. Cyril Connolly, Robin Maugham, T.C. Worsley, Robert Graves, Simon Raven: they had all had their Cartwrights. And the novels! Dozens of them. *Lord Dismiss Us*, *The Loom of Youth*, *The Fourth of June*, *Sandel*, *Les Amitiés Particulières*, *The Hill* . . .

He was one of a long line of mimsy and embittered middle-class sensitives who disguised their feeble and decadent lust as something spiritual and Socratic.

And why not? If it meant he had to end his days on some Mediterranean island writing lyric prose for Faber and Faber and literary criticism for the *New Statesman*, running through successions of houseboys and 'secretaries', getting sloshed on Fernet Branca and having to pay off the Chief of Police every six months, then so be it. Better than driving to the office in the rain.

In a temper, he took out a large Bible, opened it at random and wrote 'Irony' down the margin in red biro. In the fly-leaf he scribbled anagrams of his name. Air and an arid nadir, a drain, a radian.

He decided to go and see Gladys. *She* would understand.

On his way he was ambushed from behind a gravestone by Rundell.

'Ha, ha! It's Woody Nightshade!'

'You took the words right out of my mouth, Tarty. Only you would know about something as disgusting as the Biscuit Game.'

'Takes one to know one.'

Adriam mimed taking out a notebook.

'"Takes one to know one," I must write that down. It might come in useful if I ever enter a competition to come up with the Most Witless Remark in the English Language.'

'Well I beg yours.'

'You can't have it.'

Rundell beckoned with a curled finger. 'New wheeze,' he said. 'Come here.'

Adrian approached cautiously.

'What foul thing is this?'

'No, I'm serious. Come here.'

He pointed to his trouser pocket. 'Put your hand in there.'

'Well frankly . . . even from you, Tarty, that's a bit . . .'

Rundell stamped his foot.

'This is serious! I've had a brilliant idea. Feel in there.'

Adrian hesitated.

'Go *on*!'

Adrian dipped his hand in the pocket.

Rundell giggled.

'You see! I've cut the pockets out. And no undies. Isn't that brilliant?'

'You tarty great tart . . .'

'Keep going now you've started, for God's sake.'

Adrian reached Gladys and sat down with a thump. Down below, Rundell blew an extravagant kiss and skipped off to replenish his strength before trying the game on someone else.

Why can't I be satisfied with Tarty? Adrain asked himself, wiping his fingers on a handkerchief. He's sexy. He's fun. I can do things with him I wouldn't dream of doing with Cartwright. Oh hell, here comes someone else.

'Friend or foe?'

Pigs Trotter lumbered into view.

'Friend!' he panted.

'La! You are quite done up, my lord. Come and sit this one out with me.'

Trotter sat down while Adrian fanned himself with a dock-leaf.

'I always think the cotillion too fatiguing for the summer months. Persons of consequence should avoid it. When I have danced a cotillion, I know for a fact that I look plain beyond example. The minuet is, I believe, the only dance for gentlemen of rank and tone. You agree with me there, my lord, I make no doubt? I think it was Horry Walpole who remarked, "In this life one should try everything once except incest and country dancing." It is an excellent rule, as I remarked to my mother in bed last night. Perhaps you will do me the honour of accompanying me to the card room later? A game of Deep Bassett is promised and I mean to take my lord Darrow for five hundred guineas.'

'Healey,' said Trotter. 'I'm not saying you did and I'm not saying you didn't, I don't really care. But Woody Nightshade . . .'

'Woody Nightshade,' said Adrian. '*Solanum dulcamara*, the common wayside bitter-sweet:

> They seek him here, they seek him there,
> Those masters seek him everywhere.
> Isn't he nimble, isn't he neat,
> That demmed elusive bitter-sweet.

'A poor thing, but mine own.'

'You've read his article, I suppose?' said Pigs Trotter.

'I may have glanced through it a few times in an idle hour,' said Adrian. 'Why do you ask?'

'Well . . .'

There was a catch in Trotter's throat. Adrian looked at him in alarm. Tears were starting up in his piggy eyes.

Oh hell. Other people's tears were more than Adrian could cope with. Did you put an arm round them? Did you pretend not to notice? He tried the friendly, cajoling approach.

'Hey, hey, hey! What's the matter?'

'I'm sorry, Healey. I'm really sorry b-but . . .'

'You can tell me. What is it?'

Trotter shook his head miserably and sniffed.

'Here look,' said Adrian, 'there's a handkerchief. Oh . . . no, second thoughts this one's not so clean. But I have got a cigarette. Blow your nose on that.'

'No thanks, Healey.'

'I'll have it then.'

He eyed Trotter nervously. It was cheating to let your emotions out like this. And what was a lump like Pigs doing with emotions anyway? He had found a handkerchief of his own and was blowing his nose with a horrible mucous squelch. Adrian lit his cigarette and tried to sound casual.

'So what's troubling you, Trot? Is it something in the article?'

'It's nothing. It's just that bit where he starts talking about . . .'

Trotter drew a copy of *Bollocks!* from his pocket. It was already folded open on the second page of Adrian's article.

Adrian looked at him in surprise.

'I wouldn't get caught with this if I were you.'

'It's all right, I'm going to throw it away. I've copied it all out by hand anyway.'

Trotter dabbed a finger down on a paragraph.

'There,' he said, 'read that bit.'

'"And they call it puppy-love,"' Adrian read, '"well I'll guess they'll never know how the young heart really feels." The words of Donny Osmond, philosopher and wit, strike home as ever. How can they punish us and grind us down when we are capable of feelings strong enough to burst the world open? Either they know what we go through when we are in love, in which case their callousness in not warning us and helping us through it is inexcusable, or they have never felt what we feel and we have every right to call them dead. Love shrinks your stomach. It pickles your guts. But what does it do to your mind? It tosses the sandbags overboard so the balloon can soar. Suddenly, you're above the ordinary . . .'

Adrian looked across at Pigs Trotter who was rocking forwards and tightly gripping his handkerchief as if it were the safety-bar of a roller-coaster.

'It's a misquotation from *The Lost Weekend* that bit, I think,' said Adrian. 'Ray Milland talking about alcohol. So. You . . . er . . . you're in love then?'

Trotter nodded.

'Um . . . anyone . . . anyone I'd know? You don't have to say if you don't want to.' Adrian was maddened by the huskiness in his throat.

Trotter nodded again.

'It . . . must be pretty tough.'

'I don't mind telling you who it is,' said Trotter.

I'll kill him if it's Cartwright, Adrian thought to himself. I'll kill the fat bastard.

'Who is it then?' he asked, as lightly as he could.

Trotter stared at him.

'You of course,' he said and burst into tears.

They walked slowly back towards the House. Adrian wanted desperately to run away and leave Pigs Trotter to welter in the salt bath of his fatuous misery, but he couldn't.

He didn't know how to react. He didn't know the form. He supposed that he owed Trotter something. The object of love should feel honoured or flattered, responsible in some way. Instead he felt insulted, degraded and revolted. More than that, he felt put upon.

Trotter?

Pigs can fly. This one could, anyway.

It isn't the same, he kept saying to himself. It isn't

the same as me and Cartwright. It can't be. Jesus, if I were to declare my love to Cartwright and he felt a tenth as pissed off as I do now . . .

'It's all right, you know,' said Pigs Trotter, 'I know you don't feel the same way about me.'

Feel the same way about me? Christ.

'Well,' said Adrian, 'the thing is, you know, I mean it's a phase, isn't it?'

How could he say that? How could he *say* that?

'It doesn't make it any better though,' said Trotter.

'Right,' said Adrian.

'Don't worry. I won't bother you. I won't tag onto you and Tom any more. I'm sure it'll be all right.'

Well there you are. If he could be so sure that it would be 'all right' then how could it be love? Adrian knew that it would never be 'all right' with him and Cartwright.

Trotter's wasn't the Real Thing, it was just Pepsi.

They were nearing the House. Pigs Trotter dried his eyes on the sleeve of his blazer.

'I'm very sorry,' said Adrian, 'I wish . . .'

'That's okay, Healey,' said Trotter. 'But I ought to tell you that I have read *The Scarlet Pimpernel*, you know.'

'What do you mean?'

'Well, in the book, everyone wanted to know who the Scarlet Pimpernel was and so Percy Blakeney made up that rhyme: the one you just did a version of: "They seek him here, they seek him there, Those Frenchies seek him everywhere . . ."'

'Yes?' What on earth was he on about?

'The thing is,' said Trotter, 'that it was Percy Blakeney himself who was the Scarlet Pimpernel all

the time, wasn't it? The one who made up the rhyme.
That's all.'

IV

Adrian managed to get into Chapel early next morning, so that he could sit behind Cartwright and ponder
the beauty of the back of his head, the set of his
shoulders and the perfection of his buttocks as they
tightened when he leant forward to pray.

It was a strange thing about beauty, the way that it
transformed everything in and around a person. Cartwright's blazer was outstandingly the most beautiful
blazer in Chapel, but it came from Gorringe's like
everyone else's. The backs of his ears, peeping
through the soft golden tangle of his hair, were skin
and capillary and fleshy tissue like any ears, but
nobody else's ears set fire to Adrian's blood and
flooded his stomach with hot lead.

The hymn was 'Jerusalem the Golden'. Adrian as
usual fitted his own words.

'O Cartwright you are golden, With milk and honey
blest. Beneath thy contemplation Sink heart and voice
opprest. I know well, O I know well, What lovely
joys are there, What radiancy of glory, What light
beyond compare.'

Tom, next to him, heard and gave a nudge. Adrian
obediently returned to the text, but lapsed again into
his own version for the final verse.

'O sweet and blessed Cartwright, Shall I ever see
thy face? O sweet and blessed Cartwright, Shall I
ever win thy grace? Exult O golden Cartwright! The

Lord shall play my part: Mine only, mine for ever,
Thou shalt be, and thou art.'

Six hundred hymn-books were shelved and six
hundred bodies rustled down onto their seats. At the
east end, Headman's heels rang out on the stone floor
as he stepped forward for Notices, hitching up the
shoulder of his gown.

'Boys have been seen using a short cut from the
Upper to Alperton Road. You are cordially reminded
that this path goes through Brandiston Field, which is
private property and out of bounds. The sermon on
Sunday will be given by Rex Anderson, Suffragan
Bishop of Kampala. The Bateman Medal for Greek
Prose has been won by W.E.St. J. Hooper, Rosen-
gard's House. That is all.'

He turned as if to go, then checked himself and
turned back.

'Oh, there is one more thing. It has come to my
notice that a more than usually juvenile magazine of
some description has been circulating about the
school. Until the authors of this nonsense have come
forward there will be no exeats, no club activities and
all boys will be confined to their Houses in free time.
Nothing else.'

'It's a fucking outrage,' said Adrian as they
streamed out of the Chapel into the sunshine. 'And so
pathetic, so completely pathetic. "A juvenile magazine
of some description!" As if he hasn't read it a hundred
times and trembled with fury as he read it!'

'He just wants to make it sound as if it isn't such a
big deal,' said Tom.

'Does he really think we're going to fall for that?
He's scared, he's bloody scared.'

Heydon-Bayley came up.

'Gated for the rest of term! The bastard!'

'It's just a feeble attempt to try and get the school to turn against the magazine and do his detective work for him,' said Bullock. 'It won't work. Whoever's responsible is too clever.'

Adrian was once more at a loose end that afternoon. It was a Corps day so there was no cricket and he didn't dare climb up to Gladys Winkworth in case he bumped into Trotter again. Officially he should be visiting his old lady and doing odd jobs for her, but she had died of hypothermia the previous term and he hadn't been supplied with a replacement yet. He had just decided to go down to the School Gramophone Library and practise conducting to records, a favourite legal pastime, when he remembered he had a standing invitation to tea from Biffen the French master.

Biffen lived in rather a grand house in its own grounds on the edge of town.

'Hello, sir,' said Adrian. 'It's a Friday, so I thought . . .'

'Healey! How splendid. Come in, come in.'

'I've brought some lemon curd, sir.'

There were about six boys already in the sitting room, talking to Biffen's wife, Lady Helen. Biffen had married her at Cambridge and then taken her back to his old school when he joined as a junior master. They had been here ever since, objects of great pity to the school: an Earl's daughter tied to a no-hope, slow-lane pedagogue.

'I know you!' boomed Lady Helen from the sofa.

'You are Healey from Tickford's House. You were Mosca in the School Play.'

'Healey is in my Lower Sixth French set,' said Biffen.

'And he mobs you appallingly, Humphrey dear. I know.'

'Er, I've brought some lemon curd,' said Adrian.

'How kind. Now, who do you know here?'

Adrian looked round the room.

'Um . . .'

'You'll certainly know Hugo. He's in your House. Go and sit next to him, and get him to stop spoiling my dog.'

Adrian hadn't noticed Cartwright sitting at a window seat, apart from the main group, tossing bits of cake at a spaniel.

'Hi,' he said, sitting down next to him.

'Hi,' said Cartwright.

'Did you pass your exam then?'

'Sorry?'

'Your Grade Three piano. You remember. Last term.'

'Oh, that. Yes thanks.'

'Great.'

More immortal dialogue from the Noël Coward of the seventies.

'So,' said Adrian, 'do you come here . . . er . . . is this something you've been to many times?'

'Most Fridays,' said Cartwright. 'I've never seen you here before.'

'No, well . . . I've not been invited before.'

'Right.'

'So . . . er . . . what happens exactly?'

114

'Well, you know, it's just a tea-party, really.'

And so it had proved. Biffen had instigated a book game in which everyone had to own up to books they'd never read. Biffen and Lady Helen called out titles of classic novels and plays and if you hadn't read them you had to put your hand up. *Pride and Prejudice*, *David Copperfield*, *Animal Farm*, *Madame Bovary*, *1984*, *Lucky Jim*, *Sons and Lovers*, *Othello*, *Oliver Twist*, *Decline and Fall*, *Howards End*, *Hamlet*, *Anna Karenina*, *Tess of the D'Urbervilles*, the list of unread books that they managed to compile had made them all giggle. They had agreed that by the end of term the list would have to be much more obscure. The only two books that had been read by everyone present were *Lord of the Flies* and *Catch 22* which, Biffen remarked, said much about English teaching at prep schools. It was all a transparent, and to Adrian rather wet, device to get everyone to read more, but it worked.

Adrian, despite the gentility of it all, had rather enjoyed himself and was fired with an enthusiasm for outreading everyone on the Russians, who always sounded the most impressive and impenetrable.

'I mean,' he said to Cartwright as they walked back to Tickford's, 'this place can really get you down. It's not a bad idea to have a sanctuary like that to go to, is it?'

'He's going to be my tutor next year when I'm in the Sixth Form,' said Cartwright. 'I want to go to Cambridge and he's the best at getting you through Oxbridge Entrance apparently.'

'Really? *I* want to go to Cambridge too!' said Adrian. 'Which college?'

'Trinity, I think.'

'God, me too! My father was there!'

Adrian's father in fact had been to Oxford.

'But Biffo thinks I should apply to St Matthew's. He has a friend there he was in the war with, a Professor Trefusis, supposed to be very good. Anyway, we'd better get a move on. Don't forget we're gated. It's nearly five already.'

'Oh shit,' said Adrian, as they broke into a run.

'Did you read the magazine, then?' he asked as they jogged up the hill to Tickford's.

'Yes,' said Cartwright.

And that was that.

'It was practically a conversation, Tom!'

'Great,' said Tom. 'Thing is . . .'

'It's all settled. He'll join me at Cambridge in my second year. After we've graduated we'll fly to Los Angeles or Amsterdam to get married – you can there, you know. Then we'll set up house in the country. I'll write poetry, Hugo will play the piano and look beautiful. We'll have two cats called Spasm and Clitoris. And a spaniel. Hugo likes spaniels. A spaniel called Biffen.'

Tom was unimpressed.

'Sargent was in here ten minutes ago,' he said.

'Oh pissly piss. What was he after?'

'Tickford wants to see you in his study straight away.'

'What for?'

'Dunno.'

'It can't be . . . does he want to see you as well? Or Sammy or Bollocks?'

Tom shook his head.

'He's got nothing on me,' said Adrian. 'He can't have.'

'Stout denial,' said Tom. 'It works every time.'

'Exactly. Brazen it out.'

'But I tell you,' warned Tom, 'there's definitely something up. Sargent looked scared.'

'Rubbish,' said Adrian, 'he hasn't the imagination.'

'Shit-scared,' said Tom.

The Housemaster's study was through the Hall. Adrian was surprised to see all the Prefects standing about in a cluster near the door that connected the boys' side of the House to Mr and Mrs Tickford's living quarters. They stared at him as he went through. They didn't jeer or look hostile. They looked . . . they looked shit-scared.

Adrian knocked on Tickford's door.

'Come in!'

Adrian swallowed nervously and entered.

Tickford was sitting behind his desk, fiddling with a letter-opener.

Like a psychopath toying with a dagger, thought Adrian.

The window was at Tickford's back, darkening his face too much for Adrian to be able to read his expression.

'Adrian, thank you for coming to see me,' he said. 'Sit down, please sit down.'

'Thank you, sir.'

'Oh dear . . . oh dear.'

'Sir?'

'I don't suppose you have any idea why I have sent for you?'

Adrian shook his head, a picture of round-eyed innocence.

'No, I should imagine not. No. I hope word has not got out.'

Tickford took off his glasses and breathed anxiously on the lenses.

'I have to ask you now, Adrian . . . oh dear . . . it's all very . . .'

He replaced the glasses and stood up. Adrian could see his face clearly now, but still he couldn't read it.

'Yes, sir?'

'I'm going to have to ask you about your relationship with Paul Trotter.'

So *that* was it!

The moron had gone and blabbed to someone. The Chaplain probably. And vicious Dr Meddlar would have been only too keen to repeat it to Tickford.

'I don't know what you mean, sir.'

'It's a very simple question, Adrian. It really is. I'm asking you about your relationship with Paul Trotter.'

'Well, I haven't really . . . really got one, sir. I mean, we're sort of friends. He hangs around with me and Thompson sometimes. But I don't know him very well.'

'And that's it?'

'Well yes, sir.'

'It is terribly important that you tell me the truth. Terribly important.'

A boy can always tell when a master is lying, Adrian thought to himself. And Tickford isn't lying. It *is* very important.

'Well, there is one thing, sir.'

'Yes?'

'I really don't know that I should repeat this to you, sir. I mean Trotter did tell me something in confidence . . .'

Tickford leant forward and took Adrian's hand by the wrist.

'I promise you this, Adrian. Whatever Trotter may have said to you, you *must* now tell me. Do you understand? You must!'

'It's a bit embarrassing, sir . . . couldn't you ask him yourself?'

'No, no. I want to hear from you.'

Adrian swallowed.

'Well sir, I bumped into Trotter yesterday afternoon and he suddenly . . . he suddenly started crying and so I asked him what the matter was and he said he was very unhappy because he was . . . well he had a sort of . . .'

God this was hard.

'. . . he was . . . well he said he was in love with someone . . . he, you know, had a pash on them.'

'I see. Yes, of course. Yes I see. He thought he was in love with someone. Another boy, I suppose?'

'That's what he said, sir.'

'Trotter was found in a barn in Brandiston Field this afternoon,' he said, pushing a piece of paper across the desk. 'This note was in his pocket.'

Adrian stared.

'Sir?'

Tickford nodded sadly.

'The stupid boy,' he said. 'The stupid boy hanged himself.'

Adrian looked at the note.

'I'm very sorry but I couldn't bear it any more,' it read. 'Healey knows why.'

'His mother and father are on their way down from Harrogate,' said Tickford. 'What am I going to say?'

Adrian looked at him in panic.

'Why, sir? Why would he kill himself?'

'Tell me the name of the boy he was . . . he had this thing for, Adrian.'

'Well, sir . . .'

'I must know.'

'It was Cartwright, sir. Hugo Cartwright.'

Two Savile Row suits, a Tommy Nutter and a Bennett, Tovey and Steele, faced each other over a table at Wiltons.

'Good to see the Native back again,' said the Bennett, Tovey and Steele. 'I was beginning to think it extinct.'

'Now you say that,' said the Tommy Nutter suit, 'but I've got rather a soft spot for the Pacific chaps myself. They're sort of wetter *somehow, don't you think? Fleshlier if there is such a word.'*

The Bennet, Tovey and Steele did not agree. He considered it typical of the Tommy Nutter to have a loud taste in oysters.

'This Montrachet's a bit warm, isn't it?'

The Bennett, Tovey and Steele sighed. He had been brought up from his nanny's knee to believe that white Burgundies should not be overchilled. They knew him at Wiltons and took great care to present his wines just so. The Tommy Nutter would resent a lecture, however. Men of his stamp were absurdly sensitive.

'Still,' said the other. 'Who's complaining? Now then. Let's talk Mendax. GDS has had no joy, I'm sorry to say, with the Odysseus material. No joy at all.'

'No decrypt whatsoever?'

'Oh, they opened it up all right. It was an old twist-cypher. Pre-war. Absolute antique.'

'That figures,' grunted the Bennett, Tovey and Steele. 'And what was inside?'

'Names, addresses and telephone numbers. Load of harmless Osties. Lifted straight from the bloody Salzburg directory, would you believe?'

'The old bastard.'

'So the thing is,' the Tommy Nutter twisted the stem of his wine-glass coyly, 'did this Odysseus of yours bring the material out or did he leave it behind?'

'He's had nothing in the mail. We know that.'

'Your friend on the inside still paying his way?'

'Oh yes.'

'Good, because he's a greedy son of a bitch.'

The Bennett, Tovey and Steele suit ignored this. It wasn't as if the Tommy Nutter suit was paying for Telemachus. He thought he was, of course, and would probably never notice that it came directly out of the Bennett, Tovey and Steele's pocket, never to be reclaimed from the fund. It was a purely private business, but Cabinet liaison had to believe there was honey in it for them. It would not do for them to find out that the Service was being used entirely for the Bennett, Tovey and Steele's private ends.

'I think the Mendax material is still over there,' he said, 'without the walls of Ilium.'

'In Salzburg, you mean?' asked the Tommy Nutter, whose grip on codenames was weak at the best of times.

'That's right. In Salzburg.'

'This is all very much your own pigeon, you know. You are the only one who believes in Mendax. I am reminded of the operation you ran in seventy-six, also against Odysseus. What did that game come to?'

The Bennett, Tovey and Steele shot the Tommy Nutter a suspicious glare.

'What do you mean game?' he said. 'Why do you say game?'

'Keep your hair on, old man. I just meant that you seem to have a bit of a maggot in your head on the subject of Trefusis. Some of us are wondering why. That's all.'

'You'll find out yet. Listen. The point is this. I never said I did believe in Mendax. But if it doesn't exist why should the Trojans and Odysseus want us to believe that it does? That's worth pursuing surely?'

'Humph,' said the Tommy Nutter. 'It has at least been a cheap operation so far, that I will grant you. But we haven't a shred of proof that Szabó – what's he called again?'

'Helen.'

'We haven't a shred of evidence to suggest that Helen is anything other than a loyal servant of his state. The Trojans have just given him a medal for God's sake.'

'All the more reason to suspect Odysseus.'

'Why "Helen" by the way? Odd codename for a man.'

The Bennett, Tovey and Steele suit was not going to give the Tommy Nutter a free lesson in Homeric mythology. Where did the man go to school? The tie was no indication. Beaconsfield Conservatives or something equally foul, probably. Hadley Wood Golf Club. Carshalton Rotarians. Yuk.

'It seemed to make sense at the time,' he said.

'Oh ah,' the Tommy Nutter pressed a crumb into the table cloth. 'So tell me about these grandchildren.'

'Stefan is a chess-player. He's coming over here to play in a couple of months. They'll keep him on a long leash I shouldn't wonder.'

'And you want me to allocate resourcing?'

'I'd quite like some money made available, if that's what you mean. Grade Two surveillance should do it.'

'I have to interface, as they say, with the Treasury

123

tomorrow. *Cabinet next week. Oh, look, you're not going to smoke are you?'*

Christ! *thought the Bennett, Tovey and Steele. Roll on the next Labour government.*

Four

I

Tim Anderson considered the question with great care.

'I don't believe that the comparison with *Oliver Twist*, seductive and engaging as I would be the last to deny it being, is as valid as a first glance might allow.'

'But surely, Dr Anderson, the similarities *are* very clear. What we have here is a secret workhouse birth, we have a gang of boys set to work by the character Polterneck, we have the character of Peter Flowerbuck, who traces his own family connection with the Cotton twins, not unlike Mr Brownlow's quest in *Oliver Twist*, we have Flinter, who like Nancy is an agent of revenge. The parallels are surely most striking?'

Gary poured some more Meursault for Jenny and Adrian, never at any time taking his eyes off the screen.

'I am not going to consider failing to grant you the presence of narrative echoes,' Tim Anderson replied, 'but I would certainly find myself presented with personal difficulties if asked to deny that this is the mature Dickens of *Little Dorrit* and *Bleak House*. I'm sensing a fuller picture of a connected world here than we are allowed in *Twist*. I'm sensing a deeper anger, I find myself responding to a more complete symphonic vision. The chapter which describes the flood, the scene depicting the bursting of the Thames's banks and the sweeping away of the Den is a more proleptic and organic event than the reader has been confronted with in earlier novels. I would be laying myself open to a charge of being mistaken if I attempted to resist the argument that the character of Flinter is a development of both Nancy and the Artful Dodger which we can't be afraid to recognise takes us into a more terrified Dickens, a more, if you like, Kafkaesque Dickens.'

The interviewer nodded.

'I understand that the University has already sold the film and television rights of *Peter Flowerbuck*?'

'That is not substantially incorrect.'

'Are you worried that to do this before the manuscript has been officially authenticated might lay you open to future embarrassment, should it prove to be a fake?'

'As you know, we have taken on a number of new research fellows at St Matthew's who are working extensively on the text to determine its authenticity-level. They will be running linguistic particles and image-clusters through a computer program which is as reliable as any chemical test.'

'Authorial fingerprinting?'

'Authorial is the term often used, fingerprinting, that is far from wrong.'

'And how confident are you that this is genuine Dickens?'

'Let me turn that question round and say that I am not confident that it isn't Dickens.'

'Let me turn that answer round and say "bullshit",' said Adrian.

'Hush!' said Jenny.

'Well, I mean. Symphonic visions.'

'I don't think it insignificant,' Anderson continued, 'that at a time when English departments at my university and hundreds of others are being threatened with cuts, a discovery of pure scholarship like this should attract such attention and validate so completely what has quite properly been perceived as the beleaguered discipline of English studies.'

'It's a very lucrative discovery, certainly. How in fact was it made?'

'I was alerted to the existence of the text by a student of mine from Newnham College. She had been participating in my seminars on Derrida and Sexual Difference and had been pursuing a number of independent lines of enquiry into the Victorian Deviant Ethic. She found the papers in the St Matthew's College Library hidden amongst old copies of *Cornhill* magazine.'

'Did she realise what she had stumbled across?'

'She was not unaware of its potential lack of insignificance.'

'I understand that a philologist from your own department, and indeed college, Donald Trefusis, has expressed doubts as to the genuineness of the find?'

'I believe that I think it of immense value to express doubts. It is because of the Professor's repeated queries that we have been granted the necessary funding to research the manuscript.'

'Dr Anderson, many people like myself, who have read *Peter Flowerbuck* have been struck by the candour and detail with which sexual activity and the nature of Victorian child-prostitution is described. Do you think Dickens ever intended to publish?'

'We are currently trawling all biographical source materials for some clue as to the answer to that highly legitimate question. Perhaps I can turn it round, however, and ask, "Would he not have destroyed the manuscript if he never wanted it read?" Yeah?'

'I see.'

'I cannot deny myself the right to believe that he left it to be found. We therefore owe it to him to publish now.'

'It is not of course a completed work. What you have is only a fragment.'

'There is truth in that remark.'

'Do you think there is a chance of discovering the rest of the manuscript?'

'If it exists we are not doubtful of locating the residue.'

'Dr Anderson, thank you very much indeed. The three currently extant chapters of *Peter Flowerbuck*, edited and annotated by Tim Anderson, will be available from the Cambridge University Press in October, priced fourteen pounds ninety-five. The BBC serialisation, currently in production, with an ending by Malcolm Bradbury, is due to reach our screens sometime in the spring of nineteen-eighty-one.'

Jenny got up and switched off the television.

'Well,' said Gary, 'that's set the apple-cart amongst the pigeons and no mistake. What do we do now?'

'Now,' said Adrian, 'we wait.'

II

Adrian put down the cane and loosened the cravat. Gary sat down on the step and mopped his brow with a most preposterous handkerchief of bright vermilion silk. Jenny addressed them from the fire-escape.

'I have very few notes to give,' she said. 'There's an old theatrical saying, "Bad dress, good performance"; I'm sorry to have to tell you that this was an excellent dress. The mechanics of the show are all there. The greatest imponderable is the time it will take for the audience to follow Adrian into this yard. That's something we'll discover tonight. It's all there: just pace and enjoy it. We're all just waiting for the final director now – the audience. If you don't mind standing here in the sun I'll come amongst you now with individual notes.'

Jenny had approached Tim Anderson for permission to mount a production of *Peter Flowerbuck* and his gratitude to her for the discovery of the manuscript had made it impossible for him to refuse.

'Jenny, can I ask at this stage how you imagine presenting on stage what is, ultimately, not a play?'

'Didn't you once say yourself, Dr Anderson, that all the theatrical energy in Victorian Britain went not into drama but into the novel?'

'That is something I did say, yes.'

'The RSC is apparently planning a dramatisation of *Nicholas Nickleby*, surely *Peter Flowerbuck* is even more suited to the theatre? If we use the ADC we can take the audience outside with Peter as he goes to the Den. The yard at the side of the theatre is pretty much a Victorian slum already.'

'I'm insanely excited.'

'Good.'

'Jenny, may I ask you, do you need any help with the preparation or finalisation of a playtext?'

'Oh, I'm not writing it. Adrian Healey is.'

'Healey? I wasn't aware he'd been authorised to read the manuscript.'

'Oh, he's read it all right.'

She climbed down the fire-escape now and approached Adrian and Gary with a sheaf of notes.

'The Polterneck scenes are basically fine,' she told Gary. 'But for God's sake learn that scene twelve speech properly.'

'What happens in scene twelve?'

'It's where you buy Joe. Which reminds me, where's Hugo?'

'Here I am.'

'I want to rehearse the Russell Square scene with you and Adrian. It's still not right. Let's see . . . I've got some more notes for the others. If you go and run through it on stage now I'll send Bridget over and be with you in ten minutes.'

Hugo and Adrian walked into the theatre together.

'Nervous?' said Adrian.

'A bit. My mother's coming. I don't know what she'll think.'

'Your mother?'

'She's an actress.'

'Why did I never know that?'

'Why should you have done?'

'No reason, I suppose.'

It would have been a difficult scene even if Hugo hadn't been playing Joe. Adrian ran through it in his mind, like a Radio 3 announcer giving the synopsis of an opera.

Flowerbuck, he intoned to himself, has taken the boy Joe Cotton back to his house in Russell Square, convinced that he is his sister's son. Joe on arrival immediately tries to take off his clothes, unable to imagine that he would be expected to do anything else in a gentleman's house. Peter and Mrs Twimp, his housekeeper, calm him down and give him a bath. Mrs Twimp, played by Bridget Arden, injects into the scene her own brand of malapropistic comedy as they try to question Joe on the details of his early childhood. His memory is very uncertain. He recalls a garden, a large house and a fair-haired sister but very little else. At this stage, and indeed *on* this stage, Adrian Healey, playing Flowerbuck, finds his memory to be uncertain too and often starts to forget his lines.

After the bath Joe is taken to the dining room to eat. Or rather the dining room comes to them. It is that kind of production. Joe recognises in horror a portrait of Sir Christian Flowerbuck, Peter's uncle.

'That gentleman hurt me!' he cries.

It transpires that Sir Christian, Peter's benefactor and godfather, whose baronetcy and money Peter is in line to inherit, had been the first man to violate Joe.

The scene ends at night with Joe creeping from his room and slipping into Peter's bed. He knows no other form of companionship or love.

Peter awakes next morning, horrified to realise that he has lain with the boy who he is now more sure than ever is his nephew.

Adrian had had nothing to do with the casting of Hugo, at least as far as anyone knew. Jenny had bounced into his rooms one afternoon, full of excitement.

'I've just seen a perfect Joe Cotton! We don't need to get a real boy after all.'

'Who is this child?'

'He's not a child, he's a Trinity first year, but on stage he'll look fourteen or fifteen easily. And, Adrian, he's exactly as you . . . hum . . . as Dickens describes Joe. Same hair, same blue eyes, everything. Even the same walk, though I don't know if from the same cause. He came to see me this morning, it was rather embarrassing, he thought I was expecting him. Bridget must have arranged it without telling me. His name's Hugo Cartwright.'

'Really?' said Adrian. 'Hugo Cartwright, eh?'

'Do you know him?'

'If it's the one I'm thinking of, we were in the same House at school.'

Gary opened his mouth to speak, but he met Adrian's eye and subsided.

'I dimly remember him,' said Adrian.

'Don't you think he's ideal casting for Joe?'

'Well in many ways I suppose he is, yes. Fairly ideal.'

If Hugo was unnerved by correspondences between a hundred-and-twenty-year-old Victorian manuscript and an incident from his own and Adrian's life he

132

made no mention of the fact. But there was no doubt that his acting in the scene was awkward and formal.

'This is your home now, Joe. Mrs Twimp is to be your mother.'

'Yes, sir.'

'How should you like Mrs Twimp as a mother?'

'Does she want to join us, sir?'

'Join us, Joe? Join us in what?'

'In the bed, sir.'

'Bless me, Mr Flowerbuck, the lad is so manured to a life of shame, that's the fact of it, that he can't conceive no other!'

'There is no necessity for you to sleep with anyone but yourself and your Saviour, Joe. In peace and innocence.'

'No, Sir, no indeed! Mr Polterneck and Mrs Polterneck and Uncle Polterneck must have their boy-money. I am their gold sovereign, Sir.'

'Keep your clothes on, Joe, I beg of you!'

'Lord love the poor child, Mr Flowerbuck. Look at the condition of him! He should be washed and given fresh arraignments.'

'You're right, Mrs Twimp. Bring a bath and a robe.'

'I shall return percipiently.'

Jenny called across from the stalls.

'What do you think your feelings towards Joe are here?'

Adrian shaded his eyes across the lights.

'Well revulsion, I'd've thought. Horror, pity, indignation . . . you know. All that.'

'Good, yes. But what about desire?'

'Um . . .'

'You see, I think it's implicit that Peter is sexually attracted to Joe from the first.'

'Well I really don't . . .'

'I feel Dickens makes it very clear.'

'But he's his nephew! I don't think *Dickens* had any such thought in *Dickens's* head, do you?'

'I don't think we can be so sure.'

'Oh can't we?'

'Look at Joe now. He's standing in front of you, half naked. I think we should sense a sense of . . . we should sense a sense of . . . of . . . some kind of latent, repressed desire.'

'Right-ho. One sense of latent, repressed desire coming up. Do you want a side-order of self-disgust too, or hold on that?'

'Adrian, we go up in three hours, please don't start fucking about.'

'Okay. Fine.'

'Now, Hugo, what about you?'

'Well . . .'

'What's your attitude to Adrian, do you think?'

'Well he's just another man, isn't he?'

'I don't know how to love him,' sang Adrian. 'What to do, how to move him. He's a man, he's just a man and I've had so many men before, in very many ways. He's just one more.'

'I think Adrian's right there,' said Jenny. 'Despite being a quarter-tone flat. Imagine all the peculiar things you've had to do for your customers. Being bathed and clothed probably doesn't seem that new or different. You've been trained to please: your complaisance is the complaisance of a whore, your smile is the smile of a whore. I think you can afford a touch more assuredness. At the moment you're rather stiff.'

'He's only flesh and blood,' said Adrian. 'Look at who he's standing next to.'

'Adrian, please!'

'Sorry, Miss.'

Mrs Twimp entered with the breakfast tray.

—Sir, the lad can't be found . . . ooh!

She started in surprise at the sight of Joe's head nestling on the sleeping Flowerbuck's bare chest.

—Sir! Sir!

—Oh . . . good morning, Mrs Twimp . . .

—Bless me! I never saw such licence! Mr Flowerbuck, Sir, I cannot credit the account of my eyes. That you should stand exposed as an amuser of children, nought but a correcter of youth, a pedestal! A vile producer, a libertarian! That I should gaze upon such naked immortality, such disillusion.

—Calm yourself, Mrs Twimp. The child crept in at night when I was asleep. I had not the first idea that he was with me until just now.

—Sir! I beg your pardon . . . but the sight of him. I could only jump to one confusion.

—Leave us, Mrs Twimp.

—Shall you try to arouse him, sir? I think he should be aroused directly.

Adrian could feel Hugo's body tense at the laugh from the audience that greeted this line.

—I will wake him and send him down to you, Mrs Twimp.

—I shall draw some water for his absolutions.

She exited to a warm round of applause.

Adrian sat up and stared in front of him.

—Oh Lord! What have I done? What in God's name have I done?

—Good morning, sir.

—Ah Joe, Joe! Why did you come to me last night?

—You are my saviour, sir. Mrs Twimp bade me remember it most carefully. And you told me I should sleep only with my saviour.

—Child, I meant . . .

—Did I do wrong, sir? Did I not please you?

—I dreamt . . . I know not what I dreamt. Say I was asleep, Joe. Say I slept all night.

—You were very gentle to me, sir.

—No! No! No!

In the blackout and in the thunder of applause that marked the end of the act, they lay there while the bed was trundled into the wings where Jenny stood jumping up and down with excitement.

'Wonderful!' she said. 'Listen to that! The Grauniad is out there and the *Financial Times*.'

'The *Financial Times*?' said Adrian. 'Is Tim Anderson thinking of starting a Flowerbuck limited company?

'Their drama critic.'

'I didn't know they had one. Who the hell reads drama criticism in the *Financial Times*?'

'Everyone will if it's a good notice, because I'll have it blown up and put outside the theatre.'

'How long's the interval?' asked Hugo.

No one at the party was going to deny that it had been the finest production in the history of Cambridge drama, that Hugo and Gary in particular were bound for West End glory in weeks, that Adrian had done a fine job in translating Dickens to the stage and that he must write a new play for Jenny to direct the moment she joined the National, which appointment must be only days away.

'My dear Healey!' a hand was placed on Adrian's shoulder. He turned to see the smiling face of Donald Trefusis.

'Hello, Professor. Did you enjoy it?'

'Triumphant, Adrian. Absolutely triumphant. A most creditable piece of adaptation.'

'Will it do as my piece of original work?'

Trefusis looked puzzled.

'You know, the task you set me earlier this term?'

'Adapting someone's novel? Will that do as your piece of original work? You must have misunderstood me.'

Adrian was slightly drunk and, although he had planned this moment a hundred times in his head, it was always in Trefusis's rooms and without 'Hit Me With Your Rhythm Stick' playing in the background.

'Well, Professor, no. That's not what I mean,' he cleared his throat. 'I mean will *Peter Flowerbuck* the novel count as my original piece of work?'

'Oh certainly, certainly. By all means. I thought for a moment that you were . . .'

Bridget Arden, the voluptuous actress who had played Mrs Twimp with such éclat, came up and kissed Adrian on the mouth.

'Julian's rolling a joint in the downstairs dressing-room, Adey. Come and join us.'

'Ha! Very good! Rolling a joint! That's a great one!

Love it . . . er, she's just . . . you know,' explained Adrian, as they watched her falling downstairs.

'Of course she is, my dear fellow! No, I was saying. I thought for a moment you expected that I would take just the *adapting* of your novel as a satisfactory task. I accept the *writing* of it, gladly. A splendid conception. It exceeded my most optimistic expectations.'

'You mean you know?'

'Aside from the three hundred and forty-seven anachronisms that Dr Anderson and his team will uncover in time, I had the good fortune to be in your rooms one afternoon. How I could have mistaken D staircase for A, I have no idea. I am not usually so inattentive. But before I realised my error, I had stumbled across the manuscript.'

'You stumbled across a bundle of papers wrapped in a blanket hidden on top of a bookcase?'

'I am quite a stumbler when the mood is on me. I stumbled for Cambridge as an undergraduate.'

'I bet you did.'

'Absurdly remiss of me, I know. Not solely an affliction of the elderly however. I believe your friend Gary Collins once accidentally stumbled into my rooms in just the same way. In his case, I understand he even stumbled across a telephone before he noticed where he was. These confusions are not so rare as one might imagine.'

'Oh God. But if you've known all along, why haven't you . . .'

'Blown the whistle? I have my reasons and your manuscript serves them perfectly. The English department at St Matthew's has never had so many research fellows or been flooded with so many grants. The Dickens Society of Chicago alone . . . but that is of no interest to you. I am sincerely delighted. This is the second time you have failed to disappoint me. It's so hard to find a good crook these days. You're a treasure, Adrian, a real treasure. One thing I am unclear on, though. Why did you hit upon the happy idea of having the manuscript discovered in St Matthew's and not in the University Library?'

'Well, I wanted it to be college property. I assumed then that you would be the one to publicise it.'

'And *I* would be the one with egg on my face when the truth came out? I suspected as much. You are too splendid. I know we shall become friends.'

'No I didn't exactly mean . . .'

'You have done your college a great service. I will leave now, to allow space for carnival, riot, drugs and carnal frenzy to develop. Silenus and his leering wrinkles are not required when youth is sporting. Oh look, there is that man from Narborough, the one you routed on the cricket field the first time ever we met. Excellent performance, my dear Cartwright! I am not ashamed to say that I wept openly.'

Hugo nodded vaguely and came up to Adrian, flushed and swaying, a bottle in one hand, a cigarette in the other.

'Look where he comes,' said Adrian, 'the Allegory of Dissipation and Ruin.'

Hugo burped happily and gestured at Trefusis who was saying his farewells to Jenny.

'I know that old fart from somewhere,' he said.

'You are talking about the old fart that I love. That old fart is a genius. That old fart won a thousand pounds by backing Chartham Park against Narborough Hall. You must remember the cricket match.'

'Oh yes, that's right. You cheated.'

'Cheated?'

'Donald Trefusis. Philip Slattery's uncle. Friend of old Biffo Biffen's from school. I don't forget anything, me. Mnemosyne was, let us not forget it, the mother of the Muses.'

Adrian looked at him in surprise. 'Well, quite.'

'At least according to Hesiod. So what is the old fart that you love doing here?'

'He's the ADC treasurer.'

Jenny came up with Gary.

'For God's sake stop drinking, Hugo. You'll look forty tomorrow instead of fourteen if you carry on at this rate.'

'A man who has just exposed himself to four hundred people, including his mother, has every right to drink.'

'God yes, I forgot the famous Helen Lewis was in,' said Adrian. 'How did she like it?'

'She was highly complimentary about everyone except me.'

'She didn't like you?' Jenny asked.

'She just didn't mention me, that's all.'

Jenny consoled him with the thought that it was probably professional jealousy. Adrian beckoned to Gary, who was pogo-ing with a lighting technician.

'Trefusis knows all,' he said. 'The bugger burglarised our rooms. But it's all all right.'

'What does Trefusis know?' said Hugo, who had overheard.

'Nothing, nothing.'

'He's the old fart that Adrian loves,' Hugo confided to Jenny and the rest of the room. 'I used to be the old fart that he loves. Now it's Trefusisisisis.'

'That's right, Hugo, time for bye-byes.'

'Really?' said Jenny. 'I thought *I* was the old fart he loved.'

'Adrian loves everybody, didn't you know? He even loves Lucy.'

'And who the hell is Lucy?'

'Oh my goodness, is that the time? Jenny, if we're going to hit Newnham tonight we should . . .'

'Lucy is his dog. He loves Lucy.'

'That's right. I love Lucy. Starring Lucille Ball and Desi Arnaz. Now I really think . . .'

'Do you know what he did once? In Harrogate. He pretended to . . .'

'Oh shit, he's about to throw,' said Gary.

Adrian caught the brunt of the vomit, which, in an unusual fit of humility, he rather thought he deserved.

III

'So let me see if I understood you, Dr Anderson.' Menzies removed his spectacles and pinched the bridge of his nose like a rep actor in a court-room drama. 'Not one word, not one syllable of this document is in fact the work of Charles Dickens?'

'It certainly looks as if the paper and writing materials are modern. The handwriting however . . .'

'Oh for goodness' sake, if the ink is twentieth-century how can the manuscript be in Dickens's own hand? Or are we now to authorise research grants that will establish the use of the retractable biro in Victorian Britain? Perhaps you even believe that Dickens is still alive?'

'I think I should remind the governing body,' said Clinton-Lacey, 'that the film is due to be premièred next week. Some kind of statement is going to have to be made.'

'The college will be a laughing-stock.'

'Yes indeed,' said Trefusis. 'Sketches on *Not The Nine o'Clock News*, a cartoon by Marc. Calamitous.'

'Well it's your department, Donald,' said Menzies. 'Rather than sit back and enjoy this cataclysm, why don't you come up with a solution?'

Trefusis stubbed out his cigarette.

'Well now, that is precisely what I have taken the liberty of doing,' he said. 'With your permission I shall read a statement that the press might be offered without too much embarrassment.'

Everyone around the table murmured assent. Trefusis took a piece of paper from his satchel.

'"Using a linguistic analysis program pioneered by the English faculty in collaboration with the Department of Computing Science,"' he read, '"Dr Tim Anderson, Fellow of St Matthew's College and Lecturer in English at the University, has refined and perfected techniques which have allowed him to determine precisely which parts of the play *The Two Noble Kinsmen* were written by Shakespeare and which by Fletcher."'

'Er . . . I have?' asked Tim Anderson.

'Yes, Tim, you have.'

'What on earth has Shakespeare got to do with it?' cried Menzies. 'We are talking about . . .'

'"Comparing textual samples of known Shakespeare

against the writings of the Earl of Oxford, Francis Bacon and Christopher Marlowe, he is also in a position to prove that all the plays of the Shakespearean canon are the work of one hand, William Shakespeare's, and that Oxford, Bacon and Marlowe are responsible for none of it. There are, however, some intriguing passages in three of the plays which would appear not to be by Shakespeare. Dr Anderson and his team are working on them now and should soon have positive results. An interesting by-product of this important work is the discovery that the novel *Peter Flowerbuck* is not by Charles Dickens, but is almost certainly the work of a twentieth-century writer. There is evidence, however, that the story is based on an original Dickens plot. Dr Anderson's team is following up this suggestion with great energy." I think that should meet the case.'

'Ingenious, Donald,' said Clinton-Lacey. 'Quite ingenious.'

'You're too kind.'

'I don't see what's so ingenious about it. Why bring Shakespeare in?'

'He's diverting attention, Garth,' Clinton-Lacey explained. 'Bring out the name Shakespeare and it's even bigger copy than Dickens.'

'But all this guff about Dr Anderson working on bits of Shakespeare and the plot lines being original Dickens? What's that about?'

'Well you see,' said Trefusis. 'It shows that we are currently researching all this important material, that there may be *something* in *Peter Flowerbuck* after all.'

'But there isn't!'

'We know that, but the newspapers don't. In a

couple of months' time the whole thing will be forgotten. If they do make enquiries about our progress we can say that Dr Anderson is still working on the problem. I'm sure Tim will be able to bemuse the press.'

'He will be the one to make the announcement then?'

'Certainly,' said Trefusis. '*I* have nothing to do with the affair.'

'I'm unsure as to what the tension between the ethical boundaries and the margins of pragmatism might announce themselves to be in a situation which . . .' Anderson began.

'You see? Tim will do splendidly. His is the only major European language I still find myself utterly unable to comprehend. The press will be bored. It isn't quite enough of a hoax story to excite them and is too rigorous and scientific to have any human interest.'

'But all this means that we will have to keep funding the extra staff,' Menzies complained. 'For appearances' sake.'

'Yes,' said Trefusis dreamily, 'there is that drawback of course.'

'That's outrageous.'

'Oh I don't know. As long as they're kept busy lecturing, teaching undergraduates and authenticating documents that will be sent to us from all over the world – now that we are acknowledged as the leading university for authorial fingerprinting – I'm sure we'll find a use for them. They may even pay their way.'

IV

'You're lying,' said Gary. 'You've got to be lying.'

'I wish I were,' said Adrian. 'No, that's not true, I wouldn't have missed it for worlds.'

'You're telling me that you sold your arse down the Dilly?'

'Why not? Someone's got to. Anyway it wasn't my arse exactly.'

Gary paced up and down the room while Adrian watched him. He didn't know why he had told him. He supposed because he had been stung once too often by the accusation that he had no idea what the real world was like.

It had started when Adrian had mentioned that he was seriously considering marrying Jenny.

'Do you love her?'

'Look Gary. I'm twenty-two years old. I got here by the skin of my teeth, because I awoke from the bad dream of adolescence in the nick of time. Every morning for the next, God knows, fifty years, I'm going to have to get out of bed and participate in the day. I simply do not trust myself to be able to do that on my own. I'll need someone to get up for.'

'But do you love her?'

'I am magnificently prepared for the long littleness of life. There is diddley-squat for me to look forward to. Zilch, zero, zip-all, sweet lipperty-pipperty nothing. The only thought that will give me the energy to carry on is that someone has a life which would be diminished by my departure from it.'

'Yes, but do you love her?'

'You're beginning to sound like Olivier in *The Marathon Man*, "Is it safe? Is it safe?" "Sure it's safe. It's real safe." "Is it safe?" "No, it's not safe. It's incredibly unsafe." "Is it safe?" How the hell do I know?'

'You don't love her.'

'Oh piss off, Gary. I don't love anyone, anything, or anybody. Well, "anyone" and "anybody" are the same, but I can't think of a third "any". Which reminds me . . . that bloody Martini advert, it's bugged me for years. "Any time, any place, anywhere." What the fuck difference is there between any place and anywhere? Some advertising copy-writer was paid thousands for that piece of rubbish.'

'This is a change of subject on a cosmic scale. You don't love her, do you?'

'I just said. I don't love anyone, anything or any body, any time, any place, anywhere. Who does?'

'Jenny does.'

'Women are different, you know that.'

'I do as well.'

'Men are different too.'

'Gay men, you mean.'

'I cannot believe I am having this conversation. You think I'm like Emma, don't you? "Adrian Healey, handsome, clever and rich, with a comfortable home and happy disposition, seemed to unite some of the best blessings of existence; and had lived nearly twenty-three years in the world with very little to disturb or vex him."'

'*Distress* or vex, I think you'll find. It's as good a description as any.'

'Really? Well, I may have missed some of Jane

Austen's subtler hints, but I don't think Emma Wood-house spent part of her seventeenth year as a harlot in Piccadilly. I haven't read it for a couple of years of course, and some of the obliquer references could have passed over my head. Miss Austen also seems to fight very shy of describing Emma's time in chokey on remand for possession of cocaine. Again I'm perfectly prepared to concede that she *did* and that I have simply failed to pick up the clues.'

'What the fuck are you going on about?'

And Adrian had told him something of his life between school and Cambridge.

Gary was still indignant. 'You plan to marry Jenny without telling her any of this?'

'Don't be so bourgeois, my dear. It doesn't suit you at all.'

Adrian was growing disillusioned with Gary. He had started on his History of Art, or History O Fart, as Adrian liked to call it, at the beginning of the year and ever since he had begun to evolve into something else. Bondage trousers had given way to second-hand tweed jackets with Hermès silk flourishing from the breast pockets. The hair returned to its natural dark, slicked back with KY jelly; knives and forks dangled no more from the lobes. The Damned and The Clash were less likely to blast across the court from the rooms now than Couperin and Bruckner.

'It only needs a moustache for you to look like Roy Strong,' Adrian had told him once, but Gary hadn't been moved. He wasn't going to be the world's little piece of pet rough any more and that was that. And now he was lecturing Adrian on the ethics of personal relations.

'Anyway, why should I tell her? What difference would it make?'

'Why should you marry her? What difference would it make?'

'Oh let's not go round in circles. I've tried to tell you. I've done all my living. There's nothing to look forward to. Do I go into advertising? Do I teach? Do I apply to the BBC? Do I write plays and become the voice of the Bland Young Man generation? Do I consider journalism? Do I go to an acting school? Do I have a shot at industry? The only justification for my existence is that I am loved. Whether or not I like it, I am responsible for Jenny and that is something to get up in the morning for.'

'So it's a life of sacrifice. You're afraid that if you don't marry her, she'll top herself? I hate to wound your vanity but people don't behave like that.'

'Oh don't they? Don't people kill themselves?'

Jenny entered without knocking.

'Hiya, bum-holes, I cleared your pigeon-holes on the way in. Exciting jiffy-bag for you, big boy. Could it be the clitoral exciter we ordered?'

'Morning toast more like,' said Gary, taking the package and passing it over.

Adrian opened it while Gary explained to Jenny the history of Toast By Post.

'You taught a boy two years ago and he *still* has this crush on you?'

'His faithful little heart overflows with love.'

'Nonsense,' said Adrian. 'It was never more than an elaborate joke. If anything the parcels mock me.'

'Do you think he wanks into them before he seals them up?'

'Gary!' Jenny was shocked.

'As in "I'm coming in a jiffy", you mean? No, I do not, though I grant you the toast is a bit soggy. What else have we? A little pot of apricot jam, a pat of butter, a note which says, "And Conradin made himself another piece of toast . . ."'

'That boy is weird.'

'Who's Conradin?' Jenny asked.

'Reach down my index, Watson, and look under "C". Dear me, what villainy is grouped under this letter alone! There's Callaghan, the politician to whose door we traced what you in your memoirs gave the somewhat fanciful title the "Winter of Discontent", Watson. Here's Callow, the second most dangerous actor in London, any one of whose grimaces may be fatal, Lewis Collins, Charlie Chester, Leslie Crowther of dread memory, Marti Caine, what a catalogue of infamy is here . . . but no Conradin. Peter Conrad, who invented opera, William Conrad, whose Cannon was a Quinn Martin Production, but no Conradin.'

'I think it's from a Saki short story,' said Gary. 'Sredni Vashtar, the polecat.'

'Oh yes, you're quite right. Or was he a ferret?'

'And what's the relevance to you?' asked Jenny.

'Well, there we have to peer into the dark, dripping mind of Hunt the Thimble. The chances are that it is simply a literary reference to toast, and he is fast running out of those. But there could be a Meaning.'

'Conradin was a boy who had a horrible, repressive aunt,' said Gary. 'So he prayed to Sredni Vashtar, his polecat . . .'

'Or ferret.'

'He prayed to his polecat or ferret and his prayers were answered. Sredni Vashtar killed the aunt.'

'And meanwhile Conradin calmly made himself another piece of toast.'

'I see,' said Jenny. 'The polecat is a kind of phallic symbol, do we think?'

'Honestly, dear,' said Gary, 'you're so obsessed, you'd think a *penis* was phallic.'

'Well Sredni Vashtar is a monster from the Id, at the very least,' said Adrian. 'The dark, hot-breathed stink of the animal that Conradin would one day release from its dark hiding-place to wreak its revenge on the chintz and teacups of his aunt's drawing-room life.'

'Do you think this boy is trying to tell you something?'

'Perhaps his thimble is a thimble no more, but a long, furry savage beast that wriggles and spits and mauls aunts. I'll write and ask him.'

He looked through the rest of his post. A cheque from his mother was always welcome, a cheque from Uncle David for five hundred pounds even more so. He slipped it quickly into his jacket pocket. Reminders that Billy Graham was in Cambridge and would preach in Great St Mary's were always monumentally unwelcome, as were invitations to hear *Acis and Galatea* played on original instruments.

'But not sung,' he suggested, looking through the rest of his mail, 'on original voices. I suppose in two hundred years' time they'll be giving Beatles concerts on ancient Marshall . . . oh and a letter from old Biffo, bless him.'

Biffen was the only master from school with whom

Adrian stayed in touch. The man was so fluffy and white and decent and had taken so much pleasure in the news of Adrian's scholarship to St Matthew's which had somehow filtered through to the school the year before, that it would have been a positive cruelty not to write to him from time to time to let him know how it was all going.

He glanced through the letter. Biffen was full of the news of the Dickens manuscript.

'Donald writes me that there may be some doubt about it. I do hope not.'

'I'd forgotten Biffo knew Trefusis,' said Adrian, laying the letter aside. 'Hello! What have we here?'

There was a crumpled handwritten note for him. 'Please come to tea at C5, Great Court, Trinity. Alone. Hugo.'

'How is Hugo?' asked Jenny. 'I haven't seen much of him since *Flowerbuck*.'

'I remember him being rather naff in Bridget's production of *Sexual Perversity In Chicago*,' said Gary. 'He kept forgetting his lines and tripping over. He hasn't been in anything since.'

Adrian put the note down and yawned.

'He's probably been swotting for his Part One's. He was always that kind of creep. Hand me Justin and Miroslav.'

Adrian noticed that the permanent puddle in the passageway between King's and St Catharine's had iced over. Spring was having to make a fight of it. He wrapped Miroslav, his cashmere scarf, closer round him as he stepped out into the icy gale that blasted along King's Parade. They used to say that Cambridge was the first stopping place for the wind that swept down from the Urals: in the thirties that was as true of the politics as the weather.

Adrian wondered whether he mightn't become political himself. Always one to walk the other way from trends, he sensed that left-wingery was about to become very unfashionable. Long hair was out, flared jeans were out, soon there would be no more cakes and ale, canapés and Sancerre at best, Ryvita and mineral water at worst. Trefusis complained that the modern undergraduate was a cruel disappointment to him.

'They're all getting firsts and married these days, if you'll forgive the syllepsis,' he had said once. 'Decency, discipline and dullness. There's no lightness of touch any more, no irresponsibility. Do you remember that damning description of Leonard Bast in *Howards End*? "He had given up the glory of the animal for a tail-coat and a set of ideas." Change tail-coat to pin-stripe and you have modern Cambridge. There's no lack of respect today, that's what I miss.'

As Adrian hurried past the Senate House he noticed two old men standing outside Bowes and Bowes. He put an extra spring in his step, a thing he often did when walking near the elderly. He imagined old people would look at his athletic bounce with a misty longing for their own youth. Not that he was trying to show off or rub salt into the wounds of the infirm, he really believed he was offering a service, an opportunity for nostalgia, like whistling the theme tune from *Happidrome* or spinning a Diabolo.

He skipped past them with carefree ease, missed

his footing and fell to the ground with a thump. One of the old men helped him up.

'You all right, lad?'

'Yes fine . . . I must have slipped on the ice.'

Using Justin, his umbrella, as a walking-stick, he hobbled down Trinity Street, ruthlessly mocking himself.

'Adrian, you're an arse. In a world of arses, you are the arsiest by a mile. Stop being an arse at once, or I'll never talk to you again. So there.'

'Is there a problem, sir?'

'Oh sorry, no . . . I was just . . . humming to myself.'

He hadn't realised he'd been talking out loud. The Trinity porter stared at him suspiciously, so as Adrian limped into Great Court, he broke into more definite and deliberate song to prove his point.

'How do you solve a problem like Maria?' he fluted. 'How do you catch a cloud and pin it down? How do you find a word that means Maria? A flibbertigibbet, a will o'the wisp, a clown.'

Hugo's rooms were in the corner tower. The same tower where Lord Byron had kept his bear, arousing the wrath of the college authorities, who had told him sniffily that the keeping of domestic animals in rooms was strictly forbidden. Byron had assured them that it was far from a domestic animal. It was an untamed bear, as wild and savage as could be, and they had been reluctantly obliged to let him keep it.

'How do you solve a problem like Maria? How do you hold a moonbeam in your hand?'

Hugo opened the door.

'I brought a jar of anchovy paste, half a dozen

153

potato farls and a packet of my own special blend of Formosan Oolong and Orange Pekoe,' said Adrian, 'but I was set upon by a gang of footpads outside Caius and they stole it all.'

'That's all right,' said Hugo. 'I've got some wine.'

Which was about all he seemed to have. He poured out two mugfuls.

'Very nice,' said Adrian, sipping appreciatively. 'I wonder how they got the cat to sit on the bottle.'

'It's cheap, that's the main thing.'

Adrian looked round the room. From the quantity of empty bottles about the place he supposed that cheapness must indeed have been the deciding factor in Hugo's wine-buying policy. The place was very meanly appointed; apart from the usual college tables and chairs, the only things of interest that met Adrian's inquisitive scrutiny were a photograph of Hugo's actress mother on the table, a *Peter Flowerbuck* poster on the wall which showed Adrian in a tall hat leading Hugo away from a snarling Gary, a handful of Penguin classics, a guitar, some LPs and a record-player.

'So anyway Hugo, my old penny bun. How is everything?'

'Everything,' said Hugo, 'is terrible.'

It didn't look it. Drink never shows in the faces of the young. Hugo's eye was bright, his complexion fine and his figure trim.

'Work is it?'

'No, no. I've just been thinking a lot lately.'

'Well, that's what we're here for, I suppose.'

Hugo filled up his mug with more wine.

'I just want to see if I've got you straight. You

seduce me in my first year at school and then ignore me completely until you make up a lie about Pigs Trotter having been in love with me . . . Julian Rundell told me the truth about that, by the way. Then you seduce me again by pretending to be asleep. Years later, after having cheated my prep school out of a cricket victory, you tell me that you weren't really asleep that night, which I *didn't* in fact know, even though I said I did. Then what happens? Oh yes, you write a fake Dickens novel describing a character who looks like me and just happens to make love to someone who looks like you while that person just happens to be asleep. I think that's everything. You see, all I want to know is . . . what have I done?'

'Hugo, I know it seems . . .'

'It worries me, you see. I must have done something terrible to you without knowing it and I'd like it all to stop now, please.'

'Oh God,' said Adrian.

It was so hard to connect this man with Cartwright. If Hugo had taught at another prep school and gone to another university, the memory of him wouldn't be muddied by a sight like this alien Hugo who trembled and wept into his wine. It *was* another person of course, molecularly every part of the old Cartwright must have been replaced dozens of times since he had been the most beautiful person who ever walked the earth. And the old Adrian who had loved him was not the same as the Adrian who beheld him now. It was like the philosopher's axe. After a few years the philosopher replaces the head, later he replaces the shaft. Then the head wears out and he replaces it again, next the shaft again. Can he go on calling it the

155

same axe? Why should this new Adrian be responsible for the sins of the old?

'It's so easy to explain, Hugo. Easy and very hard. Just one word covers it all.'

'What word? *No* word could explain it. Not a whole Bible of words.'

'It's a common enough word, but it might mean something different to you than it does to me. Language is a bastard. So let's invent a new word. "Libb" will do. I libbed you. That's all there is to it. I was in libb with you. My libb for you informed my every waking and sleeping hour for . . . for God knows how many years. Nothing has ever been as powerful as that libb. It was the guiding force of my life, it haunted me then and haunts me still.'

'You were in *love* with me?'

'Well now, that's your word. Libb has a great deal in common with love, I admit. But love is supposed to be creative, not destructive, and as you have found out, my libb turned out to be very harmful indeed.'

Hugo gripped the rim of his mug and stared into his wine.

'Why can't you . . .'

'Yes?'

'I mean . . . everything you do . . . that bloody magazine, the being asleep, the cricket match, that Dickens novel . . . everything you do is . . . is . . . I don't know what it is.'

'Duplicitous? Covert? Underhand? Sly? Devious? Evasive?'

'All of those things. Why have you never come out and said anything or done anything in the open?'

'I'm fucked if I know, Hugo. I'm seriously fucked

if I know. Perhaps because I'm a coward. Perhaps because I don't exist except in borrowed clothes. I used to think everyone but me was a fraud. It's simple logic to realise that, except to a madman, the opposite must have been the truth.'

'Hell's bells, Adrian. Have you any idea how much I admired you? Any idea at all? Your talent? You used to come into the changing-room sometimes dressed as Oscar Wilde or Noël Coward or whoever and stride up and down like a prince. You used to make me feel so *small*. All the things you can do. My mother thinks I'm a bore. I used to wish I could be you. I fantasised being you. I would lie awake at night imagining what it would be like to have your tall body and your smile, your wit and words. And of course I loved you. I didn't libb you or lobb you or lubb you or labb you, I loved you.'

'Oh lord,' sighed Adrian. 'If I find a way of expressing adequately now what I am thinking and feeling you will take it to be a piece of verbal dexterity and the latest in a long line of verbal malversations. You see! I can't even say "deceit". I have to say "verbal malversations". Everyone's honest but me. So perhaps I should just whine and moan wordlessly.'

Adrian opened the window and howled into Great Court like a demented muezzin, taking the performance so far as to produce real tears. When he turned to face back into the room Hugo was laughing.

'What they call keening, I believe,' said Adrian.

'Well, there's always the cliché,' Hugo said, extending his hand. 'We can be just good friends now.'

'Here's looking at you, kid.'

'Here's looking at you, kid.'

157

'We'll always have Paris.'

'We'll always have Paris.'

Adrian raised his mug of wine. 'Here's death to the past.'

'Death to the past.'

A Tweed, a Shapeless Green Needlecord Jacket and an Eau
de Nil Chanel Suit sat in conference in the Savile Club Sand
Pit.

'I'm very much afraid that someone in St Matthew's is
not to be trusted.'

'Garth, you think?' asked the Shapeless Green Needlecord.

'Garth is much as he was in your day, Humphrey.
Maddening, sour, truculent and asper. Not a natural player,
I feel. Not a concealer. It is also very unlikely that he would
have been introduced at this late stage.'

'Have you heard from Bela?' the Chanel Suit wanted to
know.

'Not a whisper. He knows that the Budapest network
have him under the tightest possible surveillance. Pearce is
playing for very high stakes this time.'

'Don't I know it!' said the Eau de Nil Suit. 'My bag
burst in the middle of Waitrose's yesterday.'

The others giggled like schoolchildren.

'Oh dear me,' said the Tweed. 'However did you explain
it?'

'I didn't. I just fled, leaving my shopping behind. I don't
know if I can ever show my face in there again.'

They drank tea in companionable silence.

'Who then?' asked the Needlecord suddenly. 'If not Garth?'

The Tweed made a suggestion.

'Donald, no!' protested the Eau de Nil Suit.

The Tweed shrugged apologetically.

'What a howling shit.'

'Well, perhaps his insertion into play may turn out to be rather a useful development.'

'I don't see how.'

'He's plasticine.'

'Outdated you mean?'

'Not Pleistocene, Humphrey. Plasticine. We had all considered him as a possible player for the future, had we not? We know what a shifty little soul he is. Much better to have him as an enemy than as a friend. This is all turning out to be much more fun and much more complex than I had anticipated. The plot thickens like finest Devon cream.'

'If Pearce is going to play dirty like this, Donald, shouldn't we do the same?'

'Humphrey's right, you know,' said the Chanel Suit. 'Why don't I ask Nancy and Simon if they can't lend a hand?'

'Tug of loyalties?' the Tweed wondered. 'I mean Simon works for Pearce, after all.'

'I like to hope,' said the Eau de Nil Chanel Suit, 'that Simon's real loyalties go deeper than that.'

'Very well then. Recruit them and familiarise them with the ground rules. Stefan is due in England soon. He will have news from and of Bela. You know, this is all highly satisfactory.'

'It's not going to get out of control is it?' asked the Needlecord. 'I'm not sure I like the introduction of killing. Pearce cannot bear to be beaten, you know.'

'No more can I,' said the Tweed. 'And I won't be.'

Five

'You were his best friend,' Mrs Trotter said. 'He talked about you a great deal, how clever and amusing you were. He was very fond of you.'

'Well, Mrs Trotter,' said Adrian, 'I was very fond of him. We all were.'

'I do hope you and . . . and the other boy . . . Cartwright . . . can come to the funeral.'

She looked just like Pigs when she cried.

That evening the whole House was already in a slightly hysterical state by the time Tickford broke the news officially at House Compline.

'Some of you, I don't know . . . may know,' he said, '. . . may have heard, I don't know, that there has been a tragedy here. Paul Trotter took his own life this afternoon. We have no idea why. We don't know. We just don't know. We can't know.'

Fifty pairs of eyes swivelled towards Adrian, wondering. Why had be been sent for first? Why had he been shut up with Tickford and Pigs's parents for so long?

Cartwright had not yet been spoken to. He knew nothing and his eyes turned towards Adrian too, large and full of awe.

'I'm afraid he must have been very unhappy,'

continued Tickford, apparently to the ceiling. 'Very unhappy, I don't know why. But we shall say a prayer for him and commend his soul to God. Almighty Father . . .'

Adrian felt a thigh being pressed against his as he knelt to pray. It was Rundell.

'What?'

'I saw him,' whispered Rundell. 'Yesterday afternoon in the cemetery, he went up and sat next to you!'

'So what?'

'Refresh him with your Mercy, cleanse him with your Love . . .'

'And then you came down together and he was crying.'

'That has nothing to do with it.'

'In the name of your Son who died that all might have eternal life . . .'

'Oh, yeah?'

'Amen.'

Tom asked no questions and Adrian couldn't bring himself to tell him anything.

Biffo had sent a note the next morning. 'What terribly upsetting news, terribly upsetting. Helen and I were so distressed. I taught Trotter last year; such a delightful boy. I do hope you feel free to come and talk to me about it. If you would like to, of course. Helen and I would be delighted if you could make more of our Friday afternoon visits this term. With every sympathy at this dreadful time. Humphrey Biffen.'

Tom and Adrian were playing cribbage during the afternoon when there was a knock at the door.

'Avanti!'

It was Cartwright, looking frightened.

'Can I have a word with you, Healey?'

Tom saw the expression on Cartwright's face and reached for a book and a pair of sunglasses.

'I'd better grow.'

'Thanks, Thompson.' Cartwright stood looking at the floor and waited for Tom to close the door behind him.

'Sit down do,' said Adrian.

'I've just been to see Tickford,' said Cartwright, either not hearing or not heeding the invitation.

'Oh, ah?'

'He said Trotter had some sort of . . . a kind of crush on me. And that you told him that.'

'Well, that's what Trotter told me.'

'But I didn't even know him!'

Adrian shrugged.

'I'm sorry, Cartwright, but you know what this place is like.'

Cartwright sat down in Tom's chair and stared out of the window.

'Oh hell's bells. It'll be all over the school.'

'Of course it won't be,' said Adrian. 'Tickford won't tell anyone. I certainly won't tell anyone. I mean, I haven't even told Thompson and I tell him everything.'

'But Tick says I've got to go to the funeral. What will people think of that?'

'Well . . .' said Adrian, thinking fast. 'I'm going to

163

the funeral too. I'll put it around that your parents are friends of Trotter's parents.'

'I suppose that'll do,' said Cartwright, 'but why did you have to tell Tick in the first place?'

'It was suicide! He left a note. It said "Healey will explain" or something like that. What else could I do but tell the truth?'

Cartwright looked up at him.

'Did Pigs, did Trotter say . . . did he tell you how long he'd had this, this *thing* for me?'

'Since you came to the school apparently.'

Cartwright dropped his head and stared at the floor. When he looked up again there were tears in his eyes. He looked angry. Angry and to Adrian more beautiful than ever.

'Why did he tell *you*?' he cried. 'Why couldn't he have told me? And what did he have to go and kill himself for?'

Adrian felt taken aback by the anger in Cartwright's voice.

'Well, I suppose he was scared in case . . . in case you rejected him or something. I don't know how these things work.'

'More scared of me rejecting him than he was of killing himself?'

Adrian nodded.

'So now I'm going to have to wake up every morning for the rest of my life knowing that I'm responsible for someone's suicide.'

The tears splashed down his face. Adrian leant forward and held his shoulder.

'You must never think of it like that, Hugo. You mustn't!' he said.

He had never called him Hugo before and he hadn't touched him since their brief how-do-you-do in the House lavs, which was before Adrian had known he was in love.

'I'm as responsible as you are, really,' Adrian said. 'More responsible, if anything.'

Cartwright stared in surprise.

'How do you mean?'

'Well,' said Adrian, 'I could have advised Trotter to tell you, couldn't I? I could have told him not to bottle it up.'

'But you weren't to know what was going to happen.'

'And nor were you, Hugo. Now come on, dry your eyes, or people will really know something is wrong. We'll go to the funeral and then in a couple of weeks we'll have forgotten all about it.'

'Thanks, Healey. I'm sorry to be so . . .'

'Adrian. And there's nothing to be sorry about.'

Between that day and the day they travelled up to Harrogate they hadn't exchanged a word. Adrian had seen him mobbing around with his friends as if nothing had happened. The House did its best to forget the whole embarrassment. Trotter was thought of with the kind of contempt and revulsion young Englishmen of the right type reserve for the sick, the mad, the poor and the old.

The funeral was set for ten in the morning, so Tickford had decided that they should travel up the evening before and spend the night in a hotel. For the whole duration of the journey Cartwright stared out of the window.

He's beginning to resent Trotter's posthumous power over him, Adrian thought.

The Tickfords didn't speak much either. This was a duty they did not relish. Adrian, never a tidy traveller, twice had to ask Ma Tickford, who was driving, to stop the car so that he could be sick.

He couldn't imagine why he had dropped Cartwright in it the way he had. A kind of revenge he supposed. But revenge for what? And on whom? A revenge on the ghost of Trotter or on the living, breathing Cartwright?

He wasn't Woody Nightshade, he was Deadly Nightshade. Everybody who had anything to do with him was lethally poisoned.

But they don't exist, he kept repeating to himself as they rattled up the A1. Other people don't exist. Trotter isn't really dead because he was never really alive. It's all just a clever way of testing me. There's no one in these cars and lorries driving south. There can't be that many individual souls. Not souls like mine. There isn't room. There can't be.

But suppose Trotter's ghost watched him? Trotter would know everything by now. Would he forgive him?

From now on, I conform.

He should have guessed that Tickford would give him and Cartwright a twin room at the hotel. The bill was being settled by the school, after all.

Their room was at the end of a creaking corridor. Adrian opened the door and bowed Cartwright in.

Manly, unconcerned and businesslike, he told himself. Two healthy English school chums sharing digs.

Holmes and Watson, Bunny and Raffles. Nothing else.

'So, Cartwright old boy – which bed do you fancy?'

'I don't mind really. This one'll do fine.'

'Okay. Bags the bathroom first, then.'

Like all the English hotels Adrian had ever stayed in, this one was appallingly overheated. He undressed and slipped naked into bed while Cartwright brushed his teeth in the bathroom.

Now then, Healey, he warned himself. You're to behave. Understand?

He switched out the light above his bed just as Cartwright came out, magnificently clad in sky-blue pyjamas of brushed cotton, swinging a sponge-bag from his wrist.

'Night then, Cartwright.'

'Night.'

Adrian closed his eyes. He heard Cartwright shuffle off his slippers and get into bed.

Don't let him turn his light off. Make him pick up a book. Please, God, please.

He strained his ears and caught the sound of a page turning.

Thank you, God. You're a treasure.

During the next five minutes Adrian allowed his breathing naturally to deepen into a slow rhythm until any observer would swear that he was fast asleep.

He then began to give the impression of a more troubled rest. He turned and gave a small moan. The eiderdown fell to the floor. He rolled over far to one side, causing the top sheet to come away. A minute later he turned the other way violently, kicking with his foot so that the sheet joined the eiderdown.

He was now naked on the bed, breathing heavily and writhing. Cartwright's light was still on but the pages had stopped turning.

'Adrian?'

It had been a light whisper, but Cartwright had definitely spoken.

'Adrian . . .' Adrian mumbled in return, half snoring the word as he turned to face Cartwright, mouth open, eyes closed.

'Adrian, are you all right?'

'No one left in the valley,' said Adrian, flinging out a hand.

He heard Cartwright's bed creak.

Here we go, he thought to himself, here we bloody well go!

Cartwright's feet padded across the room.

He's next to me, I can sense it!

'I'll eat them later . . . later,' he moaned.

He heard the rustle of a sheet and felt the eider-down being pulled on top of him.

He can't just be going to tuck me up! He can't be. I've got a stiffy like a milk-bottle. Is he flesh and blood or what? Oh well, here goes. Nothing ventured, nothing gained.

He arched his body and thrashed his legs up and down.

'Lucy?' he called, quite loudly this time.

Where he got the name Lucy from, he had no idea.

'Lucy?'

He swept out an arm and found Cartwright's shoulder.

'Lucy, is that you?'

The eiderdown was slowly pulled away from him

again. Suddenly he felt a warm hand between his thighs.

'Yes,' he said, 'yes.'

Then soft hair brushing against his chest and a tongue licking his stomach.

Hugo, he sighed to himself. Hugo! and out loud, 'Oh Lucy – *Lucy!*'

He was awoken by the sound of a lavatory flushing. The eiderdown was on top of him and the sun was shining through a gap in the curtains.

'Oh God. What have I done?'

Cartwright came out of the bathroom.

'Morning,' he said brightly.

'Hi,' mumbled Adrian, 'what the hell time is it?'

'Seven thirty. Sleep all right?'

'Jesus, like a log. And you?'

'Not too badly. You talked a lot.'

'Oh sorry,' said Adrian, 'I do that sometimes. I hope it didn't keep you awake.'

'You kept saying Lucy. Who's Lucy?'

'Really?' Adrian frowned. 'Well, I used to have a dog called Lucy . . .'

'Oh, right,' said Cartwright. 'I wondered.'

'Works every time,' Adrian said to himself, turning over and going back to sleep.

It was a small funeral. A small funeral for a small life. Trotter's parents were pleased to see Adrian again and were polite to Cartwright, but they couldn't entirely disguise their distaste for him. His beauty, pale in a dark suit, was an affront to the memory of their pudgy and ordinary son.

After the ceremony they drove to the Trotters'

farmhouse five miles outside Harrogate. One of Pigs Trotter's sisters gave Adrian a photograph of himself. It showed him lying on his stomach watching a cricket match. Adrian tried hard but couldn't remember Pigs Trotter taking it. No one commented on the fact that Trotter kept no photographs of Cartwright.

Mr Trotter asked Adrian if he would come and stay in the summer holidays.

'You ever sheared sheep before?'

'No, sir.'

'You'll enjoy it.'

Tickford took the wheel for the homeward journey. Adrian was allowed in the front next to him. They didn't want to risk him being sick again.

'A sorry business,' said Tickford.

'Yes, sir.'

Tickford gestured over his shoulder towards Cart-wright, who was leaning against Ma Tickford and snoring gently.

'I hope you haven't told anyone,' he said.

'No, sir.'

'You must get on with the term now, Adrian. It has not started well. That disgusting magazine and now this . . . all in the first week. There's a bad spirit abroad, I wonder if I can look to you to help combat it?'

'Well, sir . . .'

'This may be just the jolt you need to start taking yourself seriously at last. Boys like you have a pro-found influence. Whether it is used for good or evil can make the difference between a happy and an unhappy school.'

'Yes, sir.'

Tickford patted Adrian's knee.

'I have a feeling that I can rely on you,' he said.

'You can, sir,' said Adrian. 'I promise.'

It was four o'clock when they got back. Adrian returned to his study to find it empty. Tom was obviously having tea somewhere else.

He couldn't be bothered to track him down, so he made toast on his own and started on some overdue Latin prep. If he was going to turn over a new leaf then there was no time like the present. Then he would write back to Biffo. Attend all his Friday afernoons. Read more. Think more.

He had hardly begun before there came a knock at the door.

'Come in!'

It was Bennett-Jones.

'Really, R.B.-J. Flattered as I am by your fawning attentions I must ask you to find another playmate. I am a busy man. Virgil calls to me from across the centuries.'

'Yeah?' said Bennett-Jones with a nasty leer. 'Well it just so happens that Mr Tickford calls to you from across his study, an'all.'

'Dear me! Five minutes' separation and already he pines for me. Perhaps he wants my advice on demoting some of the prefecture. Well, I am always happy to look in on dear Jeremy. Lead the way, young man, lead the way.'

Tickford was standing behind his desk, his face deathly white.

'This book,' he said, holding up a paperback, 'does it belong to you?'

Oh Christ . . . oh Jesus Christ . . .

It was Adrian's copy of *The Naked Lunch*.

'I . . . I don't know, sir.'

'It was found in your study. It has your name written in it. No other boy in the school has a copy in their study. On the instructions of the headmaster the prefects checked this morning. Now, answer me again. Is this your book?'

'Yes, sir.'

'Just tell me one thing, Healey. Did you write the magazine alone or were there others?'

'I –'

'Answer me!' shouted Tickford, slamming the book down onto the desk.

'Alone, sir.'

There was a pause. Tickford stared at Adrian, breathing heavily from his nostrils like a cornered bull.

Oh cuntly cunt. He's going to hit me. He's out of control.

'Go to your study,' said Tickford at last. 'Stay there until your parents come for you. No one is to see you or talk to you.'

'Sir, I –'

'Now get out of my sight, you poisonous little shit.'

A Peaked Cap, waving a sheet of typescript, hurried into the Customs office where a Dark Grey Suit was watching television.

'Comrade Captain,' he said. 'I have the inventory of the delegation's luggage.'

'You can cut out the Comrade crap for a start,' said the Dark Grey Suit, taking the proffered sheet.

'Szabó's articles are itemised at the top, sir.'

'I can read.'

The Dark Grey Suit scanned the list.

'And you searched the rest of the team just as thoroughly?'

'Just as thoroughly Com— Captain Molgar, sir.'

'The chess books have been checked?'

'They have all been checked and replaced with identical copies in case of . . .' the Peaked Cap gestured hopefully. He had no idea what the original chess books might have contained. 'In case of . . . microdots?' he whispered.

The Dark Grey Suit snorted contemptuously.

'This radio in Ribli's luggage?'

'A perfectly ordinary radio, Captain. Comrade Ribli has taken it abroad many times. He is not under suspicion also?'

The Dark Grey Suit ignored the question.

'Csom's suitcase seems to be very heavy.'

'It is an old case. Leather.'

173

'Have it X-rayed.'

'Yes, sir.'

'Yes, Captain.'

'Yes, Captain.'

'That's better.'

The Peaked Cap coughed.

'Captain, sir, why do you let this Szabó out of the country if he is . . .?'

'If he is what?'

'I-I don't quite know, sir.'

'Szabó is one of the most talented young grandmasters in the world. The next Portisch. All this checking is simply a routine test of your efficiency, nothing more. You understand?'

'Yes, Captain.'

'Yes, Comrade Captain.'

'Yes, Comrade Captain.'

The Dark Grey Suit hummed to himself. He did not know what they were looking for either. But the British had been paying him a great deal for many years and now that they suddenly wanted him to work for his money he supposed he had no business complaining. This was not dangerous work, after all. He was doing no more than his usual duty and if the authorities discovered his unusual interest in Szabó they would be more likely to reward him for his zeal than shoot him for his treachery.

He had hoiked out Szabó's file that morning to see if there was anything there to justify this sudden British directive. There was nothing there: Stefan Szabó, a perfectly blameless citizen, grandson of a Hungarian hero and a great chess hope.

The solution came to the Dark Grey Suit in a blinding flash. Stefan Szabó was planning, sometime during the tournament in Hastings, to defect. The British needed to check that he was an honest defector, that he was not bringing any equipment out with him that would suggest a darker purpose.

But why should a successful chess-player need to defect? They made plenty of money, which they were allowed to keep, they were granted unlimited travel abroad, foreign bank accounts. Hungary was not Russia or Czechoslovakia, for God's sake. The Dark Grey Suit, who had betrayed his country for years, felt a stab of resentment and anger against this young traitor.

'Little shit,' he thought to himself. 'What's wrong with Hungary that he needs to run away to England?'

Six

Just as Adrian was getting thoroughly bored, the President started to wind up the meeting.

'Now,' he said, 'it's getting rather late. If there is no further business, I would like to – '

Garth Menzies rose to his feet and smiled the smile of the just.

'There is one thing, Master.'

'Can't it wait?'

'No, sir. I don't believe it can.'

'Oh, very well then.'

Adrian cursed inwardly. They all knew the subject Menzies was going to raise and Menzies knew that they knew. They had been given the chance to raise it themselves but they hadn't. So be it. Very well. Other men might shrink from their duty, but not Garth Menzies.

He barked his throat clear.

'I am amazed, Mr President, absolutely amazed that this meeting can contemplate adjournment without first discussing the Trefusis Affair.'

A dozen heads looked sharply down at their agenda papers. A dozen pairs of buttocks clenched tightly together.

He had said it. The man had said it. Such a want of delicacy. Such wounding impropriety.

At the far end of the table a mathematician specialising in fluid dynamics and the seduction of first year Newnham girls blew his nose in a hurt manner.

Those parts of Adrian that weren't already looking sharply down or clenching tightly together contrived to quiver with disfavour.

How incredibly like Garth to bring up the one subject that everyone else in the room had been so elegantly avoiding. How childish the rhetoric with which he claimed to be amazed at that avoidance.

'I find myself wondering,' said Menzies, 'how we feel about having a criminal amongst us?'

'Now, really Garth – '

'Oh yes, Master, a criminal.'

Menzies, tall and thin, face as white, shiny and bold Roman as the cover page of the quarterly journal of civil law it was his pride to edit, had placed his left thumb along the lapel of his coat and now he stooped forwards from the waist, waving in his right hand, in what he hoped was a brandish, a copy of the *Cambridge Evening News*.

Adrian found himself chilled by the sight of a grown man trying so transparently to strike the forensic pose of a glamorous barrister. No matter how he aged, and there was not now one dark hair on his head, Menzies could never look any grander than a smart-arsed sixth-former. A smart-arsed *grammar-school* sixth-former, Adrian thought. He cut a dreadful sort of Enoch Powell figure. A kind of adolescent Malvolio, all elbows and shiny temples. Adrian found

Menzies as tiresome as his archetypes; unspeakable to behold, dangerous to discount.

Menzies resented his widespread popularity because he felt it sprang from illogical and irrelevant factors like his breath, his voice, his sniffs, his gait, his clothes, his whole atmosphere. For that reason he devoted himself with all the dismal diligence of the dull to giving the world more legitimate grounds for dislike. That, at least, was Adrian's interpretation. Donald always claimed to like the man.

If Donald had been present to witness him now, newspaper in hand and destruction in mind, Adrian was sure he would have altered his opinion.

President Clinton-Lacey, at the head of the table, looked down at his agenda and shaded his eyes. From under his hand he waggled a covert eyebrow at Adrian like a schoolboy sharing a joke under a desk-lid. But there was an urgency and seriousness in the look which told Adrian that he was being given some kind of signal.

Adrian wasn't sure if he could interpret it. He stared ahead of him, perplexed. Did the President want him, as a friend of Donald's, to speak up? Was he warning Adrian not to let his feelings get the better of him? What? He returned the look with a questioning lift of his own eyebrows.

In reply the President gave a 'yackety-yack' gesture with his hand.

Clinton-Lacey's Boltonian sense of humour was notorious but surely he meant something more than 'Oh, that Menzies, he does go on, doesn't he?'

Adrian decided it must be a demand for him to do some filibustering. He swallowed nervously. He was only an undergraduate after all and these were not the sixties. The days of genuine student representation on the boards of governors of the colleges were long gone. It was understood that he was a constitutional hiccough that it would have been embarrassing to cure. He was there to listen, not to comment.

However.

'Don't you think, Dr Menzies,' he began, not daring to look up, 'that the word "criminal" is a bit strong?'

Menzies rounded on him.

'Forgive me, Mr Healey, you are the English student. I am just a lawyer. What on earth would I know about the word criminal? In my profession, out of ignorance no doubt, we use the word to describe someone who has broken the law. I am sure you could entertain us with an essay on the word's origin that would prove conclusively that a criminal is some kind of medieval crossbow. For my purposes however, in law, the man is a criminal.'

'Now, gentlemen . . .'

'Dr Menzies' clumsy sarcasm aside,' said Adrian, 'I have to say that I know full well what criminal means and it is a perfectly ordinary English word, not a legal term, and I resent it being used of Donald. It makes him sound like a professional. One crime doesn't make a criminal. It would be like calling Dr Menzies a lawyer just because thirty years ago he practised briefly at the Bar.'

'I have every right in the world, Mr President,' shrilled Menzies, 'to call myself a lawyer. I believe my reputation in the legal field has done nothing but reflect credit on this institution –'

'Perhaps it wouldn't be unfitting if I said something

here,' said Tim Anderson. His book on Jean-Luc Godard had recently been exceptionally well reviewed by his wife in *Granta* magazine and he was in a less solemn mood than usual.

'I think it would be immensely unfitting,' snapped Menzies.

'Well that's a not uninteresting point, certainly,' said Anderson, 'but I was thinking more that I don't know many people who couldn't express doubt about the strategies that the authorities adopt in situations not a million miles dissimilar to this one and I just don't think that's something we shouldn't be unafraid to shirk addressing or confronting. That's all.'

'I have just been told by a student that I have no right to call myself a lawyer, Master,' said Menzies. 'I await an apology.'

'Dr Menzies is an academic,' said Adrian. 'He is a teacher. I'd have thought that that was quite enough of a profession for one man. I maintain that he is not a lawyer. Law just happens to be the subject he teaches.'

'I am not absolutely sure that I see the relevance of this,' said the President and something in the tone of his voice made Adrian look at him again. He was rolling an eye in the direction of the corner of the room.

The cameras!

Since the beginning of this, Adrian's third and final year, St Matthew's had put up with a television crew on the premises. Their technique, that of becoming part of the furniture, was working so well that they had become appallingly easy to ignore. They had lived up to the name of fly-on-the-wall and only the odd irritating buzz reminded the college of their existence.

It was clear that the President did not want Adrian to forget them. He could not possibly allow anything of the Trefusis Affair to be seen on national television. Adrian's duty lay clear ahead of him. He had to find a way of doing or saying something that would make the film of the meeting, or this part of it, unsuitable for family viewing.

He took a deep breath.

'I'm sorry, Master,' he said, snapping a pencil, 'but the point is that I won't sit here and hear my friend insulted, not if the accuser is the Director of Public Prosecutions, the Procurator Pissing Fiscal and the Witchfinder Fucking General all rolled into one.'

A splutter of incredulity from a middle-aged Orientalist met this unusual outburst.

'Donald has been called a criminal,' Adrian went on, warming to his theme. 'If I run down the street to catch a bus, does that make me an athlete? If you yodel in the bath, Master, does that make you a singer? Dr Menzies has a tongue like a supermarket pricing-gun.'

'Twisting my words won't help.'

'Untwisting them might.'

'Well untwist these words, then,' said Menzies, forcing his copy of the newspaper under Adrian's nose.

'What the yellow rubbery fuck do you think you're up to now?' said Adrian, pushing the newspaper away. 'If I want to blow my nose, I'll use a frigging snot-rag.'

'Healey, have you run mad?' hissed Corder, a theologian, sitting next to Adrian.

'Stick it up your heretical arse.'

'Well!'

'Explain it to you later,' said Adrian in an undertone.

'Oh, it's a game!'

'Sh!'

'Splendid!' whispered Corder, and then sang out, 'Oh, do come on, Garth, get a sodding move on.'

'Well,' said Menzies. 'I have no idea what childish motive you have for hurling abuse at me, Mr Healey. Perhaps you think it is funny. At the risk of being told that I have no sense of humour I am quite prepared to suggest that even an undergraduate audience would remain unmoved by the spectacle of a student insulting one more than twice his age. As for Dr Corder, I can only assume that the man is drunk.'

'Piss off, you fat tit,' said Corder primly.

'Mr President, are they to be allowed to continue in this fashion?'

'Dr Corder, Mr Healey, let Dr Menzies have his say, please,' said the President.

'Right you fucking are, Mr President,' said Adrian, standing up and immediately sitting down again. He had noticed that the microphone boom was only a few inches higher than his head. If he kept standing up he had a notion it would appear in shot and spoil the footage.

'You have the floor, farty,' said Corder.

'I think I'd better say for my own part,' said Tim Anderson, 'that notwithstanding – '

'Thank you,' said Menzies.

Adrian burped loudly and felt with his feet for the TV cabling which ran under the table.

'Now, for those of you have not seen it,' Menzies continued, fishing his spectacles out of his jacket pocket, 'there is an article in this evening's local paper which is of exceptional interest to this college. I shall read it to you.

'"Professor Donald Trefusis,"' he intoned, in that awful declamatory chant reserved by politicians for public readings of I Corinthians 13, '"holder of the Regius Chair in Philology and Senior Tutor of St Matthew's College, appeared at Cambridge magistrate's court this morning charged with gross indecency . . ."'

Menzies broke off. While he had been speaking a large electric lamp in the corner of the room had begun to totter on its base. It creaked on its stand, unable to make up its mind whether to crash to the ground or return to an upright position. By the time a technician had noticed and started to run across to save it, it had decided on the floor. It was the noise of the ten kilowatt bulb exploding that had interrupted Menzies' flow.

'Oh dear,' said Adrian, standing up, distraught. 'I think my feet may inadvertently have become tangled up in your cables for a moment. I'm so sorry . . .'

The BBC director smiled at him through clenched teeth.

'If Mr Healey can manage to sit still for just three minutes,' Menzies continued, 'I shall resume . . .'

'You had got as far as gross indecency,' said Adrian.

'Thank you. ". . . charged with gross indecency. The Professor had been arrested in the Parker's Piece men's toilet at three o'clock the previous night. A youth, described as in his late teens, escaped after a struggle with police. The Professor (66) pleaded guilty. The President of St Matthew's College was unavailable for comment this morning. Donald Trefusis, who is well-known for his articles and broadcasts, told the *Evening News* that life was very extraordinary."'

'Yes, well thank you, Garth,' said the President, 'I think we're all pretty much aware of the details of this morning's court-room drama. I suppose you think something should be done about it?'

'Done?' said Menzies. 'Of course something should be done!'

Adrian stood up.

'Hoover, Wrigleys, Magicote, Benson and Hedges, Sellotape, Persil, Shake and Vac, Nestlés Milky Bar,' he said and sat down again. He had a vague idea that brand names couldn't be mentioned on the BBC.

'Thank you, Adrian,' said the President, 'that will do.'

'Yes sir, Mr President, sir!' said Adrian.

Tim Anderson spoke.

'I don't think I'd be wrong in detecting – '

'If an undergraduate were compromised in this fashion,' said Menzies, 'we would have no hesitation in sending him down. Professor Trefusis is a member of the college just like any student. I submit that under the college ordinance of 1273 and subsequent statutes of 1791 and 1902 we are duty bound to take disciplinary action against any Fellow who brings the good name of the college into disrepute. I move that this meeting of the Fellows immediately invite Professor Trefusis to relinquish the post of Senior Tutor and furthermore I move that they insist he withdraw from any active teaching post in this college for one year. At the very least.'

'Nice subjunctives,' murmured Adrian.

'Now steady on, Garth,' said the President. 'I'm sure we're all as shocked as you are by Donald's . . . Donald's . . . well, his behaviour. But remember where we are. This is Cambridge. We have a tradition of buggery here.'

'Bottomy is everywhere, you know,' the ninety-year-old treble of Emeritus Professor Adrian Williams sang out. 'Wittgenstein was a bottomist, they tell me. I read the other day that Morgan Forster, you remember Morgan? Next door, at King's. Wrote *A Passage to India* and *Howards End*. Wore slippers into Hall once. I read that *he* was a bottomite too. Extraordinary! I think everyone is now. Simply everyone.'

A red-faced statistician thumped the table angrily.

'Not I, sir, not I!' he thundered.

'I don't think we should be unafraid not to discuss the gay dialectic as an energy and the homophobic constraints that endorse its marginalisation as a functionally reactive discourse,' said Tim Anderson.

The cameraman in the corner tilted his camera from one end of the table to the other, quite unable to decide on whom to concentrate his lens.

'If I can speak,' said Adrian.

He had just unwrapped a packet of cigarettes and now scrunched up the cellophane so loudly that the microphone boom, which had just reached him, swung away like a startled giraffe and struck Menzies on the head.

A production assistant with a clipboard giggled and was rewarded with a look of foul contempt from the President.

Menzies was not to be put off.

'The fact is this, Master. There are laws. Homosexual acts are only permitted amongst consenting adults in private.'

'Are you allowed in law, Dr Menzies,' asked Adrian, 'to defecate in public?'

'Certainly not!'

'How would I be charged if I did?'

'Gross indecency, beyond question, the case of the Earl of Oxford – '

'Exactly. But would I be arrested for taking a crap in a public lavatory?'

'Don't be ridiculous.'

'So a public lavatory is, in law, a private place?'

'You're twisting words again, Healey.'

'But again, the words are already twisted. Either a municipal bog is a private place or it isn't. If it is a private place in which to shit, how is it not a private place in which to fellate?'

'Oh, it was fellatio, was it?' the President seemed surprised.

'Well, whatever.'

'Who was doing it to whom, I wonder?'

Menzies' hold on his temper was weakening.

'Either the law is the law or it is not! If it is your intention to campaign for a change in that law, Healey, very good luck to you. The fact remains that Professor Trefusis has brought into disrepute the good name of this college.'

'You never liked him did you?' Adrian couldn't

help saying. 'Well, here's your chance. He's down. Kick him good and hard.'

'Mr President,' said Menzies, 'I have proposed a motion to the Fellows. That Donald Trefusis be stripped of his Senior Tutorship and suspended from the college for a full year. I demand it to be put to the question.'

'Mr President,' said Adrian, 'surely Dr Menzies can't have forgotten that a motion cannot be voted on unless saving that it howmay shall as thus *nem con*, *ne plus ultra* before these presents, as witness the hand thereunto, be seconded?'

'Er . . . quite right,' said the President. 'I think. Do we have a seconder?'

Silence.

'I ask again. Do we have a seconder for Dr Menzies' proposal that Donald Trefusis be relieved of his college duties for the period of one year?'

Silence.

Menzies' chalk-white cheeks were lit with the pin-prick of crimson which, for him, passed for a manly blush.

'Madness, absolute madness! The college will live to regret it.'

'Thank you, Dr Menzies,' said the President.

He turned to the film crew.

'That is the end of the meeting. I'll ask you to go now, as we have one or two private college matters to discuss which cannot possibly be of relevance to your film.'

The crew silently gathered their equipment. The director glared at Adrian as he left the room. The female assistant with the clipboard winked.

'I'm in there,' Adrian thought to himself.

'Now then,' said the President, when the last of the crew had gone. 'I'm sorry to keep you all, but I received a letter from Professor Trefusis this morning and I think you had better hear it.'

He took a letter from his inside pocket.

'"Henry,"' he read. '"By the time you read this I am very much afraid that my improvidence will already have been made known to you. I feel I must first offer the profoundest of apologies for the embarrassment I have caused to you and the college.

'"I will not burden you with reasons, excuses, denials or explanations. I have no doubt in my mind however that it would be a sensible thing for me to ask you if I might take advantage of my right to a sabbatical year. I had intended to ask this of you in any case, as my book on the Great Fricative Shift impels me to visit Europe for research materials. May I therefore take this opportunity to beg your permission to leave Cambridge immediately a sentence, which I am assured will at worst take the form of nothing more inconvenient than a small fine and at best a reprimand from the bench, has been passed upon me?

'"Perhaps you will be so kind as to let me know of your decision in this matter as soon as possible, Henry, for there are many arrangements to be made. Meanwhile, in all contrition I remain, Your good friend Donald."'

'Well,' said Menzies at last, 'how ironic. It seems that Professor Trefusis can be credited, in some regards at least, with more decency than the rest of the fellowship.'

'Up your crack, you fat runt,' said Corder.

'The game's over now, Alex,' said Adrian. 'The film crew has gone.'

'I know,' said Corder, stuffing his briefcase with detritus from the meeting. 'That was for real.'

In a small bedroom a Striped Nightgown had been talking to a Donkey Jacket.

The tape of the conversation was being listened to by a Dark Grey Suit. He felt sorry for the Donkey Jacket having to cope with the ruined husk of a once fine mind.

The old fool was babbling of bacon and cheese.

'It's all right, Grandfather, you should rest now.'

'Steffi's cheese is in the ice-box, you see,' whimpered the Striped Nightgown.

'That's right,' soothed the Donkey Jacket. 'Of course it is.'

'Your cheese is in the pantry.'

'In the pantry, that's right.'

'I saw God yesterday, he's very kind. I think he likes me.'

'I really think you should sleep, you know.'

The Donkey Jacket sounded very distressed. The Dark Grey Suit heard the sound of the old man crying.

'Told him that I hadn't had a shit in two weeks, Martin. "You won't need to in Heaven," he said. Wasn't that kind?'

'Very kind. Very kind indeed.'

'Take two kinds of cheese. Always two kinds. One for the mouse and one for the ice-box.'

'That's right.'

'Bit of pörkelt wouldn't hurt. With some egg-dumplings and red cabbage. No sugar though.'

'Off to sleep now.'

The Dark Grey Suit heard the Donkey Jacket rise from the bed. Heard him kiss the forehead of the Striped Nightgown. Heard the Donkey Jacket's footsteps make for the door. Heard . . . a strained whisper? The Dark Grey Suit turned up the volume of his tape-recorder to maximum.

'Martin! Martin!' A hoarse, urgent command from the old man.

The Donkey Jacket's footsteps stopped near the door.

'Sew it into the lining of your jacket!'

So the old bastard was sane after all. The Dark Grey Suit reached for a pad and composed a cypher for London.

Seven

Crossing the river by way of the Sonnet Bridge on a direct course from the President's Lodge to Donald Trefusis's room in Hawthorn Tree Court, Adrian slapped each stone ball that marched along that noble structure's span in frustration. He had hated that meeting, hated the relish with which Garth Menzies had read out the article in the *Cambridge Evening News*, hated the bubbling looks of salacious amusement on the faces of the BBC crew. All of them laughing at Trefusis.

Hell and hot shit, he said to himself, Donald of all people.

The Tea Room Trade they called it in America; in English, Cottaging. Putting yourself up for quick sex in a public loo.

'Bad news, Adrian,' the President had said that morning. 'Donald has gone and popped up in the guise of a lavatory cowboy. He tells me he's due in court at ten thirty. The *Evening News* is sure to cover it. And tomorrow the nationals. What the hell are we going to do?'

Adrian remembered the times he had sprawled on Donald's chesterfield of a summer evening, hot from a game of cricket. Or the weeks they had shared hotel rooms in Venice and Florence and Salzburg during last year's long vacation. The man had never so much as touched Adrian's shoulder. But then why on earth should he have? There were plenty of lanky, languid undergraduates in the University more appetising than Adrian. Anyway, maybe Donald's tastes were more Orton than Auden. Perhaps it was only anonymous rough trade that lit his fire. Live and let live, of course: but better he should paw Adrian than kneel before some greasy truck driver to whom the name Levi Strauss meant nothing but jeans and, by blowing him, blow a reputation, a career and a way of life.

It was Adrian's last summer, but whenever he crossed the bridge, no matter how occupied he might be, he could never prevent himself from looking across at the Backs, the green train of lawn and willow that swept along the river behind the colleges. With a late afternoon mist descending on the Cam, the absurd beauty of the place depressed him deeply. Depressed him because he caught himself failing to react properly to it. There had been a time when that blend of natural and human perfection would have caused him to writhe with pleasure. But now human affairs and the responsibilities of friendship had claimed that part of him that was capable of feeling and there was nothing left over for nature or the abstract.

Donald Trefusis, a urinal Uranian, a bog bugger. Who'd've thought it?

Adrian, no stranger to sexual adventurism, had never been struck by the charms of the public lavatory as an erotic salon. There had been an occasion, not long after his expulsion from school, when he had found himself forced to answer the griping of his bowels in a Gents in the bus-station at Gloucester.

Sitting there, gently encouraging his colon, he had suddenly become aware of a note being fed through an uncomfortably large hole in the wall that divided him from the neighbouring cubicle. He had taken and read it more in an innocent spirit of good citizenship than anything else. Perhaps some unfortunate disabled person had got into trouble.

'I like young cock,' the note said.

Shocked, Adrian looked at the hole. Where the note had been there was now a human eye. Because he couldn't think of anything else to do under the circumstances, or because he was born foolish, Adrian smiled. A winning smile, accompanied by a friendly, faintly patronising wink: the kind of beaming encouragement you might give a toddler who has presented you with an incompetent drawing.

There immediately followed a shuffle of feet next door and a clink of belt buckle hitting concrete. After a brief pause, a bulky and rather excited penis pushed itself through the hole and twitched urgently.

Without pausing for hygiene and comfort, Adrian had yanked up his trousers and fled in panic. For the next half-hour he wandered Gloucester looking for a place in which he might wipe himself, not daring to risk another public convenience. To this day Adrian failed to see any allure in the lavatory. Apart from anything else the smell. And the risk . . . but risk was the whole point, he supposed.

But nonetheless, the Trefusis that he knew – the man with startled white hair and Irish thorn-proof jackets, patched at the elbows, Trefusis the Elvis

Costello fan and Wolseley driver, Trefusis the sports fan and polyglot – it wasn't easy to imagine that Trefusis frenziedly gobbling at a trucker. It was like trying to picture Malcolm Muggeridge masturbating or Margaret and Denis Thatcher locked in coital ecstasy. But hard to imagine or not, these things had all presumably happened.

Adrian hopped across the lawn of Hawthorn Tree Court, a precaution learnt from schooldays.

'Healey, can't you read?' they used to shout after him.

'Oh yes, sir. I'm very good at reading, sir.'

'Then can't you see that it clearly says, Don't Walk On The Grass?'

'I'm not walking, sir. I'm hopping.'

'Don't be clever, boy.'

'All right, sir. How stupid would you like me to be, sir? Very stupid or only quite stupid?'

He threw himself up the stairs and thumped on Trefusis's oak. College rooms had two doors and if the oak, the outer door, was closed, it was generally held to be bad form to clamour for entrance. Adrian reckoned that circumstances warranted the solecism.

From within he heard a muffled curse.

'Donald, it's me. Adrian. Won't you let me in?'

After a sigh and a creak of floorboards the door opened.

'Really, couldn't you see that my oak was sported?'

'I'm sorry, but I thought – '

'I know. I know what you thought. Come in, come in. I was recording.'

'Oh, sorry.'

Donald's irregular broadcasts on the radio, his

'wireless essays' as he called them, had recently given him a modest amount of fame that had kindled the resentment felt by men like Garth Menzies. Adrian found it hard to believe that, after the events of last night and this morning, Trefusis could contemplate continuing with them. He was even now rewinding the tape on his Uher recorder.

'Sit down,' he said. 'There's a rather comical Bâtard-Montrachet on the side. You might pour out two glasses.'

Now he poured out two glasses of wine and threaded his way through the librarinth towards the small study-within-a-study which contained Donald, his desk, his computer and his tape-recorder. The study was in the centre of the room and made up an inner sanctum no more than six foot square and eight foot high entirely constructed of books, mostly books in Romanian, it appeared. There was even a door. This had been made as part of the set for a student production of *Travesties*, which Trefusis had enjoyed. The director, Bridget Arden, a pupil of his, gave him the door as a present. It had required large stage weights to keep it upright at first, but with books stacked all round its frame it was soon as firmly wedged in place as could be.

One advantage of this strange inner room, Trefusis claimed, was that it made an excellent soundproof chamber for his broadcasts. Adrian's view was that it satisfied a vague agoraphobia, or at least claustraphilia, that he would never admit to.

Trefusis was speaking into the microphone as Adrian tiptoed through with the glasses.

'. . . and since this embarrassment in all its noble

and monumental proportions will be known to you by now through the kind offices of the press, I shall, for the moment, spare you a description of its more gaudy details, although I look forward to sharing them with you in a frank, straightforward and manly way before the year is quite out. For the time being I will, if I may, take a break from these wireless essays and see something of the world. When I have found out what the world is like, be sure that I will let you know, those of you who are interested, of course, the others will simply have to guess. Meanwhile if you have been, then continue to and don't even think of stopping.'

He sighed and put the microphone down.

'Well, it's all very sad,' he said.

'Where shall I put the wine?' said Adrian, looking around for a free space.

'I should try your throat, dear boy,' said Trefusis, taking his glass and drinking it down. 'Now. I suppose you have come to tell me about the meeting?'

'It was outrageous,' said Adrian. 'Menzies was after your blood.'

'The dear man. How silly of him, it wasn't there, it was in here all the time, running through my body. He should have come and asked for it. Was he terribly cross?'

'He wasn't too pleased by my tactics, anyway.'

Trefusis looked at him in alarm.

'You didn't say anything reckless?'

Adrian explained how the meeting had gone. Trefusis shook his head.

'You are a very silly boy. Clinton-Lacey read out my letter, I suppose?'

'Yes, it rather took the wind out of Menzies' sails. But it wasn't necessary, Donald, no one else wanted you to step down. Why did you write it?'

'The heart has its reasons.'

'You've got to watch Menzies. I bet he'll fight your reappointment next year.'

'Nonsense, Garth and I simply overflow with love for each other.'

'He's your enemy, Donald!'

'He most certainly is not,' said Trefusis. 'Not unless I say so. He may dearly want to be my enemy, he may beg on bended knee for open hostility of the most violent kind, but it takes two to tangle. I choose my own enemies.'

'If you say so . . .'

'I do say so.'

Adrian sipped at the wine.

'Buttery, isn't it? The vanilla comes as a late surprise.'

'Yes, yes it's excellent . . . um . . .'

'You have a question?'

This was rather difficult.

'Donald?'

'Yes?'

'About last night . . .'

Trefusis gazed at Adrian sadly.

'Oh dear, you are not going to ask me an embarrassing question, are you?'

'Well, no,' said Adrian, 'not if it does embarrass you.'

'I meant *you*,' said Trefusis. 'You are not going to embarrass yourself, are you?'

Adrian gestured helplessly.

'It just seems so . . . so . . .'

'So squalid?'

'No!' said Adrian. 'I didn't mean that, I meant it seemed so . . .'

'So *unlike* me?'

'Well . . .'

Trefusis patted him on the shoulder.

'Let's go to the Shoulder,' he said. 'I'm sure Bob will find a nice quiet table for us.'

The Shoulder of Lamb was very crowded. Choral Scholars from St John's, limp with Pimms from an early May Week garden party, were singing an *a capella* version of 'Message in A Bottle' in one corner, a pair of millionaire computer designers poked each other heatedly on the chest in another. Adrian remembered how two years ago one of them had bummed cigarettes off him in the Eagle. Now his company was worth sixty million pounds.

The landlord stepped crisply forward and winked.

'Professor Trefusis, sir, and young Mr Healey!' he said, rolling his head back on his neck like a sun-struck sergeant-major. 'Bit busy this evening, sir.'

'So I see, Bob,' said Donald. 'Is there somewhere . . .?'

'I'll take you upstairs, sir.'

Bob led them through the front bar. One or two people stopped talking when they caught sight of Trefusis. Adrian was amazed at the blithe calm with which he greeted them.

'Evening, Michael! I did so enjoy your Serjeant Musgrave. Quite to the purpose. Such boots, too.'

'Simon! I see that your results were posted. A Third! You must be thrilled.'

Bob took them up the stairs.

'We was all most proud to read of your exploits in the paper, sir.'

'Why, thank you, Bob.'

'Reminds me of my old Adjutant when we was on household duties at the Palace. Fuckingham Palace we used to call it then, of course.'

'I'm sure.'

'Dear oh dear, St James's Park was a sink in those days, sir. Wasn't a bush that didn't have at least one guardsman and customer in it. Course, you'll remember Colonel Bramall, won't you, sir?'

'Thank you Bob, this room will do splendidly. Perhaps Nigel could be induced to bring up a couple of the Gruaud Larose?'

'Certainly, sir. How about a nice veal and ham pie? Spot of chutney?'

'Ludicrously ideal.'

'He'll be with you in a breath, sir.'

When they had disposed of the veal and ham pie, but not the chutney, which Trefusis warned would have a most ruinous effect on the palate, he poured out two glasses of wine.

Adrian gulped at his greedily, determining that drunkenness was the only state in which to cope with his discomfort. If the Wizard of Oz was going to reveal himself as a sad and bewildered old man, Adrian didn't want to be sober when it happened.

To be fair, Donald looked about as sad and bewildered as the Laughing Cavalier as he sipped his claret and dipped his head in appreciation.

'A purist might recommend another year of ageing

for the tannin to smooth out its rougher edges,' he said. 'I think it already supernacular, however.'

'It's fine,' said Adrian, pouring himself another glass.

Trefusis watched him contentedly.

'A good wine is like a woman,' he said. 'Except of course it doesn't have breasts. Or arms and a head. And it can't speak or bear children. In fact, come to think of it, a good wine isn't remotely like a woman at all. A good wine is like a good wine.'

'I'm rather like a good wine too,' said Adrian.

'You improve with age?'

'No,' said Adrian, 'whenever I'm taken out I get drunk.'

'Except that in your case you get laid down after drinking, not before.'

Adrian blushed.

'Oh dear,' said Trefusis, 'that was not a sexual allusion. Merely frivolous paronomasy on the theme of alcoholically induced unconsciousness. I was particularly pleased with "in your case". Are you to be discomfited by the potential for erotic interpretation of every remark I might make?'

'I'm sorry,' said Adrian. 'I've a feeling I'm a bad vintage.'

'That's nonsense, but very graceful. We were talking of drink, I've always believed it right for young people to drink. Not be alcoholic of course, that is a passive state of being, not a positive action. But it is good to drink to excess. That sounds like a toast. To excess.'

'To excess,' said Adrian, bumpering. 'Nothing exceeds like it.'

'Your strenuous tongue is bursting Joy's grape against your palate fine, and that's just as it should be.'

'Keats,' burped Adrian. 'Ode to Melancholy.'

'Keats indeed,' said Trefusis, refilling their glasses. 'Ode *on* Melancholy in fact, but we are beyond pedantry here, I hope.'

'Bollocks,' said Adrian, who hated being corrected, even kindly.

'Now,' said Trefusis, 'we should talk.'

'For the moment,' he said, 'I have nothing to say on the subject of last night. One day, when the world is pinker, I will a tale unfold, whose lightest word would harrow up thy soul, freeze thy young blood, make thy two eyes, like stars, start from their spheres, thy knotted and combined locks to part, and each particular hair to stand on end, like quills upon the fretful porpentine, and generally make you go all of a dither. But for the moment, shtum, you can keep all thoughts on the topic to yourself: zip your lip. However I do have a proposition to put to you which I would like you to consider very seriously. You have no fixed plans for next year, I think?'

'That's right.'

Adrian had made up his mind to wait until after his Finals before deciding what to do with himself. If he got a First he still planned to stay at Cambridge, otherwise he supposed he would look for a teaching job somewhere.

'How would it be, I wonder, if you were to spend the summer travelling with me?'

Adrian goggled. 'Well, I . . .'

'As you know, I shall be doing a little research for

my book. But I have something else to do. There is a problem that needs sorting out, a noisesome problem but not unchallenging. I believe you will be able to offer me material assistance with it. In return I will naturally take care of all expenses, hotels, flights and so forth. It will, I think, be a tour not wholly devoid of interest and amusement. At journey's end we will both deposit ourselves back in England, you to become Prime Minister or whatever lowly ambition you have set your sights on, me to pick up the threads of a ruined and disappointed career. How does that strike you as a plan?'

It struck Adrian as Roscoe Tanner struck a tennis-ball, but how it struck him as a plan he couldn't say. His mind reeled with questions. Had Trefusis run mad? What would his parents say? Should he tell them? Did Donald expect him to share his bed? Is that what it was all about?

'Well?'

'It's . . . it's unbelievable.'

'You don't like it?'

'Like it? Of course I like it, but – '

'Excellent!' Trefusis poured out two more glasses of wine. 'Then you're game?'

If I refused to sleep with him, thought Adrian, would he just kick me out and abandon me in the middle of Europe without a penny? Surely not.

'God yes!' he said. 'I'm game.'

'Wonderful!' said Trefusis. 'Then let us drink to our Grand Tour.'

'Right,' said Adrian draining his glass, 'our Grand Tour.'

Trefusis smiled.

'I'm so very pleased,' he said.

'Me too,' said Adrian, 'but . . .'

'Yes?'

'This problem you mentioned. That I may be able to help you with. What exactly . . .?'

'Ah,' said Donald. 'I'm afraid I am not yet fully at liberty, as they say, to disclose the details.'

'Oh.'

'But I don't suppose there's any harm in my asking you to cast your mind back to last summer. You remember the Salzburg Festival?'

'Vividly.'

'I am sure you haven't forgotten that terrible business in the Getreidegasse?'

'The man in the Mozart museum?'

'That same.'

'I'm hardly likely to forget it. All that blood.'

Bob appeared at the door.

'Sorry to disturb, gents. Thought you might appreciate some of this superior Armagnac brandy.'

'How solicitous!' said Trefusis.

'May I enquire, sir, whether everything went well?'

'Everything went splendidly, Bob. Splendidly.'

'Oh goody-good,' said Bob, taking three small brandy glasses from his jacket pocket. 'I'll join you then, if I may.'

'Please do, Bob, please do. Desperate times call for desperate measures, so pour us each one desperate measure.'

Bob complied.

'We were just talking about Salzburg.'

'Ooh, nasty business that, sir. Poor old Moltaj.

Throat slit from ear to ear, they tell me. But then you both saw it in the flesh, didn't you, sirs?'

Adrian stared at him.

'I know you'll do right by old Moltaj, Mr Healey,' said Bob, clapping him on the shoulder. 'Course you will, sir.'

also contains
five propellant

A St Matthew's Tie with Liberty silk handkerchief flamboy-antly thrust into the breast pocket was bent double in Corridor Four of the third floor of Reddaway House next to the door marked '3.4.CabCom'. He seemed to be taking an unconscionable time in doing up the laces of his black Oxford shoes. It was almost impossible for him not to hear voices coming from behind the door.

'I was just thinking, sir, that what with the Bikini alert over Iran and everything . . .'

'Bugger the bloody Persians, Reeve – I have a Limit Zero Cabinet Appro on this.'

'Copeland is very keen that we should co-operate.'

'Listen to me. The Hairy Mullah is there to stay. You know it, I know it. Neither Copeland nor anyone at Langley nor over here has got a choirboy's chance in Winchester of doing anything about it. Checkmate, d'you see? I don't suppose you know what checkmate means?'

'Well . . .'

'Of course you don't, you went to Oxford. Checkmate comes from the Arabic "shah mat" – the King is dead. Well the Shah is mat, all right, he's as mat as a bloody doornail, and I don't propose to waste time feeding the ambitions of his whining progeny – they can live it up in Monaco and Gstaad for the rest of their lives as far as I'm concerned. Clear the

board, put the chessmen back in their box, we've got bigger
capon to baste.'

'Right, sir.'

'Right. So. Report?'

'Well, sir. I'm sorry to have to make report that the
ObSquad lost Castor for a day.'

'What?'

'Er . . . if you take a look at this, sir. It's a Cambridge
police report.'

The St Matthew's Tie heard the wobble of a cardboard
wallet being opened.

'Castor and Odysseus, eh?'

'We rather think so, sir.'

'So are you telling me that Odysseus has got the whole box
of tricks now?'

'No, sir . . . if you remember our signal from Locksmith
in Budapest, Castor may have given one part of Mendax to
Odysseus but the other half will be with Pollux, sewn into
the lining of his jacket.'

'And Pollux is still in Troy?'

'Not exactly sir. Vienna Station received another signal
from Locksmith this morning, fully prioritised.'

'Fully whatted?'

'Er . . . prioritised, sir.'

'Christ.'

'It seems that Pollux left Troy last night.'

'Headed for the Greek camp?'

'Best guess, sir.'

There was a long pause.

The St Matthew's Tie straightened himself to allow a
little blood to flow down from his head.

'If you're right, Reeve, Odysseus will make his way
Greekwards in the next few days too.'

'With Telemachus, do you think?'

Another long pause was followed by the sound of a folder being dropped on a desk.

The St Matthew's Tie stooped to do up another shoe-lace.

'Well, nothing to keep me in England now that Botham seems to have lost us the blasted Ashes. I'll fly over the moment anything develops.'

'Cricket not going too well then, sir?'

'The man's a bloody disgrace. He couldn't captain a paraplegic netball team.'

'Will you be around for initialling appropriation orders later in the afternoon, sir?'

'Well, young Reeve, after a brief lunchérising and half an hour's memorandorising Cabinet, I'll be at Lord's.'

'Right, sir.'

'So if you want me to signatorise anything, send Simon Hesketh-Harvey round, he's a member. Now I must go and lavatorise. And while I'm away for God's sake try and learn to speak English.'

The St Matthew's Tie hurried along the corridor to his office. He heard the door of 3.4.CabCom opening. A voice hailed him.

'Ho there, young Hesketh-H!'

The St Matthew's Tie turned. A Bennett, Tovey and Steele Suit was standing in the corridor.

'Morning, sir.'

'Snap.'

They looked at each other's neck-ties with a smile.

'You may have to change that for the good old orange and yellow this pip emma,' said the Bennett, Tovey and Steele.

'Sir?'

'If you're a good boy, Reeve will send you over to me at Lord's this afternoon to watch the final death throes.'

208

'Good-o,' said the St Matthew's Tie. 'I shall enjoy that, sir.'

'Right. Oh, by the way – '

'Sir?'

'Prioritise. Ever come across that one?'

'Ugh!' said the St Matthew's Tie. 'Langley?'

'No, that arse Reeve, of course. Last week it was "having a meet-up with", God knows what new linguistic macédoine he's going to serve up next.'

'One shudders to think, sir.'

'All right then, Simon, off you pop.'

Eight

I

'I have taken much care in packing,' said Trefusis as he pushed shut the boot of the Wolseley. 'A tin of barley-sugar for you, Castrol GTX for the car, figgy oatcakes for me.'

'Figgy oatcakes?'

'Oatcakes are very healthy. Hotels, restaurants, cafés, they all take their toll. Salzburg is not kind to the figure. At my age travel broadens the behind. A steatopygous Trefusis is an unhappy Trefusis. The buns and tortes of Austria are whoreson binders of your whoreson stool. But a figgy oatcake laughs at constipation and favours rectal carcinoma with a haughty stare. In the grammar of health, while cream may hasten the full stop, porridge will ease the colon.'

'Oh, ah,' said Adrian. 'And curry creates the dash, I suppose.'

'Oh, I like that. Very good. "Curry creates the dash." Yes, indeed. Most . . . most . . . er, what is the word?'

'Amusing?'

'No . . . it'll come to me.'

The interior of the car smelt of Merton Park

thrillers, Bakelite headsets and the Clothes Ration. It only needed the profile of Edgar Wallace or the voice of Edgar Lustgarten to sweep Adrian and Trefusis, with bells ringing, into a raincoat and Horlicks Britain of glistening pavements, trilbied police inspectors and poplin shirts. So familiar was the odour, so complete the vision it evoked as they swung with a whine of gears out of the college gates and onto the Trumpington Road, that Adrian could almost believe in reincarnation. He had never smelt that precise smell before, yet it was as known to him as the smell of his own socks.

Trefusis would not be drawn on the purpose of their mission to Salzburg.

'You knew that man who was killed then?'

'Knew him? No.'

'But Bob said . . .'

'I do hope the Bendix doesn't give out. The Wolseley 15/50 is a marvellous saloon, but the Bendix is most terribly susceptible to trouble.'

'Well if you didn't know him, how come you know his name?'

'I suppose one could call such an affliction bendicitis.'

'When I first arrived in Cambridge there was a rumour that you recruited for MI5. Either that or for the KGB.'

'My dear fellow, there is not a don over the age of sixty who is not said to be the fourth, fifth, sixth or seventh man in some improbable circle of spies, double agents and ruthless traitors. You should pay no attention.'

'You worked at Bletchley during the war though, didn't you? On the Enigma code.'

'So did Beryl Ayliffe the college librarian. Are we to believe that she is an MI5 . . . what's the word . . . operative?'

Adrian pictured the chain-smoking chatelaine of the St Matthew's library.

'Well no, of course not,' he conceded. 'But . . .'

'Ha, ha. More fool you, because she *is*!'

'What?'

'Or is she?' mused Trefusis. 'So damned difficult to tell in this damned deadly game we play. Anyway, what does it matter? Isn't it all the bloody same? Left, right? Right, wrong? The old distinctions don't matter a damned damn any more, damn it.'

'All right, all right,' said Adrian, stung by the mockery. 'I grant you it all sounds a bit stupid. But we did see a man killed last year. You can't get away from that.'

'Assuredly.'

'And that's why we're going back to Salzburg?'

'I don't think we'll eat until we get to France. There's a surprisingly good restaurant at the railway station at Arras. See if you can find it on your map, there's a dear.'

II

Adrian had never eaten *foie gras* before.

'I thought it was just pâté,' he said.

'Oh no, the pâté is quite inferior. These are the livers themselves. Flash fried. I think you'll be pleased.'

Adrian was.

'It just literally melts in the mouth!' he exclaimed. 'Unbelievable!'

'You'll find the Corton Charlemagne an excellent accompaniment. Perfectly served at last. I have an ex-student who is likely to become the next editor of the *Spectator*. On his succession I shall offer for publication a little article on the iniquity of the British habit of over-chilling white Burgundies. If one's young friends are going to disgrace themselves by writing for such low periodicals the least they can do is assuage their guilt by providing a platform for advanced ideas. I make it a point to teach all my pupils to believe in properly served wine.'

Adrian listened with half an ear to the Professor's flow of conversation. A young man and woman had entered the restaurant a moment earlier and now floundered in the middle of the room, waiting for someone to show them to a table. Adrian's eyes narrowed suddenly. He leant across to Trefusis.

'Don't look now, but that couple behind you who've just come in . . .' He lowered his voice to a whisper. '*They were on the boat with us!* I swear it's the same two. They were behind us in the car queue. In a green BMW.'

Trefusis tore a bread roll in half and looked speculatively into a large mirror over Adrian's shoulder.

'Really? Bless my soul, it's a small world and no mistake.'

'You don't think . . . you don't think they might be . . . *following* us?'

Trefusis raised his eyebrows. 'It's possible of course. It's always possible.'

Adrian grabbed Trefusis's arm across the table. 'I could go and have a pee and put their car out of action. What do you say?'

'You think micturating over their car would put it out of action?'

'No, I mean *pretend* to have a pee but actually wrench out the rotor arm or take the distributor cap or whatever it is you do.'

Trefusis gazed at him with only the trace of a smile on his face. 'Do you know how they make *foie gras*?'

'Donald, I'm serious. I'm sure they're following us.'

With a sigh, Trefusis put down the fragment of *brioche* he had been buttering.

'I'm serious too. It's time, young Healey, that you knew what this trip was all about.'

'Really?'

'Really. Now, I'll ask you again. Do you know how to make *foie gras*?'

Adrian stared at Trefusis. 'Er . . . no. No I don't.'

'Very well then, I'll tell you. You rear a goose from a puppy or calf or whatver a goose is when young.'

'Chick? Gosling?'

'Quite possibly. You take a young Strasbourg goose-cub, chick or gosling and you feed it rich grain in a mashy pulp.'

'Fatten it up, you mean?'

'That's right, but the mashy pulp is placed, you see, in a bag.'

'A bag?'

'That's right. A bag or sack. The bag or sack has some species of nozzle or protuberance at the narrow end, which is forced down the goose's gullet or throat. The bag or sack is then squeezed or compressed and the meal or fodder thus introduced or thrust into the creature or animal's crop or stomach.'

'Why not just let it feed normally?'

'Because this procedure is undertaken many times a day for the whole of the poor animal's life. It is force fed on a massive scale. Force fed until it is so gorged and gross that it can no longer move. Its liver becomes pulpy and distended. Ideal, in fact, for flash frying and presenting with a glass of spacious Montrachet or fat, buttery Corton Charlemagne.'

'That's horrific!' said Adrian. 'Why didn't you tell me that before?'

'I wanted you to taste it. It is one of the highest pleasures known to man. Wasn't it Sydney Smith who had a friend whose idea of heaven was eating it to the sound of trumpets? Like most of our highest pleasures, however, it is rooted in suffering; founded in an unnatural, almost perverted, process.'

Adrian's mind raced forward, trying to think of the relevance of this to their situation. He ran a storyline through his head. A European cartel of *foie gras* manufacturers, determined to prevent the Common Market from outlawing their product. Prepared to·kill in order to protect what they saw as their God-given right to torture geese for the tables of the rich. Surely not? That sort of thing simply did not happen. And even if it did, it was scarcely the sort of affair in which Trefusis would interest himself.

'So what exactly . . .?'

'This forcing of a goose is an image I want you to hold in your head while I tell you of something else . . . ah . . . *le poisson est arrivé.*'

Trefusis beamed as two large dishes, each covered

215

with an immense silver *cloche*, were set before them. The waiter looked from Adrian to Trefusis with an expectant smile and – now sure of their attention – he swept each *cloche* clear with a flourish, releasing clouds of delicately fishy steam.

'*Voilà! Bon appetit, messieurs!*'

'Enlightening that what we call John Dory the French call Saint Pierre, the Italians San Pietro and the Spanish San Pedro.'

'Who was John Dory, do you think?'

'Oh, I imagine the Dory is from *doré*, gilded or golden. Of course we do sometimes call it St Peter's fish, I believe. *Merci bien.*'

'*M'sieur!*' The waiter bowed smartly and strutted away.

'Howsomever that may be,' said Trefusis. 'Some time ago I was contacted – I believe that's the right word? – by an old friend of mine, Tom Daly. Tom used to be the garden steward at St Matthew's and a fine gardener he was too, as green-fingered as . . . as . . .'

'As a Martian with septicaemia?'

'If that pleases you. It fell out that in nineteen-sixty-two Tom pleached, plashed and entwined himself with one Eileen Bishop. In due course he pollinated her and there sprung up a fine young son. In a simple but affecting ceremony in Little St Mary's later that year I agreed to renounce the world, the flesh and the devil in order to cleanse my soul in readiness for the task of standing sponsor to their freshly budded sprig, whom they had decided to baptise Christopher Donald Henry.'

'This gardener married and had a son and you are his godfather?'

'I believe that's what I said,' said Trefusis. 'Then in nineteen-seventy-six, to the distress of us all, Tom left the college to take up the post of chief borough gardener in West Norfolk. When next you admire the gay rampage of tulips at a roundabout in King's Lynn or the giddy riot of wayside lobelia in central Hunstanton, you'll know whom to thank. Be that as it may. Beyond the usual silver porringer at birth and the bi-annual five-pound note, my contribution to Christopher's moral welfare has been scant. I have to confess that Christopher, my godson, is a child of whom I stand rather in awe.'

Adrian tried to picture the Professor standing rather in awe of anything.

'The boy is remarkably gifted you see,' said Trefusis, gently laying a sliver of fish-bone on the side of his plate. 'His mathematical ability as an infant was simply astounding. From an early age he exhibited almost supernatural powers. He could multiply and divide long numbers in seconds, calculate square and cube roots in his head, do all the circus tricks. But he had a fine mind as well as an arithmetically prodigious brain and it was assumed that he would make his way to Trinity and contribute something to the field of pure mathematics before he was thirty or whatever age it is that marks the Anno Domini of mathematicians.'

'I believe they're pretty much over the hill by twenty-six these days,' said Adrian. 'How old is he now?'

'Eighteen or so. He is lucky, you might think, to

have a father proud of his gifts and who, moreover, would have been happy for him to employ them academically, in the service of scholarship, for the sake of the pure art of pure mathematics. Many fathers of comparably modest incomes would have looked on a clever son as a route to riches. My son the financier, my son the barrister, my son the accountant. Tom stood quite ready and without rancour to explain the child away as my son the loopy mathematician with the scurfy hair and bottle-end spectacles.'

'And . . .?'

'Three years ago Christopher was awarded a scholarship to a public school in Suffolk: the money came from an organisation Tom Daly had never heard of. It now seems that this organisation is proposing to put Christopher through Cambridge. He will read not Pure Maths there, but Engineering. What is worrying Tom is that the organisation is only interested in Christopher because of his potential as a brain. After university they want him to go into industry.'

'What is the organisation?'

'I'll come to that. Tom believes that Christopher shouldn't be committed so early. He is frightened that this organisation is, in effect, buying his son. So he came to me and asked if I knew anything of them. I was able to confirm that I did. I have known of them for some time.'

'Who are they?'

'Let's settle up. I will tell you the rest on the road. What would be an adequate lagniappe, do you think?'

Adrian looked out of the rear window.

'They *are* following us!'

'How frustrating for them. All that power under

their bonnet and they are forced to hold their pace down to our niggardly fifty-five miles per hour.'

As Trefusis spoke, the BMW moved out to the left and swept past them. Adrian caught a glimpse of the driver's face, alert and tense behind the wheel.

'The same man all right. British number plates. Right hand drive. GB sticker on the back. Why's he passed us, though?'

'Perhaps a relay,' said Trefusis, 'someone else will take up the pursuit. It is scarcely a problem to identify a car of this age and distinction.'

Adrian looked at him sharply. 'You admit that we're being followed then?'

'It was always a possibility.'

Adrian popped a lump of barley-sugar into his mouth. 'You were telling me about this organisation. That paid for your godson to go through school.'

'I have become increasingly aware in recent years,' said Trefusis, 'of what can only be called a conspiracy on a massive scale. I have watched the most talented, the most able and most promising students that come through St Matthew's and other colleges in Cambridge and other universities in England . . . I have watched them being bought up.'

'Bought up?'

'Purchased. Procured. Acquired. Gotten. Let us say an undergraduate arrives with phenomenal ability in, for example, English. A natural candidate for a doctorate, a teaching post, a life of scholarship or, failing those, a creative existence as poet, novelist or dramatist. He arrives full of just such ambitions and sparkling ideals but then . . . they get to him.'

'They?'

'Two years after graduation this first class mind is being paid eighty thousand pounds a year to devise advertising slogans for a proprietary brand of peanut butter or is writing snobbish articles in glossy magazines about exiled European monarchs and their children or some such catastrophic drivel. I see it year after year. Perhaps a chemist will arrive in the college. Great hopes are held out for his future. Nobel Prizes and who knows what else besides? He himself is full of the highest aspirations. Yet even before his final exams he has been locked and contracted into a job for life concocting synthetic pine-fresh biological soap powder fragrances for a detergent company. Adrian, someone is getting at our best minds! Someone is preventing them from achieving their full potential. This organisation I told you of is denying them a chance to grow and flourish. A university education should be broad and general. But these students are being *trained*, not *educated*. They are being stuffed like Strasbourg geese. Pappy mush is forced into them, just so one part of their brains can be fattened. Their whole minds are being ignored for the sake of that part of them which is marketable. Thus they have persuaded my godson Christopher to read Engineering instead of Mathematics.'

'How long has this been going on?'

'I cannot tell how long. Years, I suspect. I first began to take real notice fifteen or twenty years ago. But it is getting worse. More and more brilliant students are being diverted from work that could be of real benefit to mankind and their country. They are being battery farmed. Young Christopher Daly is just one of thousands.'

'My God!' said Adrian. 'You know who's behind this? We've got to stop them!'

'It's a conspiracy of industrialists, of certain highly placed economists and of members of governments of all political colours,' said Trefusis.

'But how can we prevent it? And what has it got to do with Salzburg?'

Trefusis looked across at Adrian, his eyes filled with grave concern. Suddenly he burst out laughing. Shaking his head from side to side, he snorted and struck the steering wheel. 'Oh Adrian, I *am* cruel! I'm wicked, naughty, dreadful and digraceful. Please forgive me.'

'What's so funny?'

'You silly, *silly* boy. What I have just described is the way the world works! It's not a conspiracy. It is called Modern Western Civilisation.'

'W-what do you mean?'

'Of *course* the best brains are lured into industry, advertising, journalism and the rest of it. Of *course* universities are adapting to the demands of commerce. It's regrettable and there's little we can do about it. But I think only a Marxist would call it an international conspiracy.'

'But you said an organisation . . . you told me that a specific organisation had offered that boy Christopher a scholarship.'

'The state, Adrian. A state scholarship. And the state will hope in return that he goes into something productive once he has obtained his degree. He will be incented by money, recruitment drives and the general thrust and tenor of the times. That is all.'

Adrian fumed in silence for a while.

'And this has nothing to do with what we're going to Salzburg for?'

'Nothing at all.'

'You are impossible, you know that?'

'Improbable perhaps, but not impossible. Besides, whilst what I described may not be a conscious intrigue, it is happening nonetheless and is vexatious in the extreme.'

'So you're still not going to tell me what we are in actual fact doing here?'

'All in actual good time,' said Trefusis. 'Now the Cardinal is getting thirsty; if memory has not fully quit her throne I believe there should be an amenable garage and *routier* in about eighty kilometres or so. In the meantime, we can tell each other the story of our lives.'

'All right,' said Adrian. 'You first. Tell me about Bletchley.'

'Little *to* tell. It was set up as a wartime decrypting station and filled up with mainly Cambridge personnel.'

'Why Cambridge?'

'The closest university town. At first they recruited philologists and linguists like myself.'

'This was when?'

'Nineteen-forty. Round about the time of the Battle of Britain.'

'And you were how old?'

'Tush and bibble! Is this then to be an interrogation? I was twenty-two.'

'Right. Just wondered.'

'Young and fizzing at the brim with ideals and theories about language. Now, who else was there with me? Dozens of girls who filed and clerked away with great brilliance and flair. The chess master Harry Golombek was on the team of course, and H.F.O. Alexander, also a magnificently dashing player. It was all rather cosy and fun at first, wrestling with enemy cyphers that had been intercepted all over Europe and Africa. It soon became clear, however, that the Enigma encryption device that German Naval Intelligence was using would need mathematicians to crack it. Acquaintanceship with the decryption techniques of the last war, the ability to do the *Times* crossword while shaving and a mastery of Russian verbs of motion were not enough any more. So they brought in Alan Turing, of whom you may have heard.'

Adrian had not.

'No? What a pity. Brilliant man. Quite brilliant, but very sad. Killed himself later. Many credit him with the invention of the digital computer. I can't quite remember how it came about. There was some pure mathematical problem which had faced the world of numbers for fifty years, I think, and he had solved it as a young man by positing the existence of a number-crunching machine. It was never his intention to build such a thing, it was merely hypothesised as a model to help solve an abstract difficulty. But unlike many mathematicians he relished the physical application of numbers. His hut in Bletchley was soon filled with rows and rows of valves. You remember valves? Tubes they call them in America. Little vacuum bulbs that glowed orange.'

'I remember,' said Adrian. 'It used to take televisions ages to warm up.'

'That's right. Well Alan had thousands of them all

linked together in some impossibly complicated fashion. Got them from the Post Office.'

'The Post Office?'

'Yes, the GPO had been experimenting in electronics before the war and they seemed to be the only people who really knew about it. The clever thing about the Enigma machine was that, although it was purely mechanical, it changed daily and the number of permutations was so grotesquely huge that the old techniques of decryption wouldn't work. Alan cracked it quite brilliantly. But that was only the first stage of course. He still needed to know the code before he could read the cypher.'

'What's the difference between a cypher and a code then?'

'Well, that is readily explained,' said Trefusis. 'Imagine a system in which a number refers to a letter of the alphabet. A equals one, B equals two, C equals three and so on, thus "Adrian" would be "One – four – eighteen – nine – one – fourteen", you understand?'

'Right . . .'

'That is a very basic form of cypher and a message written in it could be cracked by anyone of the meanest intelligence in seconds. But suppose that between us we two had personally prearranged that a word . . . "Biscuits", for example, was going to mean "nineteen-hundred hours", and that another word, for instance "Desmond", should signify "The Café Florian in St Mark's Square, Venice".'

'Got you . . .'

'I would then only have to signal to you: "Please send me some biscuits today, love Desmond," and you would know that I wanted to meet you at seven o'clock that evening at Florian's. That is a code and would be impossible to crack unless someone overheard us arranging it, or one of us was foolish enough to commit it to paper.'

'I see,' said Adrian. 'Then why not only use codes if they're uncrackable?'

'Unfortunately in wartime one needs to signal an enormous amount of unpredictable and detailed information. The receiver couldn't be expected to memorise thousands of different code words, and to write them down would be insecure. So it became practice to mix the two systems. A complicated cypher would be used which could only be cracked if one knew a key word, a code, which would change daily. That is how Enigma operated. So even when Enigma had been solved we needed Intelligence to help provide us with clues so that we could crack the daily code. That is where I came in, and of course, your old friend Humphrey Biffen.'

'Humphrey Biffen?'

'I believe he taught you French once.'

'Good Lord! Did Biffo work at Bletchley too?'

'Oh indeed. And Helen Sorrel-Cameron whom he later married. Guessing the daily key words was very much our speciality.'

'But however did you manage?'

'Well now, the Germans were so very confident that Enigma was uncrackable that they became remarkably sloppy about the assignation of the daily key. Intelligence furnished us with the names of operators and cypher clerks in German Naval Intelligence and Humphrey and I would make guesses. We used to keep immensely detailed files on each clerk:

their likes, their loves, their families, mistresses, lovers, pets, tastes in music and food . . . oh, everything. Each day we would try out different ideas, the name of that particular operator's dog, their favourite kind of pastry, their maiden surname, that sort of thing. We usually got there in the end.'

'But the Germans must have discovered that you had cracked it, surely?'

'Well that's the peculiarity of this kind of work. Our job was simply to furnish Military Intelligence with everything we decrypted. They would then, as a rule, fail to act upon it.'

'Why?'

'Because they could on no account let the enemy know that they were reading their most secret transmissions. It is generally believed, for instance, that Churchill had prior warning of the impending Luftwaffe raid on Coventry but neglected to tell the army and air force for fear of extra defences in the area revealing to the Germans that it had been known about in advance. This is not strictly true, but it demonstrates the principle. Some believe, of course, that Admiral Kanaris, the head of German Naval Intelligence, was perfectly well aware that we were reading Enigma all along, but that he was so pro-British and distressed at the behaviour of the Führer that he simply let it happen.'

'Fascinating,' said Adrian. 'God I wish I could have been around at a time like that.'

'Oh, I don't know,' said Trefusis. 'I think you might have been bored.'

Trefusis peered at the landscape and the road-signs. 'Still another fifty or so kilometres before our service station. Now it's your turn. What has happened in your young life? Plenty, I make no doubt.'

'Oh not so much,' said Adrian. 'I was arrested for the possession of cocaine once.'

'Really?'

'Yes. I had been living with an actor after a few months of being a rent-boy.'

'A rent-boy?' said Trefusis. 'How enterprising! And possession of cocaine? Were you imprisoned?'

'Well first I should tell you how I was expelled from school. That should take us twenty kilometres. Then I'll tell you what happened after that.'

Nine

I

He had stared at the first paper for the whole three hours, unable to write a thing. One of the girls came up to him afterwards.

'I saw you, Adrian Healey! Couldn't you answer any of the questions, then?'

Two years in this stupid college that called its pupils 'students' and its lessons 'lectures'. How had he stood it? He should never have given way.

'I think it's the right thing, darling. It'll give you so much more independence than a school. Father agrees. You can get the bus in to Gloucester and be home with me every night. And then after you've got the "A" levels, you can sit the Cambridge entrance. Everyone says it's an awfully good college. The Fawcetts' boy – David is it? – he went there after he was . . . after he left Harrow, so I'm sure it's all right.'

'What you mean is, it's the only place for miles around that'll take boys that've been expelled.'

'Darling, that's not . . .'

'Anyway, I don't want "A" levels and I don't want to go to Cambridge.'

'Ade, of course you do! Just think how you'd regret it if you missed the opportunity.'

He had missed the opportunity, and the lectures. Instead there had been the ABC cinema and the Star Café, where he played pin-ball and three-card brag.

Discuss Lawrence's use of external landscape in relation to the internal drama of Sons and Lovers.

Only connect . . . How are the Schlegels and Wilcoxes connected in Howards End?

Compare and contrast the different uses of landscape and nature in the poetry of Seamus Heaney and Ted Hughes.

Suddenly his plausible wit was of no use to him. Suddenly the world was dull and sticky and unkind. His future was behind him and he had nothing to look forward to but the past.

Goodbye Gloucester, goodbye Stroud. He was at least following a literary example. When Laurie Lee had walked out on his midsummer's morning he had had a guitar and the blessings of his family to accompany him. Adrian had a paperback copy of Anouilh's *Antigone*, which he had intended to read at lunchtime as some kind of feeble preparation for the afternoon's French literature paper, and fifteen pounds from his mother's handbag.

In the end he got a lift from a lorry driver who was going all the way to Stanmore.

'I can drop you somewhere on the North Circular, if you like.'

'Thanks.'

North Circular . . . North Circular. It was some kind of road, wasn't it?

'Er . . . is the North Circular anywhere near Highgate?'

'You can catch a bus from Golder's Green pretty quick.'

Bollocks lived in Highgate. He might be able to cadge a couple of nights there while he sorted himself out.

'I'm Jack, by the way,' said the driver.

'Er . . . Bullock, Hugo Bullock.'

'Bullock? That's a funny one.'

'I once met a girl called Jane Heffer. We should've got married.'

'Yeah? What went wrong?'

'No, I mean her being called Heffer. It's the female of bullock.'

'Oh right, right.'

They drove on in silence. Adrian offered Jack a cigarette.

'No thanks, mate. Trying to give 'em up. Don't do you any good in this game.'

'No, I suppose not.'

'So, what, you running away then, are you?'

'Running away?'

'Yeah. How old are you?'

'Eighteen.'

'Get away!'

'Well, I will be.'

Bullock's mother stood in the doorway and eyed him suspiciously. He supposed his hair was rather long.

'I'm a friend of William's. From school.'

'He's in Australia. It's his year off before going to Oxford.'

'Oh yes, of course. I just . . . wondered, you know. Not to worry. Happened to be passing.'

'I'll tell him you called if he rings. Are you staying in London?'

'Yes, in Piccadilly.'

'Piccadilly?'

What was wrong with that?

'Well, you know, more just *off*.'

The pin-ball machines in Piccadilly had more sensitive tilt mechanisms than those he was used to in Gloucester, and he wasn't getting many replays. At this rate he wouldn't be able to afford to carry on for more than an hour.

A man in a blue suit came down behind him and put down a fifty-pence piece.

'It's yours,' said Adrian, smacking the flipper buttons in frustration as his last silver ball rolled out of play. 'That was my last. I just can't seem to get the hang of the bloody thing.'

'No, no, no,' said the man in the blue suit, 'the fifty is for you. Have another go.'

Adrian turned in surprise.

'Well, that's awfully kind . . . are you sure?'

'Yes indeed.'

The fifty was soon used up.

'Come and have a drink,' said the man. 'I know a bar just round the corner.'

They left the chimes and buzzes and intense, haunted concentration of the amusement arcade and walked up Old Compton Street and into a small pub in a side street. The barman didn't question Adrian's age, which was an unusual relief.

'Haven't seen you before. Always good to meet a new face. Yes, indeed.'

'I'd've thought everyone was a stranger in London,'

said Adrian. 'I mean, it's mostly tourists round here, isn't it?'

'Oh, I don't know,' said the man. 'You'd be surprised. It's a village really.'

'Do you often play pin-ball?'

'Me? No. Got an office up the Charing Cross Road. I just like to look in most evenings on my way home. Yes, indeed.'

'Right.'

'I thought you were a girl at first with your hair and . . . everything.'

Adrian blushed. He didn't like to be reminded how long beard growth was in coming.

'No offence. I like it . . . it suits you.'

'Thanks.'

'Yes indeed. Yes indeedy-do.'

Adrian made a note, somewhere in the back of his mind, to get a haircut the next day.

'You sound a bit public school to me. Am I right?'

Adrian nodded.

'Harrow,' he said. He thought it a safe bet.

'Harrow, you say? Harrow! Dear me, I think you're going to be a bit of a hit. Yes indeed. You got anywhere to stay?'

'Well . . .'

'You can put up with me, if you like. It's just a small flat in Brewer Street, but it's local.'

'It's terribly kind of you . . . I'm looking for a job, you see.'

That's how simple it had been. One day a lazy student, the next a busy prostitute.

'Thing is, Hugo,' said Don, 'soon as I clapped eyes on you I thought, "That's not rent, that's the real

232

thing." I've been around the Dilly for fifteen years and I can spot 'em, indeedy-dumplings, I can. Now I'm sorry to say that I won't fancy you next week. Unplucked chicken is my speciality and I'll be bored stiff with you Thursday. Bored limp, more like. Hur, hur! But you cut your hair a bit – not too much – keep your Harrovian accent fit and you'll be clearing two ton a week. Yes indeed.'

'Two ton?'

'Two hundred, sunshine.'

'But what do I have to do?'

And Don told him. There were two principal amusement arcades, there was the Meat Rack, which was an iron pedestrian grille outside Playland, the more active of the arcades, and there was the Piccadilly Underground itself.

'But you want to watch that. Crawling with the law.'

Don wasn't a pimp. He worked at a perfectly respectable music publishing house in Denmark Street. Adrian paid him thirty pounds a week which covered his own accommodation and the use of the flat for tricks during the day. At night it was up to the tricks to provide the venue.

'Just don't start chewing gum, shooting horse or looking streetwise, that's all.'

At first the days passed slowly, each transaction nerve-racking and remarkable, but soon the quiet pulse of routine quickened the days. The young can become accustomed to the greatest drudgeries, like potato-harvesting or schoolwork, with surprising speed. Prostitution had at least the advantage of variety.

Adrian got on pretty well with the other rent-boys. Most of them were tougher and beefier than he was, skinheads with tattoos, braces and mean looks. They didn't regard him as direct competition and sometimes they even recommended him.

'Do you know of anyone less . . . chunky?' a punter might ask.

'You want to try Hugo, he'll be doing the *Times* crossword down the Bar Italia this time of the morning. Flared jumbo cords and a blazer. Can't miss him.'

Adrian was intrigued by the fact that the most prosperous, pin-striped clients went for the rough trade, while the wilder, less respectable tricks wanted more lightly muscled boys like him. Opposite poles attracted. The Jacobs wanted hairy men and the Esaus wanted smooth. It meant that he more than most had to learn to spot the sadists and nutters who were on the lookout for a sex-slave. One of the last things Adrian wanted was to be chained up, flogged and urinated over.

He liked to think that his rates were competitive but not insulting. A blow-job was ten quid to give, fifteen to receive. After a week he made up his mind to forbid anything up the anus. Some could take it and some couldn't: Adrian decided that he belonged to the latter category. A couple of boys tried to convince him, as he hobbled down Coventry Street after a particularly heavy night complaining that his back passage felt like a windsock, that he would soon get used to it, but he resolved – financially disadvantageous as it might be – that his rear section was to be firmly labelled a no-poking compartment. This was a proviso he had to make clear to clients at the opening of negotiations: between the thighs was fine – the intercrural method was, after all, endorsed by no less an authoritative source than the Ancient Greeks themselves – but he was buggered if he was going to be buggered. As long as he could get it up he didn't mind sodomising a client, but his own bronze eye was closed to all comers.

When business was slack he and some of the others would mix with the journalists and professional Soho drinkers in the French House in Dean Street. Gaston, the implausibly named landlord, had no objection to their presence so long as they didn't tout for custom there. The Golden Lion next door was for that. The regulars however – embittered painters and poets for whom the seventies were an unwelcome vacuum to be filled with vodka and argument – could be savagely impolite.

'We don't need your kind of filth in here,' a radio producer, whose watery seed Adrian had spat out only the previous night, shouted one afternoon. 'Get the fuck out!'

'How ill-bred!' Adrian had exclaimed as Gaston ejected the radio producer instead.

Like Adrian, most of the boys were self-employed; one or two had ponces, but in general pimping was a feature of the more highly structured sister profession of female prostitution. The boys were free to come and go as they pleased, no one was going to tell them where they could set up their stall, no one was going to take a cut of their hard-earned cash. The cash did come in at a pleasing rate but Adrian found he had little to spend it on. Drink didn't really appeal to him much and he was too afraid of drugs to be tempted to take so much as a single pill or a single puff of anything illegal. Every day he would walk to the post office behind St Martin's-in-the-Field and deposit his earnings into an account he had opened under the name of Hugo Bullock. It was all building up rather nicely.

Chickens worried him, though. These were the children of eleven, twelve and thirteen. Some were even younger. Adrian was no Mother Teresa and far too much of a coward to beg them to go home. They were tougher than he was and would have told him to get lost anyway. Besides, they had left their homes because life there was worse, in their eyes at least, than life on the streets. If there was one thing those children knew, it was where and when they were unhappy: there was no cloud of morality obscuring the clarity of their states of mind. They weren't popular with the majority of rent-boys, however, because they attracted television documentaries, clean-up campaigns and police attention, all of which interfered with and militated against the free flow of trade. Their customers, known not unnaturally as chickenhawks, were more nervous and cautious than Adrian's brand of client, so the chickens would have to do much more of the running than he could ever have dared to do. They would spot when they were being eyed up and step boldly forward.

'Lend us ten p for the machine, mister.'

'Oh, yes. Right. There you are.'

'Second thoughts, Dad, let's go away from here.'

It was unsettling to think of them being the same age as Cartwright. Cartwright would be sixteen going on seventeen now of course, but the Cartwright he would always know was thirteen going on fourteen.

The chickens leant up against the Meat Rack pushing their tightly denimed bums against the rails when, if only the stork had dropped them down a different chimney, they could have been clothed in white flannels, driving the ball past extra cover for four runs or wrestling with ablative absolutes in panelled class-rooms. If there was an accurate means of measuring happiness, with electrodes or chemicals, Adrian won-dered if the schoolboy would prove to be happier than the rent-boy. Would he feel less exploited, less shat upon? Adrian himself felt freer than he ever had, but he had never been sure that he was representative.

After three weeks he decided to take advantage of his flexible hours and spend five days at Lord's watching Thompson and Lillee tear the heart out of the English batting in the second Test. He arrived at the Grace Gate early and walked round to the back to see if he could get a glimpse of the players warming up in the nets.

As he made his way past the Stewards' Offices and the members' stands he thought he caught a glimpse of a familiar figure striding towards him. He turned and started to walk in the opposite direction.

'Adrian! My God, Adrian!'

He quickened his step, but found himself blocked by the incoming tide of spectators.

'Adrian!'

'Oh, hello, Uncle David.' Adrian smiled weakly up into the thunderous face of his mother's brother.

'Where the hell have you been this last month?'

'Oh, you know . . .'

'Have you been in touch with your mother and father yet?'

'Well . . . I have been meaning to write.'

Uncle David grabbed him by the arm.

'You come along with me, young man. *Sick* with worry your mother's been. *Sick*. How you could have *dared* . . .'

Adrian had the lowering experience of being publicly dragged into the MCC offices like an errant schoolboy, which he supposed was by and large what he was.

'Morning, David, caught a yobbo have you?' someone called as he was pulled up the steps.

'I certainly have!'

They bumped into a tall blond man in a blazer coming the other way who smiled at them.

'Morning, Sir David,' he said.

'Morning, Tony, best of luck.'

'Thanks,' said the tall man and walked on. Adrian stopped dead as it suddenly dawned on him who it had been.

'That was Tony Greig!'

'Well who did you expect to see here, you idiot? Ilie Nastase? This way.'

They had reached a small office whose walls were covered with prints of heroes from the Golden Age of cricket. Uncle David closed the door and pushed Adrian into a chair.

'Now then. Tell me where you are living.'

'Muswell Hill.'

'Address?'

'Fourteen Endicott Gardens.'

'Whose house is that?'

'It's a bed and breakfast place.'

'Do you have a job?'

Adrian nodded.

'Where?'

'I'm working in the West End.' The 'in' was redundant, but Uncle David was unlikely to be impressed by the truth.

'Doing what?'

'It's a theatrical agency in Denmark Street. I make the coffee, that kind of thing.'

'Right. There's a pen, there's paper. I want you to write down the address in Muswell Hill and the address in Denmark Street. Then you are to write a letter to your parents. Have you any idea what you've put them through? They went to the police, for God's sake! What the hell was it all about, Adrian?'

Here he was in another study, in another chair, facing another angry man and being asked another set of impossible questions. 'Why do you do this sort of thing?' 'Why can't you concentrate?' 'Why can't you behave like everyone else?' 'What's the matter with you?'

Adrian knew that if he answered 'I don't know' in a sulky voice, Uncle David would, like dozens before him, snort and bang the table and shout back, 'What do you *mean*, you don't know? You must know. Answer me!'

Adrian stared at the carpet.

'Well?' asked Uncle David.

'I don't know,' Adrian said sulkily.

'What do you *mean*, you don't know? You must know. Answer me!'

'I was unhappy.'

'Unhappy? Well why couldn't you have *told* someone? Can you imagine how your mother felt when you didn't come home? When no one knew where you were? That's *unhappy* for you. Can you imagine it? No, of course you can't.'

Beyond a pewter mug at his Christening, a Bible at his Confirmation, a copy of Wisden every birthday and regular bluff shoulder-clapping and by-Christ-you've-grown-ing, Uncle David hadn't taken his sponsorial duties to Adrian with any spectacular seriousness, and it was unsettling to see him now glaring and breathing heavily down his nostrils as if he had been personally affronted by his godson's flight. Adrian didn't think he'd earned the right to look that angry.

'I just felt I had to get away.'

'I dare say. But to be so underhand, so . . . sly. To sneak away without saying a word. That was the act of a coward and a rotter. You'll write that letter.'

Uncle David left the room, locking the door behind him. Adrian sighed and turned to the desk. He noticed a silver letter-opener on the desk in the shape of a cricket bat. He held it to the light and saw the engraved signature of Donald Bradman running obliquely across the splice. Adrian slipped it into the inside pocket of his blazer and settled down to write.

Under a Portrait of Prince Ranjitsinhji,
A funny little office near the Long Room,
Lord's Cricket Ground,
June 1975

Dear Mother and Father,

I'm so sorry I ran away without saying goodbye. Uncle David tells me that you have been worrying about me, not too much I hope.

I'm living in a Bed and Breakfast place in 14
Endicott Gardens, Highgate, and I have a job
in a theatrical agency called Leon Bright's, 59
Denmark Street, WC2. I'm a sort of messen-
ger and office-boy, but it's a good job and I
hope to rent a flat soon.

I am well and happy and truly sorry if I have
upset you. I will write soon and at length to
explain why I felt I had to leave. Please try
and forgive

Your doting son

Adrian

PS I met the new England Captain, Tony
Greig, today.

Twenty minutes later, Uncle David returned and
read it through.

'I suppose that will do. Leave it with me and I'll see
that it's posted.'

He looked Adrian up and down.

'If you looked halfway decent I'd invite you to
watch from the Members' Stand.'

'That's all right.'

'Come tomorrow wearing a tie and I'll see what I
can do.'

'That's awfully kind. I'd love to.'

'They give you days off to watch cricket, do they?
From this place in Denmark Street? Just like that?'

'Like the Foreign Office, you mean?'

'Fair point, you cheeky little rat. And get your hair cut. You look like a tart.'

'Heavens! Do I?'

Adrian did not return to Lord's the next day, nor any of the other days. Instead he had gone back to work and found time to hang around the Tottenham Court Road catching Tony Greig's ninety-six and Lillee's maddening seventy-three on the banks of televisions in the electrical appliance shop windows.

The risk of meeting people he knew was acute. He remembered how Dr Watson in the first Sherlock Holmes story had described Piccadilly Circus as a great cesspool into which every idler and lounger of the Empire was irresistibly drained. It seemed now that as the Empire had dwindled in size, so the strength of the Circus's pull had grown. Britain was a draining bath and Piccadilly, its plug-hole, now seemed almost audibly to gurgle as it sucked in the last few gallons of waste.

It was part of Adrian's job, in the centre of the whirlpool, to scrutinise every face that eddied past. Innocent passers-by tended not to meet the glances of strangers, so he usually found himself able to turn away in time if there was someone he knew in the area.

One rainy afternoon, however, about a fortnight after the meeting with his Uncle David, while sheltering in a favourite pitch under the columns of Swan and Edgar, touting for business, he caught sight of Dr Meddlar, without his dog collar but unmistakable nevertheless, coming up the steps from the Underground.

Term must be over, Adrian thought as he concealed himself behind a pillar.

He watched Meddlar look left and right before crossing over to Boots the Chemists under the neon signs. Greg and Mark, a couple of skinheads that Adrian knew, were going about their unlawful business there, and he was amazed to see Meddlar stop and talk to one of them. He was trying to look casual, but to Adrian's knowing eye it was perfectly clear that formal discussions were taking place.

Hopping through the traffic, Adrian approached from behind.

'Why, Dr Meddlar!' he cried, slapping him bonhomously on the back.

Meddlar spun round.

'Healey!'

'My dear old Chaplain, how simply splendid to see you!' Adrian shook him warmly by the hand. 'But let me give you a piece of advice – *verb sap* as we used to say at the dear old school – if they're asking more than a tenner for you to suck their cocks, you're being ripped off.'

Meddlar went white and stepped backwards off the kerb.

'You're leaving?' Adrian was disappointed. 'Oh, if you must. But any time you're in need of rough sex let me know and I'll fix you up with something. But as the man said in *Casablanca*, "Beware, there are vultures everywhere. Everywhere, vultures."'

Meddlar disappeared into a mess of spray and car horns.

'Remember the Green Cross Code,' Adrian called

after him. 'Because I won't be there when you cross the road.'

The skinheads were not pleased.

'You bastard, Hugo! We were about to score.'

'I'll pay you in full, my dears,' said Adrian. 'It was worth it. Meanwhile let me stand you both a Fanta in the Wimpy. There's no action going on in this bloody rain.'

They sat by the window, automatically scanning the crowds that blurred past.

'Why did he call you "Healey"?' asked Greg. 'I thought your name was Bullock?'

'Healey was my nickname,' said Adrian. 'I used to do impressions of Denis Healey the politician, you see. It sort of stuck.'

'Oh.'

'What a silly billy,' Adrian added, by way of proof.

'That's just like him!'

'Well, it's just like Mike Yarwood anyway.'

'And that guy really was a vicar?'

'School Chaplain, on my life.'

'Bloody hell. He was asking Terry and me if we'd tie him up. And him a bleeding Collar.'

'"I struck the board and cried No More!" said Adrian, folding his hands in prayer.

'You what?'

'George Herbert. A poem called "The Collar". It must have passed you by somehow. "Have I no garlands gay? All blasted? All wasted? Not so my heart: but there is fruit, and thou hast hands."'

'Oh. Right. Yeah.'

'You were the garlands gay, the fruit. And his hands were about to lay themselves on you, I suspect.

244

He must have forgotten how it ends. "At every word, Methought I heard one calling, *Child!* And I replied, *My Lord*."'

'You don't half rabbit, do you?'

'It's a splendid poem, you'd love it. I can sprint down to Hatchards and buy a copy if you'd like.'

'Fuck off.'

'Yes, well, there is that side to it too, of course,' Adrian conceded. 'Now, if you'll forgive me, I've got to nip next door to Boots and get myself some more lotion for the old crabs.'

About two months later he was picked up by an actor.

'I know you,' Adrian said, as they sat back in the taxi.

The actor took off his sunglasses.

'Christ!' Adrian giggled. 'You're – '

'Just call me Guy,' said the actor. 'It's my real name.'

A famous trick! Adrian thought to himself. I've turned a famous trick!

He stayed the night, something he had been warned against. Guy had woken him up with smoked salmon and scrambled eggs and a kiss.

'I couldn't believe you were trade, honey,' he said. 'I saw you walk from Playland to the Dilly and I couldn't fucking *believe* it.'

'Oh well,' said Adrian modestly, 'I haven't been at it long.'

'And Hugo, too! My favourite name. It's always been my favourite name.'

'One does one's best.'

'Will you stay with me, Hugo baby?'

The invitation couldn't have come at a better time for Adrian. Three days before he had caught sight of himself in the mirror of the Regent Palace Hotel cloakroom and been shocked to see the face of a whore looking back at him.

He didn't know how or why he had changed, but he had. Only the tiniest amount of bumfluff grew on his chin and when he shaved it off he was still as smooth as a ten-year-old. His hair was shorter, but not coiffured or poncey. His jeans were tight, but no tighter than any student's. Yet the face had screamed 'Rent'.

He smiled engagingly at the mirror. A cheap invitation leered back.

He raised his eyebrows and tried a lost, innocent look.

Fifteen quid for a blow-job. Nothing up the arse, his reflection replied.

A couple of weeks out of the Dilly would give him a chance to bring back some of the peaches and cream.

Guy lived in a small house in Chelsea and was about to start shooting a film at Shepperton Studios. He had been cruising Piccadilly for a last treat before throwing himself into five weeks of rising at six and working till eight.

'But now I've got a friend to come home to. It's wonderful, honey, wonderful!'

Adrian thought that to have someone to answer the telephone, do the shopping and keep the place tidy for him was indeed wonderful.

'I had an Irish cleaner once, but the bitch threatened to go to the press, so I don't trust anyone to come in now. I trust you, though, cutie-pie.'

The public school accent. If only they knew.

'I may be right, I may be wrong,' he sang to himself in the shower, 'But I'm perfectly willing to swear, That when you turned and smiled at me, A prostitute wept in Soho Square.'

So Adrian stayed and learnt how to cook and shop and be charming at dinner parties. Guy's friends were mostly producers and writers and actors, only a few of them gay. Adrian was the only one who called him Guy, which added a special and publicly endearing touch to the friendship. Guy was thirty-five and had been married at the age of nineteen. The child from this marriage lived with the ex-wife, an actress who had taken Guy's announcement of homosexuality very badly, instantly remarrying and denying Guy any access to his son.

'He must be about your age now, couple of years younger perhaps. I bet he's a screaming madam. It would serve the bitch right.'

One evening Guy's agent, Michael Morahan, and his wife Angela came to dinner. They arrived before Guy had returned from Shepperton so Adrian did his best to entertain them in the kitchen where he was chopping peppers.

'We've heard a lot about you,' said Angela, dropping her ocelot stole onto the kitchen table.

'Golden opinions, I trust?'

'Oh yes, you've done Tony nothing but good.'

Michael Morahan opened a bottle of wine.

'That's a seventy-four,' said Adrian. 'It'll need to be decanted or at least breathe for an hour. There's a Sancerre in the fridge if you'd rather.'

'Thank you, this will be fine,' was the blunt reply. 'I understand from Tony that you're an O.H.?'

Adrian had already noticed the Old Harrovian tie around Morahan's neck and had his answer prepared.

'Well, to tell you the truth,' he said, 'that's a rumour that I sort of allowed to get around. Security,' he said, tapping the side of his nose. 'I may as well tell you that Hugo Bullock isn't my real name either.'

Morahan stared unpleasantly.

'So. A mystery man from nowhere. Does Tony know that?'

'Oh dear, do you think he should?'

'I'm sure not,' said Angela. 'Anyone can tell you're trustworthy.'

They went through to the sitting room, Adrian wiping his hands on a blue-and-white-striped butcher's apron he liked to wear when cooking.

'I have to look after him, you see,' said Morahan. 'Under age and anonymous is worrying.'

'I'll be eighteen in a couple of weeks.'

'You'll still be under age by three years. A man's career can be ruined. It nearly happened last year.'

'It wouldn't exactly do *my* career any good either, would it? So we're in a position of mutual trust, I'd've thought.'

'What do you have to lose exactly?'

'The bubble, reputation.'

'Really?'

'Yes, really.'

Angela intervened.

'It's just that we have to be sure . . . I'm sure you understand, Hugo darling . . . we have to be sure that you're not going to . . . to *hurt* Tony.'

248

'But why on earth should I?'

'Oh come on, man!' Morahan snorted. 'You know what we're saying.'

'You're saying that Guy, who is thirty-five years old, rich, famous and experienced in the ways of the world, is a poor trusting innocent to be protected and I, half his age, am a corrupting devil who might hurt him? Blackmail him, I suppose is what you mean.'

'I'm sure Michael never meant that . . .'

'I shall go to the kitchen and crush a garlic.'

Angela followed him in.

'It's his job, Hugo. You must understand.'

It might have been the garlic and the onions that he was chopping, it might have been anger, it might have been nothing more than performance – because it seemed dramatically the right thing to do under the circumstances – but for whatever reason, tears were in Adrian's eyes. He wiped them away. 'I'm sorry, Angela.'

'Darling, don't be ridiculous. Everything's going to be fine. Michael just wanted to . . . find me a cigarette would you? . . . he just wanted to be sure.'

They heard Guy coming up the stairs.

'Yoo-hoo, honey-bear! Daddy's home.'

Adrian winced at the language. Angela squeezed his arm.

'You love him, don't you, darling?' she whispered.

Adrian nodded. He might as well have this awful woman on his side.

'Everything's going to be fine,' she said, kissing him on the cheek.

Adrian displayed just the right kind of affection towards Guy over dinner. Not whorish, but adoring;

not clinging or possessive, but happy and trusting. Michael and Angela went away full of praise for his cooking, his wit and his discretion.

Guy was very touched. He nuzzled up to Adrian on the sofa.

'You're my very special puppy and I don't deserve you. You're magical and wonderful and you're never to leave.'

'Never?'

'Never.'

'What about when I'm fat and hairy?'

'Don't be a silly baby. Come bye-byes with Guy-Guy.'

On the evening before his last day of filming, Guy asked Adrian to take an envelope to a house in Battersea and bring back the reply. Zak, the man to whom he was to deliver the envelope, would be expecting him, but he was a famous Dutch pop-star, shy of publicity, so Adrian shouldn't be surprised if he behaved oddly.

Adrian couldn't think of any Dutch pop-stars who needed to be shy of publicity in South London, but Guy's manner and lack of soupy terms of endearment suggested that this was a serious business, so he said nothing and next morning went happily on his way.

Zak was friendly enough.

'Boyfriend of Tony? Hi, good to meet you. You got something for me?'

Adrian handed him the envelope.

'Guy . . . I mean Tony . . . said there'd be a reply.'

'A reply? Sure, I've got a reply. You wait here one moment.'

The envelope containing the reply was sealed and

Adrian walked back over Chelsea Bridge, debating with himself whether or not to steam it open and read it when he got back to the house. He decided against it. Guy trusted him and it would be exhilarating to be so honest for a change. Instead he pulled out his copy of *Antigone* and read as he walked. It was something of a pose, he liked the idea of being seen reading a book in French, but he also wanted to keep fluent. It always caused a sensation in the Dilly when he was able to give directions to French tourists or, indeed, to do business with them.

He reached the King's Road and turned left. There was some kind of a scuffle going on outside the King's Tavern. A group of glue-sniffers was fighting with spray cans. One of them sprayed red paint over Adrian as he tried to hurry past.

'Oh, look what you've done!' he cried.

'Oh, look what you've done!' they shouted back, mimicking his accent. 'Fuck off, arsehole.'

They were not in a mood to be spoken to, so Adrian moved smartly away. But they decided to abandon their game and give chase.

Oh shit, Adrian thought to himself, as he ran into Bywater Street. Why did I say anything at all? You idiot, Adrian! You're going to get twenty types of crap beaten out of you now. He could hear them catching up with him. But then . . . joy of joys! He heard the wee-waa, wee-waa of a police car drawing up.

Two of the kids scattered, with an officer sprinting after them. But the other three were pushed against a wall and searched.

'Thank God,' panted Adrian.

'Against that wall,' said a sergeant.

'Sorry?'

'Against that wall.'

'But I'm the one they were chasing!'

'You heard me.'

Adrian spread his legs against the wall and assumed the position.

'What's this?'

'What's what?' said Adrian. All he could see was a brick wall.

'This,' said the policeman, turning him round and holding up an envelope.

'Oh, it's a message. Belongs to a friend of mine. It's private.'

'A message?'

'That's right.'

The policeman ripped the envelope open and pulled out a polythene sachet of white powder.

'Funny kind of message.'

'What is it?' asked Adrian.

The policeman opened the sachet and dipped a finger into the powder.

'Well, flower,' he said as he sucked the finger, 'I'd say it was two years. Two years easy.'

A table, two chairs, a door that squeaked, cigarette smoke, no window, yellowing gloss paint, the distant murmur of the King's Road, the unblinking brown eyes of Detective Sergeant Canter of the Drug Squad.

'Look, you say it's not yours. You were delivering it for a friend. You've never used the stuff yourself. You didn't even know what it was. Frankly, Hugo, I believe you. But if you don't tell us the name of this friend, then I'm sorry to say that you'll be drowning in a bucket of hot shit without a life-belt.'

'But I *can't*, I really can't. It would ruin him.'

'It's not going to do you a lot of good, either, is it?'

Adrian clutched his head in his hands. Canter was friendly, amused, indifferent and tenacious.

'I've got to think up a charge, you see. What can I choose? There's possession. Let me see . . . how much was it? Seven grammes of Charlie . . . bit dodgy, that. Rather a lot for personal use. But first offence, you're young. Reckon we could get away with six months DC.'

'DC?'

'Detention Centre, Hugo. Not nice, but quick. Short sharp shock. Then there's possession with intent to supply. You're looking at two years straight away, now. Then we have to think about trafficking. They throw away the key for that one.'

'But . . .'

'The thing is, Hugo, I've got a problem here you have to help me with. You've already told me that you don't take it yourself, so I can't really charge you with possession, can I? If you don't powder your own nose, you must have been intending to flog it to someone else. Stands to reason.'

'But he wasn't paying me! It was just an errand, I didn't know what it was.'

'Mm.' Sergeant Canter looked down at his notes. 'Rather a lot of cash in your post-office account, isn't there? Where's all that from, then?'

'That's mine! I've . . . I've saved it. I've never had anything to do with drugs. I promise!'

'But I look down at my notes and I don't see any

names. All I see is "Hugo Bullock nicked in possession of a quarter ounce of best Bolivian Marching Powder." No one else for my charge-sheet. Just Hugo Bullock. I need the name of the man you collected it from and I need the name of your friend, don't I?'

Adrian shook his head.

The detective sergeant patted him on the shoulder.

'Lover is he?'

Adrian blushed.

'He's just . . . a friend.'

'Yeah. That's right. Yeah. How old are you, Hugo?'

'Eighteen next week.'

'There you go. I think I better have his name, don't you? He corrupts a nice well-brought-up young kid and he sends him to pick up his cocaine for him. The court will weep big tears for you, my son. Probation and sympathy.'

Adrian stared down at the table.

'The other man,' he said. 'The man I got it off. I'll give you his name.'

'Well, that's a start.'

'But he mustn't know that I told you.'

He had a sudden vision of a Godfather-like revenge being wreaked against him. Adrian, the man who grassed, beaten to a pulp in a prison, a brown-paper parcel of two dead fishes sent to his parents.

'I mean he won't ever know, will he? I won't have to give evidence against him or anything?'

'Calm down, Hugo, old lad. If he's a dealer we put him under surveillance and we catch him in the act. Your name never comes into it.'

Sergeant Canter leant forward, gently raised Adrian's chin with a finger, and looked into his eyes.

'That's a promise, Hugo. Believe me.'

Adrian nodded.

'But you'd better start talking quick. Your boy-friend is going to be wondering where you are by now. We don't want him to call his dealer friend up on the blower, do we?'

'No.'

'No. He'll be out of it quick as shit off a shovel and then Hugo Bullock will still be the only name on my list.'

'He . . . my friend won't miss me until the evening.'

'I see, what's his job?'

'Look, I said. I'm only going to tell you about the other man.'

'My pencil is poised, Hugo.'

After Adrian had signed his statement they brought him a cup of tea. A detective inspector came in to read through it. He glanced at Adrian.

'Looks like you're in a bit of luck, Bullock. Zak is not exactly a stranger to us. About five nine, you say?'

'Well I said I thought he was about the same size as Sergeant Canter.'

'Stud in the left ear?'

'I'm pretty sure it was the left.'

'Yeah. We lost the bastard a couple of months ago. If he's where you say he is you've done us a bit of a favour.'

'Oh well. Anything to help.'

The detective inspector laughed.

'Get him charged and sorted out with a brief, John. Possession.'

'What's a brief?' asked Adrian when the inspector had gone.

'Solicitor.'

'Oh. I thought . . . you know, legal aid. Don't you provide one?'

'A boy like you . . . your parents are going to want to appoint one.'

'My parents?'

'Yeah. What's their address?'

'I'd . . . I'd much rather keep my parents out of it. They don't know where I am you see and I've put them through enough really.'

'They file you as a missing person?'

'Yes . . . I mean, I think they did go to the police. I bumped into my godfather and he said they had.'

'I think they'd be happier knowing where you are then, don't you?'

But Adrian remained firm and was led to the desk to be charged as Hugo Bullock.

'Empty your pockets on the desk, please.'

His possessions were examined and itemised in a ledger.

'You have to sign so that when you get them back you know we haven't robbed you,' said Canter.

'Oh lordy lord, I trust you,' said Adrian, who was beginning to enjoy himself. 'If a chap can't consign his chattels to an honest constable without suspicion then what has the world come to?'

'Yeah, right. We'll need your signature anyway. Oh, and there's one other thing, Adrian.'

'Yes?'

'Ah,' said Canter. 'So it's Adrian Healey, is it? Not Hugo Bullock.'

Damn, shit, bollocks and buggery-fuck.

D.S. Canter was holding up Anouilh's *Antigone*. Adrian's name was written on the fly-leaf.

'Clever lad like you, falling for a trick like that,' he tutted. 'No Bullock on the missing persons list, you see. But I bet there'll be a Healey, won't there?'

II

A bell rang in the corridor, doors slammed and voices rose in anger.

'Watch yourself, Ashcroft, one more sound out of you and you're on report.'

'But what did I do?'

Adrian shut his eyes and tried to concentrate on the letter he was writing.

'Right! I warned you. Loss of privileges for a week.'

He took a piece of paper and spread it flat on the table. A cold wind blew outside and the sky had darkened to gunmetal grey. Snow was on the way.

'Please Mr Annendale, may I get a book from the library?'

'If you hurry.'

Adrian picked up a pen and began.

13th February 1978

Dear Guy,

I have been meaning to pluck up the nerve to write to you for some time. I was finally pricked into action by seeing you in *The Likeness* the other night. You were brilliant as always. I loved you in both parts – though the Good Shelford reminded me more of the Guy I Know (up in the gallery) . . .

I wonder if you found out what happened to me? I have a feeling that you imagined me skipping off with your money. But perhaps you heard the truth. The fact is that after I had been to see your friend Zak I was arrested by the police in possession of your end-of-shoot cocaine – you were just finishing *The Red Roof* if you remember. You'll be pleased to know, by the way, that Zak wasn't ripping you off – the haul was described in court as seven grammes of highest quality Andean flake.

It may be that you've been suffering from a guilty conscience about my innocent involvement in the whole affair, but if you have, I can now cheerfully relieve you of that burden. I was treated well and never put under pressure to reveal any names.

The old parents rallied round with character witnesses – godfathers, bishops, generals, even my old Housemaster at school would you believe? – and with squads of armed and dangerous solicitors. What chance did the magistrates stand? It was only by calling on all their reserves of pride and self-control that they managed to summon up the nerve even to put me on probation. I think one of them was so overcome by my quiet dignity and round-eyed innocence that he came within an ace of recommending some kind of civilian award for me.

Since then I have been to a crammer's in Stroud, passed exams and find myself filling in time teaching at a prep school in Norfolk before going off to St Matthew's College, Cambridge – not quite poacher turned game-keeper . . . slave turned slave-master? Something like it. Boy turned man, I suppose.

My name, as you probably know, is as far from Hugo Bullock as a name can be without actually falling over, but I won't bother you with it. This is just to wish you well and thank you for a month or two of unsurpassable fun and frolic.

I hope you are now treating your nostrils as well as you treated

Your very own

Hugo Bullock

There was a knock on the door.

'Please, sir, can I ask a question?'

'Newton, I distinctly heard with my own two ears – these, the ones I put on this morning because they go so well with my eyes – that Mr Annendale gave you permission to go to the library and get a book. I did not hear him give you permission to come to my room.'

'It's just a quick question . . .'

'Oh, very well.'

'Is it true, sir, that you and Matron are having an affair?'

'Out, out! Get out! Out before I slash your throat with a knife and hang you dripping with blood from the flag-pole. Out, before I pull your guts from your body and stuff them down your mouth. Out, before I become mildly irritated. Go, hence, begone. Stand not upon the order of your going, but go at once. Run! run quickly from here, run to the other side of Europe, flee for your life nor give not one backward glance. I never hope to see you again in this world or the next. Never speak to me, never approach me, never advertise your presence to me by the smallest sound, or by the living God that made me I will do such things . . . I know not what they are but they will be the terrors of the earth. Flee hence, be not here, but somewhere in a vast Elsewhere to which I have no access. Boys who rub me up the wrong way, Newton, come to a sticky end. Be removed, piss off, *heraus*, get utterly outly out.'

'Thought so.'

'Grr!'

Adrian flung a book at the hastily closing door, signed the letter and lit a pipe. The snow had started to fall.

He had no more duties for the day so he decided to do a bit more work on *The Aunt That Exploded*, a play for the end of term that he had been cajoled into writing.

If Harvey-Potter was going to play Aunt Bewinda, something would have to be done about preserving his soprano. A definite fissure had appeared in his larynx at breakfast and a tenor Bewinda would be worse than useless. He should talk to Clare about deliberately shrinking the boy's underpants in the laundry. Anything to keep nature at bay for two months.

He still had to work on Maxted, the only master who had so far refused to participate.

'You can kick my arse from here to Norwich, Adrian, I'm not going to dress up in shorts for any man living.'

The principal idea of the play was that boys played grown-ups, parents, aunts, doctors and schoolmasters, and the staff played boys and, in the case of Matron, a little girl.

'Come on Oliver, even the Brigadier has agreed. It'll be wonderful.'

'If you can tell me in one word what's wrong with *The Mikado*?'

'No, can't do that. "It's crap" is two words and "It's complete crap" is three.'

'Of course *The Mikado* is crap, but it's good healthy stodgy crap. Your blasted play is either going to be horrible pebbly crap or a great gush of liquid crap.'

'I'll do all your duties this term. How about that?'

'No you bloody won't.'

That hadn't been such a clever offer. Maxted *enjoyed* being on duty.

'Well I think you're a heel and a stinker and I hope that one day you'll be found out.'

'Found out? What do you mean?'

'Ho hee!' said Adrian, who knew that everyone lived in fear of being found out.

But Maxted was not to be moved, which was a

nuisance because, set off in shorts and school-cap, his paunch and purple complexion would have been terrifically striking. Perhaps Adrian himself would have to play Bewinda's nephew. Not ideal casting: he was still closer in age to the boys than to any of the staff.

But it was a snug problem, the perfect sort of problem for a man in a tweed jacket, sitting in a fire-lit room with a good briar pipe between his teeth, a glass of Glennfiddich at his elbow and a blizzard whipping up outside, to ponder over. A clean problem for a clean man with a clean mind in the clean countryside.

He rubbed his fingers against the grain of his stubble and thought.

All gone. All anger quelled, all desire drained, all thirst slaked, all madness past.

There would be cricket next term, coaching and umpiring, teaching the young idea how to deal with the ball that goes on with the arm, reading them Browning and Heaney on the lawn when the sun shone and it was too hot to teach indoors. The rest of the summer would be spent discovering Milton and Proust and Tolstoy ready for Cambridge in October where, like Cranmer – but with a bicycle instead of a horse – his mind and thighs would find exercise. A handful of civilised friends, not too close.

'What do you make of that bloke in your college, Healey?'

'He's hard to get to know. I *like* him, but he's private, he's unfathomable.'

'Detached somehow . . . almost serene.'

Then a degree and back here or to another school –

his own perhaps. Stay on at Cambridge even . . . if he got a First.

All gone.

He didn't believe himself for a moment, of course.

He looked at his reflection in the window. 'It's no good trying to fool me, Healey,' he said, 'an Adrian always knows when an Adrian is lying.'

But an Adrian also knew that an Adrian's lies were real: they were lived and felt and acted out as thoroughly as another man's truths – if other men had truths – and he believed it possible that this last lie might see him through to the grave.

He watched the snow building up against the window and his mind caught the tube to Piccadilly and climbed the steps from the Underground.

There stood Eros, the boy with the bow poised to shoot, and there stood Adrian, the schoolmaster in tweeds and cavalry twills, looking up at him and slowly shaking his head.

'Of course you know why Eros was put in the Circus in the first place, don't you?' he remembered saying to a sixteen-year-old who was sharing his pitch outside the London Pavilion one July evening.

'Named after the Eros Strip Club, was it?'

'Oh that's close, but I'm afraid I can't give it you, I'll have to pass the question over. It was part of a tribute to the Earl of Shaftesbury: a grateful nation honours the man who abolished child labour. Alfred Gilbert, the sculptor, positioned Eros with his bow and arrow aiming up Shaftesbury Avenue.'

'Yeah? Well, fuck all that, there's a trick over there been eyeing you up for the past five minutes.'

'Had him. Overuses the teeth. He can find someone

else to circumcise. The point is, it's a kind of visual pun, Eros burying his shaft up Shaftesbury Avenue. You see?'

'Then why's he pointing down Lower Regent Street?'

'He was taken down and cleaned during the war and the fools who put him back up didn't know buggery ding-dong shit.'

'He could do with cleaning again.'

'I don't know. I think Eros should be dirty. In Greek legend, as I'm sure you are aware, he fell in love with the minor deity Psyche. It was the Greek way of saying that, in spite of what it may believe, Love pursues the Soul, not the body; the Erotic desires the Psychic. If Love was clean and wholesome he wouldn't lust after Psyche.'

'He's still looking this way.'

'His bottom is, at any rate.'

'No, the trick. He's started cruising me now.'

'I will clear away for you. Too many cocks spoil the brothel. Have him with my blessing. Just don't come crawling to me with your glans half hanging off, that's all.'

'I'll give him a minute to make up his mind.'

'Do that. I'm bound to wonder, meanwhile, was there any life more futile and perfectly representative than that of Lord Shaftesbury? His own adored son killed in a schoolboy fight at Eton while his national monument daily supervises child labour of a nature and intensity he would never have guessed at.'

'I'm definitely on here. See you later.'

Adrian dropped a log on the fire and stared into the flames. He was as secure as anyone: a real teacher with a real name, real references and real qualifications. No forgeries or tricks had brought him here, only merit. No one on earth could bang into the room and drag him to judgement. He really was a schoolmaster in a real school, really stirring a real fire in a safe and snug common room that was as real as the winter weather that really raged in the real world outside. He had as much right to pour a finger of ten-year-old malt and puff a soothing pipeful of the ready-rubbed as anyone in England. The grown-up didn't live who had the power to snatch away the bottle, confiscate the pipe or reduce him to stammered excuses.

Yet the sparks that spat up the flue spelt Wrigleys and Coke and Toshiba in Piccadilly neon; the escape of steam from the logs hissed a meeting of prefects plotting punishment.

He knew he could never jingle change in his pocket or park his car like a confident adult, he was the Adrian he had always been, casting a guilty look over a furtive shoulder, living in eternal dread of a grown-up striding forward to clip his ear.

But there again, when he sipped at the whisky his eyes failed to water and his throat forgot to burn. The body shamelessly welcomed what once it would have rejected. At breakfast he demanded not Ricicles and chocolate spread, but coffee and unbuttered toast. And if the coffee was sugared he leapt from it like a colt from an electric fence. He ate the crust and left the filling, guzzled the olives and spurned the cherries. Yet inside he remained the same Adrian who fought down the urge to stand and shout 'Bollocks' during church services, smelt his own farts and wasted hours skimming through *National Geographic* on the off-chance of seeing a few naked bodies.

He turned back to his work with a sigh. God could worry about what he was and what he wasn't. There was the tea-party scene to be written.

He hadn't been working for more than ten minutes when there came another knock at the door.

'If that is anyone under the age of thirteen they have my permission to go and drown themselves.'

The door opened and a cheery face peered round.

'Wotcher, cock, thought I'd come and cadge a drink.'

'My dear Matron, you can't have run out of Gees linctus again.'

She came and looked over his shoulder.

'How's it going?'

'The agony of composition. Got to keep everyone satisfied. I'm preparing a huge part for you.'

She massaged his neck.

'I can take it.'

'Oh you proud, snorting beauty, how I love you.'

It was a private joke that the boys had somehow got wind of. She was a thoroughbred filly and he was her trainer. Adrian had started it when he found out that her father bred race-horses for a living. She looked the part too, with a great mane of chestnut hair and dark eyes that she rolled in mock passion when Adrian patted her hindquarters.

She had come to Chartham as an assistant matron at the age of sixteen and had been there ever since. There were rumours amongst the staff that she was a lesbian, but Adrian put that down to wishful thinking on their part. She was now such an attractive twenty-five-year-old that they had to find some excuse for not desiring her and her liking for jeans and jackets over skirts and blouses made sapphic preferences an obvious escape route for them.

She had latched onto Adrian as soon as he had arrived.

'She always pretends to pant after new masters,' Maxted had said. 'It's just showing off to the boys to disguise her dykery. Tell her to bog off.'

But Adrian enjoyed her company: she was brisk and clean. Her breasts were high and handsome, her thighs strong and supple and she was teaching him to drive. Despite the heat of their language they had never come close to anything physical, but the thought beat its wings in the air whenever they were together.

He watched her wandering around his room, picking things up, examining them and putting them down again in the wrong place.

'She's restless, she needs a good gallop over the downs,' he said.

She went to the window.

'It's really settling, isn't it?'

'What is?'

'The snow.'

'I find it unsettling as a matter of fact. I'm on duty tomorrow and I shall have to find something for the boys to do. The rugger pitch will be four foot under if it carries on at this rate.'

'The school was cut off from the outside world for a whole week in seventy-four.'

'And it's been cut off ever since.'

She sat on the bed.

'I'm leaving at the end of the year.'

'Really? Why?'

'I'll have been here nearly ten years. It's enough. I'll go home.'

Every member of staff spoke regularly about leaving at the end of the year. It was their way of showing that they weren't stuck, that they had a choice. It meant nothing, they always came back.

'But who will spoon out the little darlings' malt? Who will paint their warts and kiss the place and make it well? Chartham needs you.'

'I mean it, Ade. Clare is fretting in her loose-box.'

'It's time some stallion was found to cover you, certainly,' Adrian agreed. 'The colts here have been very disappointing and the staff are all geldings.'

'Except you.'

'Ah, but I've still a few seasons of racing left in me before I get put out. After I've won the Cambridge Hurdles my stud fees will be that much higher.'

'You're not a queer are you, Adrian?'

He was startled by the question.

'Well,' he said, 'I know what I like.'

'And do you like me?'

'Do I like you? I'm flesh and blood aren't I? How could anyone not be thrilled by your tightly fleshed points, your twitching hocks, your quivering neck, your shining hindquarters, your heaving, shimmering flanks?'

'Then for God's sake, fuck me. I'm going mad.'

For all his talk, Adrian had never experienced a human being of another gender before and writhing around with Clare, he was astonished by the strength of her desire. He hadn't expected that women actually felt the kind of urge and appetite that drove men. Everyone knew, surely, that females went for personality, strength and security and were resigned to the need to be penetrated only if that was the price for keeping the man they loved? That they should arch their backs, spread wide the lips of their sex in hunger and urge him in was something for which he was not prepared. Adrian's room was at the top of the school and they had locked the door, but he couldn't help feeling that everyone would be able to hear her squeals and roars of pleasure.

'Bang me, you bastard, bang me hard! Harder! Deeper and harder, you lump of shit. God that's good.'

It explained all those jokes about bedsprings. The sex he had taken part in up until now didn't build up these colossal pounding rhythms. He found himself driving faster and faster and joining in her shouts.

'I . . . think . . . that . . . I'm . . . about . . . to . . . wheeeeeee! . . . whooooo! . . . haaaaaaa . . .'

He collapsed on her as she thrashed herself calm. Panting and sweating, they wound down together into a kind of breathless quiet.

She gripped his shoulders.

'You beautiful fucking son of a bitch. My God I needed that. Woof!'

'As a matter of fact,' gasped Adrian, 'I think I did too.'

Clare taught him a great deal that term.

'Sex is meaningless,' she said, 'if it's silent and mechanical. You have to think about it and plan it, like a dinner party or a cricket match. I tell you when to put in, how it's feeling, you tell me what you like, when you're coming, how you want me to move. Just remember that you have never thought a thought or imagined an act that is so dirty and depraved that I won't have thought of it thousands of times myself. That's true of everyone. When we stop talking and joking we'll know it's over.'

Two nights after the last day of term the headmaster and his wife had gone out to a dinner party, so Clare and Adrian found they had the whole school to themselves. It was cold, but they had run naked around the classrooms where she had thrown herself over a desk to be spanked, into the kitchens where they had hurled jam and lard at each other, into the staff common room where he had pumped her up with the football pump, into the boys' showers where she had urinated over his face and finally into the gymnasium where they had rolled and rolled over the mats, shrieking and slithering and jerking in frenzy.

He lay looking up at the climbing ropes that hung from the ceiling. During the act all his senses had been suspended, but now it was over he felt the bruise on his shoulder where he had barged into a door, smelt the sour lard and urine and jam that was all over him and heard the hot-water pipes rattling under the floor and the bubbles of wind building up in Clare's bowels.

'Bath,' he said. 'Bath then bed. God I'm going to need these holidays.'

'Stay with me here for a while.'

It was their one point of disagreement. Adrian had never been able to luxuriate in the afterglow.

'Time for my tub.'

'Why do you always want to have a bath the

moment after you've made love to me? Why can't we wriggle in our dirt for a while?' she said.

He fought down his customary post-coital irritation and contempt.

'Don't go looking for something psychological that isn't there. I have a bath after any kind of strenuous exercise. It doesn't mean I feel dirty,' though he did, 'it doesn't mean I'm trying to wash you out of my life,' though he was, 'it doesn't mean guilt, shame, repentance or anything like that,' though it did. 'It just means I want a bath.'

'Queer!' she shouted after him.

'Lesbian!' he yelled back.

When he came back next term, she was gone. Her replacement was a forty-year-old with one breast who most certainly *was* lesbian, which allowed the rest of the staff the free luxury of finding her irresistibly desirable. They spent their days saying she was a grand old girl and their evenings attempting to coax her down to the pub.

'Your girlfriend has gone, sir,' said Newton. 'Whatever are you going to do?'

'I shall devote the rest of my life to beating you into a purée,' said Adrian. 'It will help me forget.'

III

The morning of the match, Hunt had put a message under Adrian's toast as usual. This time it was a large heart-shaped piece of paper covered in kisses. This was going too far.

In theory, the boy on clearing duty should be the one to make masters' toast, but Hunt had long since decided that no one but he was going to make Adrian's. He fought everyone for the right. Whenever Adrian came down there would be two pieces on his side plate, and under them would be a message, usually nothing more dreadful than 'Your toast, sir . . .' or 'Each slice hand-grilled the traditional way by heritage craftsmen'. But love-hearts were too much.

Adrian looked round the hall to where Hunt was sitting. The boy pinkened and gave a small wave.

'What's Hunt the Thimble given you today, sir?' asked Rudder, the prefect next to Adrian. Hunt was known as the Thimble for the obvious reason and because he was said to be rather under-endowed.

'Oh nothing, nothing . . . the usual drivel.'

'I bet it isn't, sir. We told him that it was Valentine's Day today.'

'But Valentine's Day, Rudder dearest, falls on February the fourteenth and lies there until the fifteenth of that month. Unless I have become so bored by your anserine conversation and fallen asleep for four months, this is currently the month of June we are enjoying. What else, after all, could explain your cricket whites?'

'I know, sir. But we told him Valentine's Day was *today*. That's the joke.'

'Ah! Well, if the Queen can have two birthdays, why cannot Hunt the Thimble be granted the right to celebrate two Valentine's Days?'

'He told me,' said Rudder, 'that if he didn't get one back from you, he was going to hang himself.'

'He said *what*?' said Adrian, going white.

'Sir?'

Adrian grabbed Rudder's arm.

'*What* did he say?'

'Sir, you're hurting! It was just a joke.'

'You find the idea of suicide amusing, do you?'

'Well no, sir, but it was just . . .'

There was a silence. The boys at his table looked down at their cereal bowls. It wasn't like Adrian to be angry or violent.

'I'm sorry my angels,' he said, with an attempt at a laugh. 'No sleep last night. Working on the play. Either that or I'm turning mad. It was a full moon you know, and there's a history of lycanthropy in my family. Uncle Everard turns into a wolf every time he hears the *Crossroads* theme tune.'

Rudder giggled. The uncomfortable moment passed.

'Well, looks like a fine day today. I vote we load a crate of Coke onto the minibus before we go. You know what Narborough match teas are like.'

A mighty cheer now. The other tables looked across enviously. Healey's lot was always having fun.

The atmosphere in the minibus was tense. Adrian sat with them and tried to appear sunny and confident. It was no good his telling them to remember that it was only a game when he was as nervous as a kitten himself.

'We'll take a look at the pitch,' he told Hooper, the captain, 'and we'll decide then. But unless it's decidedly moist, put them in the field if you win the toss. "Knock 'em up, bowl 'em out" . . . it never fails.'

He was pleased with what he had done to the cricket eleven. He had never been much of a player himself but he knew and loved the game well enough to be able to make a difference to a schoolboy team. Everyone had agreed, watching his first eleven play a warm-up match against a scratch Rest of the School side, that he had done a tremendous job in two weeks.

But now they faced their first real opposition and he was worried that against another school they would fall to pieces. Last year, Hooper told him, Chartham Park was the laughing- stock of the whole area.

The bus whined up the Narborough driveway.

'Who's been here before?'

'I have, sir, for a rugger match,' said Rudder.

'Why are other schools always so forbidding? They seem infinitely bigger and more serious and their boys all look at least forty years old.'

'It's not a bad place, sir. Quite friendly.'

'Friendly? The maws of the heffalump are open wide, but don't believe that it betokens friendliness. Trust no one, speak to no one. As soon as you've heard this communication, eat it.'

There was a boy in a Narborough blazer waiting to show the team where to go. Adrian watched them stream off to the back of the house.

'See you there, my honeys. Don't accept any hand-rolled cigarettes from them.'

An old master bustled out to welcome Adrian.

'You're Chartham Park, yes?'

'That's right. Adrian Healey.'

'Staveley. I'm not Cricket. Our man's giving the team a pep talk. It's morning break at the moment. Come through to the staff room and savage a Chelsea bun with us.'

The staff room was baronial and crowded with

what seemed to Adrian like a greater number of masters than Chartham had boys.

'Ah, Chartham's new blood!' boomed the head-master. 'Come to give us a spanking, have you?'

'Oh well, I don't know about that, sir,' Adrian shook his hand. 'They tell me that you're hot stuff. Double figures would satisfy us.'

'That false modesty doesn't do, you know. I can smell your confidence. You're St Matthew's bound, I understand?'

'That's right, sir.'

'Well then, you'll be pleased to meet my Uncle Donald who's staying here until Cambridge term begins. He'll be your Senior Tutor at St Matthew's of course. Where is he? Uncle Donald, meet Adrian Healey, Chartham Park's new secret weapon, he's joining you at Michaelmas. Adrian Healey, Professor Trefusis.'

A short man with white hair and a startled expression turned and surveyed Adrian.

'Healey? Yes indeed, Healey. How do you do?'

'How do you do, Professor?'

'Healey, that's right. Quite right. Your entrance paper was very encouraging. Pregnant with promise, gravid with wit.'

'Thank you.'

'And you're a cricketer?'

'Well, not really. I've been trying to coach a bit, though.'

'Well best of luck, my dear. My nephew Philip has a youth like yourself on the staff – he'll be going to Trinity – who is said to have done much with the

Narborough side. Quite the young thaumaturge, they tell me.'

'Oh dear. I think that means we can expect to be marmalised. I was hoping Narborough would have sunk into over-confidence.'

'Here he comes now, you'll be umpiring together. Let me introduce you.'

Adrian turned to see a young man in a cricket-sweater making his way towards them.

It had to happen one day. It was bound to have done. Adrian always imagined that it would be in the street or on a train. But here? Today? In this place?

'I already know Hugo Cartwright,' he said. 'We were at school together.'

'Hello, Adrian,' said Hugo. 'Ready to be pounded into the dust?'

They put on their white coats and walked down to the ground.

'What sort of a wicket have you got for us?' Adrian asked.

'Not bad, slight leg-to-off slope from the pavilion end.'

'Got any bowlers who can use it?'

'We've a little leg-spinner I have hopes for.'

Adrian winced: he hadn't properly inoculated his team against leg-spin. It could run through a prep-school batting line-up like cholera through a slum.

'Does he have a googlie?'

'Ha-ha!' said Hugo.

'Bastard.'

He looked different but the same. Adrian's eyes could see the real Cartwright not too far beneath the surface. Behind the strengthened features he saw the smoother lines of the boy, within the firmer stride he read the former grace. His memory could scrub off four years of tarnish and restore the shining original. But no one else would have been able to.

If Clare had been with him and he had said, 'What do you think of that man there?' she would probably have wrinkled her nose and replied, 'Okay, I suppose. But I always think blond men look sinister.'

Everyone has their time, Adrian thought. You can meet people of thirty and know that when their hair is grey and their face lined, they will look wonderfully at their best. That Professor, for one, Donald Trefusis. He must have looked ridiculous as a teenager, but now he has come into his own. Others, whose proper age was twenty-five, grew old grotesquely, their baldness and thickening waistlines an affront to what they once were. There were men like that on the staff at Chartham, fifty or sixty years old, but whose true characters were only discernible in hints of some former passion and vigour that would come out when they were excited. The headmaster, on the other hand, was a pompous forty-one, waiting to ripen into a delicious sixty-five. What Adrian's own proper age was, he had no idea. Sometimes he felt he had left himself behind at school, at other times he thought he would be at his best in tubby and contented middle age. But Hugo . . . Hugo he knew would always be growing away from his fourteen-year-old perfection: the clues to his former beauty would become harder to find as each year passed, the golden hair would seem pale and weak at thirty, the liquid blue of the eyes would harden and set at thirty-five.

Summer's lease hath all too short a date, Hugo old boy, thought Adrian, but your eternal summer shall not fade. In my imagination you are immortal. The man walking beside me is merely The Picture of Hugo Cartwright, ageing and coarsening: I have the real Hugo in my head and he will live as long as I do.

'I think we'll bat first, sir,' the Narborough captain announced after winning the toss.

'That's it, Malthouse,' said Hugo. 'Knock 'em up and bowl 'em out.'

'Trust me to lose the toss,' said Hooper. 'Sorry, sir.'

'Don't be a dafty-trousers,' said Adrian. 'It's a good wicket to bat second on, it'll dry out all through the afternoon.'

He threw the ball to Rudder, Chartham's opening bowler, before taking his position at the stumps.

'Remember, Simon,' he said, 'straight and on a length, that's all you have to do.'

'Yes, sir,' said Rudder, swallowing.

The ground was in a kind of valley, with the looming Gothic of Narborough Hall on one rise and the church and village of Narborough on another. The pavilion was whitewashed and thatched, the weather perfect with only the faintest of breezes luffing the fielders' shirtsleeves. The grim seriousness of the children preparing to play, the detached amusement of Hugo at square leg, the church clock chiming mid-day, the round circles of fine gang-mown cuttings in the outfield, the sun winking off the roller by the sight-screen, the distant clatter of spiked shoes on the pavilion concrete, the open blue of the wide Norfolk sky, the six pebbles in the hand of Adrian's outstretched arm, this whole monstrous illusion froze, while to Adrian the world seemed to hold its breath as if uncertain that such a picture could last. This fantasy of England that old men took with them to their death-beds, this England without factories and sewers or council houses, this England of leather and wood and flannel, this England circumscribed by a white boundary and laws that said that each team shall field eleven men and each man shall bat, this England of shooting-sticks, weather-vanes and rectory teas, it was like Cartwright's beauty, he thought, a momentary vision glimpsed for a second in an adolescent dream, then dispersed like steam into the real atmosphere of traffic-jams, serial murderers, prime ministers and Soho rent. But its spectral haze was sharper and clearer than the glare of the everyday and, against all evidence, was taken to be the only reality, its vapour trapped and distilled in the mind, its image, scents and textures bottled and laid down against the long, lonely melancholy of adulthood.

Adrian brought down his arm.

'Play!'

Rudder bowled a ball of full length and the batsman swept his bat elegantly forward in defence. But the ball had already gone through him and Rice the wicket-keeper was leaping in glee. The batsman looked round in disbelief to see his off-stump lying on the ground. He returned to the pavilion shaking his head, as if Rudder had been guilty of some appalling social blunder. There was a liquid spatter of applause from the boundary. The school were in lessons and wouldn't be watching until after lunch.

Adrian tossed a pebble into his right hand and smiled across at Hugo.

'I got him, sir!' said Rudder, polishing the ball against his leg. 'I bloody got him. Golden bloody duck.'

'You beat him for pace, old love,' said Adrian, drawing him aside. 'The next batsman will be scared, bowl him two very quick ones just outside the line of off-stump and then a slower ball on middle, but disguise it.'

'All right, sir.'

Adrian wondered if it was a breach of etiquette for an umpire to coach during play. But then he saw Hugo, who had been replacing the bails at the other end, whispering urgently to the incoming number three. Very well then, they would fight it out between them, like First World War generals.

Rudder did as he was told for the first two balls, letting them fly at the new batsman, who played and missed at the first and left the second alone. He came thundering up for the third ball, grunting and stamping like a buffalo. The batsman quaked.

'Subtle disguise I don't think,' Adrian said to himself.

The ball was let go of early and seemed to float in at half the speed. The batsman had nearly completed his defensive stroke by the time it got to him, with the result that the ball was knocked from his bat gently back to Rudder who threw it up in the air with a yell of triumph.

'Caught and bowled! And hast thou slain the number three? Come to my arms, my beamish boy. Two for none, oh frabjous day, calloo callay!'

Hugo was furious at lunch. His side had been bowled out for fourteen runs. He couldn't believe it.

'I'll kill them!' he said. 'I'll castrate them and hang their scrotums from the score-board.'

'Don't worry,' said Adrian. 'We'll probably be all out for ten.'

'I'm going to replace the whole team with boys from the scholarship Sixth. At least they'll have some brains. What good is ball sense without common sense? I mean, trying to square cut a straight half-volley! It makes me want to throw up.'

Adrian was sure that he himself wouldn't sulk quite as gracelessly if it had been his side that had been dismissed for fourteen. But then Cartwright had always been ambitious. He remembered the time they had walked back from Biffen's tea-party and Cartwright had talked about going to Cambridge. That had been the same day that Trotter had hanged himself.

Adrian smothered a sudden desire to rap his spoon on the table, call for quiet and announce, 'This man opposite me here, my fellow umpire, I thought you might like to know that he sucked me off one night in a hotel when he thought I was asleep.'

'Funny old game,' he remarked instead.

'Look,' said Hugo. 'If you do cream us straight after lunch, how would you feel about making it a two-innings match?'

'Well . . .'

'It'll go down as your victory of course, but we do need the practice.'

'All right,' said Adrian. 'I'll check with my team first.'

Hooper was doubtful.

'We've never played two innings before, sir. What happens when we pass their first score?'

'We make as many runs as possible before we're all out.'

'Sir, suppose they can't get us all out?'

'That's when you have to declare, dear. Make sure you judge it so that there's time to put them in again, bowl them out and then pass their total before stumps. We don't want a draw.'

'When are stumps?'

'Narborough's Mr Cartwright and I agreed on seven o'clock. I'll have to ring the school and check with the headmaster. You'll be late for bed of course, but it'll all be the most super-duper fun.'

The whole school turned out to watch after lunch. As Adrian had feared, Narborough's leg-spinner, Ellis, completely baffled his boys. Once they had got used to the ball bouncing and spinning one way, he would send down top-spin and undetectable googlies that made the ball fly off to the waiting close field. Chartham was all out for thirty-nine after an hour and a half of tortured embarrassment. Hugo looked very smug as Narborough prepared for their second innings.

'We're only twenty-five ahead,' said Adrian.

'That's all right, isn't it, sir?' said Rudder. 'If we get them out for fourteen again we'll have won by an innings and eleven runs.'

'If.'

The Narborough openers stalked to the wicket looking determined and confident. They were playing in front of their home crowd now and had experienced the satisfaction of seeing the Chartham team writhe.

Rudder's first ball was a wide. Adrian signalled it, with raised eyebrows.

'Sorry, sir,' said Rudder with a grin.

His next ball was driven to the mid-off boundary, the next was hooked for six. The fourth, a no-ball, was late-cut for two which became six after four overthrows had been added. The next two were both glanced for four. Rudder turned to Adrian to collect his sweater.

'Two more balls yet, Simon.'

'Sir?'

'There was a wide and a no-ball in there. Two more balls.'

'Oh. Yes, sir. I forgot.'

The next two were each smacked for four over Rudder's head.

'What's going wrong, sir?'

'What's going wrong is you're not bowling properly. Line and length, darling, line and length.'

For the next two hours the opening pair batted freely and fiercely, putting on a hundred and seventy-four, until one of the batsmen, the same man Rudder had clean bowled first ball of the morning, retired to let some of his friends enjoy the slaughter.

Hugo's merriment was unbearable over tea, for all the whiteness of his teeth and the sparkle in his eyes.

'Well that's a bit more like it,' he said. 'I was beginning to get worried this morning.'

'Dear old friend of my youth,' said Adrian, 'I'm afraid you've discovered our principal weakness.'

'What, you can't bowl you mean?'

'No, no. Sympathy. My boys were simply devastated by your glumness at lunch, so we decided to cheer you up by letting you have some batting practice. I take it you're declaring over tea?'

'You bet. Have you out of here, tail between your legs, by half past five.'

'Is that a promise?' said a voice behind them. It was Professor Trefusis.

'Certainly, sir,' said Hugo.

'What do you think, Mr Healey?'

'Well let me see . . . two hundred and thirty-nine to make before seven. I think we can do it all right, if we don't panic.'

'Ellis isn't tired, you know,' said Hugo. 'He can bowl for hours at a stretch.'

'My boys were beginning to read him by the end,' said Adrian. 'We can do it.'

'I have just placed a bet with my nephew Philip,' said Trefusis. 'Two hundred pounds on Chartham to win at odds of five to one against.'

'What?' said Adrian. 'I mean . . . what?'

'I liked your entrance papers, most amusing. I don't see how you can fail.'

'Well,' said Hugo, as Trefusis ambled away, 'what a bloody idiot.'

'Oh, I don't know,' said Adrian, popping a sandwich into his mouth, 'smart investment if you ask me. Now, if you'll forgive me, I have to go and brief my platoon.'

'Want a side bet?' Hugo called out after him.

'Right,' said Adrian to his team. 'There's a man out there who is so sure, based on the evidence of what he's seen, that you can do it, that he has bet two hundred pounds that you will blow these bastards out of the water.'

They were padding up in the pavilion, forlorn but brave, like Christians preparing for an away match against Lions.

'But what do we do about Ellis, sir!' said Hooper. 'He's impossible.'

'That's a trough of piss. You step up to him and you cart him all over the park, is what you do. Just don't get pushed against your stumps. Aim for the close-in fielders, if you miss the ball you might manage to belt them with your bat on the follow-through.'

'Isn't that a bit unsporting, sir?'

'Arseholes. Whistle, hum, look unconcerned, look bored. When he's ready to bowl, you step forward and say you're not ready. Disturb his rhythm, demonstrate contempt. Don't forget, I'm out there, and he'll want to bowl from my end because of the slope.'

'You won't *cheat* will you, sir?'

'Cheat? Good heavens. This is an amateur cricket match amongst leading prep schools, I'm an Englishman and a schoolmaster supposedly setting an example to his young charges. We are playing the most artistic and beautiful game man ever devised. Of course I'll cunting well cheat. Now, give me my robe and put on my crown. I have immortal longings in me.'

Out in the middle, little Ellis took the ball and flipped it from hand to hand with the disturbing competence of a born spinner of the ball.

Adrian patted his head.

'Good luck, little chap,' he said. 'Don't get upset if they punish you a bit. It's only a game, eh?'

Ellis looked puzzled. 'Yes, sir.'

A sporting round of applause from the Narborough boys welcomed Chartham's opening pair to the wicket.

'Here they come now. They're both rather savage hitters of the ball, I'm afraid. But if you don't lose your head you should be able to cut it down to ten or so an over. A word of advice, though. Try and do something about disguising that googlie of yours a bit better . . . sticks out like a sore thumb.'

Ellis tweaked the ball out of the side of his hand uncertainly.

'Thank you, sir.'

'All right, here we go. Don't be nervous.'

Frowde and Colville, the openers, had certainly taken the game-plan literally. They surveyed the field with lofty disdain and smiled faint patronising smiles at the short leg and silly point crowded around them, nicely blending admiration for their physical courage and doubt for their mental capacity. They were welcome to stand there and be cut in two, but they had been warned.

'Play!' said Adrian.

Ellis stepped forward. Frowde at the other end threw up a hand and bent to do up his shoe-laces.

'Sorry!' he called. 'Won't be a sec.'

Ellis turned back to his mark and waited.

'All right, Frowde?' said Adrian.

'Fine thank you, sir. Just don't want to get tangled up when I start running.'

'Quite so,' Adrian dropped his arm. 'Play!!' he boomed.

Ellis bowled a full toss which Frowde hooked straight over the boundary. The short leg fielder glared at Ellis: the ball had nearly decapitated him.

Adrian signalled a four to the scorer.

'It was a six,' said Hugo at square leg.

'Sorry?'

'It was a six!'

'Are you sure?'

'Of course I'm sure! It went clean over.'

'Well if you're sure,' said Adrian, signalling a six. 'I didn't want to give ourselves two extra runs. That was a six, scorer!' he yelled, just as Ellis next to him was catching the return from deep mid-wicket. The blast in his ear made him drop the ball. Adrian picked it up for him.

'Try and get them to bounce on the ground first,' he said helpfully. 'That way it's harder for the batsman to hit quite so far.'

Ellis's second was a long hop square-cut for four.

'You see?' said Adrian. 'That's two fewer already.'

The next was on a good length and driven straight to close extra cover.

'There might be a couple here,' shouted Frowde to his partner.

'Genius,' thought Adrian, as they ran one run after the extra cover fielder fumbled the ball in his amazement at the possibility that anyone was going to run at all.

Ellis was made of stout stuff. His next ball was an excellent leg-break that nearly had Colville stumped.

Adrian stepped forward and patted the pitch.

287

'You must watch your feet after you've bowled,' he said to him. 'You're not allowed to run on in the area between the two wickets. It kicks up rough stuff and helps the bowler at the other end.'

Little Ellis was aghast at the possibility that Adrian might think he had been trying to cheat.

'I'm very sorry, sir,' he said. 'I didn't mean . . .'

'I'm sure you didn't, my dear fellow. That was just a warning, that's all. I'm sure it won't happen again.'

Ellis knocked the next ball from so wide of the stumps that it glanced straight across Colville for four byes.

He was taken off after three more catastrophic overs and retired to long on, blinking back tears and fending off the jeers of his home supporters on the boundary.

Cricket, thought Adrian. It's so character-building.

After the collapse of Ellis the outcome was never really in doubt. The fast man at the other end was competent but soon exhausted. Weirder and wilder alternatives were tried, boys who dropped slow balls from a great height, boys with violent actions like windmills that produced gentle long hops, boys who bowled balls that bounced twice before reaching the middle of the pitch, but to no avail. The openers put on a stand of a hundred and twelve and the fourth-wicket partnership of Rice and Hooper scored the final runs as Narborough church clock struck six.

Adrian watched it all with raised eyebrows and an impartial smile. Hugo boiled and seethed and glared, glancing miserably from time to time at the stony figure of his headmaster who sat perched on a shooting-stick next to Professor Trefusis.

'An instructive match,' said Adrian as he and Hugo

pulled up the stumps. 'I thought we were in real trouble at one stage.'

'I can't understand what the hell went wrong with Ellis,' said Hugo. 'I really thought he was the most gifted cricketer in the school. An England prospect even.'

'He's young yet. Temperament is the problem there, I fancy. I tried to calm him down and encourage him to get on with his natural game, but he was a bit overawed. Don't give up on him, he's learnt a lot today.'

'He'll learn a bloody sight more after I'm through with him.'

The Narborough team, hot and limp with exertion and defeat, saw them off in the driveway. Hugo stood with them, sipping at a can of beer.

'Three cheers for Chartham Park,' called Malthouse, their captain, raising his arm with an attempt at casual gallantry. 'Hip-ip.'

'Ray!' murmured Narborough.

'Hip-ip!'

'Ray!'

'Hip-ip.'

'Ray.'

'Three cheers for Narborough Hall,' shouted a flushed and triumphant Hooper, punching the air. 'Hip-Hip!'

'Hooray!' bellowed Chartham.

'Hip-Hip-Hip!'

'Hooray!'

'Hip-Hip-Hip-Hip!'

'HOORAY!'

'Goodbye then, Hugo. See you for the return match.'

'We'll pulverise you.'

'Of course you will.'

A madness suddenly possessed Adrian. With a pounding heart he leant forward and whispered in Hugo's ear.

'I was awake, you know.'

'What?'

'That night in Harrogate. I was awake all the time.'

Hugo looked annoyed.

'I know you bloody were. Do you think I'm an idiot?'

Adrian stared open-mouthed and then burst out laughing.

'You total . . . you complete . . . you . . .'

Trefusis stepped forward.

'Well, young man, you've earned me a thousand pounds. Here's two hundred, my original stake.'

'Oh really,' said Adrian. 'I couldn't.'

'Of course you could,' he pushed a bundle of notes at him. 'Tremendous display.'

'Yes, they're not a bad bunch, are they?' Adrian looked on affectionately as his team climbed into the minibus.

'No, no, no. You!'

'Professor?'

'I knew that the man who wrote those artfully disguised second-hand essays, who disgorged such specious and ill-thought-out nonsense with such persuasive and brilliant flair wouldn't let me down. You've clearly a genius for deceit and chicanery. I look forward to seeing you next term.'

Ten

'Well!' said Trefusis when Adrian had finished. 'Did I really say that? "A genius for deceit and chicanery"? Did I really? And we had only just been introduced. How rude.'

'I didn't take it so.'

'Well of course not.'

Trefusis groped about with his right hand in the driver's side glove compartment until he found a figgy oatcake, which he inspected carefully, blowing off a piece of fluff before popping it into his mouth. 'My goodness, Adrian,' he mumbled through the crumbs, 'that was all so much more than I had bargained for. Tell me . . .'

'Yes?'

'The girl who was the Matron at Chartham . . .'

'Clare? What about her?'

'Did you really . . .? I mean the lard and the football pump and the jam and the urine and so . . . and so on . . . you really *did* . . .?'

'Oh yes,' said Adrian. 'Isn't that usual?'

'Well now, *usual*. Usual isn't the word I'd've . . .' Trefusis wound down the window distractedly.

'Well anyway,' said Adrian, 'there it all is.'

'Young people sometimes give me the impression that I have never lived at all.'

'Surely you must have had experiences of a similar nature?'

'Oddly, no. Of a similar nature? No. It is profoundly strange I know, but I have not.'

'Well apart from . . .'

'Apart from what, dear boy?'

'Apart from, you know . . . that night in the lavs in Cambridge.'

'I *beg* your pardon? Oh . . . oh yes, of course. Apart from that, obviously.' Trefusis nodded contentedly. 'Now, unless I am more hugely mistaken than God, our service-station should be just around the corner. Ah! here we are. Petrol and lemon tea, I think. The car could do with a fill up and we could do with a fillip, hee-ho.'

Adrian, as the car swung off the road, marvelled, like many an English traveller before him, at the trimness and appealing order of continental service-stations. Euro-colours might be a little too bright and primary, but better this luminous cleanliness than the drab squalor of British motorway stops. How could they afford to have all the litter swept up and the paintwork so freshly maintained? Everything neat, from the little hanging-baskets of geraniums to the merry pantiled roofs that offered shaded parking to hot and weary travellers . . . a metallic gleam suddenly caught Adrian's eye. He gaped in astonishment.

Down the end of the same row into which Trefusis was inexpertly manoeuvring the Wolseley was parked a green BMW with British licence plates and a Hoverspeed 'GB' sticker.

'Donald, look! It's them.'

'I should hope so too. I was most specific as to time.'

'You were what?'

'And don't forget, dearest lad, that the verb "to be" takes a nominative complement.'

'What?'

'You said "it's them". What you meant of course was, "it's they".' Trefusis pulled up the handbrake and opened the door. 'But that's unbearable pedantry. Who, in their right mind, says "it's they"? No one. Well? Are you going to sit in the car or are you going to come along with me and hear me practise my Luxembourgeois?'

They took their trays of tea and buns to a table near the window. The couple from the BMW was sitting in a non-smoking section at the other end of the dining area.

'It won't do to talk to them,' said Trefusis. 'But it's good to know they are there.'

'Who *are* they?'

'Their names are Nancy and Simon Hesketh-Harvey and they have been kindly provided by an old friend of mine.'

'They're on our side then?'

Trefusis didn't answer. He bobbed his teabag up and down in its glass and thought for a moment.

'After the war,' he said at length, 'Humphrey Biffen, Helen Sorrel-Cameron, a mathematician called Bela Szabó and I had an idea.'

'At last,' said Adrian. 'The truth.'

'You shall judge. We had all of us worked together

on Enigma and become increasingly interested, in our own ways, in the possibilities of language and machines. Bela knew very well that the path to what is now called computing had been opened up in Britain and America and that digital machines would one day be capable of linguistic programming. Turing's work at Bletchley had shown that the old Höllerin-based punched-card systems would soon be a thing of the past. Algorithmic, low-level mathematical languages would be followed by higher level modular intelligent languages giving rise, ultimately, to heuristic machines.'

'Heuristic?'

'Capable of learning by mistakes, of operating, like human beings, through trial and error. My interest in all this was not mathematical, nor especially social. I was not frightened of machines becoming cleverer than human beings, nor of their in some way "taking over". I was however *very* interested in the development of new languages.'

'On account of your having learnt all the existing ones and being in danger of growing bored?'

'You exaggerate charmingly. Bela returned to Hungary after the war, Humphrey married Lady Helen, as you know, and became a schoolmaster. I stayed on at Cambridge. But we continued to work, where possible, on our idea for a perfect high level language that could be spoken by both machines and human beings. The dream, you see, was to invent an international language, like Esperanto, that would also serve as a *lingua franca* between man and machine.'

'But surely the ideal solution would be to teach a machine to speak English?'

'Well I'm very much afraid that this is what will happen. We had no way of predicting the arrival of the microprocessor, or perhaps I should say, we lacked the imagination to predict its arrival. The cost of computing has been reduced by a factor of a million in ten years. It is simply astonishing. This means that you can now buy for one pound processing ability that would have cost you a million pounds in nineteen-seventy-one.'

'But isn't that good?'

'Marvellous, simply marvellous. But of no use to me. There are now dozens of languages at work in computing. Cobol, Forth, C, Lisp, Superlisp, Fortran, BASIC, Pascal, Logo, simply scores of the wretched things. We have a new Babel. This will sort itself out as soon as computing power comes still further down in price. Before the end of the century we shall have computers that recognise existing human languages.'

'So what's the problem?'

'Oh, there's no problem. None at all. We spent thirty years mining what turned out to be a barren seam, that's all. Nothing wrong with that. That's academe-biz, as they say. I tell you this to give you the background of my relationship with Szabó. We stayed in touch, do you see? He in Budapest, I in Cambridge.'

Adrian said that he saw.

'Two years ago Szabó made a curious discovery. He had shifted the focus of his attentions over the years from pure mathematics to electronics, acoustic engineering and any number of invigorating related fields. Hungary is very good about that sort of thing.

That coloured cube that everyone is playing with at the moment is Hungarian, of course. I suspect that it is the advantage of speaking a language understood by so few that has turned the Magyars into such experts in numbers and shapes and dimensions. There is even a Hungarian mathematician at the moment who is close to achieving what was once thought to be the impossible. He is on the brink of squaring the circle. Or is it circling the square? Whichever.'

'A Hungarian is the only man who can follow you into a revolving door and come out first,' quoted Adrian.

'Exactly. Szabó is just one such hornery cuss. He had been working, during the seventies, on cures for the common stutter, experimenting with ways of playing back the speech of a stutterer into their ears as they spoke. Apparently if a subject hears his own voice back a split second after he has spoken and while he is moving on to the next thing he wants to say, his stutter will be eliminated.'

'How baroque.'

'Baroque? If you say so.'

'But not very practical to go about the place in headphones, I should have thought.'

'Quite so. Far from a feasible cure for the affliction. Experience in this area, however, did lead Bela towards what turned out to be immensely fruitful researches into the speech centres of the brain. The subject that most interested him was that of lying or, as it were, *saying the thing which is not*. He wanted to find out what happened in the brain when people said things which were not true; to see, for example, whether there is any difference between telling a lie, making a mistake in memory and inventing a fiction, all of which involve, in one way or another, saying the thing which is not. Thus a man might say: "I have to work late tonight, darling," or "The German for a chive is *ein Zwiebel*," or "Once upon a time there was a fabulous trouser-eating dragon called Geoffrey." These might all be taken to be examples of a lie. The speaker is in fact *not* going to be working late that night, he is instead going to the flat of his mistress there to conjoin with her in carnal riot. That is an Alpha-type lie. In the second case the man's *brain* knows full well that *Zwiebel* is in fact the German for "onion" and that the word he is groping for is *Schnittlauch*, but his mind is unable for the moment to gain access to that information. His statement that *ein Zwiebel* is the German for "a chive" is therefore a Beta-type lie. And lastly, there never was a fabulous trouser-eating dragon called Geoffrey, once upon any time and what is more the speaker knows it: a Gamma-type pseudology. The Alpha-type, the first kind of lie, the moral lie, if you like, the lie that disturbs the conscience of the speaker, might well be detectable using a polygram machine, the other two most certainly will not be.'

'Your friends are leaving,' said Adrian.

The BMW couple had stood up and were making for the exit.

'Excellent!' said Trefusis. 'That means we really *are* being followed.'

'How do you mean?'

'If Nancy and Simon leave the rendezvous first it is a sign that we are not alone. If they let *us* leave first, it means that we go unobserved.'

'Moscow Rules, George. Moscow Rules all the way.'

'I beg your pardon?'

'Nothing. So who is following us?'

'I dare say we shall find out. Drink your tea precipitately. We must not lag too far behind.'

Out in the car park the BMW had gone. Trefusis opened the driver's side door of the Wolseley, while Adrian looked around for signs of other cars preparing to start up in pursuit.

'Can't see any likely looking candidates,' he said.

Trefusis stooped and picked something from the ground. He came up holding a thick oblong of folded paper which he handed to Adrian across the top of the Wolseley.

'This was wedged in the hinges of the door. What does it say?'

Adrian unfolded the oblong and spread it over the roof.

'I think it must be in code, or cypher, rather. Or whichever one was which. Either way it's gibberish to me. You take a look.'

Adrian revolved the sheet of paper to face Trefusis.

'Young Nancy takes after her mother,' he said. 'It's in Volapük.'

'In what?'

'Volapük. A very silly international language devised at least a hundred years ago by a charming man called Johann Schleyer. "Vol" means world in his language and "pük" means speak. If he had known that in English it meant vomit, he might have chosen more carefully.'

'And what does the note say?'

'It seems that we are being followed by two cars, one a French-registered blue Lemon BX, whatever that might be, the other a white Swiss Audi Four.'

'They must mean a Citroën BX and an Audi Quattro, I should think.'

'That would seem to make sense. Well, this is refreshing to know, is it not?'

'What, that we're being followed?'

'Yes.'

'But we stick out like a sore thumb in this bloody jalopy.'

'I hope so. The element of surprise is absolutely crucial.'

'What element of surprise?'

'Exactly!' beamed Trefusis as he edged onto the autoroute and pointed the Wolseley towards Germany. 'That is what is so surprising.'

The staccato rush of cars travelling in the opposite direction reminded Adrian of interminable childhood journeys to the coast. He would gaze at his father's cocked wrists on the steering wheel or count all the four-legged animals in the fields as they passed, one for a sheep or cow, two for a horse, yawning repeatedly in a giddy cloud of car-sickness. He had had a trick of covering his ears with his hands and removing them rhythmically in time to the whoosh of each car as it passed the window.

He tried it again now.

'Are we there yet, Daddy?'

'Why do people always say that on car journeys?' asked Trefusis.

'It reminds them of when they were young.'

'Humph.'

'Anyway,' said Adrian. 'We were talking about lies.'

'So we were. Light me a cigarette, there's a good fellow.'

Adrian lit two from Trefusis's cigarette case and passed one over.

Trefusis took in a deep lungful of Gold Leaf.

'We can be fairly certain,' he said, 'that animals do not lie. It has been both their salvation and their downfall. Lies, fictions and untrue suppositions can create new human truths which build technology, art, language, everything that is distinctly of Man. The word "stone" for instance is not a stone, it is an oral pattern of vocal, dental and labial sounds or a scriptive arrangement of ink on a white surface, but man pretends that it is actually the thing it refers to. Every time he wishes to tell another man about a stone he can use the word instead of the thing itself. The word bodies forth the object in the mind of the listener and both speaker and listener are able to imagine a stone without seeing one. All the qualities of stone can be metaphorically and metonymically expressed. "I was stoned, stony broke, stone blind, stone cold sober, stonily silent," oh, whatever occurs. More than that, a man can look at a stone and call it a weapon, a paperweight, a doorstep, a jewel, an idol. He can give it function, he can possess it.'

'Surely when a bird uses a twig for nesting material it is doing the same thing?'

'Birds collect for nests much as we expand our lungs a dozen or so times a minute in order to suck in air or, in our case, tobacco smoke. It is, or so I am reliably informed by those who know, an entirely instinctive mechanism. Animals do not have the lying capability of man.'

'Keats's negative capability?'

'To some extent, yes. Within our brains connections are made and stored all the time. This word signifies this thing, this fact actually occurred, this experience was in truth undergone; the whatness and whichness of everything is established. Thus I ask you, "What did you drink just now?" and you reply "lemon tea" because lemon tea and your recent drinking are connected. If you deliberately wish to lie you *think* "lemon tea" – you can't help that because the link is there – but you search for some other drinking material and say, for example, "apple juice". A link is now made between your recent drinking activities, lemon tea and apple juice. The strongest link, however, is between the drinking activity and lemon tea because it is the true one. The link between what you drank and apple juice exists, because you created it. But it only exists through the link with the lemon tea. Are you following me?'

'Like a panther,' lied Adrian.

'The details of a lie are harder to recall than the truth, because they are less strongly linked in the mind. The act of remembering is literally just that: the act of reassembling the members of something. If the members are illusory it is naturally more difficult to enact this mental reconstruction.'

'So your friend Szabó discovered what happens in the brains of people when they lie and has invented some kind of lie-detector, is that it?'

'No, no. He did much more than that. He discovered a lie-*deflector*!'

Adrian watched the smoke from his cigarette being sucked through the quarter-light of the car. He had an awful feeling, deep down inside him, that he was somehow more than a passenger on this journey, more than an observer.

'A lie-deflector?' he said.

'Let us suppose that all true things are connected in the brain by pathways called A-type pathways and all untrue things are connected by B-type pathways.'

'Okay.'

'Imagine a machine which inhibits the brain from making any B-type connections. When under the influence of such a machine, the subject is simply unable to lie.'

'And this is what your friend Szabó has come up with?'

'Such is his claim.'

Adrian thought for a moment.

'There are some lies,' he said, 'which you tell . . . which people tell . . . so often that they believe them themselves. What about those?'

'However much you may consciously believe what you are saying, your brain knows the truth, and has made connections accordingly. You may imagine, for instance, that on holiday in Sardinia you witnessed a gang of twelve bandits robbing a bank with machine guns and hand grenades, you may repeat this story to the dismay of all your acquaintances at every dinner party to which those friends have made the rash mistake of inviting you, such that you believe it surely and wholly. Nonetheless, buried under the dead neural weight of all these convictions, your brain knows perfectly well that in fact there were only two bandits with nothing more than a water-pistol and a spud-gun between them. Your brain was there too, you see, and it has registered the truth.'

'I do see. I do.'

'Szabó claims the machine is in fact as much a memory- retrieval device as a lie-inhibitor. It can just as easily make the subject disinter the German for "chive" as disgorge the details of his true whereabouts on the night in question.'

'Wow.'

'W, as you rightly remark, ow. Or, as they say in Poland, "Vov".'

'And where do *you* fit into all this?'

'Nowhere in the development of the machine. Bela and I have corresponded over the decades, and a little over a year ago he began to include in his letters to me references to his development of Mendax, as he has fancifully dubbed this fruit of his intellectual loins. Last July Istvan Moltaj, a violinist friend of his, left Hungary to take part in the Salzburg Festival. Bela entrusted him with a sheaf of papers relating to Mendax. The idea was that Moltaj should give the papers to me. We had an appointment to meet at Mozart's Geburtshaus in the Getreidegasse. It is apparent that someone had either been following Moltaj or had intercepted Bela's letter to me arranging the rendezvous. He was there most unpleasantly killed, not ten yards away from us, as we both have cause to remember.'

'And he never got to give you the papers?'

'Moltaj had taken the sensible precaution of leaving a package for my collection at the reception desk of the Goldener Hirsch Hotel. The package contained a sheaf of musical manuscript paper. A duet for piano and violin. The music was cacophonous in the extreme but the notes corresponded to letters which spelt out a text in classical Volapük.'

'So you got it?'

'You may remember that on our return to England last year we were robbed?'

'They took your briefcase!'

'They did indeed.'

'But, Donald, if I may say so . . .'

'Yes?'

'Why didn't you post the papers or something? If they were willing to cut a man's throat in broad daylight . . . I mean just to go round with them in a briefcase in your car! Not exactly tradecraft, old man.'

'Tradecraft?'

'You know. Not how Sarratt would train Circus men to operate in the field.'

'Adrian, I'm rather afraid that you are gibbering.'

'Le Carré. Operational procedures. A good field man would have taken the papers and shoved them in a DLB or DLD.'

'A what?'

'A Dead Letter Box or Dead Letter Drop.'

'Oh.'

'Moscow Rules, George, old boy. Moscow Rules all the way.'

'Yes, no doubt a Dead Letter Drop would have answered perfectly. I should have thought of that. Instead I made a false copy of the manuscript and left the real one in Salzburg.'

'You did?'

'It seemed sensible,' said Trefusis.

'So the papers in the briefcase that was stolen . . .?'

'Were drivel. It must have taken them a long time to discover, read it which way they might, that the manuscript they took from us contained nothing more illuminating than pages three-two-three to three-six-seven of the Salzburg telephone directory.'

'And what exactly did you do with the real manuscript?'

'There was a very nice chambermaid at the hotel. She said she would look after it for me. Was that bad tradecraft too?'

'Well,' said Adrian. 'If she's still got it, it was good tradecraft, if she hasn't, it wasn't.'

Trefusis inclined his head gratefully. 'Don't look behind you,' he said, 'but there has been a white Citroën two cars behind us for the last twelve kilometres. As to whether it's a BX or not, I really couldn't say.'

Adrian looked behind him.

'You still haven't told me,' he said, 'who was responsible for cutting this violinist's throat . . . what was his name again?'

'Moltaj.'

'Right. Do you know who killed him?'

'So many people would love to get their hands on a machine that can inhibit pseudology, mendacity and falsehood. The police, Intelligence services, all sorts and conditions of interested agencies and institutions. Bela, like any good scientist, is worried that he may have opened the door to something rather frantic, something rather ghastly.'

'What have I done? What have I done? Have we

any business taking away people's right to lie? That sort of thing.'

'Questions of free will certainly do seem to arise. It is perfectly possible to live a life from cradle to grave that is entirely dishonest. One might never reveal one's true identity, the yearnings and cravings of one's innermost self, even to the most intimate circle of family and friends; never really speak the truth to anyone. Priests and psychotherapists may believe that the confessional-box or the analysis session reveals truths, but you know and I know and every human being knows that we lie all the time to all the world. Lying is as much a part of us as wearing clothes. Indeed, Man's first act in Eden was to give names to everything on earth, our first act of possession and falsehood was to take away a stone's right to be a stone by imprisoning it with the name "stone". There are in reality, as Fenellosa said, no nouns in the Universe. Man's next great act was to cover himself up. We have been doing so ever since. We feel that our true identities shame us. Lying is a deep part of us. To take it away is to make us something less than, not more than, human. So at least Bela fears.'

'Yes,' said Adrian. 'You still haven't told me who killed Moltaj.'

'The Hungarians have a wonderful word,' said Trefusis. 'It is *puszipajtás* and means roughly "someone you know well enough to kiss in the street". They are a demonstrative and affectionate people, the Hungarians, and enthusiastic social kissers. "Do you know young Adrian?" you might ask and they might reply, "I *know* him, but we're not exactly *puszipajtás*."'

'I have no doubt whatever in my mind,' said Adrian, 'that all this is leading somewhere.'

'A few weeks ago Bela's grandson arrived in England. He is a chess-player of some renown, having achieved grandmaster status at last year's Olympiad in Buenos Aires. No doubt you followed his excellent match against Bent Larsen?'

'No,' said Adrian. 'I missed his match against Bent Larsen and somehow his matches against Queer Karpov and Faggoty Smyslov and Poofy Petrosian also managed to pass me by.'

'Tish and hiccups. Bent is a perfectly common Danish Christian name and it would do you no harm, Master Healey, to acquire a little more patience.'

'I'm sorry, Donald, but you do talk *around* a subject so.'

'Would you have said that?' Trefusis sounded surprised.

'I would.'

'I will then straight to the heart of the matter hie me. Stefan, the grandson of Bela, came to England a fortnight ago to play in the tournament at Hastings. I received a message to meet him in a park at Cambridge. Parker's Piece to be exact. It was ten o'clock of a fine June night. That is not extraneous colour, I mention the evening to give you the idea that it was *light*, you understand?'

Adrian nodded.

'I walked to the rendezvous point. I saw Stefan by an elm tree clutching a briefcase and looking anxious. My specifying that the tree was an elm,' said Trefusis, 'is of no consequence and was added, like this explanation of it, simply to vex you. The mention of the lad's anxiety, however, has a bearing. The existence of the briefcase is likewise germane.'

'Right.'

'As I approached, he pointed to a small shed or hut-like building behind him and disappeared into it. I followed him.'

'Ah! Don't tell me . . . the small shed or hut-like building was in fact a gentlemen's lavatory?'

'Meeting for the first time one of his grandfather's oldest friends, a man of whom he had heard much, Stefan naturally embraced me, bestowing a friendly kiss on each cheek. We were *puszipajtás*, do you see? Stefan then knelt to open his briefcase. It was at this point that two policemen emerged from a cubicle, making unpleasant insinuations and an arrest.'

'Is that a zeugma or a syllepsis?'

'It was an impertinence and an inconvenience.'

'It was in a convenience certainly . . . But you can hardly blame them. I mean, two men kissing in a lavatory and then one of them getting down on his knees . . . what was he thinking of?'

'The job in hand,' said Trefusis coldly.

'Oo-er!'

'Adrian, it is a long walk back to England. I suggest you keep your putrid sense of humour in check.'

'I'm sorry.' Adrian clamped his mouth shut.

'It is possible, I grant you,' Trefusis continued, 'that a person stumbling upon such a *tableau* might be tempted to place constructions of a deleterious nature upon it, but only if their minds were already composed of stuff so gross and rank in nature as to be themselves guilty of as much impropriety as the most shameless erotic miscreant in the land. Stefan, at any rate, found himself wholly perplexed by events. I managed to communicate to him in Hungarian, however, as we awaited the police van. I . . . er . . . created a scene and he was able to grab his briefcase and "make good his escape" as the newspapers have it.'

'What sort of a scene?'

'A scene-y sort of a scene. Just a general, you know, scene.'

'What sort of a scene?'

'Does it matter what sort of a scene?'

'Come on, Donald. What sort of a scene?'

'Oh very well. If you must know, I let out a screech of animal lust and attempted to remove the trousers of the officer detaining me.'

'You did *what*?'

'Well I have no doubt you could have dreamt up a dozen more appropriate schemes, Adrian, but it was all that occurred to me under the duress of the moment. I scrabbled at the unfortunate man's trouser-ings and while his companion leapt forward to rescue him from this parlous circumstance, Stefan found himself temporarily deoppilated. He returned to the Shoulder of Lamb where he left the item he had come up expressly to deliver and which I have with me now. Bob then arranged for his safe return to Hastings'

'Yes, I was meaning to ask you. How come Bob is involved in all this?'

'Bob is a friend.'

'Bletchley?'

'Bob has been involved in all kinds of things in his time. He had his tongue ripped out by the Japanese.'

'*What?*'

'Yes, but he doesn't talk about it.'

'Oh ha frigging ha. You *still* haven't told me who the enemy is.'

Trefusis reached for a figgy oatcake.

'Enemy?'

'Yes, enemy. The people who robbed us in Germany and stole your briefcase. The people who killed Moltaj and who are,' Adrian craned his neck round, 'still hot on our arses.'

'Well now, it would seem we have two "enemies", Adrian. Moltaj was killed by a servant of the Magyar Republic of Hungary, I think there is no doubt of that. Bela's employers have no intention of letting his invention leave their country.'

'And now they are following us?'

'No, we are being followed by enemy number two. It was they who robbed us in Germany last year.'

'And who are they?'

'Well,' said Trefusis, 'I was rather hoping *you* might know that, Adrian.'

Eleven

I

In the corridor, Rudi nearly collided with an enomously fat man with a small head and lank hair. Rudi managed, with a supreme effort of balance and co-ordination, learnt on the ski-slopes of Innsbruck, to avoid the calamity of dropping the drinks tray he was carrying and proceeded, trembling, on his way, cursing under his breath the rudeness and clumsiness of the guests as he went. Probably a music journalist in Salzburg for the Festival; such gracelessness was to be expected from the press.

Rudi tapped gently on the door to the sitting room of the Franz-Josef Suite and listened for a reply. This was his first week at the Österreichischer Hof and he was not certain if it was done simply to knock and enter as he would have done at the Hotel der Post in Fuschl-am-See where he had learnt his trade. The Österreichischer Hof was altogether smarter than the Hotel der Post and things were done here on the international scale, with taste, style, courtliness, discretion and just a *Schluck* of Austrian *Gemütlichkeit*.

There was no reply from within. Yet someone had ordered a bottle of Absolut lemon vodka and three glasses, someone had commanded room-service. Surely it was reasonable to suppose that someone was in the room? He knocked again and waited.

Still nothing. Most puzzling.

Rudi balanced the tray on his shoulder, leant forward towards the door, and coughed purposefully.

From inside he heard a voice. An English voice.

'*Entschuldigen Sie* . . .' Rudi called through the keyhole.

He could sense that his husky tones were not penetrating the thick wood of the door. Rudi was a little nervous. In the kitchens yesterday he had caused a beautiful puff-ball of Salzburger Nockerl, the hotel's speciality, to deflate by dropping a fork into it by mistake, and two days ago – Rudi blushed at the memory – two days ago in the dining room he had spilt some kirsch down the shirt-front of Signor Muti, the famous conductor. Fortunately the *maestro* had been wearing one of his famous black polo-neck shirts and the stain had not shown up so much, but the memory was painful to Rudi.

English people. Were they deaf?

'Excusing me!'

Rudi knocked again, his head leaning against the door. He heard the voice still.

'. . . incontinently and savagely beautiful, not unlike a small chaffinch, but much larger and with less of a salty after-tang . . .'

This Rudi could not understand. The word 'beautiful' was familiar certainly. English girls who came to stay with their families at the Hotel der Post liked to say that it was 'a very beautiful morning this morning, Rudi', that the mountain and the lake and the Schloss were 'simply beautiful' and sometimes, when he had been lucky, that his hair and eyes and his legs and his *Schwanz* were so 'beautiful'. Beautiful he knew, but what was this 'chaffinch'? Of course! a green vegetable, like *Kohl* or *Kraut*, that was chaffinch. A strange conversation this man was having.

'. . . a certain degree of *Schadenfreude* under the circumstances is inevitable perhaps . . .'

'*Schadenfreude!*' He could speak German.

Rudi knocked until his knuckles were raw.

'*Entschuldigen Sie bitte, mein Herr. Hier ist der Kellner mit Ihren Getränken!*'

'. . . a message delivered by motor-bicycle. A curious new phenomenon these despatch riders . . .'

Rudi could wait no longer. He swallowed twice, turned the handle and entered.

A beautiful suite, the Franz-Josef. Herr Brendel the pianist had stayed there last week and the Bösendorfer Grand that had been installed for him had not yet been collected. They should keep the piano here always, Rudi thought. With the flowers and the cigarette boxes and long flowing curtains, it conspired to give the room the look of a film set from the nineteen-thirties. With great care he set down his drinks tray on top of the piano and listened again to the English voice.

'. . . this rider, standing in the threshold holding out a clipboard to be signed, reminded me at first of a copy of Izaac Walton's *Compleat Angler* that I have in my possession. Bound in leather, lavishly tooled and a lasting joy . . .'

'Your drinks are arrived, my sir.'

'. . . of the package that he delivered I can say only this . . .'

The voice was coming through from the bedroom. Rudi approached nervously.

'. . . it shocked me right down to my foundation garments. From stem to stern I quivered . . .'

Rudi straightened his bow-tie and tapped loosely on the half-open bedroom door with the back of his hand.

'Sir, your drinks that you have ordered . . .'

Rudi broke off.

The door he had knocked on so lightly had swung open to reveal a man sitting on the end of the bed, soaked from head to foot in blood. He faced a writing table on which stood a small radio.

'. . . I suppose there are degrees of startlement, much as there are degrees of anything. If there is an official scale comparable to, for example, the Beaufort, Moh or Richter Scales and if that scale be measured from one to ten, I would say that on this Trefusian Scale of Abject Bestartlement I scored at least a creditable 9.7, certainly from the European judges. The East Germans would probably have been less generous, but even they could not have failed to give me 9.5 for artistic impression . . .'

Rudi hugged the door-handle and half swung from the door, staring at the dead man with innocent surprise and wonder, like a child watching donkeys copulate.

A knock on the sitting-room door brought him to his senses.

A high English voice called through the sitting room.

'Martin! Are you there? Martin!'

Rudi jumped. This was witchcraft.

Two men had entered the sitting room, one silver-haired, the other closer to Rudi's age. They were smiling.

'Ah, lemon vodka on the piano. Very much Martin's poison.'

Rudi gasped.

'*Sie sind . . . sie sind!*' said Rudi, pointing at the older man.

'*Was bin ich?*' the man asked in surprise.

So he was German, this man. But the voice. The voice was . . .

Rudi pointed to the bedroom.

'*Da drinnen sitzt ein Mann!*'

'Is there something wrong with him, Donald?'

'*Er ist tot!*'

'Oh dear,' said Trefusis, hurrying forwards. 'Please not. Please not!'

Adrian followed him into the bedroom.

'. . . I will let you know, those of you who are interested, of course, the others will simply have to guess. Meanwhile if you have been, then continue to and don't even think of stopping.'

'Well, as the Professor has just told us, that was the last of the current series of *Wireless Essays from the Desk of Donald Trefusis*. Half an hour of World News in a moment, followed by *Meridian*. BBC World Service. This is Lond – '

Adrian switched off the radio and brought his gaze to bear upon the young man on the bed.

His throat had been cut in a wide crescent from one ear to the other. It was as if a second mouth had been cut beneath the chin. Even the lining of the poor man's jacket had been ripped open. As with Moltaj the previous year, the flap of skin had a gruesomely false, plastic, made-up appearance. Adrian supposed that just as genuine gunfire was said not to sound realistic, so genuine death had a falser air than the gore of the movies.

Rudi gestured towards the radio: '*Das waren Sie, nicht wahr?*'

Trefusis nodded vaguely. '*Jawohl, das war ich.*'

'*Sind Sie Österreicher oder Deutscher?*'

'*Engländer.*'

'*Echt?*'

'*Echt,*' said Trefusis. '*Hast du die Polizei schon telefoniert?*'

'*Nein . . . ich bin nur zwei Minuten da . . .*'

'*Also.*'

Trefusis crossed over to the writing table and picked up the radio.

'*Und hast du jemanden gesehen?*'

'*Nein . . . nie – Moment! Ja, ein dicker Mann . . . sehr dick . . .*'

'*Mit kleinem Kopf and schlichten Haaren?*'

'*Ganz genau!*'

'This young gentleman and I will await the police, Adrian.'

Adrian nodded. He felt sick, deeply sick. Sicker than when he had witnessed the death of Moltaj in Mozart's house, sicker than he had ever felt in his life. It was his fault. It was all his fault. From liar to murderer, like in the Æsop fable.

Trefusis had sat at the table and was scribbling on a sheet of hotel writing-paper. Adrian steeled himself to turn and look at the dead man again. The torn throat and the blood soaking into the sheets were disgusting enough, but somehow the savage shredding of the viscose lining of the jacket seemed a world more obscene. It revealed a wanton animal fury that struck fear into Adrian's soul.

'Adrian, I want you to deliver this note to the British Consulate,' said Trefusis. 'It is to be placed into the hands of the addressee himself. None other.'

Adrian looked at the name written on the envelope.

'Are you sure, Donald?'

'Quite sure, thank you. The Consulate is situated in number four Alter Markt. This has all gone quite far enough.'

II

Adrian made his way across the Makart Steg bridge that connected the Österreichischer Hof with the old town. The Salzach flowed beneath him, traffic flowed past him on the Staatsbrücke, crowds of holiday-makers flowed around him and dark, dreadful thoughts flowed within him.

Some of the shops on the Franz-Josef Kai had begun to place posters in their windows of the con-ductors and soloists due to appear in the Festival. An umbrella and luggage shop by the taxi-rank where Adrian waited was tricolated in the yellow and black livery of the Deutsche Gramophon Gesellschaft. A huge photograph of von Karajan glowered out at him, distrust apparent in the deep frown and clenched brows, contempt all too clear in the upward thrust of the chin and the sour wrinkle about the mouth. Two-horse fiacres flicked past him, bearing tourists and Festival-goers along the Müllner Hauptstraße. A bruised sky bore down. Adrian saw an image of the whole scene through a camera that was zooming outwards and outwards with himself in the centre diminishing and diminishing until he was a frozen part of a postcard pinned to a cork noticeboard in a warm suburban kitchen in England, eternally trapped, blessedly unable to move forwards or backwards in time or space.

At last, after twenty minutes, just as he was preparing to go in the shop and ask about buses, a Mercedes taxi drew up into the empty rank beside him.

'*Britisches Konsulat, bitte. Alter Markt vier.*'

'*Aber man kann es in zwei Minuten spazieren.*'

'*Scheiße.* Never mind. *Das macht nichts.* Take me there anyway. *Es sieht nach Regen aus.*'

Indeed, as Adrian spoke, the first drops began to fall, and by the time the cab drew up outside the Alter Markt, which would indeed have taken only a few minutes to reach on foot, the rain was pouring heavily. The taxi had not been able to go right to the door of the Consulate, so Adrian had to thread his way through the market itself, where people were gathering for shelter under a stall that sold artificial flowers. Number four itself was a small doorway next to the Oberbank a few doors down from Holzermayer's, which sold the *Mozartkugeln*, small chocolate marzipans wrapped in silver-foil portraits of Salzburg's most famous son. Adrian had bought a box for his mother there the previous summer.

'Sir David who?'

The woman at the desk was not helpful.

'Pearce. I know he's here, could you just tell him that . . . hang on.' Adrian took a Festival brochure from a pile on the desk and wrote in a white space on the back. 'Just show him that. I'm sure he'll see me.'

'Well I'm sorry, Mr . . . Telemackles, does it say?'

'Telemachus.'

'No one called Sir David anything at the Consulate. Never has been.'

'He's here. He must be here.'

'You're in trouble, I suppose? Want to borrow money?'

'No, no, no. Look, could you call the Consul and tell him that Telemachus insists on seing Sir David Pearce. Just tell him that.'

'I'll try his secretary,' she said, with a sniff.

Adrian tapped the desk with his fingers.

'Hello, Mitzi? It's Dinah at the front desk. Have a young gentleman here who says he wants to see a Sir David Pearce. I told him we . . . oh . . . I'll ask him.'

The receptionist favoured Adrian with a combative scowl.

'What was that name again, please?'

'Oh, Healey. Adrian Healey.'

'That's not what you said.'

'Never mind, just say Adrian Healey.'

'Mitzi? He says Adrian Healey . . . yes, I'll hold.'

She turned to Adrian again. 'Could you not do that?'

Adrian smiled. His fingers stopped tapping against the desk.

'Yes, dear? All right. You'll send someone down will you?'

'Everything all right?' Adrian asked.

'You're to wait. Chair over there.'

The words had hardly left her lips before Adrian heard a door closing upstairs and footsteps descending the stairs. A greasy-haired man in a powder-blue safari suit bounded towards him with hand outstretched.

'Adrian Healey?'

'We've met before, I think,' Adrian said. 'On the Stuttgart to Karlsruhe Autobahn.'

'Dickon Lister. Simply delighted. Come on up, why don't you?'

Adrian followed Lister up the central staircase and into a vast reception room. Sitting on a sofa, hunched over a small radio set, an earpiece plugged into his left ear, was a man in a Savile Row suit and St Matthew's College tie. Dickon Lister winked at Adrian and left the room.

'Hello, Uncle David.'

'It's unbelievable, Adrian, simply unbelievable!'

'I really don't see how . . .'

Uncle David waved him to silence.

'That's it! That must be it. Lillee has gone, that *must* be it.'

'What . . .'

'Haven't you heard? *Headingley*, man! Botham and Dilley put on one hundred and seventeen for the eighth wicket yesterday. Simply unbelievable. And now . . .' He clapped his thighs ecstatically. 'You won't believe this, Adrian, but Australia needed only one hundred and thirty to win today and they went from fifty-six for one to seventy-five for eight. Willis

320

has run through them like a tornado. What? No . . .
Chilly, you *cunt!*'

'What is it?'

'Chris Old has just dropped Bright. Wake up man!'
he boomed at the radio. 'It was five hundred to one
against an England victory in the betting tent today,
can you credit it? And if it wasn't for you and your
bloody Trefusis I'd be up there now watching the
most exciting Test Match in history. But oh no . . .'

He relapsed into silence again, wincing and grim-
acing at the radio.

Adrian settled himself on the edge of the sofa and
stared into the empty fireplace. He could hear a faint
hiss from Uncle David's earpiece. A clock ticked
slowly on the mantelpiece. Adrian felt the same
molten surge of guilt in his stomach he had felt so
often in the past. He could not for anything imagine
the outcome of the next twenty-four hours, but he
knew that it would be dreadful. Simply dreadful.

Finally Uncle David let out a great roar.

'That's it, that's it! Willis has taken eight for forty-
three! England have won! Ha, ha! Come on, my boy,
cheer up! Let's get Dickon to bring us in some
champagne, what do you say?'

'I think you should read this first.'

'What is it?' Uncle David took the envelope. 'A
demand for more money, Ade?'

Adrian watched Uncle David's face, as he read the
letter through, change from benign indifference to
irritation, anxiety and anger.

'Damn him! Damn him to Spitzburg in a cork-
bottomed raft. Where is he now?'

'Österreichischer Hof.'

'With Pollux?'

'No,' said Adrian. 'The thing is Pollux was dead when we got there. His throat had been . . . you know . . . like Moltaj.'

'Shitty damn. Police?'

'Not yet. There was a waiter though, so I suppose . . .'

'Doublefuck, hell and arse-tits. *Lister!* Where the hell is that man when you need him? *Lister! !*'

'Sir?'

'Get on to Dunwoody at Vienna. Tell him to fix the Salzburg Polizei soon, sooner, soonest. Pollux has been bollocksed in the Österreichischer Hof. Suite?' He clicked his fingers at Adrian. 'Come on boy! Suite? Room number!'

'Franz-Josef it was called, I think,' said Adrian. And don't call me sweet, he added to himself.

'You *think*? Was it or wasn't it?' Uncle David shook him by the shoulders.

'Yes!' shouted Adrian. 'The Franz-Josef.'

'Got that Lister? Full diplo tarpaulin over the whole farting mess. And a car for me and laughing boy here to be at the Goldener Hirsch by six o'clock this pip emma. You'd better come along as well.'

'Armed?'

'No,' said Adrian.

Uncle David's right hand slammed lazily into the side of Adrian's face.

'Don't give orders to my men, Ade, there's a dear.'

'Right,' said Adrian, sitting down on the edge of the sofa. 'I'm sorry.' Uncle David's signet-ring had caught the flesh above his left eyebrow and he blinked as a drop of blood oozed into his eye. The blinking only caused the blood to sting his eyes more, so tears sprang up to wash it away.

Uncle David nodded to Lister.

'Armed,' he said, 'and ever so slightly dangerous.'

Twelve

At one end of the Schubert Banqueting Room at the Goldener Hirsch Hotel a small platform had been arranged on which stood a chair and a table. On the table were set a gavel, a medicine bottle of purple liquid, a metal waste-paper bin, a box of matches, two small radio sets and a pair of headphones. The chair was set to one side, facing out into the rest of the room. Behind the stage a grey curtain obscured the back wall, trimly pleated like a schoolgirl's skirt. The impression given might have been that of a village hall in Kent preparing to host a Women's Institute lecture. Only the tondo portrait of Franz Schubert who gazed down at the room over round spectacles with an affable, academic and Pickwickian air and the collection of antlers distributed on the walls betrayed the Austrian bloodlines of the setting.

A cluster of people stood against the tall window at one side and twittered quietly to each other like shy early arrivals at a suburban orgy. Humphrey Biffen, white-haired and awkwardly tall, stooped like an attentive stork to hear his son-in-law Simon Hesketh-Harvey relate the details of the extraordinary cricket match that had taken place earlier that day in Yorkshire. Lady Helen Biffen was clucking sympathetically at a pale young man with red-rimmed eyes. Amidst them bustled Trefusis with a bottle of Eiswein.

At precisely the moment a gilt and porcelain clock on a plaster corbel by the window chimed six o'clock with dainty Austrian insistence, Sir David Pearce strode in, followed by a smiling Dickon Lister and an ovine Adrian.

Pearce looked about him, failing quite to conceal his satisfaction at the silence his arrival had caused to descend on the room. His manufactured angry glance flashed across at Biffen and his son-in-law, then back to Trefusis who was hurrying forward with three glasses and a bottle.

'Donald, you old barrel of piss!' barked Sir David. 'What are you doing with my man Hesketh-Harvey?'

'Ah, David. Prompt almost to the second! So grateful, so grateful.'

Trefusis proffered Lister a glass, blinking up at him.

'Have we . . .?'

'Lister, Professor. How do you do?'

'If you take hold of these two glasses, Adrian, then I can pour.'

Trefusis looked enquiringly at the swelling over Adrian's eye. Adrian inclined his head minimally towards Pearce and twisted his own ring-finger to indicate the cause of the cut. Trefusis bobbed with comprehension and began gingerly to pour the wine.

'I think you'll like this, Mr Lister . . . oh dear, "Mr Lister"! How inelegant of me. That's worse than "Lord Claude" isn't it? Or "Professor Lesser", come to that. This is called Eiswein, by the way. Are you familiar with it?'

'Ice vine?'

'Eiswein, yes.' Adrian watched with amusement the light of lecture come into Trefusis's eyes as he backed Lister into a corner and began to preach. 'They allow, you know, the full effects of the *pourriture noble*, or *Edelfäule* as they call it here, to take effect on the grape, such that the fruit simply glistens with rot and sugar. They then take the most audacious risk. They leave the grape on the vine and await the first frost. Sometimes, of course, the frost comes too late and the fruit has withered; sometimes too early – before it is yet fully purulent with botrytis. But when, as in this vintage, the conditions concatenate ideally, the result is – I'm sure you'll agree – vivid and appealing. One's sweet tooth returns with age, you know.'

Lister sipped his wine with every evidence of appreciation. Trefusis poured a glass for Sir David and one for Adrian. The overpowering bouquet of thick, honeyed grape almost made Adrian, his head still buzzing from the blow he had received from Uncle David, his mind still dizzy with apprehension, swoon. As he blinked and steadied himself, his focusing eyes met the sad, solemn gaze of Humphrey Biffen who smiled sweetly from the corner and looked away.

'Hum ho,' said Trefusis. 'I am supposing that we had better proceed. Adrian, I wonder if you wouldn't mind accompanying me to the dais?'

Adrian drained his wine-glass, handed it with what he hoped was a flourish to Dickon Lister and followed

Trefusis to the platform. He could not rid himself of the suspicion that this whole charade had been rigged to expose him. But exposure as what, to whom or to what end, he could not for the life of him figure out.

'If you would sit here,' said Trefusis indicating the single chair. 'I think we might be ready to bully off.'

Facing his audience like a conjuror's stooge, with Trefusis behind him at his prop-table, Adrian looked down at his shoes to avoid the stare of expectant faces that were turned towards him. Enticing sounds floated up through the window from the central courtyard bar below; the prattle of drinkers; tinkles of ice and glasses and laughter; a horn concerto by that same Mozart who was born three and half centuries after this hotel had been built and almost exactly two centuries before Adrian had gulped his first lungful of air. The funeral march of Siegfried would have suited his mood better than this foolishly exuberant gallop.

Behind him Trefusis cleared his throat. 'If I might have everyone's attention . . .?'

An unnecessary request, thought Adrian. Every eye in the room was already fixed firmly on the stage.

'Do sit down, everyone, I beg. There are chairs for all. So! That is much better.' Lister had ignored Trefusis's invitation to be seated and stood in the doorway with his legs apart. Whether he imagined he was deterring entrance or egress, Adrian could not decide.

'Perhaps I can prevail upon you to lock the door, Mr Lister . . . ah, I see that you have already done so. Excellent! Now then, I think we all know Adrian Healey. He is Sir David Pearce's nephew, on the distaff. Sir David, of course, is a well-known servant of the government, by which I mean he is not well-known at all, for his department is a clandestine one. His assistant Dickon Lister you see guarding the doorway like Cerberus. They, on behalf of their government, are most interested in a system devised by my friend Bela Szabó. Sir David as an old tutee of mine from university has long known of my association with Szabó, whose distinguished grandson, Grandmaster Stefan Szabó, is with us today.'

Adrian looked at the young man with eyes fresh from weeping who sat between Biffen and Lady Helen. Nothing in the shape of his head or the set of his expression indicated anything of the abstract or logical genius that marked out the chess champion. A rather ordinary, innocent looking fellow. But sad: very, very sad.

'I had hoped that Bela's other grandson, Martin, would be with us too. As I think you all know he was killed today.'

Five sets of eyes bored into Adrian, who coloured and looked down again.

'Also with us are Humphrey Biffen and his wife Lady Helen, old friends and colleagues of Bela and myself. Their son-in-law, Simon Hesketh-Harvey, is here too. As it falls out Simon works in the same department as Sir David.'

'Or at least did until six o'clock this evening,' growled Sir David. 'I'll have your arse for a plate-rack, Hesketh-Harvey.'

'But then of course Simon and Mr Lister are not the only people to have been in your employ, are they, Sir David? I believe I am right in saying that young Master Healey here has been drawing a stipend from you for the last two years at least.'

Adrian closed his eyes and tried to concentrate on Mozart.

'But let us get things in order. Two years ago, Szabó, when still an obedient Hungarian scientist, had been to Salzburg for a conference. There he had hidden papers relating to his Mendax machine. And not a moment too soon. Six months following his return to Budapest, the Hungarian authorities had found out about his work and were demanding to be shown the fruits of it. Your department, David, had heard of Mendax too and became determined that Britain must certainly do its best to gain possession of so intriguing a device – if only as a means of impressing your American *confrères*. The world had just learnt about poor dear Anthony Blunt, we must remember, and I am sure there must have been an overwhelming desire within your Service to win gorgeous trophies to lay before the feet of your betters. You supposed that were Szabó to try to dispose of Mendax then I, as his oldest friend outside Hungary, would in some manner be involved.'

'And so you were, old love.'

'It is true that Szabó sent me a letter last year. He wrote of his wish for me to collect the documents he had hidden in Salzburg. I was requested to be at Mozart's Geburtshaus at two p.m. on the seventh of July where a contact would be awaiting me by a diorama of the supper scene from *Don Giovanni*. I have no doubt you intercepted this letter to me, Sir David. Quite right too, I don't complain of that.'

'Too bloody bad if you did, Professor.'

'Neatly put. So, what happened next? Well, Adrian, the eyes and ears of Sir David Pearce, accompanied me to the rendezvous. My contact at the Geburtshaus was to be a friend of Szabó's named Istvan Moltaj, a violinist officially present in Salzburg for the Festival. So far so splendid.'

'So far so obvious.'

'Well, now to something rather less obvious perhaps.'

Adrian wondered why this meeting seemed to be developing into a public dialogue between Donald and Uncle David.

'I wonder if you have ever heard, Sir David, of Walton's Third Law?'

'No matter how much you shake it, the last drop always runs down your leg?'

'Not quite. It was a wartime SIS convention. If a meeting is set up and a time for it given in the twelve-hour clock – using an a.m. or p.m. suffix – then the meeting is understood to be called for a time thirty-three minutes earlier than that designated. What Adrian would call tradecraft, I believe. Accordingly Moltaj met me not at two p.m. on the appointed day, but at one twenty-seven p.m. At this meeting he told me where to find the Mendax papers. They were to be collected by me from the reception desk here at the Goldener Hirsch. Moments after imparting this information, Moltaj's throat was cut by someone, I must assume, who was blessedly unfamiliar with Walton's Third Law. A few days later, your man Lister, acting, I have no doubt, on information received from Adrian, made a rather vulgar attempt to relieve me of the papers in an Autobahn lay-by in West Germany.'

Sir David leant back in his chair and looked round at Lister, still standing in the doorway. 'Were you vulgar, Lister? I'm sorry to hear that. See me afterwards.'

'Vulgar and unsuccessful. I had left the papers here. I knew perfectly well that Adrian was not to be trusted. That is why I ensured that he was always by my side. Was it not Don Corleone who kept his friends close, but his enemies closer? How could Don Trefusis do less?'

Adrian opened his mouth to speak, but decided against it.

'The technical data on Mendax were securely locked in the safe here at the hotel. But Szabó had also built a working Mendax machine, which he had split into two and entrusted to his grandsons, Stefan and poor Martin. Stefan smuggled out his half in a radio set belonging to another member of his chess delegation and presented it to me in a Cambridge public lavatory a fortnight ago. Martin was to have given me the other half this afternoon in the Hotel Österreichischer Hof, but his throat was cut before he was able to do so. It seems that by this time the killer had worked out how Walton's Third Law operated. That, my dears, is the brief history of Szabó's attempt to get Mendax to me. Does anyone have any questions?'

'If you had left the entire business to us, Tre-blasted-fusis, this whole sordid shambles would have been avoided,' said Sir David.

'I wonder. A problem that has been exercising me mightily is the killing of Moltaj. He was an innocent musician delivering a message for a friend. We have no reason to imagine that he knew about Mendax, no grounds for supposing that he presented a threat to anyone. The Hungarians are not nowadays noted for their savagery in these matters – unlike the East Germans or the British. What conceivable ends could the death of Moltaj serve? It seems to me that this is far from being a trivial issue.'

Trefusis lit a cigarette and allowed the import of his question to sink in. Adrian had done with his inspection of the floor and had now started on the ceiling. He tried to believe that he was a thousand miles and years away.

'Well, we will return to the "Why" later,' said Trefusis. 'The "Who" is interesting also. I saw the killer, as it happens. A very fat man with lank hair and a small head.'

'Who cares?' said Pearce. 'Some bloody Hungo knife artist. Probably halfway across Czecho by now.'

'I think not-o, David-o.'

Sir David put his hands behind his head. 'Donald, give me listen. If you press that wonderful mind of yours into service you will find, after due stock-taking, adding up, taking away, knitting, purling and tacking, that the score is one and a half to half in your favour. You are in possession of the technical bumf and the one half of the machine that your chess-playing friend Castor here gave you in your bog in Cambridge. That's the major haul, old darling. The other half, which the Hungoes got ahold of this afternoon, is n.f.g. without the book of words that you have so cunningly kept clasped to your sagging bosom. You're ahead of the game. Give your winnings to us like a good boy and expect a knighthood by return of post. Failing that, shove it on the open market and make yourself a millionaire. But don't fucking horse around with us. We're busy men. You follow me?'

'Now why should you think that I have only the *one* half of Mendax?'

'Donny dear, you just said, did you not, that the knife artist got to Pollux before you? I take it he didn't kill him just for the fun of it – saving your grief, young Stefan.'

'No, as it happens you are right.' Trefusis picked up the medicine bottle from the table and unscrewed the lid. 'The lining of Martin's coat had been ripped open. I am forced to assume that something was taken.'

'There you are then, so why don't you . . . what the Nigel Christ?'

Trefusis was pouring the purple contents of the bottle into the waste-paper bin on the table in front of him.

'A little prestidigitation to entertain you,' said Trefusis. He struck a match and dropped it into the bin. A great ball of blue and green flame blossomed upwards up for an instant and then shrank away into thick smoke.

'And so we say farewell to Bela's Mendax papers,' said Trefusis.

'You great flapping clitoris,' said Sir David. 'You pointless, fatuous, drivelling old man. What the hell do you think you're playing at?'

'I know what's worrying you, David, but you may rest easy. The smoke alarm has been disconnected. I saw to it earlier this evening.'

'Of course you realise now that you can kiss good-bye to any chance you ever had of getting onto the BBC Board of Governors, don't you?'

'I had no idea I was in the running.'

'All you're in the running for now, matey, is ten years of tax inspectors waking you up at dawn twice a week and policemen stopping your car four times for every two miles you drive.'

'Don't be dismal, David,' said Trefusis. 'I have merely eliminated the vigorish. The game is now even. I have one half of Mendax, while the killer would appear to have the other.'

'Damn you to Hull and all points north.'

'Well, possibly. For the meantime, however, perhaps young Simon can help us out with the identity of this knife artist, if that really is the current jargon. Who is the Hungarians' best assassin, Simon? Not your desk I know, but you've worked there.'

'The artist they like to use is actually a German, sir. Sets up his stall under the name of Alberich Golka.'

'I see. And is this man, I wonder, fat at all?'

'Very fat, sir. That's about the only thing we know about him. He's fat, he's German and he's very expensive.'

'So this costly, full-figured Teuton was employed by the Hungarians to intercept Mendax and, it seems, to kill anyone remotely connected with it. I return to my original question. Why? Why kill Moltaj?'

'Well, sir, it's what killers do. They kill.'

'Only to order. Why *order* this Golka to kill an innocent violinist?'

Simon shrugged politely; Humphrey and Lady

Helen shifted themselves into a more upright position, like churchgoers demonstrating their attentiveness to a sermon; Sir David Pearce yawned; Stefan gazed forlornly out of the window and Dickon Lister continued to bar the door. Adrian wondered when attention was going to be paid to him.

'I ask myself,' said Trefusis, 'why people are ever murdered. They are murdered for reasons of revenge, retribution and rage. They are murdered as a means of winning secrecy and silence, they are murdered to satiate a psychotic lust and/or to achieve a material gain. None of these grounds satisfactorily explains the immense expenditure of monies and risk that was involved in putting a period to the existence of a harmless Hungarian fiddler. Consider too the *manner* of the murder. So grisly, so public, so violent, so uncomely.'

'Perhaps the killer didn't like his face,' suggested Pearce.

'Oh, but it was a lovely face. No, there is only one motive that strikes me as necessary and sufficient. Moltaj's murder was directed at *me*.'

'Golka mistook him for you, sir? That's hardly . . .'

'No, no, Simon. I meant precisely what I said. Moltaj was murdered *at* me, to frighten me.'

Sir David rose, stretched and made his way to the sideboard.

'More of this wine anyone?' he called out to no one in particular.

'Yes please,' said Adrian.

Sir David ignored him, poured himself a glass and resumed his seat. Adrian flushed and scrutinised his shoe-laces.

'I believe,' continued Trefusis, 'that the killing of Moltaj was designed to impress upon me the savage and remorseless lengths to which the Hungarians were prepared to go in order to acquire Mendax. If they mean to kill for it, I was supposed to say to myself, then I had better let them have it at once. But what a footling stratagem! I am not, I hope, so old and feeble an old quiz as all that. If I was truly scared – and I must pause here to assure you that indeed I was as pitifully afraid as ever I have been – then surely the natural course of action for me to have taken would have been to deliver the Mendax papers to Sir David and to rely on his department for protection. The Hungarians are not the kind to set murderers on one's tail simply to exact revenge. They are not MI5, for heaven's sake. Then again, nor are they such idiots as to imagine that they could ever panic me into giving Mendax to *them*, they could only panic me into giving it to my own people. That is when I realised, of course, that this is precisely what was intended. I was meant to be cowed into present-ing Mendax not to the Hungarians, but to Sir David Pearce. Sir David Pearce had been running Golka. Sir David Pearce had ordered the death of Moltaj as a means of frightening me out of the game and Sir David Pearce had ordered the identical death of Martin Szabó that he might maintain his fiction of bloodthirsty Hungarians running riot throughout Salzburg.'

'I'll call for a nurse,' said Sir David. 'You lot keep him talking. And for God's sake humour the poor bastard before he turns violent.'

Trefusis dipped his head sorrowfully. 'No, David,

I don't think anyone will be calling for nurses. Not just now.'

Sir David met the stares of the others in silence and then burst into laughter.

'Oh for God's sake, look at you all! You can't possibly be serious! The man's babbling and you know it.'

'Perhaps we should ask Golka,' said Trefusis.

'Ooh, yes, *what* a good idea. Let's ask Golka. Or Florence Nightingale perhaps, or the Nabob of Bhandipur.'

'Well, Golka?' said Trefusis. 'You are the one who did the killing. Perhaps you could tell us on whose orders?'

Lister did not alter his expression at all. He shifted his weight from his right to his left leg and remained silent.

Adrian felt his gut churning. Ten minutes ago he had not imagined getting out of this session with his integrity unscathed, now he was beginning to doubt that he would get out of it alive.

Simon Hesketh-Harvey coughed and raised a tentative hand.

'Um, excuse me, sir. I hate to seem dim, but are you suggesting that *Lister* is Golka?'

'Oh, there can be no doubt of that. I recognise him, you see.'

'Mm. He's . . . not very *fat* though, is he, sir?'

'Well of course not. Such a *noticeable* thing to be, isn't it, fat? Far from ideal, one might therefore think, for the successful pursuit of the dreadful trade Golka has chosen. But you see, while a fat man can never make himself thin, a thin man may easily make himself fat.'

'*Padding*, do you mean, sir?'

'Quite. His face might not properly match the corpulence of his body, but it is not uncommon, after all, to see men who are fatter in frame than in feature. Is that not right, Mr Lister?'

Lister said nothing.

Adrian stared at him, trying to picture where on his person a gun might be concealed. Or his knives.

'Are you absolutely certain, sir? I mean . . .'

'Oh for God's sake!' exploded Sir David, his voice setting the bells of the gilt and porcelain clock on the wall to chime. 'You work to *me* Hesketh-Pisshead-Harvey! You sir *me*, do you understand? You do not sir this sack of rotting tweed. You sir me!'

Simon did not turn to look at Pearce during this outburst. 'As you say, sir,' he said stolidly. 'You are suggesting then, Professor, that in order to acquire Mendax, Sir David hired Golka?'

'Yes, because he has been operating privately, I think. He wants Mendax for himself. A supplement to the nugatory pension he might expect from his masters. If he had succeeded in frightening me into offering Mendax to Her Majesty's Government, he would have made sure, I have no doubt, that Golka crashed the handover and took Mendax away, apparently from the both of us. It had to look like the Hungarians had won, you understand.'

'This is so stupid of you, Donald,' said Sir David. 'So very stupid. You see, if your analysis is correct, I already have one half of Mendax, the half that Lister

338

took from Martin this afternoon. It seems natural that I should trouble you for the other half.'

'Oh but you don't have one half of Mendax, David. That is the whole point. I have both halves.' Trefusis looked down at the two radio sets on the table in front of him.

Adrian watched as Uncle David's eyes froze into a momentary stare of panic before slowly relaxing into a smile.

'Bad bluff, Donald. V. bad bluff.'

'I am afraid not. You see, there is something else of which you and Lister or Golka – whichever he prefers – are in ignorance. Walton's *First* Law.'

'Oh hell!' said Humphrey Biffen suddenly.

Everyone turned to stare at him.

'Ever since you mentioned the Third Law I've been sitting here racking my brains trying to remember the others,' said Biffen with an apologetic shake of the head. 'I remember Two and Four of course, but what on *earth* was One?'

'Oh come on, Humpty!' his wife nudged him playfully. '"Whatever is on the person is not true." How could you forget?'

'Oh *yes*!' cried Biffen with satisfaction. 'I *am* an old fool. So sorry, Donald.'

'My dear fellow, not at all. Lady Helen is of course quite right. "Whatever is on the person is not true." I wonder, Sir David, if you ever listen to the little wireless essays with which from time to time I infest the air waves? They may be heard domestically every Saturday morning on Radio 4. They are also broadcast around the globe by the BBC World Service.'

'I know that. Anyone who's ever tried to listen to the cricket knows that. To their bored cost.'

'Ah, then it is possible that you heard this week's essay? It was transmitted in Europe this morning at oh three hundred hours and again at fifteen hundred this afternoon.'

'Yes, I heard it,' said Sir David. 'By God, this had better be leading somewhere.'

'Indeed it is. You might recall a reference to a chaffinch in my piece. Chaffinch is my name for Martin Szabó. Stefan here is Coaltit, I am Bald Eagle, Adrian is Lyre Bird.'

Adrian blushed again. Why 'Liar Bird'? It didn't seem fair.

'And you, Sir David,' continued Trefusis, 'are · Duvet, I don't know why, but you are. I hope that doesn't upset you.'

'I've been called worse things.'

'Oh, surely not?'

'Just get on with it, will you?'

'Very well. In this same broadcast I also uttered these words . . . let me see . . . the sentence went like this . . . "reminded me at first of a copy of Izaac Walton's *Compleat Angler* that I have in my possession". Yes, I think that was it. This was an instruction to Martin to obey Walton's First Law: Whatever is on the person is not true. "Reminded me at *first* of a copy of Izaac *Walton's* . . ." I knew, you see, that if you or Golka did intercept Martin you would expect to find your treasure in the lining of his coat. In his last interview with his grandson in Hungary, Szabó had deliberately told Martin that this was where Mendax should be secreted. Your department's man in Budapest has a contact inside the Hungarian secret police. Simon tells me he is called "Locksmith". "What you want will be in the lining of Martin Szabó's jacket," Locksmith no doubt signalled to London, as Bela intended him to. You briefed Golka accordingly: "Expect to find Mendax in the lining of Pollux's coat," you will have said. Martin did indeed create an inner pocket to his jacket in which he hid a piece of microcircuitry. This Lister gratefully took after he had cut the poor boy's throat. I believe you will discover that what you killed that boy to obtain controls the spin cycle of a tumble drier. The wireless set on Martin's dressing table would have yielded a much richer secret. I have it here.'

Trefusis held up the second of the two radios.

'There we have it, you see. Mendax. I know how badly you want it, David, and I am so terribly sorry that I am not in a position to oblige you. Humphrey and Lady Helen, like myself, are old friends of Bela Szabó and we feel that we have the prior claim. Simon's loyalty, naturally, is to his parents-in-law and to me, the devoted godfather of his wife Nancy. Stefan here, as Bela's heir and the brother of Martin, whom you so pitilessly slew, must decide on what punishment should be meted out to you. Lister, I'm afraid, cannot be allowed to live.'

Sir David rose to his feet. 'This has all been most instructive,' he said. 'A tidy operation on your part, Donald. I congratulate you. I must now ask you to present Mendax to me. Mr Lister, *if* you please.'

Adrian watched as Lister's right hand went slowly to his left side and brought out, from under the lapel of his powder-blue safari jacket, an automatic revolver. At least Adrian supposed it was an automatic revolver. It was certainly some form of hand gun, and it was pointed very directly at the head of Professor Trefusis. Adrian had imagined that he had a lifetime before him in which to acquire all kinds of facts, including a basic knowledge of firearms, enough for instance to be able to tell the difference between a pistol, a revolver, an automatic or a semi-automatic. But now he was to be killed by one such instrument before he had the chance to find out what it might be.

'Mendax,' said Trefusis with no indication of concern, 'is of course yours to keep or dispose of as you will, Sir David. I have no argument against bullets. But I must ask you to allow me to finish my address. Then you may kill us all, as kill us all you surely must, for I am sure I speak for everyone in this room when I say that I have every intention of informing your political masters of the entirely reprehensible part you have played in this affair.'

'Oh certainly I shall kill you all,' said Sir David. 'With the greatest pleasure in the world I shall kill you all.'

'Naturally. But I cannot allow you to purchase Mendax, even at the bargain price of six bullets, without offering you a demonstration of its prodigious abilities. You cannot be expected to buy a pig in a poke, Sir David . . . sight unseen. That, after all, is why Adrian is with us here.'

Sir David folded his arms and reflected.

'Very well,' he said. 'If it amuses you.'

'Thank you,' Trefusis bent down over the table. 'Now correct me if I am wrong, Stefan, but I believe that all we need do is connect these two radio sets like so . . .'

Adrian forced his eyes away from the gun in Lister's hand and round towards Trefusis behind him. He had prised open the battery compartments of each radio. From one a ribbon of parallel connecting cable now protruded, ending in a plug. As Trefusis pushed this plug into the battery compartment of the other it snapped home with a soft plastic click. He plugged the headphone jack into one of the radios and looked enquiringly towards Stefan, who was shaking his head.

'Not this, it must be the other. Certainly the other.'

'Thank you, my boy.' Trefusis unplugged the headphones from the first radio and attached them to the minijack socket of the second. 'Two hundred and fifty metres, I think?'

'Sure,' said Stefan. 'You will hear noise.'

Trefusis held the headphones up to one ear and turned the tuning wheel on the first radio set. 'Aha!' he said at length. 'Adrian, if you would be so kind . . .'

Adrian took the headset with trembling hands. He looked up at Trefusis, who returned the gaze affectionately.

'Must be done, my dear,' he said. 'I don't believe you will be harmed in any way.'

As soon as the headphones were over his ears, Adrian felt reassured. A gentle hiss filled his head, foregrounded by brighter, sharper little sounds that were like an aural equivalent of spots in front of the eyes. It was very pleasant, very relaxing; a bath for the brain. He heard too, quite clearly, the real external sound of Trefusis pressing a button on the device behind him. The effect of this was to cause the hiss, and the dancing little sounds in front of it, to be replaced by a wider, deeper hum. Slowly Adrian lost all sensation of physical contact with the world. He knew quite clearly that he was sitting in a chair, but he could not feel which parts of his body were touching it. Somewhere in the centre of this warm, weightless pool of sound hung the voice of Donald Trefusis.

'Tell me how you feel, Adrian.'

Adrian knew how he felt. He knew everything. Suddenly nothing in his mind was mystery; all was open and clear. It was as if he was swimming through the lobes, folds, neurones, synapses, chambers and connectors of his own brain.

'I feel fucking great,' he declared. 'Sort of swimming feeling like the time I had that grass round at Mark's place in Winnet Street – that must have been years ago – I can see the outline of Lister's cock the way he's standing there – very badly cut safari suit I suppose – small circumcised as well – and after we had the grass I was really sick all over Mark's duvet – when Uncle David came to stay and I was twelve I found magazines under his bed I remember – that fluff smell under the spare-room bed – I smelt it again when we stayed in the hotel on Wednesday on our way to Salzburg – I had to pretend I knew the difference between grass and resin which I didn't which is pathetic because it's so fucking obvious isn't it – I wish I hadn't taken Uncle David's fucking money – why on earth Donald calls him Duvet – the word for the unit of thermal insulation in duvets is

344

tog – Donald will know where it comes from – come to think of it I haven't had a wank in two days – Lister can't kill us all can he – I mean this is mad completely mad – they might sell KY jelly in a chemist's somewhere in the Getreidegasse – all that blood – if I *do* die it won't matter anyway because I'm such a cunt I won't notice – Uncle David is listening to me and looking at me as if I was a fish in a tank and I can hear Donald talking to me so I suppose if none of you minds I had better shut up and listen to what he's saying – big helmet but tiny cock – you've hardly said anything Biffo and your wife hasn't said much either – showing through his togs – what are you doing here anyway – I suppose Donald asked you to follow him as well when we were driving here – I'm asking you a question Mr Biffen and you aren't answering – or rather I suppose you *are* answering because your mouth is opening and closing but I can't hear you – awful white spittle you have in the corners of your mouth – I've just had this gross image of you and Lady Helen snogging can you imagine – someone is telling me to be quiet I can hear them – I think I had better stand up now – no I can't because the headphones would slip off – I mean grass looks like grass and resin doesn't but I thought it was a trap I suppose – Lister wearing padding and looking fat – I wonder if Simon is armed and is going to try and shoot Lister before he can fire at Donald – Lister has heard me say that now and he will probably shoot Simon first just in case – me and my big mouth – can't be an automatic revolver come to think of it doesn't sound right – somebody is still telling me to be quiet – thirty-eight that must be it a thirty-eight automatic though

whether that's thirty-eight millimetres or inches I
have no idea – wasn't there someone called Lister at
school – Hugo is turning into an alcoholic because of
me – it really is a *very* small cock that Lister has got
perhaps that is why he is a killer – if Donald knew all
along that I was being paid by Uncle David then he
has never liked me and if he has never liked me then
perhaps it's just as well Lister is going to shoot us all
– do you remember that time when you made me
write to Mother Uncle David and I saw Tony Greig
– I hope Lister shoots the others first so I can watch –
that's disgusting but then I am disgusting I suppose
everyone is – I'm so happy – I really like all of you
you know that – I simply must have a fuck before I
die there was a girl on the footbridge with simply
astonishing tits – Stefan's got quite a cute bum it has
to be said oh for God's sake Adrian he's just lost a
brother – I don't know why but I like you all but I
am glad that we are all going to die and be together –
I like you too Uncle David I always – the magazine
under your bed was called *Lolita* wasn't it completely
hairless vaginas – I can't imagine how you spell Golka
but it is rather an impressive name – I suppose it gets
bigger when he's excited – when he's cutting someone's throat probably – as big as a thirty-eight slug I
suppose – looks like a slug at the moment – this is an
amazing experience – I probably love Donald – not
like Hugo or Jenny – not like wanting to go to bed
with him – ha can you imagine that Donald – me
going to bed with you – no I don't mean that but I
think I love you in every other way and of course you
hate me don't you as you should because I am such a
cunt – everyone watching me and listening to me and

me making a total arse of myself because I can't help it though it's good to get it off my chest – of course it's never going to end because – '

'Thank you, Adrian, I think that will do.'

Trefusis pulled off the headphones and the air seemed to scream into Adrian's head with a huge kicking electric shock. He gasped like a skin diver breaking the surface. He felt Donald's hand on his shoulder and the stares of everyone else in the room piercing him through to the brain. Rocking backwards and forwards in his chair, he buried his head in his hands and began to cry.

Through the close snivel of his weeping he heard re-establish themselves the sounds of the room: the music in the courtyard below, the ticking of the clock and Uncle David's crude heckling.

'What bloody use is this? The boy's done no more than drool and blub like a maniac. I don't need a machine to make him do that. One swift kick in the balls would be enough.'

'I imagine,' said Trefusis, 'that had we left the machine attached for longer, every truth in Adrian's brain would have been disgorged.'

'What a revolting thought.'

Adrian leant back in his chair and opened his eyes.

'May I stand up please?' he asked in a small voice. 'I think my leg may have gone to sleep.'

'Yes, yes, of course. Walk around the room a little, my boy.'

Avoiding the eyes of Stefan, Simon and the Biffens, Adrian stepped down from the dais.

Sir David gave the wide shrug of a man who believes himself to be surrounded by fools. 'Well I dare say it might work,' he said. 'Just leave it where it is and walk away from the table, will you?'

'In a moment, David,' said Trefusis. 'First I have to do this . . .'

Trefusis raised the gavel like a benevolent judge and brought it down onto the coupled radios. Splinters of broken plastic flew across the room. Sir David stiffened.

'You're dead, Donald,' he hissed. 'Do it, Dickon!'

'No! No, no, no, no, no!'

With a screech that tore his throat Adrian threw himself at Lister, knocking him to the floor. He fell on him with a roar, banging his head down onto his chest, barking and bellowing into his face.

'I'll kill you! Kill you! I'll kill you!'

He felt the sharp profile of the gun against his stomach, and pressure upwards as Lister's gun hand tried to free itself from the weight of Adrian's body.

Through the background clamour of upraised voices, Adrian thought he heard Simon Hesketh-Harvey shout, 'Pull him off!'

Hands pulled roughly at his shoulders, trying to tug him away. Why the hell didn't they run? Why couldn't they leave him be? What was the point of sacrificing yourself like this if your allies stayed around to watch? This was their chance to flee. Did they *want* to be killed?

Adrian kicked his knee into Lister's stomach and the gun exploded with a dull boom.

For a second Lister and Adrian stared at each other. Someone, it could have been Uncle David, said, rather impatiently, 'Oh for heaven's *sake*!'

Adrian felt hot blood surge against his stomach like

a discharge of semen and wondered whether it was his or Lister's.

'Oh shit,' he said as Lister rolled away. 'It's mine.'

'It's not my fault!' someone close to him cried. 'He just . . .'

Adrian's eyeballs slid upwards and he fell forward. 'I'm so sorry,' he said.

As he fell into unconsciousness he thought he heard the voice of Bob, the landlord of the Shoulder of Lamb.

'You silly arse, sir. I had him covered all the time.'

But as Adrian slipped away, Bob's voice, if it had ever been there, tapered and dissolved into the only sound that accompanied Adrian into the darkness, the sound of Trefusis wailing.

Thirteen

Professor Donald Lister's face hung above Adrian like a great white balloon. Adrian forced his eyes wider open and tried to remember who Professor Donald Lister could be. He had not realised that such a person was.

The balloon moved away and split itself into two, like the dividing of a gigantic cell.

'You should sleep, my boy,' said Trefusis.

'Sleep,' echoed Dickon Lister.

The two new balloons separated and disappeared from Adrian's line of vision.

A little while later he opened his eyes again to find Istvan Moltaj and Martin Szabó gazing down upon him. Their throats were pure and unscarred, their brown eyes round with compassion.

'Very pale, Helen. Is it right he should be so pale?'

'Only to be expected,' said the voice of Lady Helen Biffen.

Adrian smiled. 'Thank you for welcoming me here,' he said. 'I had always known that death would never be the finish. I hope we can stay friends throughout eternity.'

He realised with a flick of annoyance that although he had uttered the words quite plainly they had sounded only inside his head. His lips had not moved nor had his larynx stirred. Perhaps there was a special technique up here that he would have to master in order to be able to communicate. He dwelt on the possibility for a while and contemplated with drowsy satisfaction the prospect of the infinite time now available to him.

Adrian awoke from his dreams in some discomfort. The bedroom was very familiar. The dressing table at the end of the bed he had seen before only recently. He hauled himself up onto his elbows to get a better view, then yelped in agony as a sharp pain shot through his stomach. Footsteps hurried towards him from a connecting room. As he sank back, spent, the thought came to him that he was in the same suite of the Hotel Österreichischer Hof that Martin Szabó had stayed in, that he was lying on the very bed that Martin Szabó had sat on when his throat had been cut.

'Adrian, you shouldn't try to move,' said Trefusis.

'No,' said Adrian. 'Sorry.' He closed his eyes in order to concentrate on framing a question but the question eluded him and he fell asleep.

He came round a little later to find Trefusis sitting by his bed.

'Morning, Donald. If it is morning.'

'Yes,' said Trefusis. 'It is morning.'

'I'm alive then?'

'I think we can go that far.'

'What day is it?'

'Wednesday.'

'Wednesday. How long have I been here?'

'No more than a few hours.'

'That's all?' Adrian was surprised. 'They got the bullet out, did they?'

'Bullet? There was no bullet.'

'But I was shot.'

'Yes, you were shot, but there was no bullet.'

Adrian pondered this.

'What's hurting me then?'

'You lost some blood. I should imagine your stomach will be a little sore for a while. The plaster from your dressing will be pulling at your skin.'

'I'm quite hungry.'

'Rudi will bring you something.'

'Good-o,' said Adrian and fell asleep again.

Two days later Adrian sat at the piano in the Franz-Josef Suite and picked his way through Beethoven's Minuet in G. There was a plate of sandwiches and a glass of beer in front of him. His suitcases were assembled in the middle of the room ready to be taken down to reception. He had felt fully fit enough to bear Donald company for the long drive home in the Wolseley but Trefusis had insisted he go by air.

Adrian's stomach was healing very well, the raw little eruptions where the embedded wadding had been picked out with tweezers were capped with fresh scar tissue and he could now touch the long soft tongue of burn-tissue on his left side without wincing.

He closed the piano lid and straightened himself. It was a companionable kind of pain, clean and sharp as Pilsner; a better pain than the crushing leaden ache of guilt he had carried around with him for as long as he could remember.

There was a hearty knock at the door and Simon

Hesketh-Harvey came in, followed by a beaming Dickon.

'*Grüß Gott*,' said Adrian.

'And how's the lad?'

'The lad's fine thank you, Dickon,' said Adrian. 'And looking forward to going home.'

'That's the ticket,' said Simon.

'No,' said Adrian, pulling a travel wallet from his jacket pocket, 'this is.'

A long table had been prepared in the upstairs room of the Shoulder of Lamb. Nigel the barman was serving soup under the vigilant eye of Bob, the landlord. Trefusis sat at one end, with Adrian at his left hand side and Lady Helen Biffen on his right. Martin and Stefan Szabó, Humphrey Biffen, Dickon Lister, Istvan Moltaj and Simon and Nancy Hesketh-Harvey were all present, chattering and laughing with the hysterical bonhomie of businessmen at a Christmas party. There was one empty chair halfway down the table on Lady Helen's side.

'But why did you have to go to such lengths?' Adrian was asking Trefusis. 'I mean why couldn't you just *tell* me what was going on?'

'It was very necessary, I am afraid, that you acted in complete ignorance of the whole affair. David Pearce was paying you to spy on me after all. You believed you were acting in the interests of his department. That was how it had to remain. We knew he wanted Mendax for himself, not for his country but for his own enrichment. It was expedient that you should be unaware of this.'

'What about Lister? Is he really Golka?'

353

'Lister used to work as a junior official at the British Council in Bonn. Simon found out that Pearce had inexplicably seconded him to the Consulate in Salzburg. This puzzled Simon. He picked Lister up and questioned him with some force. Lister is indeed Golka – between ourselves,' said Trefusis, lowering his voice, 'not a very pleasant man, I'm afraid. It became apparent that Sir David was quite prepared to kill for Mendax. This was wholly unacceptable to us. We made Lister an offer. He was to keep us informed of Pearce's plans, much as you were keeping Pearce informed of ours, and we would arrange that he need only *pretend* to kill Moltaj and Martin.'

'As long as I witnessed these killings?'

'Oh yes, that was very necessary. Your description of them to your Uncle David would be of the utmost importance. It had to seem to him that, although he had just failed to get hold of the Mendax papers, he had at least succeeded in getting hold of one half of the device itself. When he knew that I had the rest he would come out into the open and reveal his true motives.'

'There's one thing,' said Adrian. 'When you attached Mendax to me I heard nothing through those headphones but white sound. I felt no compulsion to do anything but fall asleep. All that guff I came out with, it was just a put on. I made it up.'

'Of course!' said Trefusis. 'Haven't you understood it yet? Mendax doesn't exist.'

'What do you mean?'

'It's a nonsensical notion, absolutely nonsensical. But we had to make Pearce believe it could really work.'

'But you hooked me up to it!'

'That's right.'

'I might have blown the whistle. Simply announced that it wasn't doing anything for me, just hissing in my ear. How could you know that I wouldn't?'

'I relied on the fact that you are a chronic liar. Once you were attached to a device that was supposed to make you tell the truth but didn't work, you would naturally do the dishonest thing and pretend that it did. It was mixture of suggestion on my part and appalling dishonesty on yours. Not that it mattered whether you went through that charming and absurd act or not. Pearce had shown his hand by this time. I am only sorry that you decided to behave in such a peculiar fashion as to throw yourself at Lister's gun.'

'It was very brave of the poor darling,' said Lady Helen. 'And it was criminally foolish of Lister to have loaded blank charges. They can be very dangerous.'

'It might have been necessary for him to appear to shoot one of us,' said Trefusis.

'A toast!' cried Simon Hesketh-Harvey. 'To Adrian Healey, saint and hero.'

'Adrian Healey, saint and hero.'

'Thank you,' said Adrian, touched. 'It was nothing, really.' He beamed around the room. 'So the invention of Mendax was merely a ruse.'

'Some of us,' said Simon Hesketh-Harvey, 'had been entertaining doubts as to Sir David's trustworthiness over a number of years. Donald came up with the idea of Mendax. Over a two- year period he corresponded with Bela on the subject, knowing that Sir David would eventually get to hear of it. An old hand like Donald must expect his mail to be interfered

355

with. He never expected that one of his own students would be set to spy on him, however. That was a tremendous bonus.'

'Steady on,' said Adrian. 'David is my uncle you know. Blood is thicker than water after all.'

'Not thicker than friendship I might have hoped,' said Trefusis. 'But there! No recriminations. You acted splendidly.'

Bob, the landlord, leant forward and winked. 'I had a great big gun pointed at Sir David from behind the curtain all the time, Master Adrian, sir.'

'Well, you might have told me,' said Adrian. A wave of tiredness came over him and he gave a huge yawn, the effort pulling at his stomach muscles and reawakening the wound.

Humphrey Biffen must have read the momentary twinge of pain in Adrian's face, for he was instantly on his feet. 'You are still weak, Adrian. One of us should take you back to St Matthew's.'

Adrian rose as steadily as he could. 'That's all right,' he said. 'The walk will clear my head.'

Cambridge in the long vacation had a forlorn, slightly embarrassed appearance, like an empty theatre. It was a warm night. Adrian looked up at St John's College chapel and at the stars beyond. The soft summer air refreshed him. Perhaps he would not go straight home to bed after all. There was a great deal to think about. In his pocket he had a letter from Jenny. It had awaited him in his pigeon-hole at St Matthew's on his return from Gatwick that afternoon. It seemed that she had got herself a job as an assistant director at Stratford. Adrian crossed the road, sat on the low stone wall opposite the pub and lit a cigarette.

He found that the letter could be read both as a farewell and as a plea for his return.

'I cannot decide whether or not you have grown up yet. What *is* this fantasy world that men inhabit? I don't think there is anything so wonderful about hard-nosed realism or remorseless cynicism, but why must you always revert to type? Have you already become an irretrievable "Enemy of Promise"? I was rereading it the other day. What is that final phrase about all Englishmen . . . that they become "Cowardly, sentimental and in the last analysis homosexual"? It was written fifty years ago for God's sake! It can't still be true can it – after a world war, a social revolution, rock and roll and all the rest?

'I was so in love with you last year. I believed we were the most remarkable couple anywhere. All my friends thought I had it made, that's a terrible phrase I know, but you know what I mean. I don't think you quite believe that women exist. To you they're a kind of difficult boy with surplus flesh in some places and missing flesh in others. I'm not even sure if you ever enjoyed my company, but then I don't know if you ever enjoyed anyone else's either, including your own. I know you hate amateur psychology but there it is.

'"Little girls grow up to be women, little boys grow up to be little boys." I can't believe that our generation is growing up to fulfil all the ridiculous stereotypes. So I'll become an earth mother and you will loll in front of the television watching cricket and Clint, is that it? Then why the years of education? Why a youth at all? Why read books and try to puzzle things out if it all ends in the same way?

'To you and your kind your youth and upbringing

take on this great mystique, the quality of myth. The first twenty years of my life are an open book, school and home, home and school, some friends here, some friends there. To you they are the backdrop to a gigantic world of fantasy to which you have endlessly to return. "Dearest creature, you do not understand . . ." I hear you say, as generations of men have always whined to their women. But that is the point! I do not understand. Nor, even if you had more persuasive powers of exposition than you already do, could you ever make me understand. Because there is nothing *to* understand. That is what *you* have to understand. You grew up, you went to this school and that one, you made these friends and those. It was nothing. The future is a much bigger deal than the past, Adrian, a much bigger deal. Not just because it has babies in it, but because there are better people in it, who are better behaved and more fun to be with; the scenery is better, the weather is better, the rewards and thrills are better. But I really am not sure that you will ever . . .'

A commotion coming from the Mitre, the pub next door to the Shoulder of Lamb, caused Adrian to look across the road. Both establishments had reached closing time. The landlord of the Mitre was escorting a boisterous group of drinkers into the street. Nigel, next door in the Shoulder, was locking up for the night. Something higher up caught Adrian's attention. One window of the room upstairs, the private dining room which he had just left, was directly above the street entrance of the pub. Adrian could see the clear silhouette of a man standing with his back to the window. Trefusis proposing a toast, perhaps. He looked harder. No, assuredly not Trefusis.

Adrian waited for the pack of drunken rejects from the Mitre to disperse. They stood jeering boozily outside the pub for what seemed an age before at last shouting and kicking their way towards Magdalene Bridge and out of sight. The street was empty. Adrian crossed over and edged his way round to the alleyway that connected the two pubs. The ground floor of the Shoulder of Lamb was empty. Adrian looked around for a box or beer crate that he could stand on. There was a plastic dustbin in the corner of the alley marked 'Mitre Only!' in white paint, the exclamation mark betraying a whole history of bitter inter-pub rivalry that Adrian had time to find both comic and pitiful. He edged the bin under the Shoulder's ground floor window and, setting his left leg onto the lid, tried to haul himself up, but the dustbin buckled and he found himself thigh deep in refuse. Pain ripped across his stomach and he gagged at the stench of garbage that rose to his nostrils. It was an abiding mystery to Adrian that all man-made rubbish smelt the same once it had been in a dustbin for any length of time. Trying hard not to breathe, he turned the bin upside down and tested if the base would be more likely to take his weight. It held and Adrian got his foot to the window ledge and straightened himself. His head was now no more than two feet below the level of the first floor window. He heard the voice of Humphrey Biffen.

'I'm still not quite sure how we score this,' he was saying.

'Excuse me?' said a Szabó.

'Well, it's Donald's victory again. No doubt about that,' said Nancy. 'Even if we take Lyre Bird out of the picture altogether. He was, after all, a shared resource. The same result would have been achieved without him. He merely added zest. You have to admit it, you failed to take Walton's Rules into account and you genuinely believed that you held one half of Mendax: you loused up, didn't you, David?'

'Bollocks to the lot of you,' growled the voice of Uncle David. 'Donald changed the game halfway through! Turned it into some half-baked fiction just so that he could put that dandiprat of a nephew of mine over his knee and give him a spanking. A spanking that he richly deserved, I will grant you.'

'Well, that's what gave you half a chance,' said Nancy. 'You were beaten all ends up and you know it.'

'Ha! You wait. Just you watch my smoke. If you're not all excessively nice to me I'll set the next round in Lebanon and then you'll know what's what.'

'What are you going to tell the department?' asked Humphrey.

'Nothing *to* tell. Wasted a tiny amount of cash on the surveillance of Stefan. A few flights to Salzburg. Activated our man Locksmith in Budapest. An idle bugger who needed a sharp toe up his totsie anyway. No harm done. The world knows you're my Moriarty, Donald. They let me have a fly at you once in a while, to humour the mad dog in me. They're relieved to see that I have a human flaw, is my view of it.'

'And when do you play your next game?' asked the other Szabó.

'We try to make each game run for at least two or

three years,' said Trefusis. 'Like any decent real life engagement. We will take the next year off before starting again. David and I are the antagonists and it is up to us to recruit as we please. I nearly always have Humphrey and Helen on my side, and David likes to use Dickon. I am the spy and David the spycatcher.'

'Donald devises the scenario and I have to stop him. Which I did in seventy-four.'

'David is at liberty to use all the facilities of his Service, but at his own risk.'

'And at yours, old love,' said David. 'The fact that you are now branded a dirty lavatory loiterer is some kind of victory for me, I venture to think.'

'That's a point,' said Simon. 'You did nearly get yourself sent to prison, Donald.'

'An unlooked-for occurrence, I admit, but these things lend lustre to the reputation of a fading don, don't you feel?'

'Can't you do something about that, David?' asked Helen. 'A word in the right ear, a review of evidence, a retraction from the arresting officer . . . *something*?'

'Of course, of course,' Uncle David's voice murmured affably.

'Really David, there's no need . . .'

'When did you start all this please?'

'When the game proper ended,' said David. 'About twenty years ago life in the Service became dull, pompous, sordid and absurd. Bloody good bouillabaisse, Bob.'

'Thank you, sir. Got the trick of it in Marseille.'

'Yum, yum.'

'Tell me a thing,' said Trefusis. 'In the car driving

over to Salzburg, Adrian told me what we might call his life story.'

'Oh ah?'

'He told me about you and Helen at school, Humphrey.'

'Yes, he came to a couple of our Friday afternoon teas, didn't he, dear?'

'He told me too, about bumping into you, David, at Lord's in . . . seventy-five or six it must have been.'

'Oh yes, that'll be the Aussie test. I remember. Don't know what he means by "bumping into me" though.'

'No?'

'His parents were going on holiday. Naturally they didn't want the little rat getting under their feet then. Shoved him onto me.'

'He hadn't . . . then . . . *run away* from home in any way?'

'Good Lord no! That what he told you? No, no. Pretty normal schooling he had as far as I can remember. Got slung out for nobbing half his house and circulating filthy drivel in a school magazine. Couple of years at the local college in Gloucester where he got his "A" levels. Taught at some prepper in Norfolk. Then St Matthew's. Why, tell you something different did he?'

'No, no. That was broadly the story as he told it me. One or two, er . . . embellishments perhaps. A lot of highly entertaining nonsense about Piccadilly and prison and so forth. I'm sure he never intended to be so insulting as to expect me to believe them.'

Adrian's foot slipped on the ledge. Scrabbling wildly to regain his balance, he kicked a toe through the window, knocked the dustbin from under him and fell backwards onto the ground. Without stopping to see what damage he had caused either to himself or to the window, he picked himself up and ran out into the street.

Fourteen

Adrian brought the tips of his fingers together and smiled gently. The girl's voice continued to read.

'*Othello* is a tragedy of privacy, a phrase that itself expresses incongruity, for, as with most Shakespearean tragedy, success is achieved by a treatment unsuited to the form. And it is the lack of suiting which makes the theme perennial; the tearing- down of a privacy is a subject which fits our age, as it might fit any age. It lets in chaos, and lets out love.'

'Oh bravo!' cried Adrian. 'Memorably phrased, Shelagh.'

The girl flushed slightly with pleasure. 'You like it Dr Healey?'

'Indeed! I liked it when I first read it . . . phew, let me see . . . must be getting on for ten years ago now . . . nineteen eighty-one, I'm pretty sure it was . . . and I like it just as much now. If anything age seems to have improved it. John Bayley, *Shakespeare and Tragedy*, published, unless I'm very much mistaken, by Routledge and Kegan Paul.'

'Oh dear,' the girl flushed again, but not this time with pleasure.

'Too memorably phrased I am afraid, my dear.'

'Thing is . . .'

'I *know* you are . . . frantically busy. But believe me, I had far rather listen to that good essay than the bad one you would have contrived without Bayley's help. All's well. I think you will manage to get yourself an adequate degree without my pestering you every fortnight for an essay, don't you?'

'Well . . .'

'Of course you will!' Adrian stood and refilled Shelagh's glass. 'A little more malvoisie for you?'

'Thank you.'

'A smoky volcanic bite that cannot disgust. You act, I believe?'

'Yes . . . that's why I get so behind with work.'

'I don't know why I say "believe" you act, I've seen you in a number of productions. My wife is down from London this weekend, you may have heard of her?'

'Jenny de Woolf, the director? Of course!'

'Then why don't you come round to our house in Trumpington this evening and say hello?'

'Really? I'd love to.'

'All right, my dear. Seven o'clock, shall we say?'

'That would be fine. Thanks!'

Adrian watched with approval as the girl gathered her bag and her scarf and made for the door. 'By the way, Shelagh . . .'

She paused enquiringly in the doorway.

'I note,' said Adrian, 'that you are a member of the University Humanist Society.'

She looked back at him with a hint of defiance and suspicion.

'Yes?'

'You take it seriously?'

365

'Very.'

'You dislike religion perhaps?'

'I loathe religion.'

'Ah, now that is interesting. I think that tonight I shall invite old Trefusis along as well, you'd like him I'm sure, and I know he'll like you. We are currently working on a . . . on a problem that may interest you.'

'Oh?'

'As you may know, the nineties have been nominated the "Decade of Evangelism" by various functionaries culled from the madder wings of the Christian church.'

The girl's mouth wrinkled in comic disgust. 'Don't remind me.'

'We have discovered that behind this weird and pitiable phrase there lies . . .' Adrian broke off. 'Never mind. I'll tell you the rest tonight. Dryden House, Trumpington. Can't miss it.'

The girl looked intrigued. 'Right. I'll see you then, Dr Healey. Er . . . bye then.'

'Goodbye, Shelagh. Oh and Shelagh?'

'Yes?'

'I'd appreciate it if you didn't mention this to anyone for the moment. You'll find out why.'

Adrian looked out of the window and watched the girl hop across the grass of Hawthorn Tree Court. He smiled to himself as he sat at his desk and wrote a short note on a sheet of writing- paper.

'To Bald Eagle. Gingerbread. Informal. I think the game may well be afoot. Love Liar Bird.'

Adrian leant back in his chair, fed the paper into his fax machine and pressed an autodial key. He watched the sheet chug through the machine before crossing to his window again.

On the other side of the court he could make out the figure of an old man through an open window on the first floor. The figure stooped down for a moment and fiddled with something on his desk and then came up bearing a ripped sheet of paper. He turned in Adrian's direction, flourishing the paper like a Morris dancer waving a handkerchief, and executed a quick little jig.

Adrian laughed and turned back into the room.

Acknowledgements

Donald Trefusis and his Wireless Essays first appeared
on the BBC Radio 4 programme *Loose Ends*. I should
like to thank the producer Ian Gardhouse, and
the presenter Ned Sherrin, for allowing the Professor
a platform for his ideas and observations.

There is no possibility that this book could ever
have been written without the violent threats and
pitiless blackmail of Sue Freestone of William
Heinemann and Anthony Goff of David Higham
Associates.

I'm grateful to my parents for their researches
into Salzburg, to Tim Rice for allowing the quotation
from 'I Don't Know How to Love Him',
to Hugh and Jo Laurie for reading the manuscript
when they had hundreds of better things to do,
and to Jo Foster for everything.

Also available from Mandarin Paperbacks

A BIT MORE
FRY & LAURIE

Following the acclaimed success of their runaway bestseller smash barn-storming ripsnorter '*A Bit of Fry & Laurie*: Raw, naked, trembling sketches from the first series of *A Bit of Fry & Laurie*', Stephen Fry and Hugh Laurie now present '*A Bit MORE Fry & Laurie*: Bowel-shattering comic sketches from the increasingly misunderstood BBC series *A Bit of Fry & Laurie*', a dazzling basket of ripe, dew-sodden comic moments, fashioned by hand using only the finest, plumpest, English words, and then lovingly acted out in front of a specially-seated audience to ensure a snug, stylish, and above all, lasting fit. Here are some of the things that have been said about *A Bit MORE Fry & Laurie*:

'*It's no good, Trevis, this kindling wood is soaked through; pass me* A Bit MORE Fry & Laurie *and some paraffin.*'

'*Damn, it's still wobbling. We need something thicker. How about that* A Bit MORE Fry & Laurie?'

'*Never mind, love. It often happens. You're nervous I expect. Flick through this copy of* A Bit MORE Fry & Laurie – *that'll get you going.*'

'*I'll show you what I mean. I draw a man on page 187 of, say, this copy of* A Bit MORE Fry & Laurie *and another on page 185, but this time his knee is a bit more bent. And so on. Then when I flick through the pages fast he gives the impression of walking. Basic animation, but at a fraction of the cost.*'

'*Tee-hee! I'll shove a copy of* A Bit MORE Fry & Laurie *down my trousers. Old Felchley can whack as hard as he likes then, but I won't feel a thing. Smirk!*'

Norman Douglas

VENUS IN THE KITCHEN

Recipes For Delectation

'About a dozen lambs' ears will make a small dish, and these must be stewed. Take a large handful of sorrel, chop it a little and stew it in a spoonful of broth and a morsel of butter. Pour in a small ladle of coulis, grate some nutmeg, and put in a little pepper and salt. Stew it a few minutes, twist up the ears nicely, and dish it up.'

When Norman Douglas died in 1952 he left behind him a number of volumes of classic travel writing, a novel, his extraordinary reputation as a hedonist and this small and exotic cookery book. *Venus in the Kitchen* is full of recipes to stiffen up the sinews and summon up the blood of gentlemen who fear their ardour may be fading. Some of the recipes will seem strange and esoteric ('Take a good quantity of leopard's marrow. . .'), inspired by the writings of the ancients, others are very palatable indeed. Here is your opportunity to try them for yourself.

'Any book that is written with such style, grace and comic sensuality, any book, in short, that dares be so different and so direct, can only be welcomed, reverenced and adored'   *Stephen Fry*

A Selected List of Humour Available from Mandarin

While every effort is made to keep prices low, it is sometimes necessary to increase prices at short notice. Mandarin Paperbacks reserves the right to show new retail prices on covers which may differ from those previously advertised in the text or elsewhere.

The prices shown below were correct at the time of going to press.

☐	7493 0159 7	**The Complete Fawlty Towers**	John Cleese & Connie Booth	£7.99
☐	7493 1436 2	**Class**	Jilly Cooper	£5.99
☐	7493 0849 4	**Angels Rush In**	Jilly Cooper	£5.99
☐	7493 1164 9	**Women and Superwomen**	Jilly Cooper	£3.99
☐	7493 1163 0	**Men and Supermen**	Jilly Cooper	£3.99
☐	7493 1703 5	**Back to Basics**	Arthur Daley	£4.99
☐	7493 1695 0	**Jeremy Hardy Speaks to the Nation**	Jeremy Hardy	£5.99
☐	7493 1896 1	**These Were Your Father's**	John Hegley	£3.99
☐	7493 3606 4	**Second from Last in the Sack Race**	David Nobbs	£5.99
☐	7493 0020 5	**Pratt of the Argus**	David Nobbs	£4.99
☐	7493 0138 4	**The Secret Diary of Adrian Mole Aged 13¾**	Sue Townsend	£3.99
☐	7493 0222 4	**The Growing Pains of Adrian Mole**	Sue Townsend	£3.99
☐	7493 0229 1	**True Confessions of Adrian Albert Mole**	Sue Townsend	£3.99
☐	7493 1863 7	**Adrian Mole: The Wilderness Years**	Sue Townsend	£4.99
☐	7493 1503 2	**Barmy**	Victoria Wood	£5.99
☐	7493 1314 5	**Up to You, Porky**	Victoria Wood	£5.99
☐	7493 0819 2	**Lucky Bag: The Victoria Wood Songbook**	Victoria Wood	£7.99
☐	7493 2046 X	**Pat and Margaret**	Victoria Wood	£7.99

All these books are available at your bookshop or newsagent, or can be ordered direct from the address below. Just tick the titles you want and fill in the form below.

Cash Sales Department, PO Box 5, Rushden, Northants NN10 6YX.
Fax: 01933 414047 : Phone: 01933 414000.

Please send cheque, payable to 'Reed Book Services Ltd.', or postal order for purchase price quoted and allow the following for postage and packing:

£1.00 for the first book, 50p for the second; **FREE POSTAGE AND PACKING FOR THREE BOOKS OR MORE PER ORDER.**

NAME (Block letters) ....

ADDRESS ....

....

☐ I enclose my remittance for ....

☐ I wish to pay by Access/Visa Card Number

Expiry Date

Signature ....

Please quote our reference: MAND